TWENTY-FOUR DAYS

Rowe-Delamagente series

By J. Murray

Other books by Jacqui Murray

Rowe-Delamagente Series
To Hunt a Sub
Twenty-four Days

Dawn of Humanity trilogy
Born in a Treacherous Time

Crossroads trilogy
Survival of the Fittest (Book 1)
The Quest for Home (Book 2—coming Summer 2019)
In the Footsteps of Giants (Book 3—coming Summer 2020)

Non-fiction
Building a Midshipman: How to Crack the USNA Application

Education
Over 100 non-fiction resources integrating technology into education available from Structured Learning LLC

Praise for the *Rowe-Delamagente* series:

A blistering pace is set from the beginning: dates open each new chapter/section, generating a countdown that intensifies the title's time limit. Murray skillfully bounces from scene to scene, handling numerous characters, from hijackers to MI6 special agent Haster. ... A steady tempo and indelible menace form a stirring nautical tale. – Kirkus Reviews

***

... a satisfying read from a fresh voice in the genre, and well worth the wait. The time devoted to research paid off, providing a much appreciated authenticity to the sciency aspects of the plot. The author also departs from the formulaic pacing and heroics of contemporary commercialized thrillers. Instead, the moderately paced narrative is a seduction, rather than a sledgehammer. The author takes time rendering relatable characters with imaginatively cool names like Zeke Rowe, and Kalian Delamagente. The scenes are vividly depicted, and the plot not only contains exquisitely treacherous twists and turns, but incorporates the fascinating study of early hominids, and one ancestral female in particular who becomes an essential character. – Goodreads reader

***

A fusion of technology, academics, and archaeology make "To Hunt a Sub" a thrilling ride. The stakes are high as a PhD student and an ex-Seal risk all to stop terrorists from stealing American submarines carrying nuclear weapons. The writing is clipped and crisp, fitting well with the genre—there's little fluff. The author's expertise in technology shines through. A quick read I finished in just a few days. Solid debut novel. – Amazon reader

***

*So last night I couldn't sleep and finally got up about 3
o'clock in the morning and thought I would just read for a
while and maybe I would get to sleep unfortunately, I read
your book. Needless to say I was only halfway done when I
started at 3 a.m. and by 6 a.m. I had finished the book! too
good to go to sleep. Excellent book. Can't wait for the next
one. WOW – Amazon reader*

***

*This is a complex layered story that successfully blends
well researched archaeology and cutting edge technology,
with a high stakes terrorist plot to steal nuclear
submarines. It's got characters to root for, and villains to
loathe. –Amazon reader*

***

*I loved the way the author combined vulnerability and
strength in her main characters. I loved where the macho
character 'Rowe' takes Kali's hand even though she pulls
away. And there is this beautiful raw, insight into what it
can cost you to be a mother. Otto is very cool too. –
Amazon reader*

Published by Structured Learning LLC

Laguna Hills, Ca 92653

This is a work of fiction. Names, characters, places, and incidents either are the product of the author's imagination or are used fictitiously, and any resemblance to actual persons, living or dead, business establishments, events, or locales, is entirely coincidental. The publisher does not have any control over and does not assume any responsibility for author or third-party websites or their content.

Design and layout for cover: Paper and Sage Inc.
Printer: Quality Instant Press

Printed in the United States of America

ISBN 978-1-942101-47-5

My sincere thanks to the following people for their support and knowledge. CDR Matthew Carr for his passionate discussions about submarines, my brother CDR John MacCrossen who shared what he could from his days hunting submarines, Dr. Philip Ender of the University of California Los Angeles for savvy insights into computers and an alternative approach to thinking, Mike Merrifield for inspiration, Roxane Teboul for her tips about being a Columbia grad student, my husband for his constant belief in my ability to tell this story, John Rowe for allowing me to use his son's name, my daughter's cerebral friends for their humorous approach to all things complicated, my anonymous friend for his anecdotal insights into radical Islam—providing a personal face to the terrorists' goals, Donald Johansen and the Leakey's for nurturing my abiding love and respect for our ancestors, and the talented members of my writing group and blogging community— thank you for unselfish hours of editing.

Please know that, while these individuals assisted in this book's development, all mistakes are my own. In some cases—particularly with Columbia University and parts of New York—I adjusted reality to reflect the needs of the script. In other cases—such as submarine protocols and other government-based details—I purposely strayed from reality to insure my story never got close to resembling national secrets.

Table of Contents

Prologue

Monday, August 7th
HMNB Devonport England

Until last month, Eyad Obeid considered himself a devout Muslim. He prayed five times a day, proclaimed God's glory in every conversation, and performed the required ablutions when confronted with uncleanliness. When his brother was executed by Israeli gunman five years ago, Obeid swore retribution. No nobler purpose could he imagine for his worthless life than dying for Allah.

But instead of a suicide vest and the promise of seventy-two virgins, the village imam enrolled him in college to learn nuclear physics, thermodynamics, chemistry, and math so complex its sole application was theoretical. Much to Obeid's surprise, he thrived on the cerebral smorgasbord. In fact, with little effort, he attained all the skills required by the Imam.

By the time he earned his PhD in Nuclear Physics, he had learned two lessons. First, he was much smarter than most people around him, and second, the western world was not what he had been told.

Now, just weeks after graduation, Eyad Obeid approached the dingy Devonport pub on the frigid southern shore of England and wondered how to explain to the man responsible for giving Eyad Obeid this amazing future that he would fulfill his obligation, but then, wanted out.

He squared his shoulders and entered the pub.

His stomach lurched. Rather than his mentor Salah Mahmud al-Zahrawi, he found the Kenyan and his three henchmen. He had first met these thugs in San Diego California where he learned to run a nuclear submarine under the friendly tutelage of British submariners. When Obeid finished his studies, the Kenyan slaughtered the Brits. No warning. No discussion, just slash, slice and everyone died.

As did Obeid's belief in the purity of Allah.

The nuclear physicist jammed his hands into his pockets, hunched his shoulders, and approached the table. The Kenyan had never introduced himself and Eyad Obeid lacked the courage to ask.

"I was expecting Salah al-Zahrawi," Obeid offered as he slipped into the booth.

The Kenyan stared past Obeid, eyes as desolate as the Iranian desert, thick sloping shoulders still, ebony skin glistening under the fluorescent lights. Danger radiated from him like the hum of a power plant. He had three new fight scars since their last encounter, like angry welts but otherwise, he looked rested, clearly losing no sleep over the slaughter of innocents.

"You have one more job before you are released." In a quiet, toneless voice, the man without a soul explained the new plan, finishing with, "If you fail, you die."

Obeid was stunned. His gut said *Run*! He risked his future—his life—staying a moment longer with this crazed zealot, but Obeid did little more than croak a strangled, "If I succeed, I will also die!" His University friends called it a Sophie's Choice.

The Kenyan shrugged. "But less painfully."

Obeid twitched as heat washed his face. As he sought an appropriate response, the waitress arrived with tea. She poured a cup for each of them, chattering to no one in particular about how she had forgotten her blarmy slicker because her boyfriend kept her up the whole bloody night, di'n he, and she was frightfully knackered. No one responded.

"Shall I tell you the specials on offer?"

The Kenyan slowly ratcheted his head toward her. "Go."

The waitress backed away, almost knocking over another server and his steaming tray of eggs, bacon, black pudding, and baked beans. "Well, aren't we in a bloody mood," and she left.

The Kenyan did not seem to notice, his flat dead eyes back on Obeid. The physicist squirmed. He was but one man. His only hope was to quietly warn the authorities. He folded his hands into his lap to hide their shaking.

"Insha Allah, I will help. What do you require?"

"Do you remember the training you received from the Parishers?"

The British submariners you butchered? Obeid nodded.

"You must ensure the sailors perform their duties after we hijack the sub."

With no further explanation, the Kenyan tossed a fistful of notes onto the table and left. As Obeid hurried after him, he surreptitiously thumbed a message into his phone and pushed send.

There was no signal.

The Kenyan parked in the crew lot outside Her Majesty's Devonport Plymouth Naval Base. Obeid changed into a uniform and emerged from the car carrying a loaded gun in a prayer rug. *Maa shaa Allah.*

The storm broke and quickly turned the parking lot slick and shiny. Obeid shivered despite the heavy pea coat with the warm fur-lined collar. How did the British stand the weather? When this ended, he would never again leave the sparkling sun and cloudless skies of his beloved Iran.

"Eyad!" It was Tariq Khosrov, with two other friends from Obeid's graduate program, all with PhDs in nuclear physics. Tariq was one of the smartest boys Obeid had ever met and the most naïve. "Are we going to steal a nuclear submarine?"

Obeid hissed, "Quiet!" and the Kenyan nudged him toward the base's thick metal gates. They had been designed to stop an AK-47 or a firebomb, even an RPG, but not the weapon Salah al-Zahrawi would use. Faithful Muslims who worked for naval personnel had replaced pictures of the dead San Diego Parishers with Obeid and the rest of the hijackers. By the time the Royal Navy realized something was wrong, *HMS Triumph* would be gone and missing.

"Next!"

The man in front of Obeid passed his ID to the bored security. He checked the man's face, his computer screen, and waved him through.

It was Obeid's turn. "ID, please."

Obeid's chest tightened as the stern-looking sentry, blonde hair trimmed close to his scalp, collar turned up against the wind, fingers like thick sausages on powerful hands, turned a flint-eyed glare to Obeid. The nuclear physicist froze and the guard's boredom became suspicion. He read the name stitched on the right breast of Obeid's uniform. "Haim is it?"

He looked Obeid up and down, as though to determine if the name matched the slight figure in front of him with wire-rimmed glasses and the thatch of black hair dripping rain down his forehead. True, he couldn't tell Obeid's stomach lacked the six-pack of muscles the real Haim had been so proud of, but he could see Obeid's slender hands and they were those of a scientist, not a sailor. Surely, the guard would say something.

Obeid fumbled, almost dropping the ID before shoving it forward.

"Anything to declare?" The guard's gaze flicked to the prayer rug.

Sweat broke out under Obeid's arms. Should he tell the guard there was an AK-47 in his prayer rug or would he shoot before listening to Obeid's explanation? No, better to deal with the problem onboard. Besides, the Kenyans claimed they were simply leveraging demands against Britain backed by the threat posed by the sub's weapons. They would never use them.

He bit his lip hard, tasting blood, and forced anger into his voice. "You suspect me because I am Muslim? Do you want to examine my prayer rug?" His voice dripped with righteous indignation as he had practiced and he extended the tightly-bound bundle, taking care to keep the ends turned away from the soldier. "Maybe I am carrying an A... K." He purposely stumbled over the name.

The sentry flushed and stepped back as though burned.

"Now I didn't mean that mate, did I? O' course you're fine," and waved Obeid through.

Across the yard, limned against the grey sky, towered the domed shape of the *HMS Triumph*, its deck slick with rain, sail glistening in the early morning light. The warheads it carried could reach the vast majority of the planet but the bustling sailors, some in oil-stained uniforms, others nattily dressed in white with jaunty officer caps, greeted each other, oblivious to the danger approaching them in the uniform of shipmates.

What had he done?

"Keep going," the scar-faced Kenyan hissed between clenched teeth.

Obeid balled his fists to stop their shaking and forced his steps to be slow and measured as if in no rush to start what would be a three-month deployment.

When the group reached the *Triumph*, they were greeted by a cherub-faced seaman. "You the Parisher blokes?" He stuck his hand out. "Name's McEwen. We're the Second crew. First came down with food poisoning."

He chuckled, eyes crinkling with merriment, brows like gray steel wool. "Brill, you think? Who wants to play hide and seek with a Diesel?"

McEwen poked the Kenyan in jovial familiarity while Obeid combed through his training for what a 'diesel' might be.

"Enough yakking. Get sorted, blokes. We leave in an hour."

Press Release: North Korea to Launch Satellite into Orbit

SEOUL, South Korea — North Korea proclaimed plans to launch a communications satellite into orbit August 30th, threatening to increase tension surrounding their nuclear weapons program.

The United States condemned the step, saying it violated UN Security Council resolutions, demanding North Korea stop launching rockets that use long-range intercontinental ballistic missile technology. "If they proceed with this launch, how will we trust a regime that egregiously violates its international commitment?" the State Department spokesperson asked.

North Korea, with the aid of their strategic partner Iran, is believed to be developing technology to mount nuclear warheads atop a missile such as the Unha-2, ultimately intended to deliver nuclear weapons as far away as North America, though analysts doubt their success. At least twice, North Korea tried and failed to loft satellites into orbit. To this day, it boasts that a satellite is in orbit, broadcasting patriotic songs praising Kim Jong Un.

Chapter One

Day Four, Thursday, August 10th,
Early morning

Zeke Rowe crouched behind a clump of creosote in a shallow Iraqi wadi. The cracked ground, baked dry by the scorching sun, might as well have been steel wool under his hands. In three hours, darkness would shroud his return to base, but until then, he must be invisible.

Something cracked and then the whisper of movement through the hot dry air. Rowe turned, M-16 at the ready, eyes darting through the brush for anything out of sync. There was a glint like sun bouncing off steel, followed by a flash of light. He scrambled, aiming while bobbing sideways, but a searing blast turned everything dark.

His head hurt. If it split open, it'd be an improvement. He tried to lift an arm to see what was drilling into his skull, but couldn't. Same with his legs, which left his eyes the sole recon available. One was swollen shut and the other felt like sandpaper as he pried it open. Focusing made his skull pound.

"You are awake, Lt. Zeke Rowe, Navy SEAL, intelligence, serial number 502861011."

The world swam and his stomach heaved. He swallowed hard and tried to make sense of the blurred image through one slitted eye. Two men—no, one, twice—feet spread, cleaning his nails with a knife.

How the hell does he know my name?

He tried for a witty response, but his tongue got in the way, dry and sticky from lack of saliva. Someone yanked his head back and dribbled water through his swollen lips. Water never tasted so good.

"What's your name?" Rowe's voice cracked. His throat burned.

The man grinned, eyeing Zeke Rowe like he might tonight's dinner. "I will start. Where is your fellow SEAL, Lt. Cdr. Duck Peters, serial number 523640248?"

Duck. The brother Rowe never had.

"Who would name a soldier 'Duck'?" The man was tall, dressed in a filthy white robe with a ragged turban around his head. He stank of goats and sweat and wore Rowe's watch.

"That's my... time..." He couldn't think clearly. The Bedouin looked back at someone and Rowe's left hand exploded. White pain arced down his fingers, up his arm. The trigger finger on his left hand was gone at the first knuckle. Blood pumped onto the parched dirt at his feet.

"We know he seeks our leader. We would like to know where." The voice was calm, kind. Not the voice of a madman.

Rowe gritted his teeth. "Duck... is... what I should have done."

Rowe's favorite story about Duck Peters popped into the SEAL's fuzzy brain. In the early days of the War, insurgents lobbed a grenade into Duck's SEAL nest. The man, a month out of BUD/S, threw himself on top of it while he bellowed for his teammates to take cover. He smothered it for five seconds, then five more, but nothing happened. Duck gingerly extracted it from beneath his belly and pitched it back toward the enemy quipping, "There goes the Medal of Honor."

Another nod from the Bedouin. This time, Rowe's right hand burst into white-hot flames.

"Do you wish to assist yet?"

"If I don't …" Rowe panted. "…you gonna chop off…" He paused as a wave of nausea rolled through his stomach. He tried to bend forward so he wouldn't choke on his vomit, but jerked back at the sight of his finger by his boot. "…another finger? …Get it …over with." He'd never rat out a brother.

The Bedouin's smile was forced this time. His eyes narrowed. "I thought a SEAL's fingers were important." He cocked his thumb and index finger to simulate a gun. "I misjudged." He spoke perfect English with a cultured British lilt.

Rowe had trouble listening. Saliva dribbled down his lip. Ants attacked his finger stubs.

A small brown man with a full beard appeared, dragging a shark-toothed Conibear trap. An image flitted across Rowe's mind of a golden retriever he had found snared in one. Her frantic efforts to escape had torn the muzzle from her face. Rowe had tried for thirty minutes to free her, but she suffocated.

The little man struggled to lever the teeth open, face dripping sweat, eyes darting from Rowe to the mangy Bedouin. He finally forced the jaws around Rowe's right knee and let go. A wet crunch announced the bite of metal into Rowe's flesh. He howled, fingers forgotten.

The little man had one more task. Rowe flailed, but two goons held him while the yawning maw of a second trap locked onto his other knee. Rowe passed out.

He didn't so much regain consciousness as sense pain, like animals chewing on his living body. Rowe tried to move and heard the clang of metal against metal. The Bedouin raised an eyebrow, popped a strawberry into his mouth and fixed Rowe with a questioning stare.

"I can help you, Mr. Rowe. By now, you should welcome assistance."

"From you? Like a case of the clap."

The man puckered like he'd eaten a lemon. "What will it hurt? Your friend will not be there anymore."

Rowe tried to ignore the throbbing tissue around the Conibear. "He'll be here soon. Stick around."

Which Rowe believed with every fiber of his being. Positions reversed, Rowe would move every sand dune from here to Kuwait to find Duck. "You want to live, let me go before he arrives."

When angered, Duck was your worst nightmare. Shoulders like a ledge, fight scars in all the right places, arms that looked like he could bench press a Volkswagen, with a neck so thick it was part of his shoulders. But his physical assets paled next to his brain. Duck had a warrior mindset. He never gave less than full throttle because war killed those in second place. What Duck really knew how to do—and he did it well—was win.

The Bedouin smiled. "We are invisible. What is it you Americans say—like finding a straw in a haystack?"

Rowe ignored the fire in his knees and the coppery scent of his own blood, and eyed his tormentor. "Duck's specialty is doing the impossible." He kept his voice soft, calm, betraying none of the pain that raged through his ravaged body.

The Bedouin laughed. "He's just one man, Zeke Rowe. We are many."

Rowe pinned the man with his working eye. "And Little Boy was just a bomb."

The Bedouin turned to his left. The small brown man approached Rowe, eyes equal mix of fear and concern. "Tell him. He will not stop."

"Neither. Will. I."

The man mouthed *I'm sorry* as he slammed a dinner plate-sized rock against the Conibear trap, driving the teeth deep into tissue and bone. Rowe bit hard on his tongue and tasted blood pool in his mouth. When he still refused to talk, the trap crunched again. And again until his tormentors were too tired to continue and left him for the night. When the camp went quiet, a mangy dog crawled in, so skinny his chest could double as a picket fence. He curled up at Rowe's side, licked the warrior's wounds, and disappeared by daylight.

The interrogation continued the next day and the next, same torture with the same results.

One morning, something clacked over Rowe's head and his arms flopped to his sides. He tried to move them without success. He heard a rattle, then a sucking noise and his legs blew up. Pain rippled through his body.

"You're not free, American. We have a new game we learned from your Hanoi Hilton."

Hanoi Hilton. The North Vietnamese house of torture for captured Americans during the Vietnam War. Rowe kept his face stoic, a mask of disinterest.

"Duck here yet?" He croaked.

Rough hands shackled his numb arms and manhandled him to his destroyed knees. Red and yellow puss oozed into puddles that stunk like rotting carrion. He swallowed a scream, rolled over to take the pressure off his broken joints and was kicked back to an upright position.

"You move, we beat you," so Rowe stayed, packaged up the pain and stowed it for later. A round three-inch tube of rebar nestled in the craw of his knees, and then his feet were tied together with a length of canvas looped around his hands. Someone yanked and his back arched like a rocking chair, forcing his hands toward his feet. Within moments, the rebar began cutting off circulation to his feet. As the pain burned through his damaged joints, he understood how this would make most soldiers talk.

But Rowe never considered himself 'most' soldiers.

"Answer and we remove the rebar."

"You mean where Duck is?" Thousands of white-hot pins burned Rowe's arms. He chased the pain and trapped it in a corner of his mind. "Last time I saw him was fucking your mother."

The strawberry-eating leader put his full weight on the rebar and Rowe failed to bite back a shudder. Every cell screamed for oxygen, the nerves firing off their last cries for help. Sweat beaded his forehead. Try as he might to hide it, he began to shake.

The leader laughed. "Tell us, Zeke Rowe, and we release your feet."

The voice came through Rowe's consciousness like rats clawing at an attic floor. He let the world dissolve into sensory overload and planned his escape.

This group was sloppy. One piece of canvas around ankles and wrists made inflicting pain easier, but if Rowe overextended his arms, almost dislocating his shoulders, he could pick the knot.

The problem was an American SEAL, baddest of the bad, was a prize never left alone. When not being tortured, soldiers spit in his face, slapped him, and laughed at his damaged body.

Rowe waited.

One morning, excited chatter filled the air about an American caravan ripe for the picking. The Bedouin leader stuck his head in Rowe's prison. "You will soon have company," and left. War cries mixed with the pounding of boots and then faded to silence. Only three tattered, gun-toting teenagers remained to guard the American with the destroyed knees and shattered hands, a man who had been tortured for days, starved, and was considered too weak to be a problem. The choking smell of excrement and gore kept them outside where the air was fresher.

Rowe had his opportunity. He arched, bone fragments from his cracked kneecaps stabbing into his flesh and muscles. He bit back a yelp, fingered his way down the canvas strip until he came to the knot that connected everything. Without the first knuckle on his index fingers, it was harder than expected, but he cajoled and wheedled until the knot unraveled. As he prepared to slip the ropes from his wrists, the Bedouin leader approached his tent. The man paused to say something to the guards giving Rowe just enough time to pitch forward to his original position.

When he entered, he stopped and studied Rowe. "Your eyes sparkle. Why?"

Rowe forced a cough. "I'm sick, you theocratic thug. I need a doctor or I'll die of whatever I caught from you. Try bathing." Rowe coughed again, "or stay away from camels."

The leader snorted. "I feared we had broken you. That would end the fun." He picked at a hangnail. "Are you looking forward to company?"

He stepped forward as he talked, eyes toggling between his finger and Rowe's face. Rowe had to distract him and did the only thing that came to mind.

He spit at the Bedouin's sandaled foot. "You're the first one I'll kill when I'm free."

The leader stepped back, shocked, eyes on his foot. Rowe rocked back on his heels and scrambled up on rubbery knees. Pain rolled through his body in waves. He tried to focus on the Bedouin, but the figure wavered in and out of focus. One moment, Rowe was standing; the next his knees buckled and he pitched forward, arms stretching for his tormentor.

The man effortlessly sidestepped Rowe's clawing fingers.

"Who untied you?" The Bedouin sounded more surprised than frightened, which meant he'd underestimate Rowe. The man pulled a knife from his belt and waggled it as he advanced.

Instinct kicked in and Rowe snatched the rebar from under his body and launched it like a spear straight into the man's left eye. The Bedouin cried out and collapsed, the knife bouncing across the room. The tent door flew up and three guards sprinted in. They froze at the sight of their dying leader.

Rowe needed a weapon, fast, before these two oafs woke up, but the leader had no gun and the knife had ended up too far away. That left the rebar embedded in his enemy's skull. He scrabbled forward and wrenched it free as the first guard clumsily unholstered his weapon. Before he could flip the safety and aimed, Rowe hobbled to his feet and swung with a strength he shouldn't possess. The guard's head popped like a melon exploding. Rowe's embattled knees gave up and he pitched forward, snatching the man's weapon and aiming it at the next guard. With his trigger finger missing, he shot awkwardly but relentlessly until the slide locked open which turned out to be eight shots more than he needed. The third guard screamed and fled.

But not far. Rowe heard a scuffle, a frantic yip, and then silence. He dropped the empty gun and dragged himself toward the knife. The flap flew open, but Rowe focused on reaching that weapon. A voice he knew laughed.

"Dammit, Duck. I spent the last three days hiding you from these goons. What are you doing here?"

Duck Peters carried an M-16 over his shoulder, a 9mm in one hand, and a K-bar and a bag of claymore mines in the other. He blinked as he stuffed the handgun into its holster and the knife into his belt.

"Usually you only need one round." His voice caught.

Rowe raised his hand. "I had to adapt," then asked, "Did you get him?" Meaning the radical Islam leader responsible for the bomb that destroyed a Marine caravan of fifty-two souls.

Duck glowed. "Dragged him right out of his spidey hole. He only had fifteen guards. Half my team never fired a shot." A team was six. Pain cut the big man's face. "I bet you feel better'n you look."

He ripped the dead Bedouin's robe into strips and then wrapped them gently around Rowe's knees and hands. "Can you make it?"

Rowe labored to his feet. "If I didn't plan on making it, why let them take my fingers."

"OK then. Let's hurry. Even these idiots will soon realize they were tricked."

It hurt to chuckle, but Rowe did. "I see. No American caravan ripe for the attack?"

Duck chuckled. "Remember that techie geek, Eitan Sun?"

Using the rebar like a crutch, Rowe snatched his watch from the dead man's wrist, then hobbled to where his backpack had been thrown a lifetime ago and hoisted it over his shoulder. "He's a myth, Duck—"

"Yeah, well that myth hacked their communications, alerted them to an American medical convoy passing through," which meant, lightly armed, "and then blocked the lines so they couldn't verify it. They took the bait."

Rowe hurt everywhere, from his head where the bullet grazed him to his hands with their raw stumps to his shoulders and chest. But his knees hurt the worst. He tried to move quickly, but settled for a shuffle.

Duck offered a shoulder, but Rowe brushed it away and focused on placing one foot in front of the other. They got a mile before barking registered through Rowe's fierce concentration.

"It's the damn dog."

"What damn dog?"

"I made a friend there."

He stopped long enough for a mangy mutt more bones than bark to limp up, dragging one leg, tongue lolling, tail wagging furiously as though he discovered a bone burial ground.

"When they finished beating me for the day, this little guy came to visit. I think he hates them as much as I do."

The wretched creature looked exhausted and hungry, but leaped up on Rowe as though to say, *Did you forget me?*

Rowe winced. "Careful, buddy. Sore knees," but he scratched behind its ears, and then placed it tenderly in his backpack. It yipped contentedly until it fell asleep.

Zeke Rowe jerked awake. The sheets wrapped his legs in a tight knot. Sweat swathed his body and his head pounded. Somewhere, a bell chimed. His hand patted under his pillow where he kept his pistol—gone. He stared hard into the darkness, wondering who knew where he stowed his weapon.

And remembered. No more SEALs. No more target on his back. No more gun under his pillow.

He blinked hard and the room swam into focus— double bed, chest of drawers that belonged to his Grandma, the roll top desk he bought to commemorate the beginning of his academic career. Was the chair in a different spot? No. He moved it last night so he could see the park where he and Survivor spent hours exploring. The dog was the only plus to come of Iraq. He still missed him.

Kali rustled next to him. "Get the phone," and curled back to sleep.

Rowe knocked the clock off the bedside table trying to get to his cell. 2:13 a.m. August 7th. Ten years since his capture and it felt like yesterday.

"What?" An empty line and then a click, like the last time and the one before.

A dog barked. Why would a dog be awake at this hour? Rowe crawled out of bed and peered through the window, thought he saw a shadow and then it disappeared.

He rubbed his sore knee. Why the nightmares again? The shrink called them guilt for killing so many, but Rowe carried no guilt. He defended himself, his buddies, and his country. He felt no shame being that man. If not for the medical discharge, he'd still be one.

But he wouldn't have Kali. They met last year when her son was kidnapped by a terrorist to force her to give up an artificial intelligence she had created. Rowe had stopped the madman, rescued Kali's son, and surprised himself by falling in love. What such a beautiful mind saw in a damaged soldier like him was a mystery but every day, he tried to show her she made the right decision by turning his back on the best life he'd ever lived and starting over.

Except Duck. There, he made an exception.

Rowe picked up a picture of the two of them on his last paleoanthropologic dig. His smile was genuine, eyes glinting with happiness, shoulders relaxed, with none of the telltale scrapes or cuts every SEAL wore like badges of honor, no wariness to his face from searching out the closest escape route. He brushed his truncated finger along the curve of her cheek, over the firm jawline, and wondered what she saw in him.

He quietly pulled on shorts and a top being careful not to awaken her, got in his car, and left.

Chapter Two

Day Four, Thursday, August 10th
HMS Triumph, *600 miles from Devonport, England*

Eyad Obeid wiped Vaseline up his nose. The smells
on *HMS Triumph* made him nauseous. The cleaner—
Amine—might keep the air breathable, but the stench clung
to his clothes and hair like stale cigarette smoke, not to
mention the constant drone of machinery.

Twenty-four hours had passed without a problem.
Obeid expected to be miserable, but found he enjoyed the
sub. For the first time in his life, he felt important. He
wracked his brain for a way to stop what al-Zahrawi had
started. Otherwise, he would share responsibility for
everything about to happen.

How had his bright dreams come to this?

Out of the eight hijackers, four were PhDs like
Obeid, participating to fulfill the *jihad* required of all
Muslim males. The other four—radical theocrats from
Kenya—were thugs, but what they lacked in intellect they
more than made up for in physical strength. Obeid begged
his colleagues to help, but they refused. When he tried to
talk to the Captain, he was too busy getting ready for the

war games. In desperation, Obeid snuck into the communications room, but lacked the proper passwords to send a message.

With no other option, Obeid ended up doing exactly what the Kenyans required which was to shadow WEPS, the officer in charge of weapons. The gangly Brit instructed Obeid keep his mouth shut and learn. This Obeid did, knowing it would take every bit of his prodigious IQ to derail this plan, but he intended, *Allah inshallah*, to do just that.

The loudspeaker blared, "The games have begun."

Triumph had reached the Dutch Annual International Submarine Command Course Competition off the coast of Del Helder Denmark where they would test the crew's skills at evasion. When *Oooga* shrieked from the speakers, Obeid jumped and slammed his head into the bulkhead.

WEPS laughed. "Bob's your uncle, Parisher. We're diving. You're a submariner now," mistaking Obeid's trepidations for fear.

Obeid's stomach churned. It was time. *Bismillah*. As the sub nosed downward at a five-degree angle, he stabbed a 9mm gun snuck aboard by one of the Kenyans into WEPS' ribs, hoping aggressive would be mistaken for power.

"Do as I say. I-I do not wish to hurt you." His voice came out pinched and unsure.

WEPS pushed his glasses up his nose. "I say, mate. What are you doing?"

Obeid ground the gun into WEPS' side and removed the armory keys from the officer's belt. "We are hijacking this submarine. Proceed to the crew's mess. Do not stop. Do not talk to anyone and you will not be injured."

To Obeid's immense relief, the man did as asked. When they reached their destination, forty of the boat's 130 crew crowded into the small room, officers and enlisted, all under the alert eyes of a gun-toting Kenyan. Obeid shoved WEPS through the hatch. The officer stumbled, righted himself, brushed his jacket smooth, adjusted his glasses and turned to the nearest Kenyan.

"Are you bloody fucking wankers trying to hijack our boat? This is—"

The Kenyan drove his left hand into the V under WEPS' ribs. The man gasped and pitched forward. Next, the Kenyan stomped hard on his exposed neck. The crunch of bones reverberated through the silence and the officer lay still. The sour stench of urine soon saturated the room.

"Boys." The cherub-faced McEwen, the one who welcomed Obeid aboard, shouted from across the room. "There are eight of them and dozens of us. What are we waiting for?"

The rat-a-tat of an AK-47 on full auto shattered the room. McEwen went down first, a line of red stitched across his chest, followed by five officers who had started forward and seven sailors. The Kenyan ran through multiple magazines without pausing. No one even tried to stop him.

The room finally fell into a stunned silence, broken by the moan of a dying sailor begging for help as blood bubbled from his wheezing chest. A sheen of red covered everything. The armed Kenyan stared into a boy's pleading eyes and double-tapped him in the head. Obeid vomited. It was San Diego all over again. "You promised no more death!"

All heads turned to him as one of the Kenyans dragged Obeid through the hatch and threw him against the bulkhead, dangling by his neck, feet hanging uselessly above the deck. The man's sweat-coated face hovered an inch from Obeid, the sour rot of bad oral hygiene making Obeid gag.

"Kindness is weakness," the henchman spit out as he smashed Obeid's windpipe until the scientist almost choked. "You are *kaffiya* from too much time in their belly. You have forgotten they are the enemy."

Obeid tried to agree, but ended up with a mangled squawk. Just as blackness began erasing Obeid's world, the Kenyan leader slapped his mate.

"He is the only one who can launch the weapons." The henchman dropped Obeid like a bag of rice. Obeid gasped, rubbing his throat.

"*Alhamdulillah*. Thank you," he rasped to the man who saved his life

The leader crouched down, smoothed Obeid's collar and smiled. "Islam is borne on a river of *jihad*, my friend. Violence is a necessary means to the end, but I understand your concern. These thugs," and he hitched a thumb over his shoulder, "are True Believers, but have no brains. I need yours."

"Yes. I am sorry. I have seen too many die for no reason."

"Do your part and no one else gets hurt. I promise. Killing too many of these blokes will make the Brits angry and we will not get what we need. But if you try something funny, more die and that will be on you. Understand?" He helped him to his feet. "I will show this group," he nodded toward the crew mess, "evidence. It is fake, but remember what Allah teaches when dealing with the infidel, that the end justifies the means. Praise be to Allah."

Obeid took a seat in the room as the leader addressed the cowed group.

"You no longer work for Her Majesty. I am your Captain. I control the Bridge, the Engine Room, Command Information Center, and the weapons. I have left those required to run the ship in position, but they will not rescue you."

He held a picture up of a pink-cheeked toddler, duct taped naked to a chair, tears streaming down his blotchy face. The body of his mother lay in a crumpled heap at his feet, her head at an impossible angle. Obeid fought to remain impassive, but panic bled out. No matter what the leader said, these images weren't fake.

"Only those who assist in the takeover of this submarine are necessary." The predatory eyes turned to Obeid. "Get weapons from the armory. The rest of you, tie each other up. If you behave, there will be nothing more dangerous than chafed wrists."

Obeid fled, WEPS' keys in his shaking hands, the Kenyan's lies echoing in his ears. Bile burned his throat as he tried to calm himself. He must treat this like a physics problem, solvable once you found the key. Obeid needed the key.

He raced down the pway and stumbled into the most violent of the Kenyan henchmen. He had pinned three submariners against the bulkhead with his AK-47. Obeid darted past, around a corner, and then froze at the next words.

"Who will tell me how to use the nuclear weapons?" Seconds passed and then an AK-47 barked followed by a shriek and a thud. "Have I changed any minds?"

A voice squeaked. "We can't even if we want to, can we. The codes are in the blarmy safe and only First Sea Lord—in London—has the combo. Th-that keeps the sub from going rogue."

Obeid could see the henchman's dull brain work through this complication. He pulled the trigger. The sailor howled.

"You're lying."

"It-t's true, mate! They used to be with the Captain, didn't they, but th-that changed!"

A phone chimed and the henchman repeated what the sailor had said. "He says you're lying," and shot the man.

The remaining sailor shrieked, skidded around the corner and caromed off the bulkheads, the Kenyan three steps behind. Calmly, he raised his weapon and pulled the trigger. The sailor arched back, hands clawing at air, then crashed forward, head bouncing once and then lay still.

"Looks like it's up to you."

Whatever good feeling Obeid had for being part of something important blew up with that boy's life. His legs shook brutally, but he squelched the backwash of emotion and made a decision. Surely, the Brits could counter a hijacking. He would act the part of a terrorist, but keep a keen eye for some way to stop them.

"*Triumph*, request your position."

This was the third call in thirty minutes. *Triumph* had been paired with *HNMLS Dolphun*, an old *Walrus*-class diesel. The game required each sub avoid detection for seven hours, which gave *Triumph* a long head start to its final destination. At this point, to find them, the Brits must scan a circumference of two hundred miles around Den Helder.

The British radioman had tried covert messages on VLF and ELF—very low- and extremely-low frequencies. Now they resorted to an open channel.

"Sir. Still nothing." The Brit radioman was so nervous, he left the line open. Someone directed, "Start a grid search."

The Kenyan leaned into the Captain. "What's that?"

"They'll methodically cover the surface based on our last known position and move out, looking for wreckage, buoys, distress signals—anything that indicates our presence. Then they'll drag the ocean floor for debris."

"They better not find us." The Kenyan drew a hand across his throat, the message as subtle as the 9mm in his hand.

The Captain punched the mic. "Noise lock down. We're being hunted."

Five minutes later, the Brit radioman announced, "SOSUS picked up a blip. Too small for *Triumph*, isn't it? A whale?"

The Kenyan grabbed the Captain. "What's this SOSUS?"

The Captain shook free, fire in his eyes, and tugged his blouse back into place. "SOund SUrveillance System is a chain of underwater sonar listening posts to notify the home country if someone crosses their ocean borders. There," and his finger traced a path across the Straits of Dover, from White Cliffs England to Calais France. "Change directions or they find us in ten minutes."

"Ten minutes. Let's see if this sub can operate as advertised."

Something tumbled across the Captain's face.

Minute by minute, they crept toward the imaginary line. Obeid was transfixed by the blip. Finally, seconds remained as *Triumph* inched toward the line. Obeid held his breath, hoping, as the final moments ticked off.

And then it passed.

The Captain muttered, "That's impossible," not believing what he'd seen.

That *was* impossible. When anything passed within range of the sonar listening posts, sound waves were bounced back to the receiver. A string of posts across an egress/ingress point wouldn't miss *Triumph*. The estimate of their position must be off.

Then eleven minutes passed. No alarms. No bells. No call from the radioman. Obeid kept his face impassive, gun pointed at the Navigator, and set his brain to work on how al-Zahrawi made a sub invisible to sonar.

"*Triumph*, requesting your position," and then, "We'll find you. If you're sunk or unable to communicate, you will not die."

The Captain sagged. "Where are we going, mate?"

When the Kenyan said nothing, the Captain shook his head. "I can't stop you, blarmy. Tell me what you're doing with my sub."

The Kenyan slammed him into the consul. "It takes only two nuclear submarines to control the planet, you and one other. In twenty-one days, Allah regains what is righteously his."

USS Virginia, *off the East Coast of the USA*

"Sir, unknown contact bearing zero-five-zero, range one thousand yards."

"On my way."

Yesterday's Top Secret briefing popped into the Captain's mind. Credible SIGINT and HUMINT indicated submarines were a terrorist target. Anything out of the ordinary should be addressed with extreme caution. The Captain had never known a US submarine to be hijacked on the open seas, thought it impossible, but he would take no chances on his first command. He was the youngest sub Captain in the Navy and wanted to be the best.

"What d'you have?" The Captain peered at the Bridge monitors and saw nothing.

Virginia had been deployed on a top secret mission, the purpose of which the Captain would find out in another week. His only hint came when maintenance added forward-looking cameras to his sleek *Virginia*-class attack sub. Something required enhanced visual even at the expense of speed. The CO had puzzled over this with his

XO, a twenty-year veteran the Captain felt lucky to have, and come up empty.

"Sonar is picking up a rhythmic noise, manmade."

"XO?"

"That's Morse code, sir. SOS."

Morse code? No one taught it anymore.

"Captain. Flash message. One of our ASDS's contacted Norfolk. Some sort of electromagnetic pulse knocked out their power. We're to render any assistance possible."

An Advanced SEAL Delivery System meant American SEALS. Odd no one mentioned it in the Captain's pre-departure briefing. Anything in his AOR, he should have been apprised of. They must have launched after *Virginia* left Norfolk.

No matter. Now, he must decide. Because subs spent so much time incommunicado, the Navy selected a Captain in part for his ability to act autonomously and correctly. Calling for advice would be admitting he was unprepared for leadership.

"Let's make sure it's ours before riding in on our titanium horse." Although, it must be. Who else would have a Navy minisub? "OOD. Close to six hundred feet for visual."

The cigar shape of an American submersible appeared, resting in the silt and teetering on the edge of the continental shelf. A stiff current would push it over and tumble it well past its crush depth. No one would find it in time to save the men aboard.

But still, he would be cautious. "Circle the submersible."

They took a quick loop. It was banged up. Maybe someone attacked it; the crew fought them off, lost power, life support, and comm in the battle. The CO squeezed his fists. His gut said these were fellow warriors in trouble, but this could go wrong so many ways.

"Damn," he muttered. "What's the world come to when we refuse assistance to fellow Americans in need? Go get those boys."

Chapter Three

Day Four, Thursday, August 10th, early evening
Adirondack Mountains, New York

"I'm going to slip into something you'll like, Baby." Candy peeked over her shoulder and winked. Bobby James, ex-high school football star, now a senior agent with the FBI known equally for his ability to intimidate felons as his salaciously single lifestyle, found himself staring like a hound dog drooling over a bone. He may have met his match in Candy Caminski.

"You know what I like." He tried for manly, but his voice came out strangled

She giggled and left the cabin's cozy living room for where James expected to spend most of this weekend— the luxurious master bedroom with its massive four-post bed, real wood fireplace, intimate Jacuzzi, and double-pane French windows with a spectacular view of Mt. Marcy, the highest point in the Adirondack Mountains. James had reserved two spots on a hiking day trip in case they felt frisky.

James put wood on the already roaring fire for something to do. The rental agency had stocked the grate with enough logs to get them through a week-long snow storm. He popped the cork on a $100 bottle of Duckhorn Special Edition Cabernet Sauvignon and then decided he might as well get comfortable also.

He slipped out of his Crockett & Jones Oxford Brogues purchased on his last visit to MI-6 London headquarters, the Hermes suit Candy had bought for him on a Paris junket (she had entertained herself shopping while James met with DGSE, France's CIA), the Anderson & Sheppard white shirt with tiny stripes coordinated with the Robert Talbott silk tie his personal shopper insisted were *de rigueur* this season, and threw on a fluffy white robe that matched Candy's. He tugged the belt around his waist, dimmed the lights and settled into the double-wide chair placed conveniently in the glow of the fireplace.

"Pour me a glass of that Duck, will you, Baby? I love wine with sex."

James gulped, hands shaking with anticipation. Why the number two swimsuit model in America wasted time on him, he had no clue. He doubted it was his six-foot 250-pounds of well-managed muscle with the tiny roll that refused to be weight-lifted away, or the receding hairline Candy said made him look 'distinguished', or even the chiseled jaw still firm despite his forty something years. No. James suspected it had more to do with the frisson of danger that surrounded a seasoned federal agent who carried a gun like others carry credit cards, awash in international terrorists and privy to the secret lives of presidents.

He poured. "The refreshments are ready, honey bun, and so am I."

She giggled.

There was a knock on the cabin door. When James ignored it, as well as the next, his cell buzzed. No one had this number except Tess, his assistant, and she had strict instructions to bother him only at the request of the

Director. He tiptoed over and peered through the peephole as he answered the phone. A tall gawky man stood hunch-shouldered in the pale moonlight, face a mottled pink, thin hair damp against his skull, a yellow stain on his Burberry collar. He held a Blackberry to his ear.

"What?"

The man jerked upright as though surprised to hear a voice. "Special Agent James? I'm Special Agent Haster, MI-6. I need your help."

Each *s* whistled like fingernails on a blackboard. James' call-waiting beeped. Speak of the turncoat.

"Excuse me a moment," and he toggled to the incoming call. "Tess. Why—"

A strident female voice cut him off, "Try unpacking your encrypted phone."

The man who was presumably SA Haster pounded on the door. "SA James. Please allow me entry."

James punched call waiting. "SA Haster. Give me a moment," and he muted the phone, looked around for his suitcase, and found it still on the couch. He flipped it open one-handed, dug through swimming trunks, a satin lounge jacket, and a toy Candy had asked him to bring, until he found the encrypted Blackberry satellite phone. He plugged in the safety protocols and called Tess.

"Who's SA Haster?"

"The Director sent him." Her words were like a whiplash. Tess cared zip James was the boss. She saw them as equals, different jobs but the same patriotic goal.

The pounding got louder. "Please open the door, SA James. It is far from private out here for the conversation you and I must have."

"Tess, hold on." He switched phones and unmuted SA Haster: "I'm not at the cabin. I'm in town, having dinner—"

"And yet your car is in the driveway, lights are on and smoke escapes the chimney."

James scowled. Hiding from a spook was difficult. "It's 9pm. Can we talk tomorrow?"

"Would I have flown across the Atlantic without my morning tea, spent two hours tracking down your whereabouts, and driven five hours through rush-hour traffic if tomorrow was soon enough?"

"I'll give you five minutes. Hold on." That's all the time James had to find out what Haster had to say. Swimsuit models like Candy had options. Forty-something spies didn't.

When he clicked back to Tess, she was still talking. "I'm sending you an email from the Director." James' Blackberry buzzed and his spirits fell.

"What's he want?"

Tess sighed. "The material is Top Secret and requires clearances I do not even want. Have fun with… Candy."

What happened in the six hours since he left? The Director never over-reacted. In fact, in James's entire intelligence career, only two emails were like this, one on 9/11 and the other when Osama bin Laden was killed.

He opened the message as he took two steps toward the bedroom to see if Candy had finished her shower. Her music played, meaning she was digging through her four suitcases to find something to wear. He had at least five minutes. The email said, '*Virginia* missed call-in. Tie-in to Brit sub?' It included a link and asked James to meet him as soon as possible.

James put aside the question of 'what Brit sub' and started with '*Virginia* missed call-in'.

The italics referred to *USS Virginia*, SSN 774, a nuclear attack submarine. Fully loaded, its warheads had six times the power of the Hiroshima atomic bomb. With 12 VLS tubes for ballistic missiles, four torpedo tubes for Mk 48 fish, it could seek and destroy enemy warships, project power ashore with fire-and-forget Tomahawk cruise missiles, carry out Intelligence-Surveillance-Reconnaissance (ISR) missions using the Advanced SEAL Delivery System—ASDS. With an admitted speed in excess of 32 knots, it ran quieter than most subs at five knots. Of all three classes of attack subs—*Los Angeles, Seawolf,* and *Virginia*—only the latter was designed for littoral assignments or penetration in shallow water. Overall, the *Virginia*-class subs were the world's most deadly weapons

James shuffled over to the bedroom door.

"Honey bunny. A man's here." The enticing sounds of a woman preparing for a romantic evening fell silent. "I need to speak to him." He chuckled with a mirth he didn't feel. "He'll be gone before you're ready." *And so will I.*

He got no response and flung the front door open. SA Haster stood there, trench coat flapped open to reveal a rumpled off the rack suit, a blue shirt that clashed with the green in the jacket, and wingtips that had needed a shine since the BREXIT vote. An image of Ichabod Crane flitted through James' brain. Most British MI-6 agents were natty dressers, believing their appearance mirrored their tradecraft. Clearly, SA Haster didn't share that opinion.

The man-bag over his shoulder reinforced the image.

With a sweep of his arm, James growled, "Five minutes, SA Haster."

James plopped into an overstuffed chair letting Haster find his own seat and considered his unwanted guest. The agent wore no wedding ring. He had long fingers, a pianist's hands with chewed off fingernails and a nicotine stain on the first and second finger of his left hand. His eyes were red, face lined with worry.

Haster shuffled from one foot to the other, arms crossed over his chest clutching an eight by ten manila envelope. James relented and motioned to a guest chair.

"What brings you to my *private* getaway?"

"Please forgive my abruptness in showing up during your holiday. Generally, I would chat a bit, have a cup of tea, but we have a situation here. Are we secure?"

"Protocol requires I sweep for bugs wherever I stay, as I'm sure you do. Tell me what type of 'situation' we have and I'll decide what's sufficient."

Haster handed a pile of pictures to James. "Two days ago, MI-5 found five bodies floating in the Channel. Flag Officer Sea Training identified them as submariners from *HMS Triumph* SSN 19."

James pulled eye glasses from the drawer where he'd hidden them and flipped through the images. The bodies were bloated, some missing chunks of flesh, others entire limbs. One had its eyes pecked out. All were dressed in the remains of British naval uniforms. James recognized one victim, but couldn't place him what with the damage.

Haster tossed over more pictures. "These arrived the same day from your San Diego Police Department. Eight bodies identified by passport photos as British sailors."

Each image in the second group exhibited a mangled sailor on a barren concrete floor, body glistening as though wet, face a grim rictus of horror. All had raw red feral gashes across their necks.

"We identified them as Parisher trainees," and he tapped the first set of photos, "and like the first five, assigned to the *HMS Triumph*."

"The British Submarine Command Course, like our Basic Enlisted Submarine School?"

Haster nodded as he fumbled a pack of cigarettes from his jacket. He looked around the room, found no ashtray, so stuffed them away and pulled a plastic sleeve from the manila envelope. It held a creased eight-by-ten sheet of white paper.

"They found a note in one of the Parisher's pockets."

James took the document out and held it to the firelight. It was twenty pound, ninety-two brightness, no watermark. The FBI had reams of it by every copy machine. The note was typed, Times New Roman 12, centered on the sheet, one-inch margins. He ran a finger over the lines of type, likely from an ink jet printer. Dark gray fingerprint dust overlapped dirt smudges. The message read, *9:5 Slay the idolaters wherever ye find them and besiege them and prepare for each an ambush. But if they repent and establish worship, then leave their way free. Lo! Allah is Merciful.*

It was signed 'Tehrik-e Taliban Pakistan'. The Pakistan Taliban.

James shot a look over his glasses at Haster. "One of their members is Number Four on our National Counterterrorism Center's Most Wanted list, responsible for the 2008 bombing of the Islamabad Marriott which killed more than fifty people and wounded another 300. They also claim responsibility for the Times Square bombing. We thought they were defanged. I guess not."

James reread the note. "This note is designed to scare the hell out of Britain. Where is the *Triumph*?"

Haster's face fell. "We've had no contact for three days. If it is hijacked, no one officially claimed it." His temple pulsed and he forced his hands to his sides.

"How the hell did they capture one of Britain's most advanced nuclear subs—"

SA Haster cut in. "*The* most advanced since its upgrade a month ago."

James mulled that over as he logged into the FBI's secure database. Within moments, he had the basics on *HMS Triumph*. The sub was a *Trafalgar*-class sub, 4740 tons, 280 meters long, admitted speed of 32 knots. It carried McDonnell Douglas UGM-84B Sub-Harpoons and Trident II D5 missiles armable with Marconi Tigerfish Mk24's or one of thirty-eight nuclear warheads.

His adrenaline spiked. "Tell me it carries no nuclear warheads."

SA Haster sighed as though explaining the obvious to a dunderhead. "Every British submarine does as part of our mandate to move nuclear weapons off the mainland. *Triumph* carries enough to destroy the world as we know it."

James bit back a string of profanities. "You might have led with that." Winston Churchill's words popped into his head unbidden, 'The only thing worse than having allies is not having allies'. James rarely applied this to his British colleagues.

"Calm down, SA James. Please. The warheads are equipped with Permissive Action Links, a gift from you Yanks, which makes them impossible to launch by accident or treachery."

"Yeah, right." James needed to finish with Haster and get back to DC.

"Baby, I'm bored." Candy purred from the bedroom door in the little girl voice that drove James wild. Twenty minutes ago, he would have moved heaven and earth to fix any problem she had. Now, he felt her slip away like a boat loose of its anchor.

"In a minute, Pumpkin." James steepled his fingers under his chin and stuffed thoughts of Candy the Swimsuit Model away. "What was *Triumph* doing when it went missing?"

"Participating in war games with a Dutch submarine."

"The two collided?"

"The Dutch say no, and we found no damage to the exterior of the *Dolphun*, their sub."

"Any chance the Dutch sank it?"

Haster snorted. "The *Dolphun* is a diesel, so quieter than some, but it could never sneak up on the *Triumph*. To be thorough, we confirmed it retained the expected armaments."

Besides, James considered it unlikely the Royal Netherlands with only four submarines and six frigates would risk war with one of the world's naval powers.

He forced himself to sit. "Walk me through what you did to find it."

"Certainly—" Haster stopped as the bedroom door opened.

"I waited a minute, Honey bun. Are you ready?" Her voice was petulant. James turned and smiled at his soon-to-be ex-date.

"Candy. Please wait in the bedroom. I'll only be a moment." He turned away, ignoring whatever argument she might have. The door slammed and music blared.

"Let's go outside, SA Haster, give Candy some space," and they stepped out into the pristine mountain air. James breathed deeply, pulling the essence of nature into his being, soaking in its calm and logic. A half-moon hung over the rocky peaks and insects chirruped as they went about their nocturnal business.

Haster seemed oblivious as he reviewed the steps taken to locate *Triumph* and thoughts on how the sub base had been infiltrated.

"But the fake Parisher IDs wouldn't match the database."

Haster set his lips in a tight line. "The real photos were replaced, the responsible party arrested. He naively considered his treachery a contribution to the anti-nuclear cause."

"He replaced a homogenous group of sub trainees with Muslims?"

Haster bristled. "Americans think all terrorists are Middle Eastern with beady eyes and prayer rugs wrapped around AK-47s. In fact, only fifteen percent of the world's one billion Muslims are Arab. All cultures embrace Islam, SA James, be they white, black, brown or yellow."

James flushed, chastened, and turned to the link from Tess. It appeared to be a blog by an Eyad Obeid, the most recent post titled "Help". It included a video.

"I'll check our satellite photos, see if we spotted *Triumph*."

"Here." Haster pulled another envelope from his jacket and handed it to James. Inside, he found an array of timed images taken by America's KH-12 satellite, one of the 30,000 pound LEO—low earth orbit—behemoths able to read a text message on a cell phone. "From your Director. These would show if *Triumph* was visible."

James took everything inside. A hip hop song boomed from the bedroom as he dressed, buttoning with one hand as he stuffed his pockets with the other. "What's the next step?"

Haster remained silent. James arched a brow as he maneuvered cuff links into place. "What?"

"*Triumph* has a chink in its armor."

James liked this man less and less. He shrugged into his jacket and asked, "What's a 'chink'?"

"We skipped the degaussing. We wanted to test our boys' evasive skills."

When a sub moved through the ocean, it squashed together the earth's magnetic fluxes, giving its enemies a way to find it. This was minimized by a process called 'degaussing'.

James's brain tingled. "So when *Triumph* gets within range of a magnetic anomaly device, it stands out like coffee at high tea."

"Quite, though we've had no nibbles. One more issue you should know."

Haster pointed to a dead sailor James vaguely recognized.

"Who is this?"

"Sir George Linley, the Third Earl of Severne. If they will kill British royalty, SA James, they will kill anyone. We must find them."

James went still. Deep inside, a dull pain awoke, not for himself but a man he considered as close a friend as any he'd ever known.

He took a long breath. "You want Otto to find *Triumph*."

Otto was an artificial intelligence capable of finding almost anything on earth that could be written into a script. After his amazing success last year stopping a disaster of unimaginable proportions by using magnetic fluxes to find a submarine, the smartest minds in government tried to replicate him and failed. Sure, they had copied every single algorithm, but much like human DNA, Otto was more than mere code. Even his inventor, Kalian Delamagente, couldn't explain how the miles of programming sparked the results they did. Her best guess had to do with his sophisticated 'learning' capacity. As a result, Otto remained a one-of-a-kind creation.

"Your Director assures me the problem with Dr. Delamagente's clearance can be solved."

"Ms.," James corrected and then snorted. 'Problem with her clearance' put it mildly. "Even if I can clear her, America doesn't force citizens to comply with government requests. We'll have to find another way."

"And if they launch those missiles before you can 'find another way', you'll accept responsibility for the bereavement of world citizens?"

James said nothing. What could he say?

Haster continued, "I'm told you two are friends. Persuade her to let you use this Otto."

James laughed a mirthless laugh. "Most of the time, she won't talk to me, which makes listening to me a challenge." In fact, the last time they talked was when she blamed him for almost getting Zeke Rowe killed.

That's where he'd start. Zeke Rowe, former-SEAL, had the uncanny ability to block out fear, extraneous information, and slow things down in his mind's eye giving himself time to calculate what the enemy would do and organize a reaction. And when Rowe found out Sir George Linley was dead, Katy bar the door. He would take those warrior skills right to the enemy. Stopping him would be like talking a herd of crazed elephants out of stampeding.

"Give me until Sunday to work out the clearance," by calling in every favor ever owed to him. "Maybe you find *Triumph* by then. Now wait so I can say goodbye to Candy."

Chapter Four

Day Five, Friday, August 11th, mid-morning
Columbia University Office of Dr. Zeke Rowe

Zeke Rowe powered through his fifth set of forty handstand pushups, cooled down with a hundred sit-ups, and limped to the worktable on his bad knee—knees, but he long ago figured out you couldn't limp on both legs—to see what new insights the endorphins would reveal about the million-year-old bones.

He rubbed his eyes, flashing back to the shadowy figure outside his window at 2 am. He found footprints too large for a neighborhood kid taking a shortcut home. He stretched his neck, trying to touch ear to shoulder. Between spies and nightmares, there soon wouldn't be enough warm milk in the world to put him to sleep.

He should have run when he couldn't' sleep. It relaxed him. He loved the anonymity of night, had since he was a boy hiding from his drunken father. Good ol' dad, a high school football star who destroyed his shoulder one bright fall day, recruiters from Notre Dame and Florida State looking on. He gambled his future on a rough sport and lost. At first, he got jobs because of his football fame.

When those dried up, he blamed his wife and son. Rowe's mother smiled through it, remembering the man she once loved, but Rowe ran until his brain had no thought other than getting oxygen into his starved lungs. Then, exhausted but satisfied, he studied how nocturnal predators hunt.

They made it look easy.

He wiped his face and neck with a towel, slowed his breathing, and then returned to the thick-boned braincase of an 800,000-year old *Homo erectus*. He ran his fingers over the rough surface, the worn teeth, sensing the creature's history and the fullness of its ancient life. He found this skull next to a protowolf, yet there were no tooth or tool marks indicating either species preyed on the other. Rowe wondered if he held the earliest example of man and dog cohabitating.

His brain tingled. Nothing captured his imagination like a mystery, which explained why he once loved the intelligence field. Where others were confused by details, Rowe buzzed with connections.

The phone rang and went directly to voice mail. He and Kali planned to have dinner this evening so they could talk. Rowe knew what 'talking' meant.

"Hey, Zeke. Been a while. Let's catch up. No pressure just because I left four messages. I'm in the neighborhood. I'll drop by."

Rowe scratched behind his left ear. He lived by the philosophy that people sucked. The only exceptions were his brothers on the Teams, Kali, George—Sir George Linley—and Bobby James. He and James had worked together during Rowe's intel days, but lost touch until last year when James needed Rowe's help on a case. It ended with Rowe blowing the world's most dangerous terrorist so far out of the sky no one could find his body. The prosecutor had to try Salah Mahmud al-Zahrawi in absentia, not an easy task when half the evidence was top secret and the other half circumstantial.

In the process, Rowe almost died and met Kali. Pretty good year by SEAL standards.

Why James needed help wouldn't matter. He had made a promise to Kali.

He turned to the wide, shallow drawers behind him stuffed to capacity with jaw bones, teeth, phalanges and other artifacts. He selected two pig jaws from the Spanish Gran Dolina dig he hoped would establish the skull's time frame. The knots in his shoulders loosened and his breathing deepened as he lost himself in a long-gone world where days were marked not by a calendar, but the rhythm of the land.

Until James strutted in like a Power Player at a hostile takeover.

"Hey, bud. I like what you did with your wardrobe. Is that paleo chic?"

The primeval figures melted away. Rowe rubbed his hands down his shorts, pockets shredded by tools and cuffs ragged from the desert landscape of his latest archeologic dig. Kali called these his comfort clothes. He never understood why James put such thought into clothes.

"It ain't easy living in your fashion orbit."

"D'you think so? My personal shopper chose these. The pants are Italian wool, just out this season, the shirt ecru broadcloth with French cuffs. You know ecru isn't white, don't you?"

Rowe returned to the bones, trying to reclaim the visceral memory. "Did you call at 2 am and say nothing?" James looked confused. "Whatever you're here for will have to wait. I have a summary due in an hour." Not true, but conversations with James always led to trouble. In fairness, when you're a predator, all the world looks like your next meal.

"Dropped in to chat with an old friend. What's wrong with that?"

"Other than I'm busy?" Rowe leaned forward with a magnifying lens and examined the calcified debris encrusted on the pig's teeth.

"I can help; pour you a beer or something."

Rowe chuckled in spite of himself. He had missed James's irreverence. "Go ahead; chat."

So James shared his God's eye view of Candy Caminski. "Not someone I'd marry—not like Kali—but my Ms. Perfect is still out there."

When Rowe's only response was a grunt, James asked, "How's Kali? We haven't talked in a few months."

James and Kali didn't talk, they argued, and refereeing made Rowe happy to be a former SEAL rather than a kindergarten teacher.

"She didn't see my best side last year. If she gets to know me, she'll like me. Not today, but someday."

"God hasn't invented that day, bud."

"I'd like to attend her competition tomorrow—Man vs. Machine."

Before Rowe blurted out an inappropriate response, James's phone buzzed. He glanced and stuffed it back in his pocket. "Eitan's running late."

Dr. Eitan Sun, the FBI's premiere intelligence expert, undercover as a Columbia University techie. What did James need with him?

As though he read Rowe's mind, James continued, "He's checking something for me."

Rowe's brain hummed, like an engine warming up. "He didn't say anything this morning when we talked."

"It's need-to-know."

Rowe processed this through a brain conditioned to reading behind words and decided James wanted to pull him in on whatever the newest emergency was. Not this time. Rowe had a job he loved and a girlfriend he planned to marry.

"That leaves me out."

James flicked a piece of lint off his collar, his face the image of serenity. "I can tell you if you're on the Task Force."

Rowe tingled again, but focused back on the bones. "Tell me the outsider version."

"It's complicated."

"Speak slowly. I'll try to read your lips."

Sweat prickled James's forehead and he shifted in his seat. "Hell, Zeke, we have a big problem. Two subs are missing."

Rowe focused on James. "What happened?"

"A Brit sub, *Triumph*, was playing war games with the Dutch off the Netherlands. They were supposed to stay dark so it took seven hours for the Brits to realize they were missing. In an unrelated incident, *Virginia* left port yesterday and hasn't been heard from since." James ran down what he learned from a British agent named Haster.

Rowe's eyes were on the skull, but his concentration on the missing submarines. "These two subs' combined weaponry theoretically can attack every location on the planet."

"Or hold it hostage. Eitan's figuring out if the hijackers can access the nuclear weapons. MI-6 and the Navy say no, but I'll believe it when Eitan says it. How does someone hijack a sub, Zeke?"

A chill went through Rowe at the thought of rogue subs with his nation in their crosshairs. He pawed through a pile of old-fashioned wood pencils, selected one and flipped it. It was a habit developed years ago to help him think.

"Submariners board the sub. No fingerprints or iris scans required. If they kill a few officers, threaten a few families, everyone knows they're serious."

"We checked. Immediate families are healthy."

"Subs have no communication with the outside world. Photoshopped images of dead wives and frightened kids are persuasive.

"Why not use your in-house intel geniuses, Bobby?"

James laughed. "You're like them but smarter."

Rowe didn't need extra smarts to know James was hiding something. He removed breccia from pig jaws while he waited for James to reach a decision. Finally, he spit it out.

"They didn't degauss *Triumph*, Zeke. Something about testing the crew's skills. Otto can find it. I'm trying to get Kali's clearance reinstated, but after what she did last year, no one's eager to give it."

Rowe forced his voice to remain calm. "Why would she help you? She kept the entire American fleet out of enemy hands and you thanked her by trying to nationalize Otto. You would have, too, except she threatened to destroy him. Your response: Pull her clearance."

"We over-reacted. You're right. I'm going to fix—"

"How do you fix a lack of trust?"

James's face flushed. "Eitan says codes protecting the nuclear weapons can be broken, given enough time. The hijackers have a day head start. I'm prepared to apologize, but we'll use Otto with or without her cooperation."

That was a hell of a plan to mend bridges.

James wandered through Rowe's lab—the table of artifacts, the drawers bursting with comparison pieces, and the piles of documentation that supported Rowe's early man research—as though he understood the weight of what he asked.

"I need your help, Zeke."

Rowe flipped his pencil, peered at his friend and made a decision. "One condition: Tread lightly with Kali."

"Don't I always?"

"Do you ever?"

Chapter Five

Yong Soon Young

Yong Soon Young was the only child of Kim Soon Young and his Iranian bride Akhtar. 'Yong' translated as 'brave' in Korean, a fitting name for the son of North Korea's most feared general, though a daunting goal for the scrawny, underweight infant who cried piteously every waking hour. *Colic*, the doctors said. *He will grow out of it.*

By the age of two, he did indeed stop crying. He also stopped eating. Nothing edible persuaded this privileged child to do more than nibble. *Failure to thrive*, his doctors intoned.

His father declared him spoiled.

On Yong's sixth birthday, his father had enough and forced the pale, stick-thin boy to join him in a review of the personal protection detail for North Korea's Supreme Ruler. For ten minutes, Yong clung to the General's leg, shaking with fear. When his father commanded he walk at his side, Yong peed his pants.

His father was furious. He rechristened the boy Gil-dong—the invisible one—fired his tutors, and enrolled him in the local primary school. Living among the populace would cure him or kill him and the General didn't care which. The boy tried to make friends, but respected no opinion other than his own. He was shocked when the other kids laughed. His father shared ideas with subordinates and they all agreed. Gil-dong fought back, pointing out to classmates—reasonably he thought—that tests proved him smarter than them so they should listen to him.

He spent the next four years hiding in the library when not in class. There he lost himself in the benevolent world of fantasy where he became the courageous, noble son his father so badly wanted.

One day, Gil-dong settled in at his usual table preparing to read yet another story about strong men with lofty goals they always achieved, when he noticed a volume discarded on the desk. The cover showed a skinny bespeckled man-boy named Trevor Fieldman. Gil-dong flipped it open and started reading. By the age of twenty-three, despite his weak body, Fieldman became one of the wealthiest, most influential men in the world—this, according to the same giants of industry and political leaders who feared and respected Gil-dong's father.

How was that possible? His father insisted success came from physical prowess, yet Fieldman had much of the former and none of the latter. As he poured through the chapters, Gil-dong discovered why. Where his father controlled people with brawn, Fieldman achieved the same results with his brain by hijacking secrets which he leveraged to achieve success. This was an epiphany. Gil-dong had never considered his astounding intellect useful beyond passing tests and impressing teachers.

Over the next two years, Gil-dong learned to use trolls and viruses as his father did soldiers. By high school, the obsequious, frightened boy with the gracile physique and darting eyes became a self-assured man who treated his tormenters as lab rats. He hacked their school records, lowered grades and changed university recommendations to scathing attacks. When the class leader confronted him, he stuffed a dead bird into his locker. When the boy complained, Gil-dong hung the body of the family's cat over the front door and smiled when the eight-year-old sister broke into tears.

Everyone learned to leave Gil-dong alone.

He hoped his cunning would curry his father's favor, but the great general equated clever to weak. That changed when a few keystrokes persuaded his father's alma mater, the prestigious Sakchu military academy, to interview him for one of their coveted spots. Gil-dong arrived at the meeting, saluted as he had practiced, sure this time he would make his father proud. A young officer greeted him, regal in his starched uniform and chestful of ribbons. Gil-dong proffered his resume, but the interviewer brushed it aside. Gil-dong must first pass the physical requirements.

He failed.

His father threw him out of the house.

Thanks to a kindly administrator who took pity on the brilliant boy, he received a four-year scholarship to the American university NYU in Abu Dhabi UAE. Gil-dong changed his name to Ankour Mohammed—a football player he read about on the internet—and vowed to never again speak to his father.

Within a month, Ankour Mohammed, né Yong Soon Young, aka Gil-dong, hated NYU. Wealth served as the school's currency much like muscle had been his father's. Once classmates discovered his poverty, he became invisible. This surprised Mohammed. He thought here in the West, with its reputation for freedom of speech and open-minded attitudes, he'd find friends who agreed with his supremacist thoughts, but as in high school, everyone shunned his extremism. Mohammed wrote it off to stupidity and jealousy. Of course they hated him. He was smarter than they.

Without friends to detract from studies, he spent his days studying and his evenings laundering and repairing the two sets of clothing he owned—white drawstring pants with a plain white t-shirt, and off-white linen pants with a black long-sleeved dress shirt. With little effort, he excelled at his courses, especially science and engineering, and graduated tenth in his class. Most graduates had jobs waiting for them or grad school positions secured through friendly professors, but not Mohammed. As he pondered his non-existent options, one of his professors invited him to lunch. Dr. Nasr Al-alah was small in stature like Mohammed, wore glasses and a poorly-made gray suit over a stark white old-fashioned Nehru shirt. During their meal, Dr. Al-alah chatted about the University, student life, even Middle Eastern politics.

Halfway through Mohammed's hot fudge sundae, Dr. Al-alah said, "Your father, Mr. Mohammed, must be proud of you."

Mohammed flushed. He carefully folded his hands in his lap and looked Dr. Al-alah in the eye, "My father is dead to me as I am to him."

Dr. Al-alah smiled and instructed Mohammed to call him Nasr.

Mohammed liked this professor who allowed a boy to greet him informally. When Nasr offered to sponsor Mohammed's grad school application, Mohammed blushed.

"I have no money, Dr—Nasr. I must leave."

"*Insha'Allah*," Nasr smiled. *If God wills.* He invited Mohammed to meet other applicants. Mohammed cringed, but Nasr stopped him.

"This group is different. Each, like you, is brilliant and wishes to pursue graduate studies in a technical major."

Mohammed reluctantly agreed and arrived at the appointed time. He found himself chatting, receiving nods of agreement, and delving into ideas as he had never done his entire life. When he confessed to the pranks he pulled, everyone laughed with him, enjoying the strength brains brought to an argument. By evening's end, Mohammed had found a family.

The next day, he received an invitation to participate in a program sponsored by Dr. Nasr Al-alah. The money he earned would cover graduate studies. The only requirement was Mohammed join a *jihad* upon graduation. All adult Muslims must do this so Mohammed willingly agreed.

Soon, Mohammed spent all his time outside of classes with these students. Never in his life had he experienced such love. With them, he became part of something big. When he shared this with Nasr, the man smiled in his calm, loving way, the one that made Mohammed feel he could do no wrong.

"Praise be to Allah, young Ankour. It is time you understand the Great Satan. We will study Sayyid Qutb whose visionary ideas inspired even the great Osama bin Laden."

In the first lesson, Mohammed learned the West considered the individual supreme. This confused Mohammed because Islam believed everyone served Allah equally. In the second lesson, Mohammed learned that the infidel considered death failure while Muslims believed it began their glorious existence with Allah.

The last lesson startled Mohammed more than any other. Where the Prophet taught Muslim beliefs were never to be questioned, the West considered compromise a cornerstone to world harmony, that it demonstrated respect for other cultures by seeking a middle ground.

When Mohammed graduated—at the top of his class again—Nasr Al-alah introduced him to the Vali-e-faqih of Iran, heir to the Prophet Muhammad. The man was tall and charismatic, older than Mohammed but younger than Nasr Al-alah, with dark curly hair framing a noble face, smooth except for a left cheek more hamburger than flesh. Mohammed prostrated himself, nose on the ground, elbows raised. The Vali-e-faqih patted Mohammed and then addressed the group.

"The time has come to begin your *jihad*. Expect it to be difficult, but Allah will guide you. Follow his lead. *Fi Amanullah*—may Allah protect you."

One by one, the Vali-e-faqih pulled each newly-minted PhD aside and explained their job. Finally, Mohammed's turn came.

"Your task, young Mohammed, is two-part. First, infiltrate an American warship. Second, forgive your father."

Mohammed collapsed inside like wet tissue paper. Moments passed before he worked up the courage to speak to the man greater than all. "He refuses to speak to me, Holy Leader."

He rested a hand on the boy's shoulder, eyes boring into Mohammed's. "Speak to his soul. *Inshallah*. If Allah wishes, your father will hear you."

Mohammed's pride swelled. The Holy Leader saw potential in a man such as he, one rejected by his father, expelled from his homeland, and new to Islam. How great the Holy Leader must be to see what Mohammed offered.

He bowed. "Praise be to Allah. I will do as required to serve Allah and his messenger." When the Vali-e-faqih left, Mohammed asked Nasr, "How am I to speak to my father's soul?"

"Thy Lord hath decreed ye must be kind to parents. Say not a word of contempt, nor repel them, but address them in terms of honor. And, lower to them the wing of humility. These are the words of Allah. Praise be to him." He left Mohammed alone in the room.

Mohammed decided to eat nothing, drink only water, and await Allah's guidance. He sat cross-legged in a corner, held his hands out in supplication and prayed.

A day later, he approached Al-alah. "I wish to call my father."

"The time for that will come when Allah wills it. First, we begin your journey into the belly of the Beast."

On the flight across the Atlantic, Al-alah explained al-Zahrawi's plan.

"You are responsible for the second of three stages in this the holiest of *jihads*. If you fail, we fail. The first is complete. We have two nuclear submarines which will soon destroy the West." At Mohammed's astonishment, Al-alah merely fluttered his hand through the air. "All is possible with the guidance of Allah."

"In the second stage, we capture an American naval vessel. You will be undercover so must sublimate your personality, opinions, and attitudes. They have no part in your jihad. Can you do this?"

In Mohammed's mind, his supremacist views were the root of his success so why would Al-alah require he hide them? Still, he answered in words spoken by every *mujahid*.

"*SubhanAllah*. If Allah wills, he will give me the strength."

"You have less than three weeks. We have arranged quarters for you in San Diego, California. There, you will befriend an officer on the American warship. If female, you will seduce her. If male, you will turn him over to Shalimar."

Mohammed blanched. "I cannot speak to females as is done in such a decadent country. I am repulsed to touch them. Is there another way?"

Al-alah took the boy's hand, "You are my star, Mohammed, but if you cannot do this, return to your father."

"N-no, I will do it." He laughed nervously. "How does one 'flirt' with a female?"

"I will teach you," and Al-alah said nothing more.

They landed, passed through customs, and exited. Al-alah put his hand on Mohammed's shoulder. "It is time to call your father. He must know you forgive him and he must forgive you."

Mohammed bowed and made the call. To his surprise, his father was friendly, as though expecting the call. They discussed his mother, his father's new position as *Wonsu*, and Mohammed's desire to serve Allah. Where Mohammed expected disgust that he abandoned the religion of his family, his father merely grunted acknowledgement and hoped Mohammed would allow him to be part of his future.

It shocked Mohammed. His father dictated, never requested. He offered a stunned, "Of course," and ended the conversation.

Al-alah now gave Mohammed final instructions. "A boy lives in the apartment building you will move to," and provided a name. "You may need to eliminate him."

He gave Mohammed a card to provide money and they went their separate ways.

Chapter Six

When Mohammed reached San Diego, California, he moved into a bachelor unit—a funny name for a room big enough for a family. He found the building's security cameras so he would know to avoid them, located the boy, pocketed the set of keys he found on the kitchen counter, and browsed through the supplies that filled the closets.

That done, he logged onto his secure account. First, he needed a list of cruisers based at the San Diego Naval base. Thanks to the internet, he came up with six. Only two fit Al-alah's requirements: *USS Bunker Hill* and *USS Princeton*. He would infiltrate both.

For no particular reason, he started with *USS Princeton*. He drove to the base, parked in a public lot near *Princeton's* dock, and trained a set of powerful binoculars on the gangway. When a group of officers left for the day, he followed them to a downtown bar called Trophy's. The males trolled for women leaving the lone female by herself. He knew he should approach her, but Al-alah had not yet taught Mohammed how to talk to a female.

Back in his apartment, he rolled this problem around in his exceptional mind. Allah provided an idea. Mohammed would copy what men did on the television to attract females. One show featured young people at a beach, laughing, romping, and talking to strangers. Since San Diego had an ocean, he would start there.

An hour later, he was sitting on a bench by the ocean surveilling couples. They laughed, held hands, kissed, shared meals, chased each other into the water, swam, sunbathed, and rubbed lotion onto each other's bodies. After enough time, Mohammed went to the local mosque. There, he prostrated himself, asking Allah for guidance. How could he do what he had seen?

When he returned to his bachelor apartment, he found a beautiful green-eyed whore awaiting him. That night, she taught him how to talk to women, touch them, and seduce them. The next day, they walked along the beach hand in hand, laughing, giggling, whispering—all the activities he had witnessed yesterday. They even shared an ice cream cone. As they drove back to his apartment, he found himself hoping she would continue his instruction. When she explained their time was over, he told her he had something for her inside. She smiled and started to walk away, but he stopped her.

"It is a bonus. You have done well. I wish to express my gratitude."

Her brow knitted in confusion, but curiosity prevailed. She allowed Mohammed to lead her inside. Once there, he slapped her so hard she crumpled to the ground, green eyes shocked, beautiful blue-black hair spilling over the red welt blossoming on her cheek.

"Do not yell. You will be safe." When she started to scream, Mohammed punched her in the stomach. Hard. She curled inward and vomited.

"No more noise or I must do something you will not like." Mohammed pointed to a chair. "Sit," which she did without hesitation. He tied her in place and slapped a piece of tape over her mouth. Now, it no longer mattered if she knew the truth.

"I cannot risk you talking."

She shook her head frantically, eyes wild, but he ignored her as he laid out a plastic sheet on the living room carpet, lifted her chair from behind to avoid her kicking legs, and placed her in the middle of the plastic. There he left her while he retrieved a knife that was as long as his forearm with a thick razor sharp blade that gleamed purity. Al-alah had provided it and Mohammed was eager to test it. He yanked the whore's head back to expose the smooth alabaster neck and sliced from ear to ear. Blood spewed, narrowly missing the edges of the plastic. He needed a larger sheet next time. Within minutes, she bled out, the stink of excrement mixed with her jasmine perfume and a yearning Mohammed had never experienced. He wrapped her carcass in the plastic, rolled it in a large rug, trundled it to his car and drove east into the Cleveland National Forest to a place called Loveland Reservoir where he dumped her body. By the time someone discovered her, it would not matter.

He cleansed himself as required after touching a female and then went back to Trophies, hoping to again find the female officer. As before, she sat alone. Mohammed sent her a drink as the whore had suggested and smiled when she came to thank him. Within minutes, she was telling him her life story. He asked questions, expressed interest, winked at her piggish eyes, and bought more drinks as he had been trained. Much to Mohammed's surprise, it worked.

Until he asked for the ship's roster. Even after six drinks and a promise of sex, she refused, reminded him he might be a terrorist plying her with drinks to get information. Then she giggled and kissed him. No matter how he ingratiated himself, she told him nothing. Mohammed had to stop himself from grabbing her by the throat and forcing her to speak. They arranged to meet later in the week. He would persuade her to be more open then.

The next night, he repeated his efforts with a female officer on *USS Bunker Hill,* failing again. Back in his apartment, he bowed low with his hands on his knees and began prayers.

"I saw Allah's Messenger—may peace be upon him—perform ablution like this ablution of mine. Then Allah's Messenger—may peace be upon him—said he who performs ablution like this ablution of mine and then stands up for the Prayer and offers two rak'ahs of the Prayer, without allowing his thoughts to be distracted, all his previous sins are expiated."

He sat up, feet folded under his body, turned left and right, saying, *"Peace be upon you and God's blessing."*

Mohammed remained seated, enjoying the feel of Allah around him. He offered a final *Peace be upon you, and God's blessing,* rose, and called Al-alah to report his failure.

"We will use Shalimar. The process has succeeded many times. Set up a Facebook account under Shalimar's name. In her profile, say she seeks consultants for a book she's writing. Find the right officer and Shalimar will handle it from there. If the officer resists, blackmail him. Believe this, once he provides one piece of information, he will provide the rest.

"Here is the address and password of a friends-and-family website for *Bunker Hill.* Find men and Shalimar will meet them."

Mohammed set up Shalimar's Facebook account and then logged into the *Bunker Hill* friends-and-family site. Each name he searched on Google, trolled their social media accounts, and dug into all online activity for details of their life. Two hours later, he had no promising officers. Today apparently was not Allah's time to reveal himself. Mohammed stretched, got a drink of water, and decided to try one more name.

The next on the list, Executive Officer Lt. Commander Kevin Taggert, was single, no children, parents dead, with many short-term girlfriends, and love of thrill-seeking activities such as skydiving and dirt bikes. Studies concluded these types of adrenaline-producing activities were favorites with traitors. Mohammed's chest tingled as he read. At eighteen, Kevin Taggert enlisted in the Navy. Two years later, after graduating from Officer Candidate School, he rose through the ranks until he achieved the second highest position on a warship.

Since then, nothing. Mohammed trolled the wealth of public documents available and many others hidden behind security walls made available by Nasr Al-alah's connections. Taggert had been reprimanded twice for tardiness in the last year and warned several times about credit issues. Small Claims Court records included five cases settled for non-payment of contractual obligations, the latest two months ago.

Mohammed tamped down his excitement and backhacked Taggert's online profile, located the man's personal IP address, and found the passwords to his financial records (in a file labeled 'Passwords'). His credit cards were maxed thanks to expensive restaurants, Las Vegas weekends, and large purchases at liquor stores. Bank records revealed a checking account balance of $142.03.

Money problems poised to sink Taggert's personal ship.

Though it was five in the morning, Mohammed friended Taggert under the guise of Shalimar and asked for his assistance with her novel, *The XO*. She needed the perspective of a successful, charismatic Executive Office. Anything he could share about his responsibilities, the price he paid with family and friends, and the risk to his life serving on a warship would be appreciated. She assured Taggert she wanted no national secrets—*only what you can post on the internet.* She ended with a smiley face as Mohammed had seen other females do.

Within five minutes, Taggert accepted the friend request. 'Shalimar' asked him to provide his PayPal email and she would send a stipend 'for expenses'. Within an hour of receiving the money, Taggert divulged *Bunker Hill's* current position (in dock), crew level (full), and deployment (wouldn't be 'for a while').

Mohammed smiled. The arrogance of Americans was predictable.

Chapter Seven

Day Five, Friday, August 11th
Columbia University Office of Kalian Delamagente

Eighteen hours to go before Man vs. Machine and Kalian Delamagente had yet to complete the programming to transfer Otto from the wall-mounted device that had been his world for two years to his sleek new mobile android bot.

If it were a simple matter of copying operating systems, she would have finished days ago, but Otto was an experiential learner. Because he modeled Kali's logical sensibilities, his arguments always made sense to her. For example, early on, Otto asked to be referred to as 'he' rather than 'it' explaining he had more in common with humans than the dumb computers with which he interfaced. He insisted on being called 'Otto' because palindromes symbolized his complex personality.

Kali's stomach growled. She checked her drawer, even though she knew the last of her emergency granola bars were long gone. She had lost ten pounds in the race to get Otto ready for the contest on time.

She tugged at an errant strand of hair, waiting for Otto to boot up, wondering how she had gone so far afield. Otto started as a tool to integrate technology into education, but became the world's most effective data mining system—which started her problems.

Well, it also brought Zeke Rowe into her life. In the past year, she went from dislike to respect to love for a man who spent most of his adult life doing things she didn't want to think about.

"Hello, Kali. How nice to see you. Did you have a pleasant evening?"

When Kali added Otto's verbal protocols, she included social graces she hoped would make people comfortable interacting with an artificial intelligence.

"Wonderful, Otto," she encouraged with a calm she didn't feel. Truth, Rowe had another bad night. He never spoke of his torture, but judging by his missing fingers and the limp, he gave much to his country—her country. He tried once to explain why he missed the SEALs, something about God-given talents and an obligation. According to James, the man was a human Otto, able to pull together incongruent scraps of information and draw the right conclusion.

It may be a God-given talent, but it tortured him.

Despite everything, she loved him. His humility and kindness, how he accepted everything without judgment, but lately he'd become distant. Though he promised never again to risk his life, she had become to doubt that was a promise he could keep.

"Kali? You were going to tell me about your evening."

She hurried through the details knowing Otto would continue prodding for one-point-five minutes—the amount of time she had programmed for the hello-how-are-you chit-chat people engaged in before getting down to business. Try as she might to tweak him, Otto failed to replicate the human ability to balance brevity with hospitality when necessary.

Ninety seconds later, she asked, "Are you ready, Otto?"

"Yes, Kali. I know tomorrow's competition against Dr. Sun is important for your thesis."

What Otto didn't know was literary agents had contacted her about a book deal if Otto defeated the nation's foremost problem solver. The event had become the geek version of chess's Deep Blue vs. Kasparov and the dollars discussed would pay off her grad school loans.

"I'm copying your operating system to the bot."

The bot would be Otto's foray into a three-dimensional world, one he'd only experienced from the flat vista of his monitor.

"When I'm mobile, the first thing I want to do, Kali, is touch something."

One of Otto's appealing characteristics was his zest to learn. He would ask questions, find holes in her theorizing, play Devil's Advocate, and offer suggestions until the initial hypothesis became bullet proof. She encouraged him to communicate using the cultural anomalies of his listener, such as when talking to Americans, use contractions.

Kali laughed. "Personally, I'd like to walk through walls as you do."

"Everyone does that in Second Life," the online world where Otto spent his free time. "I want to see what's outside your office, Kali. People race by, lights come and go. You disappear there each night and return in the morning. This room with its four walls, two desks, three chairs, nine hundred eighty-seven books, four hundred six magazines, six-thousand three emails—six-thousand four, six-thousand five—" A *ding* marked new email in her mailbox, "has been my home since you created me."

"Ms. Delamagente?"

The woman who stood at the office door, one knee bent, dressed for success in a navy blue a-line skirt, crisp white blouse, low pumps and a string of pearls around her slender neck, carried an Overnight Delivery box and wore a frown. Many serious students objected to Kali's cut-off shorts, curve-hugging tank top faded from too many washes, and the dime store thongs destroyed by Kali's dog Sandy's boundless appetite for chew toys. Kali didn't care. She had dressed for digging through wires and circuits this morning, not the weight of an intern's expectations.

And her head ached. It started this morning as a low rumble, one Kali expected to gut out. An hour ago, it had exploded like coffee in a microwave. She tried four aspirin to no avail.

Kali forced a tepid smile. "Give me a minute," she glanced at the intern's badge, "Martha."

She didn't. "This is from Berkeley Geochronology Lab, in California? The one that dates events using geology?" She sniffed. "It's important?"

Kali rubbed her temples, annoyed at how Martha posed each statement as a question. "It hasn't even been a week."

The girl's eyes turned to saucers. "Oh wow. You're working with them? My brother received a grant there, researching tectonics? He—"

"Thank you." Kali cut her off. She had no interest in Martha's brother's life story. "Where do I sign?"

"Right here?" and Martha stuck a clipboard forward. "Umm, what's in it?"

Kali scribbled her name. "Good news, I hope," and turned away before Martha asked more questions.

The girl left, whispering into her phone, "Jake! I delivered that box..." and melted around a corner.

Kali fixated on the package, afraid to open it.

"Is it bad news, Kali?"

Kali smiled at Otto. He was a kinesics expert, thanks to a body language module she installed when he told her how much the ability to grasp the unspoken word assisted in his research. His programming included programs from Jung, Briggs-Myer, and Keirsey so the AI could tailor conversations to personality types. He now asked people about their families and jobs, and commiserate over problems. No surprise, people liked talking to him. In Kali's case, even though she knew it was manipulation, he became a friend.

She had few of those.

"I'll know when I open it, which I'll do when I finish your modifications."

"The package is distracting you. If you open it, you'll work faster."

As usual, her body language was as subtle as face warts. "You're right," and she ripped open the box. It contained the ancient bones she had sent BGL, all carefully wrapped and labeled. Underneath she found an envelope.

"I can make out words, Kali. Would you like me to read them? *We are—*"

"No, Otto. Thank you." She tore it open using her finger as a letter opener.

And smiled. "The bones are 800 thousand years old, Otto."

A beep proclaimed the completion of Otto's upload. "And the rest can wait. I must install your senses."

Before she could begin, *Taps* announced a call from her advisor, Dean Porter Manfried. Her head throbbed. Time was running out.

"Hello, Dean. How are you?" She imagined his petulant face, the glistening dome of his forehead with a few straggled hairs, the portly figure stuffed into the confines of a University-issued desk chair, doubtless dressed in a suit in case a prospective donor appeared.

"Glad you're back. How did it go?" Without waiting, he continued, "Kali, you've been ABD far too long."

Kali personally knew many PhD candidates who were ABD—All But Dissertation—longer than she. Her shoulders tensed and throat tightened. "Dean—"

"I cut you slack because of your status," as a Nobel Prize short list, "though I'm beginning to think that was a fluke. True, we received some nice grants thanks to your notoriety." He forgot to mention the publication of her article last October on how Otto found submarines using geomagnetics. It was the first time a PhD candidate had ever been published in the prestigious *Journal of Scientific Research*. "But you must finish. I will give you one more month. Please, publish or leave."

"Did you get the letter from Bobby James?"

"Yes, of course. He said you're serving your country. Is he a boyfriend? Never mind. I don't care. Columbia's grad committee expects you to finish what you promised without the involvement of international criminals."

Kali started to hang up when he continued.

"And I am not your secretary. The next time you need Mr. James admitted to your office at one in the morning, do it yourself," and the line went dead.

The thought James lied to access her office made her headache throb. "Otto, did James talk to you?"

"Yes, at 12:58 this morning. He asked for the location of a British submarine, but failed to supply the correct passcode."

That did it. Breaking into her office and trying to trick Otto crossed the line. On a good day, she distrusted James. Today, an apology tied around his neck with a box of donuts wouldn't be enough.

"You appear upset, Kali. Should I have allowed him entry? I know humans have different rules for friends."

"I'm not upset at you." If only her head would stop pounding. "I'm trying to understand his purpose."

"I can help," and Otto proceeded to share every detail of the unauthorized visit, right down to James's phone call to his superiors explaining his failure, which of course, Otto overheard once James activated him. While he talked, Kali checked her voice mail. Nothing from James, but she had received a half dozen messages from someone at MI-6. Was that related?

"Thanks, Otto," she interrupted. Otto's ability to collect data outstripped anyone's ability to listen and the concept of *irrelevant* so far made no sense to his scripts.

"By the way, Kali, someone was in the hall outside this room four seconds ago."

The Bionic Man had nothing on Otto's audio receptors. "The intern?" Kali asked as she walked to the door.

"No. Her step is lighter and shorter."

Kali poked her head out into the hall as a door snicked shut. "It must have been the grad student next door."

"No, Kali. I recognize Kurdo Pham's footsteps. These correspond to an individual who weighs approximately one hundred ninety pounds."

More importantly, why had someone stood outside her door?

"Good news, Otto." Three hours and she'd made significant progress. "You have audio and visual," the former complements of a microphone in its mouth and the latter a camcorder with forty degrees of rotation both directions.

"I am sure I will have no problems in your three-dimensional world. I ran simulations in Second Life."

The video phone vibrated and Eitan Sun's melon-sized head atop a chubby, pear-shaped body appeared. He had the doughy complexion of a true geek unblemished by facial hair. Today, he wore a Giant's ball cap atop a ragged fringe of baby-fine hair that fell to his shoulders.

"Checking in on my shrewd friend, Otto."

As usual, every flat surface of his geekosphere was buried in snack food and the endless supply of reading material that fed his voracious cerebral appetite.

"I like today's t-shirt, Eitan." *If you're not part of the solution, you're part of the precipitate.* The scientist chose his t-shirts carefully and appreciated when someone remarked, which few did.

Eitan's fingers flew over three keyboards. "Will Otto be mobile soon?" His huge eyes, made more so by his thick glasses, were soft, even kind, but represented the tip of his formidable attention, intimidating those unprepared for the scientist's daunting intellect. Today, something flitted across his face. In anyone else, Kali would call it subterfuge, but Eitan was incapable of such a trait so she brushed it off to fatigue.

"Yes, but not today. Something's going on with Zeke. By the way, did Bobby check with you about using Otto this morning?"

Eitan shook his head, but Otto made the whistling sound indicating a person's words didn't match their body language.

"Um, was Kurdo in this evening?"

Keys clattered. "He didn't access the internet or servers. Why?"

"Nothing."

Riverside Church chimed 7 p.m. Damn. Zeke would be at her house in an hour.

Chapter 8

Day Five, Friday, August 11th
Columbia University
Office of Dr. Eitan Sun

Eitan Sun disconnected. It didn't bother him Otto thought he lied. Kali knew there were topics he couldn't talk about. Shrug.

Two nuclear subs missing. Technically, they might be late calling in, or exercising their prerogative to move independently, but no one on James' hastily assembled Task Force believed that, nor did they believe submarine captains from two countries would go rogue concurrently. In Sun's entire career, he'd never seen a highjacking work as flawlessly as this.

The nuclear warheads weren't Sun's greatest fear. Their complicated activation codes almost tamper-proof. No, the problem was the conventional weapons. The load-out on each sub was capable of wreaking worldwide havoc and many sailors knew how to fire them.

Sun opened the email James had forwarded, titled 'Help', sent to the FBI's general account after *Triumph's* disappearance. He bounced in his chair and stuffed a handful of Cheetos into his mouth as a smiling boy-man appeared.

> *"Hello, my friends! This is Eyad*
> *Obeid again. We've done it—NYU*
> *Abu Dhabi's newest nuclear physics*
> *PhDs." He panned over a group of*
> *squirming, happy, mostly-bespeckled*
> *men who looked like they'd hit the*
> *lottery. "We are in San Diego*
> *California, USA."*

The sky was blue bursting with fluffy white clouds. A ship's horn blew.

> *"I wish you could smell the salt on*
> *the breeze. Everywhere is green—*
> *trees, plants, grass. These are my new*
> *BFFs—trainees on the great British*
> *submarine, HMS Triumph."*

The camera zoomed out to take in Obeid's Best Friends Forever, a group of British sailors. Smiles creased their faces. A few waved. One did a quick jig for the camera. Obeid giggled.

> *"They spent two days telling me*
> *about the submariner life and then we*
> *toured the American Naval base.*
> *Now, we head for a farewell meal*
> *sponsored by Ankour Mohammed, our*
> *sponsor."*

Obeid approached a blocky warehouse indistinguishable from every other building in the industrial complex. The man identified as Ankour Mohammed put a hand over the camera.

"Turn that off!"

The video ended. Did Obeid know his new BFFs were about to die?

Sun rewound the video and paused when Mohammed came onscreen. His parents must be Asian and Middle Eastern. His eyes were cold, flat as pebbles, and devoid of emotion, like a man trained to follow orders, not think. His face was young, body solid. Sun knew the type. Properly motivated, he would see all ends as justifying the means. Sun's skin prickled.

He tapped the blog's *About* page and got another video.

> *"My name is Eyad Obeid. I was born in a tiny village in southern Iran. My family has no money, less food. There are no jobs here so my brothers did what all males in my village do when old enough—they joined the Muslim Society for World Peace. There, they received food, a place to live, the friendship of other jihadis and the warmth of Allah's love as they devoted their lives to serving His needs. Within a year, they were all dead.*
>
> *"My parents assumed I would follow that path, but our imam took a personal interest in me."*

Obeid held up a snapshot of a skinny pot-bellied toddler in the foyer of a beaten-down mosque. In his hand was a tattered Qur'an.

> *"Before I could talk, I was reading the only book available, the Qur'an. When the imam asked me questions, I bowed as I had seen others do when speaking of Allah. From that day forth, the imam fed me, educated me, and secured my acceptance into the university in Abu Dhabi UAE. In return, he asked I spread Allah's words to those who did not know his good work.*
> *"This blog is my effort to fulfill my promise, by interacting with you—who my religion calls 'the infidel'."*

Obeid's face creased in confusion, head tilted as he stared hard into the camera.

> *"My village says you are belligerent and superior, your conversations rough, and your actions amoral. I grew up on stories of your rudeness and hate. But that has not been my experience. From my first day at NYU, I found nothing but kindness, openness, and your willingness to listen. I have enjoyed our discussions on military strategy, politics, even current events, our shared struggles to learn nuclear physics, and the common wish for our futures with good spouses and honest children. As I graduate, I*

*wonder how I ever considered
differences in culture and religion as
motive for man to turn against man.
Together, we will make the world a
better place. Praise to Allah!"*

The final entry on the 'About' page displayed a
smiling clean-faced male, eyes bright with anticipation,
Summa Cum Laude scarf proudly adorning his robes,
graduation cap askew from the hugs of classmates. A tiny
bearded male in traditional Muslim garb stood next to him,
cold eyes fixed on the happy boy, hand on his shoulder as
though taking ownership of a new tool.

Sun flipped through the NYU Physics Department
pages until he found a paper written by Obeid. He opened a
proprietary program and backhacked to what likely was
Obeid's personal computer. It had no password so Sun
scrolled unobstructed through the files until he found the
email with the subject line 'Help'. For some reason, Obeid
suspected a problem and had programmed the post to
dispatch automatically to the FBI. Obeid wanted help
before it was too late.

Too late, according to Obeid, was August 30th.
Nineteen days from now.

But what—

Sun jerked. "Who's there?" The door to his lab
creaked opened, despite 'Do not enter' on a sheet of 11x17
paper. Who would ignore two primes? Sun glared as the
old man shuffled in, head down, back bent, dragging a
wheeled bucket.

"Get out!" Sun screamed. "Everything is clean!"

"My job!" The man held his nose and pointed at
crumpled candy wrappers, crushed soda cans, paper plates
of half-eaten food, even something green and fuzzy in a
pizza box. "I fix!"

"Touch nothing or I'll fire you!" The last time the cleaning crew straightened his lab, he had been unable to think for a week.

The man scowled, wrote in a notebook, and left. Why did people invade his space? Maybe if he made a larger sign—17x19 or 23x29. Those were very nice primes also.

He picked up the photo of his wife, her eyes dancing with the look that drove him crazy, wearing the string of pearls he gave her when she told him they were pregnant. He pushed 'play' on the photo. "Hello, sweetie. I have Season Six of *Star Trek Voyager* and popcorn. Get your work done and come home. I love you!"

After three iterations, Sun tucked his feet under his bottom, bounced once in his thickly padded chair, and with a flurry of keystrokes, went off into the virtual world to find the breadcrumbs *Triumph* and *Virginia* must have left. He didn't expect to find the subs themselves, rather indications of their presence like refueling ships, anomalous sightings, anything out of sync with the surroundings. With his clearances and hacking expertise, no internet-connected computer escaped his prying fingers. Data gushed like a broken anthill across the thirteen monitors in his workstation. He read twelve thousand words a minute, well short of Howard Stephen Berg's 25,000 world record, but fast enough for these data streams. He searched for spikes not as they applied to anything in particular but as they existed, or patterns or lack of patterns or one there one moment and gone the next. Sun possessed the rare ability to absorb, retain, and index large amounts of data which he could mentally comb through to find context.

Head back, mouth open, his magnificent brain browsed, tasting each bit of data for the right flavor. He scarcely registered the trill of phones, the footsteps of late-working colleagues, or the cough of the night watchman as he stuck his head in and left. A connection tripped up Sun's cognitive stream. The missing *Triumph* could reach North Korea by the projected date of a North Korean missile launch if it transgressed the Suez Canal.

Sun entered a code into his yellow keyboard and a counter popped up in the upper left corner of Monitor Thirteen.

"Hello, Armaida."

Armaida purred silently; she had no vocal program. Her sole function was to analyze the probability of relatedness among events. He redirected the data streams from his research to her queue. Ten minutes later, Armaida's counter stopped at fifty. That was inconclusive, as likely the data was related as unrelated.

Sun popped an orange segment into his mouth. Usually, the clutter of his lab, the multiple monitors, and the digital jewelry that dangled everywhere brought him peace. Not today. Something niggled from Obeid's auto-posted article. It was titled 'Help', but he mentioned nothing he needed help with. He went back to the email and perused the metadata. The video file size was larger than the content. Sun looked for Easter eggs—hidden files inserted by programmers activated with simple keystrokes. Obeid might include those to have fun with his colleagues, but none of the usual keystrokes worked.

It might be steganography, data hidden in an image file which the recipient would then extract. Using a simple program he had created, Sun quickly found a hidden video. It started where the original stopped, after Mohammed told Obeid to turn off his recorder. In fact, Obeid had simply dropped the camera into his pocket, hiding the video but preserving audio.

A door snicked closed, followed by shuffled steps, then yelps and grunts.

"What are you doing?" Obeid's voice. "Why are you beating our friends?"

"Kneel!" A new voice snarled. The camera briefly revealed four muscular males, their ebony skin glistening under fluorescent factory lighting as they waived AK-47s at a frightened row of kneeling British sailors.

Darkness again and Obeid shouted, "Stop!" Something crunched and then a painful cry from Obeid. When the camera again appeared, Obeid stood behind his University friends. All stared forward, shoulders rigid, legs stiff. Two hugged themselves. One stood in a dripping puddle Sun recognized as urine. About ten feet away were the British sailors, kneeling on a thick sheet of plastic. Mohammed sliced a knife through the air as he paced a circle around the captives' shivering bodies.

"You have the honor of being *shahid* in a glorious *jihad*," and began a litany on the greatness of Allah.

The visual disappeared, but a voice Sun recognized as Mohammed's shouted, "*La ilaha illa Allah*." *There is no deity but God,* and spouted the pro forma anti-Western rhetoric common among Muslim fringe elements.

The camera appeared again, showing Mohammed praying. Another "La ilaha illa Allah," this time parroted by Obeid's University colleagues.

"Today, your passing will provide the instrument of our *jihad*."

Mohammed approached one of the British captives. For the first time, an audio overlay of Obeid's voice came on.

"This is Haim, a nineteen-year-old boy. He enlisted in Her Majesty's Navy a year ago and planned to marry his hometown sweetheart on his next leave. Please let his family know his passing was honorable."

Mohammed closed his eyes, knife raised. "I honor you, infidel, for you are the purest of your colleagues," and slashed the boy's neck. Blood exploded, covering Mohammed's chest and face. "Take not these infidels who do not choose Allah's way to be your friends," and he sliced another boy's throat, the cut so deep, the head flopped back against his shoulder blades. "Take not from among them a friend or helper..."

Obeid leaped forward, but his colleagues pulled him back. Obeid struggled against them, shrieking as all eight Brits were slaughtered. The surviving Muslims crowded together, some praying, others blaming the Brits for bringing Allah's wrath upon them. Mohammed stripped himself of his stained clothes and replaced them with a brilliant white *thoub*, a short vest-like *bisht*, and the traditional *kufi* skull cap. The Kenyans wrapped the bodies in the plastic sheet and stuffed them into a small storage shed in a corner of the warehouse.

The screen went black, but the audio recorded Mohammed's voice, full, rich, joy overflowing. "Let us celebrate the beginning of our *jihad* over dinner," and the video ended.

A heavy darkness filled that same place where others might feel God. Sun rarely wished violence on another, but tonight, he heard Obeid's plea and promised to avenge the massacre of his friends.

A ping. Sean Delamagente, Kali's son, had agreed to Sun's terms. When the teenager started at the University of California San Diego, Sun told him to call anytime. Sun had once been sixteen and alone and wanted to support Sean in any way he could. A week later, Sean asked Sun to teach him hacking. After last year, the boy had a right to be paranoid so Sun sent him a list of ebooks and websites. Two days later, Sean asked for specific surveillance equipment. Again, Sun complied.

He heard nothing else from Sean until this morning when the boy asked Sun to run some data through Armaida related to eight homicides near the naval base. Sun wanted to ask if they were British sailors, but instead told Sean to go to the police. Sean refused, calling the evidence unconvincing. Sun acquiesced, but told the boy his terms.

He redirected Armaida to the analysis of Sean's data, expecting it to reach thirty percent, or forty. It hit forty-five which was still inconclusive.

And then it popped above fifty. Sun twisted in his chair. It would stop soon.

Fifty-eight. Sixty-two. Sun's head pounded. What had Sean stumbled on?

Sixty-eight. Sun couldn't take his eyes off the screen.

Seventy. He stared, willing it to stop.

It stopped at seventy-two, reversed and dropped to sixty-nine, sixty-eight, and froze.

He skimmed Armaida's report and found connections to not only the San Diego naval base but the missing *Triumph*. Sun hadn't purged that information from Armaida's buffers because, well, why would the two data streams intersect?

Worry. He texted Sean telling him to call the police and then told Bobby James' voicemail Kali's son was in danger.

Chapter Nine

Day Five, Friday, August 11th, afternoon
San Diego, CA
Apartment of Ankour Mohammed

"Have you decided which ship best serves Allah's purposes, Nasr?"

The *Princeton* female—she insisted Mohammed call her Muffin—had gone too far. She called him constantly. If he didn't answer, she texted. The last time they met, she grabbed his crotch. She had become a thorn in his shoe that kept him alert on a long walk, necessary but annoying. He eagerly awaited the day he could kill this fat, immoral female and lay her mutilated body next to the raven-haired whore.

"*Bunker Hill.* You have nineteen days," and he hung up.

Mohammed breathed deeply, letting Allah's goodness wash over him. He could not fail with his God guiding him. Mohammed arranged to meet Shalimar and the XO that evening. Then he called the *Princeton* female.

"Muffin? I have a surprise for you."

"Anky! You *calling* is a surprise. You have *never* done that."

"I prepared dinner. Are you available?"

He imagined her panting, fat bosom pressing against the tight uniform, double chin shaking as she visualized their evening.

"How about an hour. I want to change." She paused, catching her breath. "You never invited me over before, Anky. This must be special."

He laughed and gave her his address, then finished with, "Hurry."

The thought of how he had been forced to touch her and stroke her heathen hair disgusted him. He would like to torture her, but time had run out. He rolled industrial plastic across the living room floor, placed the saber, still crusted with the whore's blood, on the kitchenette counter, and waited.

Fifty-nine minutes after they said goodbye, she rang his bell. When he opened the door, she greeted him wearing nothing but a raincoat and a grin.

"I'm ready for dinner."

Mohammed gulped back the bile that burned his throat and invited her in, a heavy flashlight hidden at his side. Thirty minutes later, he loaded the bloody plastic sheet with her body, wrapped securely in a carpet purchased from Home Depot, into his car. How proud Allah must be of his servant.

Chapter Ten

Day Five, Friday, August 11th, early evening
Columbia University

Kali's footsteps echoed through empty hallways.
No phones rang, no people chattered, no elevator grinding
as it took students to class, only the faint thrum of music
from some party she hadn't been invited to. Again, she felt
as though someone watched her, but saw no one suspicious.
She shook it off. Her son had moved across the country.
Her best friend was still recovering from last year's trauma,
and after tonight, Zeke would probably dump her. There
were three good reasons to be nervous.

She signed out with the guard—*Sharon*, according
to his name tag—and stepped outside. The day's ninety-
degree heat had bled off to a pleasant evening, but her mind
was on her future. When she finished her PhD, she must
find a job. Most candidates ended up working for contacts
made during post-grad studies. Kali had no interest in the
FBI.

She glanced at the spot of light three stories up.
Eitan would be here until midnight or later, sleep on the
couch in his lab if he got tired, shower in the faculty lounge

in the morning, and eat breakfast from the food stands. Kali had expected him to grieve, but not for two years. She encouraged him to date, but he refused. Why would he, he asked. No one got excited when the clock showed 14:22, or the odometer reached 36912. No one saw the scintillating patterns that pulsed from data or traced their finger along the landscape of sizes and colors. *See the red one—how bright it is?* Kali wondered if the memories of his wife offset the pain. It might be a worthy trade.

Lost in her thoughts, she crashed full-bodied into a stranger. She flailed to regain her balance, flinging her purse in the process, exploding make-up and Kleenex and everything else around her feet. "Oh—excuse me!"

He pranced around her sunglasses to keep from stepping on them, tried to grab a bouncing pill box and ended up batting it further down the sidewalk. "My fault," and the stranger helped her stuff everything back into her bag. "I'm distracted. My wife… Well, there's a long story. I'm sorry," and he left, muttering about families and friends.

His voice was familiar. Kali watched as he left. He would be handsome except for a ragged red cheek, as though burned and badly. Did he wear sunglasses because he was he blind?

Kali shrugged. She had only forty-five minutes to shop, make dinner, and greet Zeke.

Kali rushed down the market aisles. The chicken smelled fresh so she put it into her basket. Same with lettuce, Brussels sprouts, rolls, and Zeke's beer. She handed over her last twenty and a handful of change and ended up putting half the beer back.

Ten minutes later she arrived at her building, an old brick multi-story squashed between two high rises and backed into a narrow alley. She crossed the lobby, a generous name for the unmanned Spartan foyer with its scarred linoleum and chipped beige walls, fumbled her key into the lock, bumped the door open with her hip, and ordered, "Down, Sandy!"

Undeterred, her fifty-pound yellow Lab clattered across the tile floor, planted his paws on her chest and swiped a wet tongue across her face while balancing on one leg.

"Nice day, huh? You always have nice days."

Kali rubbed under his neck and he sprinted to the bone shelf, wagging his entire backside in anticipation.

"You want your good boy good dog good evening bone," and she tossed him a treat which he swallowed whole, eyes begging for more.

She shook the box. "All gone."

The voicemail blinked. It better not be Zeke. She listened as she put the chicken and vegetables next to the stove and the beer in the refrigerator. "Hello, Ms. Delamagente. My name is Special Agent Haster with MI-6." She winced as his *s's* whistled. "I have a proposition for you that's already cleared with your SecNav and your friend, Special Agent Robert James. Please call when you get in."

Dropping James's name didn't work as Special Agent Haster with MI-6 hoped: She deleted all six of his messages.

Nothing from Zeke, which was OK. Nothing from Sean, which was not.

"He must call. He needs a ride from the airport."

How naïve she had been as a teenager, to think she could handle a baby. Between finishing high school, applying for college and finding a job, she struggled to bond with her son. Thankfully, grandma stepped in. By the time she passed, Kali and Sean had both grown up. Kali missed him every day. She wanted to visit, but he always said he was busy. Still, he promised to be there tomorrow for Man vs. Machine.

She jumped in the shower and stood there, hands against the wall, as the water washed over her. This weekend was about change. She and Zeke would figure out if they shared more than the past. Otto would become mobile. Man vs. Machine would climax her dissertation, and she would meet her adult son.

Cheered by a plan, she turned off the shower, thinking about the black tank dress that reached mid-thigh and the sixty-inch string of pearls she planned to wear this evening.

And heard the end of Zeke's message. "Sorry to cancel. I'm working on a ... project... See you tomorrow?"

Kali stood naked, dripping on the carpet, eyes hot as she tried not to cry. Six weeks ago, under sparkling night skies, awash in the thrill of ancient mysteries, she believed Zeke when he promised to turn is back on James.

"Damn you, Zeke! What gives you the right?"

She sobbed so hard her whole body shook. Tears spilled down her cheeks, Sandy's tail banging against her hope chest as he tried to figure out what to do. She blew her nose, threw on pajamas, shoved the chicken in the fridge and reheated soup which she ate standing up. She ended up throwing most of it out.

Dishes washed, Kali collapsed onto the couch. Sandy plopped at her feet, nose on his paws and snored contentedly, disaster averted. She was about to tuck in for the night when a news story interrupted the broadcast.

> *North Korea pressed ahead with final preparations. They warn any incursion into a 500-mile perimeter around the trajectory on launch day will be considered an Act of War. The highest ranking military officer, General Kim Soon Young, called this test more necessary than ever with the*

disappearance of two of the West's nuclear subs.

Missing subs—as in more than one? That's how James snagged Zeke. She wound a rope of hair around her index finger as the announcer continued:

> *In a show of support for a nation who has lately become a strategic partner, Iran called the western world out of control. "Islam is a peaceful religion who wishes to live in harmony with its neighbors, but we will defend ourselves as would the US and Britain if required."*

She flipped the TV off. "How's anyone lose a sub, Sandy?"

The Lab yawned and sprinted through the doggie door. As he sniffed for the perfect spot, her next door neighbor shuffled out dressed in pajamas and slippers.

"Hey, Mr. Winters. Everything OK?"

She met the retired Marine the day she moved in. He loved dogs, but considered himself too old to own one so offered to babysit Sandy. Since then, the Lab spent many sleepovers next door.

"Oh, sure. Everything's great." His glistening white capped teeth, unlined face, and thick gray hair made him look fifty instead of eighty. "A friend of yours stopped by today. Said he'd find you on campus. Did you see him?"

"Hunh. No. Who?"

"Didn't get his name. Nice looking guy, older than your usual, had a scar on his cheek like he was hit by a boiler blast—what's wrong, Kitten? Did I say something?"

It must be the man she'd run into.

"No—I did see him. Did he say anything else?"

"Like what?"

Sweat broke out on Kali's forehead. "Never mind."

"Sure, kitten. How's Sean? Doing OK in San Diego? That's a great town, San Diego. Lots of Navy people, decent folk. And what about Zeke? Sure miss talking shop with him. When's he coming by again? You two kids have fun in De-manisi?"

Kali shared highlights of the paleoanthropological dig, but kept her dark thoughts about Zeke to herself.

"I gotta go, Mr. Winters. Sandy, come!"

Sandy bounded back through his doggie door and sprinted to her bedroom while Kali checked her phone. Still no call from Sean. She brushed her teeth, locked the doors, and touched a photo of her son. He held his acoustic bass in one hand, Pernambuco wood bow in the other, and wore a crooked grin, such a whimsical period in Sean's life when his biggest decision was whether to study music at Julliard or science at MIT.

She flipped on her favorite Edgar Meyers recording—a duet with Yo-yo Ma—and opened a Robert Parker novel. Only 10 pm and already tucked into bed. Maybe she should join a chess club or attend a poetry reading. She liked poetry when she was a child.

Chapter Eleven

Day Five, Friday evening, August 11th
Little Italy, San Diego CA, Apt of Sean Delamagente

Sean Delamagente rubbed a hand over his greasy hair and caught a whiff of old sweat. *Yeah. I'll have to shower tonight before leaving or change clothes.* He sniffed again. *Or both.*

He slouched in front of his computer set-up, wearing black jeans and a Quicksilver t-shirt as he did every day and many nights to bed. He purchased ten-packs so dressing was a snap. Fashion didn't matter. He had no girlfriend.

A crash blurted from his speakers. He'd built a subroutine to locate the source of noise and zoomed in on it. Apartment 140, Harmon—drunk again. He emailed a screenshot to the landlord so he knew who broke the chair. Apartment 420 and 533 were back from TGI Fridays with doggie bags. Sean was surprised they were still dating as much as they fought. Then Apartment 310 slipped into the frame. Ankour Mohammed. He always dipped his head as though hiding from the cameras.

Sean leaned back and gazed around his bachelor unit—wrinkled clothes piled on the floor, spreadsheets and diagrams on the walls. Others might call it disorganized, but not Sean. Yeah. He rubbed his temples, worried he'd inherited his mother's headaches.

Or maybe it was stress. Probably stress. All senior year, after being kidnapped by Salah al-Zahrawi, he looked over his shoulder. If he took the subway to class events, he'd cut through two or three cars, and as the doors slammed shut, jumped off and board the next one. As he walked, he checked his reflection in storefronts. Sometimes, he started running, full speed, and then ducked behind a building. He never found anyone, but couldn't stop himself from doing it again the next time.

He never told his mom. She had enough going on with a new boyfriend, her PhD thesis, and Dean Porter. If his mother's experiences represented academia, Sean wanted nothing to do with it. He liked what Eitan did— play computers all day.

He liked what Zeke did, too, but could never be that person. First off, he had no muscles. Except in his fingers. He could type all day. No problem-o. Yeah.

When he graduated last June, he moved to California because UC San Diego had given him a scholarship. At first, his landlord rejected the idea of a sixteen-year-old living alone, but when Sean nabbed two employees stealing money, the manager hired him as Security Director, the pay: free rent. That worked for Sean. His scholarship covered tuition and books. His mom paid for food. Eitan funded the spy cams. The boy needed nothing else.

He pressed the heels of his hands into his gritty eyes and rubbed. Classes were way easy so he spent all his free time studying hackers, crackers, backhacks, traffic analysis, cryptanalysis, keyloggers, web crawlers, web spiders, and everything to do with cybersurveillance. When he moved in here, he set up cameras in the building and adjacent areas like the Dog Park. Yeah. He found three lost dogs already which made everyone happy, but Sean needed to find bad guys before they found him. Not like last year. Yeah. He was smarter each day. He almost wished al-Zahrawi was alive so he could beat him.

But today, his cone of safety had cracked. Someone had been killed and Sean was pretty sure the murderer lived in his building.

It started two weeks ago when one of his web crawlers logged that Ankour Mohammed in 310 spent a lot of time talking about the San Diego Naval Base. Yeah. Most people only did that if they worked there. Sean planted video cams in an industrial park catty-corner to the Naval Base and waited.

Today—this afternoon—his spy cam recorded Mohammed on his cell talking in Farsi. Sean got only one word when he ran it through his translator: Parisher. It would have been meaningless except for a news story about dead bodies thought to be *Parisher* trainees.

Was this the same *Parisher*? His throat tightened and a chill ran through his body. He tagged fifteen instances of Mohammed's voice in his library of surveillance tapes. To eliminate background noises, he used a free program called Waves X-Noise to block frequencies below one-hundred ten Hz and above five kHz—the range of human speech—and then erase common sounds like cars, machinery, and dog barks. He got two matches. The first was Mohammed talking to an American in Seaport Village. Yeah. Wrong location, but Sean filed it.

Before he could click on the second, something moved to his left.

"Oh—yeah, I missed your dinner." Itui, a species of electric eel called Itui Cavala, was often hungry. The snake-like creature bumped again against the wall of a six-foot aquarium, one luminous eye staring at the boy while its shining tail swished through the water, as though to ask how he had forgotten.

"Here, your favorite," and Sean dropped five pinches of brown flakes into the water, then five more while he chatted about Mohammed and Parishers and asked the fish what it thought was going on.

Itui proved good company, but Sean had purchased him for other reasons. Every day, Sean harvested its electricity. If anyone broke into Sean's unit, a device powered by this invisible energy source silently collected data which it automatically uploaded to the cloud. Yeah. If Sean failed to access it within a day, Eitan Sun received an email link to the files.

Itui satisfied, Sean opened the second file, recorded five days ago. Mohammed had been with British and Middle Eastern individuals judging by the accents. Sean identified a name—*Triumph*—as the group disappeared into a building. When they reappeared thirty minutes later, the British accents had disappeared. This time, his translator picked up *'38 44 90'* and cruiser. Was it a code? He googled them and found nothing. He got only one more sentence—*Why kill them?*

His eyes glazed over and his hands trembled on the keyboard. He gulped, trying to slow his breathing, stroked the keys, listened to the hum of the drives, let the familiarity calm him. He stuffed a handful of Tostitos from a half-full bag into his mouth as he checked his email. No word from Eitan. Sean had to get ready for his flight, but his brain wouldn't stop whirring through everything he'd seen. There was a connection he couldn't quite see.

As he was about to give up for the evening, he found something unusual. A week ago, Mohammed in Apartment 310 entertained one of the most beautiful women Sean had ever seen—deep green eyes framed by lustrous blue-black hair, skin so smooth not even pores marred the perfection. She stared into his camera as though she knew he watched. She and Mohammed left in beach clothes and returned hours later, but she never exited Mohammed's apartment. He ran an open-ended search, but found nothing. He widened it to include cars around the building the day she arrived and then compared those to the ones he logged in today.

One car stood out, in the same spot. It even had a ticket.

Where had she gone? And who was the woman now in Mohammed's apartment?

Sean would have to miss his flight.

Chapter Twelve

Day Five, Friday evening, August 11th
Imperial College, London, Lab of Dr. John Penbury

Only thirty-eight, but Oliver Najafian was already stooped under the weight of worry. His hair clung flat and dull to his skull and grey streaked the temples. Stress. It must be. His father retained rich dark hair into his sixties.

The Iranian immigrant trudged down Prince Consort Road's wide tiled sidewalk and entered the double glass doors of Imperial College's Blackett Laboratory, Physics Department. He wiggled through the stream of people rushing home, shoved his backpack into a file cabinet, and began to clean up after students who cared little for the physics Oliver had loved passionately until the world turned it into a grenade with the pin out. Tonight, he would change that.

With a doctorate in physics, Najafian had wanted to use it to better the lives of his countrymen. Iranian leaders, though, had other ideas, all focused on nuclear weapons. Najafian hastily immigrated to Britain. A future was important to him.

But there was a problem transferring his degrees. The British Education Ministry gave him a file number and promised to call. Najafian did not trust government so every Monday, he walked 2.8 meandering miles along Hyde Park, skirting Buckingham Palace Gardens, wound from Strutton Ground to Old Pye Street to St. Ann's and Great Peter Street, until he reached Marsham Street #2, home of the immigration office. There he asked about progress on his case. They always promised to tell him when they had word and he returned home.

Thanks to the intercession of his long-time colleague, Dr. John Penbury, Najafian found this job as a lab assistant while he awaited the disposition of his case. Penbury was one of two top world scholars in an area of theoretic physics called metamaterials, Najafian the other. Penbury's inquiry focused on using metamaterials to hide objects from view, not unlike Harry Potter's cloak in the famous movie. Often they chatted about the concept—refracting light rays so they flowed around an object rather than bouncing off. People saw the distraction, not the reality. They theorized that adaptations of the process would divert other rays such as shock waves or sound. Always, they focused on peaceful uses.

Until the man named Salah suggested Najafian had been misled.

Counters wiped, beakers organized, voltage probes in place, accelerometer and spectrometer secured—Najafian unlocked Penbury's windowless office and sat in front of the computer. He ran through the plan one more time knowing if this man he'd known half his life was the devil, Najafian would do everything to stop him. First, he would verify Salah's proof.

That's when the alarm blared. The building was on fire.

Chapter Thirteen

Day Five, Friday evening, August 11th
Englewood, New Jersey, Home of Zeke Rowe

The early evening sky purpled. One hand on the wheel at twelve o'clock, the other tapping out the rhythm to Trace Adkin's *Arlington*, Zeke Rowe took Van Nostrand to Summit and turned left. To one side lay the Flatrock Nature Center, on the other the multi-million dollar estates of New York's mega-rich. Nestled within this enclave was the safe house Rowe called home. It had been compensation for assisting in the capture of Salah Mahmud al-Zahrawi, number three on the FBI's most wanted list. The case remained open until the terrorist's body turned up so to Rowe's thinking, he continued to assist.

Despite himself, ever since James's visit, Rowe's brain tingled as though he was beginning a job. It came, he guessed, from a life lived on the edge, pitting his wits against those who would destroy the world he loved, and Rowe's statistical ability to stop them.

He wasn't worried about *Virginia*. An American sub had never been hijacked. Sub CO's were cowboys—supposed to be. They would do what must be done and ask forgiveness later. And the crew—God help the terrorists who thought those guys would cower, no matter the odds.

But two hijacked subs on opposite sides of the planet could control the globe.

He crept by his house, talking on an empty phone line while scanning cars, dog walkers, joggers, and a utility truck parked after hours. He'd done this since his SEAL days and couldn't shake it—didn't want to, either. Rowe knew typical. Anything else would be like perfume at an Augusta member's meeting.

Satisfied, he pulled his 1978 350 SL into the drive of the two-story wood-and-stucco house. The car had been the treasured possession of a SEAL who gave his life for his country while under Rowe's command. He had no family, so Rowe kept it until he could find its rightful home.

He studied a couple walking arm-in-arm until their faces clicked into place.

"Enjoying your visit, Mr. and Mrs. Shellock? Joe treating you right?"

They chattered back and forth a few minutes until Rowe limped into his house. He sniffed, looking for scents out of place, but otherwise, couldn't stop thinking about this evening's dinner with Kali. 'To talk' was code for the heart-to-hearts women considered necessary and men liked as much as ballroom dancing. Explaining himself was not Rowe's strength. He had planned to swear he was not the man she met last year. Now he had to explain why he would be breaking his promise.

A run would help. He threw on navy blue shorts, a sleeveless sweatshirt, and Nikes. Each time he ran, he took a different path. Today, it was a five-mile loop along Flatrock Brook, and then cut uphill into the underbrush adjacent to his house. After two miles, he increased his pace to a five-minute mile. Two miles later, knees throbbing and lungs burning, a thought struck him like lightning. He slowed, chest heaving, lungs working hard to pull in oxygen, and turned toward what would be North Korea if he could see that far. He rolled the idea over in his head. The more he did, the more it became the only thing that made sense. The best reason not to use a stolen sub was because it was in transit.

Rowe took off, covering the final mile in four-point-seven minutes and puffed to a halt in his driveway where he found James leaning against a government-issue Buick checking his Blackberry.

"You're as predictable as ever."

James grinned and stabbed a one-fingered message into his phone. "Can I get a beer?"

James's stress tell twitched. Rowe went inside with a follow-me gesture, then toweled the sweat from his neck and face while James stood before a picture of the dig that had rocketed Rowe to paleoanthropologic stardom. Finding proof of early man in that location was historic. James stared a moment longer, then settled into one of the two Lazy Boys, de rigueur in safe houses.

Rowe popped open two beers, rolled one across his forehead, and extended the second to James. The agent downed a mouthful and stared into space. Rowe waited, knowing his friend would talk when ready.

James's eye twitched again. "I'm worried about *Triumph*. Why steal a nuclear sub if not to use it? Each missile has multiple warheads, and each of those has the power of fifteen Hiroshimas."

Rowe rolled the beer can in his hands. "Relax. If the hijackers could use those warheads, they would have."

James shrugged. "That's supposition."

"But I'm right. On an American sub, the launch process for nuclear warheads requires a Presidential key, to preclude a rogue—or hijacked—sub using them. The Brits have something similar." Rowe waited for James to respond, but nothing. "Any word on *Virginia*?"

"It's still in the window which means my bosses aren't yet officially worried," and he fell silent.

Rowe decided to push. "What have the Brits done to find *Triumph*?"

James shrugged. "It can stay underwater until food runs out, which is up to six months. It could hide in the Swedish fjords where MAD" Magnetic Anomaly Devices, "can't penetrate."

Rowe sat up, elbows on his knees and fingers cathedraled. "But why, unless they're planning a surprise attack on Iceland? SOSUS will light up any exit from the area."

James wouldn't make eye contact. "Speculation is something about *Triumph* makes it invisible to sonar. They didn't demagnetize it because they wanted to see if the gadget worked—whatever 'the gadget' is. What would make a sub invisible to sonar?"

Without a word, Rowe went to his office and pawed through a pile of files on a chair.

"Metamaterials," he called as he strode back waving a magazine. "Manmade artificially engineered structures this article predicts will make warships invisible in ten years."

"Let me see." James skimmed the article. "The leading researcher is British."

Rowe took a swallow of beer and nodded toward the TV. "The press says that Britain allowing a nuclear sub to fall into terrorist's hands makes her as much a loose cannon as the hijackers."

An alertness filled James's eyes. "North Korea plans to launch a satellite August 30th. What if that isn't a satellite but a space-based weapon, and what if *Triumph*—or *Virginia*—is part of the plan? How do we stop it?"

Zeke shrugged. "We'd have to sink it, Bobby."

James's temple throbbed. "No one's ever sunk a nuclear sub."

"But nuclear subs have *sunk* with zero contamination to the seas around them. The reactor is welded into a core assembly inside a pressurized vessel. Even if that leaks, seawater dilutes the radiation at a rate of ten percent for every two feet of water. Sink it in twenty feet of water and you neutralize the effect."

James went outside to make a phone call. Rowe's thoughts drifted to the men on *Triumph*. The hijackers would cherry pick the crew, separate out the weak and kill the rest. The longer Britain took to find their sub, the more men would die.

James returned and stood there, hands in his pockets.

"There's more." Rowe's neck tingled waiting for the other shoe to drop. He sat back, laced his hands behind his head, and waited while James paced. His eye twitched. Twice. Whatever this was, was personal. A news story about Sir George Linley popped unexpectedly into his brain. George, one of the few people Rowe called friend, was following the Royal Family's proud history of military service.

"George is on *Triumph*."

James cleared his throat and explained about the dead sailors, one of which was George.

Rowe's ears started to ring. His chest got so tight he feared it would crush his heart. A wave of pain washed over his body as though hit by an explosion. He had met George at the University of Paris where Rowe taught a lifetime ago. He remembered his open smile, easy acceptance of a pacifist teacher with barely the francs for an apartment. They had beers after class one day and ended up discussing William F. Buckley's quote, *Idealism is fine, but as it approaches reality, the costs become prohibitive.* Rowe considered it the jaded opinion of an old capitalist while George, despite his youth, understood ideals often were not shield enough against the treachery man rained on his fellow man.

When Rowe's fiancée was slain by the very mob his socialist principles respected, Rowe might have self-destructed if not for George whisking him away to a thousand-year-old castle nestled in the British hinterlands. There, Rowe ate, exercised, read, and beat himself up for his naïveté. After a month, he found he could talk to people, even walk outside, but nothing touched him as it had before. He was stronger but colder, smarter but numb. When he left, he found a new home with the SEALs where emotion became a liability, where right was black or white and only victory mattered. Rowe happily rejected the romantic notion of a fair fight. SEALs used whatever tool was required to win, bringing that warrior mentality to bear for family and country.

Rowe would have done anything to save George. Now all he had was revenge.

"I need Duck."

"Already taken care of."

James left, saying he'd see him tomorrow. Rowe leaned against the kitchen counter, head hanging, and breathing ragged. He talked to Kali's voicemail and then checked the batteries on the five flashlights he'd hidden around the house. If anyone broke in, Rowe would blind them, buying time to take care of business.

Next, he went to the back of his bedroom closet, behind everything stuffed there over the last year, and pulled out his Colt, Sig Sauer, and a Springfield Armory XT, the first weapon he ever owned and in his estimation the best. He placed Hoppe's solvent, lubricating oil, Q-tips, and a wire bore brush on a newspaper, and cut an old t-shirt into cleaning patches. One after another, he field stripped and cleaned the weapons. It felt natural, soothing, like coming home. The odor of solvent and oil took him back to a time when he considered himself undressed without a gun—or two—on his person.

Everything ready, he drove to a shooting range. It had been a year since he last fired a gun. Men had lost their shooting eye in a shorter time, but all it took to clear Rowe's mind was one round downrange. The percussive pops felt right and he inhaled the burned powder. After a dozen shots, he no longer thought about it. His hands knew the way. The brass bounced at his feet as he devoured all his rounds and got a hundred more. He started at twenty-five feet, moved to fifty, then one hundred, switching from right-handed to left-handed. He worked the Sig first, switched to the Colt, and then the Springfield Armory XT.

Ninety minutes later, he went home, took the carry permit out of his safe, and stuck it in his wallet.

Chapter Fourteen

Day Five, Friday, August 11th
The* USS Bunker Hill, *San Diego CA

"FCO. Request location."

LT Paloma Chacone, Fire Control Officer, dismissing the radio call as she barreled down the pway of *USS Bunker Hill,* nearly colliding with the Auxiliary officer. "Why the rush, AUXO?"

"Change in the watchbill. Better check yours," he replied without pausing.

"Later," she muttered as she ducked into the Wardroom. It'd been ten hours since her last break. The only thing Chacone wanted more than to sit was coffee.

Her radio crackled again. "FCO. Request location."

She'd turn off the volume but XO might call. The ship's Executive Officer, second-in-command to the Captain, couldn't be ignored.

The coffee smelled scorched and old and tasted like manna from heaven. She poured more into her mug and collapsed, enthralled with the quiet, willing her muscles to relax and her brain to slow. Her eyes burned. Her shoulders ached, but nothing like her feet. She'd run fo'c'sle to fantail of the 567-foot ship ten times in four hours. She'd been up and down five flights too many times to count, raced through pways so narrow she had to stand sideways, and sweated in Auxiliary Engine Room One where temperatures reached 110 degrees or higher while replying to the Chief Engineer's questions.

Thank God the Congressionally-mandated INSURV ended today. If she answered one more what-if question, she might explode. What were the examiners doing— writing *Cruiser Operations for Dummies*?

Chacone sipped her coffee, thinking back to the path that led to this day. Two years preparing the perfect USNA application while taking the hardest classes her high school offered, the day she tore open a letter, not knowing whether it was congratulations or rejection.

The day her life changed.

Four years later, commissioned, she reported for duty to the *Ticonderoga*-class guided-missile cruiser *USS Bunker Hill*. She saluted the national ensign and the Petty Officer of the Watch, intimidated by the knowledge she walked in the footsteps of thousands before her who defended America from the decks of a warship. Her granddad served on the cruiser *Houston*, WWII's Galloping Ghost of the Java Coast. His love for the Navy convinced her to grab the last spot on the last cruiser ship selection night at the Naval Academy. He was so proud a year and a half later when she earned her Surface Warfare Officer pin.

She sighed and bit into a granola bar. At least INSURV took her mind off XO. What was up with him?

"Break time, huh?"

She cracked an eye. "Electro," the Electrical Officer.

Her civilian name was Jane Auburn, but everyone went by job titles on duty. Electro was new to the ship, right out of NROTC at Notre Dame. Decent officer, but Chacone wondered if the woman could handle pressure.

She was junior to Chacone, so Paloma shut her out, returning to a world without sailors looking for directions, senior officers looking for a scapegoat, and guys with clipboards looking for mistakes.

Electro ignored the snub. "You surviving?"

Chacone started to tell Electro to shut up, but stopped when she saw the blue-black bruise blooming on her left cheek.

"What happened?"

Jane touched it gingerly. "I fell into a pipe climbing through the catacombs of #3 GTG room. No biggie." She winced, hooked a straggle of hair behind her ear, and poured coffee. "So why'd the mess decks get a *Cheers* renovation and our wardroom got *Moby Dick*?"

Chacone smiled, comfortable in the narrow, featureless room decorated with Formica tables and Naugahyde chairs. Pre-packaged snacks littered the bland counters, available to be eaten on the run. "The enlisted guys deserve it. They work their butts off."

Electro sipped her coffee. "We're gonna pass, aren't we?" Her voice was uncertain.

Chacone thought a moment. Would the Powers That Be fail *Bunker Hill* after giving it an expensive upgrade and a new captain? She shrugged. "Everyone wants us to succeed."

Electro's mouth turned up a fraction. "XO acted weird today."

Chacone smiled absently and reveled in the caffeine churning through her veins. After a moment, she turned to Electro. "What do you mean?"

"He took a picture of a DC plate down in CCS—a flooding drill he said, but he marked the battery shop. We never practice flooding there."

DC Plates were oversized laminated canvases, suspended vertically so they could be paged through, providing deck-by-deck blueprints of the ship. Crew members used grease pencils to run disaster scenarios. It appeared XO was experimenting with flooding different spaces to see how that affected the buoyancy of the entire ship.

Or finding what could sink the ship. She was the one officer outside of the senior command entrusted with the Top Secret DC Book, one chapter of which explained how to scuttle the ship should that be necessary.

Something nibbled at Paloma's memory. She tried to catch it, but yawned instead.

"Who really knows why he does anything?" But she frowned, dug for the thread and gave up. She'd figure it out later, hopefully before a WTF moment threw it in her face.

Electro's radio screeched. "Electro. Cheng. Come to CCS."

"Be right there, sir." She gulped the last of her coffee, sketched a wave, and disappeared.

Chacone tried to return to empty thoughts, but XO nagged at her. Why take a picture when anyone with clearance to view the data had digital access on the LAN? Had she been there, she would have said something. XO would thank her—*We're in this together*, his standard response meaning everyone on the crew was cut from the same blue cloth.

No, he wouldn't. XO hated criticism. The last officer to cross him was reassigned as Departmental Operations Record Keeper—DORK in the Navy's acronym-crazy world. XO found it hilarious.

Did this have something to do with his girlfriend? Chacone had become suspicious of XO's 'consulting' job advising a writer on cruisers when it included all expenses paid research trips to Las Vegas and a new Porsche. What did he tell her to earn that?

And yesterday he announced their engagement, showing Paloma her snapshot. Paloma expected a dowdy, pasty-faced, bespeckled creature who spent fifteen hours a day at a keyboard. Instead, the woman was stunning with a heart-shaped face, a glossy ebony mane that fell in a shimmering waterfall to her waist, and eyes that spoke to the soul. XO was twenty years older with a body solidly in a no man's land between portly and overweight and he chewed his food with his mouth open. What did she see in him? No one believed it was love except XO. He told everyone Shalimar—what else would she be named?—loved men in uniform.

Now, hearing this, Chacone wondered if he had crossed the line.

Her radio squawked. "FCO. XO. Report to CIC." The Command Information Center.

"On my way, Sir."

Three hours later, two hours after her shift ended and an hour after her energy ran out, she stumbled to her car, somehow drove home without an accident, and fell through the door of the apartment she shared with Trish Andrews, an officer on the destroyer, *USS Preble*.

"Hey, Trish. We still going out?" Paloma stumbled to her bedroom as Trish mumbled something. Paloma kicked off her shoes, flipped on the TV and collapsed onto her queen-sized bed, the first piece of furniture she bought after graduation. Four years of Naval Academy bunks made sleeping in comfort critical.

A wide-eyed blonde correspondent breathily reported that, in response to the August 30th North Korean satellite launch, the Navy would deploy a Surface Action Group capable of destroying the missile/satellite should the need arise. Chacone hoped it would include *Bunker Hill*. She'd never been to Japan

Trish stuck her head in. "When you ready?"

"Give me ten minutes."

Paloma wished things were different with Trish. The women had nothing in common and were thrown together when their San Diego orders left both needing a roommate. Where Paloma loved the pride of military service and the opportunity to do something meaningful with her life, Trish wanted to finish her five years and leave.

Paloma closed her eyes. Her bed felt soft, inviting. The TV droned.

She shook herself awake, a sitcom blaring. 9pm!

"Trish!" No reply. Paloma threw on dark skinny jeans, a sequined blouse, black Manolo heels, checked her phone for a text from Trish—nothing—and flew out the door.

Ten minutes later, she dove into the overflow crowd at Hennessey's, Trish's favorite watering hole. She waved to a few shipmates as she bumped her way up to the bar and left a voicemail for Trish.

"Excuse me. Are you alone?"

Paloma jerked. A male, her age, cute with tousled blue-black hair, an olive complexion, narrow shoulders covered by a long-sleeved striped pullover. Too skinny.

"No." She turned away.

He nodded as though she said yes. "I am not either. I await a friend from work. He assured me we would meet here. Maybe he is here, but how would I find him?" The man kept his eyes on Paloma, but he was frightened.

"Yeah? What's his name?"

The man opened his mouth, shut it, and giggled. "I lied. I wanted to meet you. My name is Ankour. I am new to San Diego."

His voice sounded desperate. Paloma relented. "I'm Paloma Chacone," and she extended her hand.

His eyes widened and he froze, but recovered. His handshake felt delicate, hesitant. Did his culture not shake hands?

Before she reached a decision, Mohammed asked, "What do you do in this big city, Paloma Chacone?"

"Hey, Paloma—smile!" and a camera clicked.

"Jane—what are you doing?"

"I'm posting these on Facebook. We'll show those civvies Navy women know how to have fun!" and Jane disappeared into the crowd, punching buttons on her phone.

Here we go. If dating an officer in the Navy threatened Ankour, he'd never stick around when she shared her opinions.

"I'm an officer on *Bunker Hill*," and she waited to see what he did next.

His eyes lit up and a smile creased his face. "Wow. A woman in uniform," and spent the next two hours peppering her with questions. Paloma found herself sharing her background, her dreams and ideals, how lonely life was away from friends and family and unable to date anyone at work. He confessed to a love of cruisers, despite having attended the Air Force Academy.

When Hennessey's threw them out, they talked on the sidewalk for another thirty minutes. She christened him 'Anchor' and basked in the warm glow of a new relationship.

Later, as she drifted off to sleep, something floated through her brain. He requested the crew list, but as ex-military, he knew that was classified. Something was off about Anchor. Before she decided what, her brain blinked out and she fell asleep.

Chapter Fifteen

Day Five, Friday evening, August 11th
Mohammed, Little Italy, San Diego

Mohammed had no doubt Paloma Chacone was Allah's tool. He went to the bar to assist Shalimar, but she hadn't shown. When he saw Paloma, he decided to do what he had done so effectively with the *Princeton* female.

Paloma, though, was nothing like the other. He was captivated by the pale curve of her slender neck and the drape of her long hair over her shoulders. He struggled to concentrate until, Allah be praised, the whore's advice again worked.

That evening, he cleansed himself as he must after interacting with the infidel. First, he washed his hands thrice. Next, he washed his face, rinsed his mouth and cleaned his nose with water three times. Then he washed his right arm up to the elbow three times and his left arm in the same manner.

Mohammed sniffed and still stank of the female. He scrubbed his head, washed his right foot up to the ankle three times, and washed his left foot the same way. This time when he tested the air, he couldn't find her.

He called Al-alah for his daily check-in. Nasr greeted him with, "You have a tail."

Mohammed's eyes popped open. "No! That is impossible! I am very careful—"

"It is the boy you were asked to keep an eye on. Fix this," and Nasr disconnected.

Chapter Sixteen

Day Six, Saturday, August 12th, morning
Kali's Columbia University office

Six a.m. and already eighty degrees. Would this heat ever break? Kali wiped an arm across her forehead, decloaked Otto, plopped into her chair, and took a moment to pout.

Sean had canceled. He said he had a big test. How many times had she said the same thing when the toddler Sean wanted to play? A lump grew in her throat and her eyes burned.

"Hello, Kali. You are sick today?"

Kali swiped a tear from her face. "No, I'm fine, Otto. How was your evening?" she asked as she pulled her hair into a severe ponytail.

"Excellent. I met someone," and Kali listened for ninety seconds to an accounting of his escapades in the virtual world of Second Life

"We have only three hours until the competition. Let's get started."

"Your President Franklin Roosevelt said, *Competition is useful up to a certain point and no further, but cooperation... begins where competition leaves off.* We should call it Man and Machine rather than Man vs. Machine so we accomplish more?"

Kali hooked a cable into the drive holding Otto's operating system and connected it to the three-foot tall robot that would be his new body. It had a bulbous head with audio and visual in their equivalent human positions. Its round trunk doubled as a monitor. Sturdy roller feet provided mobility. She even added arms Otto could move to enhance the conversation.

"It's a human thing. We love pitting our skills against others. It makes us stronger, points out weaknesses, pushes us to find our limits. And, we consider it fun."

He said nothing for a moment, and then, "Why does Frank Kellogg say competition is not only a terrible burden upon people, but one of the greatest menaces to world peace?"

Ah, the challenge of arguing with a brain hooked into the internet. "Think of it this way: History proves competition enables human survival. Today, you and Eitan will help each other. I'm starting the transfer now, Otto, no talking until I finish."

After what seemed like hours, the android pinged. Kali typed in a series of commands and within moments, the big round lidless eyes lit up as electricity charged through their circuits. The globe atop a squatty neck turned toward Kali and latched onto her face with a beguiling innocence. Kali put her hands on Otto's android shoulders and smiled.

"How are you, Otto?"

A violent spasm rolled through Otto's new fiberglass body. His roller feet jerked, his jointed tubular arms flailed and eyes whirled in their machine-smoothed sockets. Kali hopped back to avoid one of his stubby arms.

"What... what... I'm afraid not well." His voice roared through the room. Kali dropped the volume as numbers scrolled down his chest-mounted monitor like a cry for help.

"Why did my arm flap, Kali?" Otto's head jerked sideways. She had programmed the bot to turn toward noise as people do, but Otto didn't know that. "Who else is here, Kali? Oh, this is far different than what I imagined."

"That's your voice, Otto," Kali said as she hammered in a series of commands. "I'm transferring it to your mouth," and she touched the circular speaker located under his olfactory sensors. "Do you understand?"

"Of course, Kali. I have a robust intellect," Otto replied as his round eye cams tried to find that spot on his face. "But I am unable to see it."

She dug her cosmetic mirror out of her purse and held it up. "See? Like mine."

Otto powered forward and slammed into it. "I see, but I do not understand what is happening."

Kali weighed responses and settled on, "We call it change, Otto. It bothers me, too."

"So I'm becoming human?"

Kali wanted to laugh, but stopped herself. "Yes, Otto. You're becoming human." She glanced at the clock. Damn. "Time to go!"

Otto spun around in a full circle in an attempt to face the door. "This turning is harder than it looks when you do it, Kali." Finally, he aimed somewhat at the exit, rolled forward, picked up speed and slammed into the wall.

"Otto! Are you alright?"

Otto churbled and wheeled backward. "Oh, perfectly. I wanted to see what it means to not be able to walk through walls. Will we go out there?" And Otto fluttered an arm at the hall.

"Follow me, intrepid adventurer. I will show you the mysteries of the hallway," and Kali took the knob that served as his hand and guided him forward.

Otto chattered about the various shades of color in the hall's eggshell-white paint, the phone calls he heard through thin walls, and the conversations that filtered from rooms too far away for the human ear. When they arrived in Eitan's lab, the room pulsed with cerebral energy as the attendees debated whether man or machine was the better problem solver. Eitan had made an effort to clean up, moving books from chairs to the floor and trash onto shelves. Kali took a quick survey of the crowd and found no Zeke. Her heart sank. First, he canceled last night. Now, he stood her up on this most important event. What was going on?

Otto pointed his hand-knob at a three-foot tall '0'. "Humans need to be told the time?"

"It's a countdown counter, and yes, people have no internal caesium clock tied to the National Institute of Standards and Technology."

Otto considered this. "Dr. Eitan Sun seems to."

Kali laughed. "Eitan is the rare individual with an autonomic sense of time, accurate to within a minute."

She pointed to screens on either side of the clock labeled *Dr. Sun* and *Otto*. "The monitors display what you and Eitan are doing."

"Kali!" She turned at the sound of Eitan's voice and saw a man dressed in dark pants, a white button-down jersey and wing tips, thin hair neatly combed over a round dome.

"What happened? Run out of t-shirts and cargo pants?"

Eitan ignored her, focusing instead on Otto. "Hello, my mobile friend. Do I see fear in your eyes?"

"No, Dr. Sun. That's the electrical charge to power my camcorders."

"Shrug. So it is. Are you ready?"

"I am always ready, Dr. Sun. It is a human trait to require a warm-up."

Eitan turned to Kali, head tilted, fingers stabbing at invisible keys on his arm. His bright, inquisitive eyes were shadowed with worry. "Where's Sean?"

"He canceled."

"OK. I need to talk to you."

She bit back a smile. "I know what's upsetting you and I understand why you lied to me last night."

Eitan shifted uncomfortably. "Well, yes, but I need to explain." A gentleman approached the pair, a wide grin across his rosy face. Eitan turned to him and back to Kali. "But first, this is my mentor from Cal Tech. He … is… visiting New York. Do you mind if he introduces you?"

Kali turned to the squatty, bespeckled man with the intelligent eyes and retro bow tie.

"Hello, Ms. Delamagente. I dabble in artificial intelligence. I'm eager to meet Otto. I promise I'll do you justice."

Kali smiled and nodded, not sure what to make of this, but she trusted Eitan. The stranger addressed the audience.

"Hello, AI enthusiasts. My name is Dr. Theodore Kaslow." Kali stumbled backward, almost falling into a chair.

"*The* Dr. Kaslow?" World-renowned in the field of AIs, on track to create the first mechanical brain. What about her interested him?

Dr. Kaslow steadied her and offered a warm smile. A murmur spread through the crowd.

"Today I introduce the woman who made this event possible. You know her as a struggling grad student, ABD for, what, Ms. Delamagente, four years?" He paused to allow her a stiff nod and then continued. "But Ms. Delamagente is no ordinary grad student. She has been shortlisted for a Nobel Laureate, the only non-PhD ever published in the Journal of Scientific Research, and the only pre-Doctor Fellow accepted by Berkeley

Geochronology Lab to do research. She requires only three hours of sleep a night and is admired by a man I hold in highest esteem, Dr. Eitan Sun.

The crowd applauded as Kali blushed.

"This brilliant woman created an artificial intelligence that defies belief. Dozens of alphabet agency experts tried to replicate Otto's programming to no avail. Further detail is classified but suffice to say, her work is ground-breaking."

He motioned Kali forward to raucous applause as Eitan retreated to his station.

"Thank you all for your attendance. I've never had an introduction quite like that." She scanned one last hopeless time for Rowe and started. "May I introduce our contestants? Otto, a Mobile Artificial Intelligence." The audience clapped and Otto churbled a greeting. "...and Dr. Eitan Sun, an extraordinary mind to all who have the pleasure of knowing him." This time, the applause was deafening, bolstered by hoots of support.

"Today we answer the question of our time: Who is the better problem solver, Man or Machine? Much is made of a machine's speed at gathering and sorting data, but can a collection of wires, algorithms, and scripts solve a common quandary man sees every day: finding solutions for situations we've never faced. That includes stone tools, the wheel, farming, and theoretic concepts like Black Holes and anti-matter. Each required visionary thinking. Can a machine do that?"

She smiled at both contestants. Otto was slamming his mechanical hand against a table top, chortling after each impact. Eitan's intense blue eyes stared unabashedly at Kali, mouth open, dribbles of something brown spotting his shirt.

"I considered using an unsolved mathematical problem such as the Collatz Conjecture, but it might have no solution, so I chose instead the ubiquitous Travelling

Salesman Problem where a salesman must come up with the most efficient route between clients in a list of cities. Formulated in 1930, it still has no general method of solution. The current leading number of cities is 7,515,789,959. I will provide Dr. Sun and Otto with the latitude and longitude for a random selection of one thousand from the list. I will add more if necessary. They will have three hours and thirty-one minutes to arrange travel to as many cities as possible. Whoever gets the furthest in the shortest distance, wins.

Kali nodded to Otto, then Eitan. Neither required a countdown. "Contestants, begin."

Eitan's keyboard burst to life and Otto rolled in circles, seemingly in search of a comfortable position. After eleven seconds, he froze, eyes down, silent except for a low hum.

People grouped around the monitors as the contestants arranged routes, changed their minds, and added stops, the travel web growing by the minute. Cheers and groans marked a favored contestant's movement in the standings. People snacked on prune juice, cola, peanuts, cashews, sausages and granola bars and chatted quietly among themselves.

Kali brought up both entries in side-by-side windows on her iPad and spent her the time verifying contestant choices until the alarm buzzed.

"Time's up. Dr. Sun won by two hundred seventeen cities."

The crowd went wild, Otto spun in circles, and the lone Columbia University reporter rushed to post his story.

Kali sidled over to Otto, "What happened? You were on par with Eitan for the first three hours. Did you get stuck?"

"Oh, no. Kali. Why would I get stuck? I considered our discussion about competition. When I saw time running out, I stopped to await the collaborative part where most is accomplished. I presumed we would reach that before the clock ran out. Did I do something wrong?"

"No, Otto. You did perfectly. Contests are most exciting when unpredictable." She patted him and approached Eitan. "Otto failed to comprehend the concept of competition—the need to beat you."

Eitan cocked his head, a slight smile on his lips. "Intriguing. How do you teach human qualities like competition, collaboration, or even humanity?"

Dr. Kaslow smiled. "I'm sorry I must leave, Ms. Delamagente. This was captivating."

"Please, call me Kali.

"If you call me Teddy. I had hoped to meet your son about whom Eitan says wonderful things. Keep me up to date on Otto. Please."

Kali started to walk out with Teddy when a strident voice stopped her.

"Kalian! A moment, please." The Dean toddled over, hair ruffled, face pink with heat. "Otto lost. How does this work for your thesis?" He said nothing about Otto's bot body.

"It certainly ruined my book deal."

Eitan tugged her arm. "Kali." She was grateful for the distraction. "Please find me when you're done. I still need to talk to you." His voice was strained.

Kali wondered what upset the first man America called when in trouble. Before she could placate the Dean, he turned on his heel, cell to his ear, and left.

"Hello, babe."

Her heart leaped. "Zeke!" There he stood, like so many times before, in a Navy pullover, gray sweatpants, sandals that should have been trashed months ago. He took her breath away. When he wrapped his arms around her, she smelled his maleness, felt the beat of his heart, his breath warm on her cheek.

And then she saw the sat phone on his belt, the one Zeke had thrown into a desk drawer as proof he and Bobby were done.

"Is that why you're late?" She tried to sound neutral, but it came out angry.

He grinned sheepishly, but his mouth remained tense, eyes cold. "Is Bobby here?"

"Why would he be? We don't like each other."

Zeke's eyes softened. "He is curious about Otto, that's all. Kali, we need to talk. Will you wait for me?" He kissed her forehead and made a beeline for Eitan.

"Sure." Her voice cracked. She stared after him, his walk brisk and fluid with no wasted movement as though saving his energy for some future emergency. Zeke never coddled her, always told the truth, but something had happened to change. The row boat they called a relationship had sprung a small, steady leak. She needed a bucket, but had no idea where to find one.

And then James arrived, immaculate as usual. Black blazer, white Oxford button-down dress shirt, black and pink striped tie, pink hankie, gray slacks, hair perfect. Before Kali could turn her back on him, a grinding noise and a thump interrupted whatever would come next. Kali turned to Otto as he toppled over, arms waving.

"I better see what's wrong," she said to no one in particular. With a deft movement, she led Otto from the room. James yelled something about needing to talk to her.

Why did everyone want to talk to her today?

Chapter Seventeen

Day Six, Saturday, August 12th, afternoon
Eitan Sun's Columbia office

Rowe caught the drift of Kali's perfume as she left, couldn't stop a memory of Dmanisi from invading. Was he still that man or had he vanished?

When he turned back, James was staring at him, a frown creasing his brow. "I got her clearance re-instated, Zeke, because we need her help," and he started after Kali.

Rowe grabbed his arm. "Let her fix Otto, then I'll talk to her."

James shrugged off Rowe's hand, but stopped. "She's your blind spot, bud."

James was right. Time to put emotion aside, at least until they found the hijackers.

Sun joined them as Rowe asked, "Have you talked to *Virginia's* Blue crew?"

"What Blue crew?"

"Every sub has two crews, Blue and Gold. Gold was aboard when *Virginia* disappeared. Blue would know about an embedded traitor."

Bobby took a note. "*Triumph* was sighted off the coast of France. From there, it can hit most of Europe."

"Or take a path through the Med and out the Suez Canal. It could reach North Korea in time for the missile launch. Who's supervising the launch?"

"There'll be three or four warships there—including a sub. Their sonar will find *Triumph* without breaking a sweat."

"Like SOSUS did."

James paused. "Point taken."

"And what if it teams up with *Virginia*?" Rowe let that hang.

James stuffed his hands in his pockets. "If we'd had access to Otto, he would have found *Triumph* yesterday."

Rowe bristled. "Or *Virginia* would have stopped you. Even without the nuclear warheads, they have Tomahawks."

James took a deep breath and let it out. "Bottom line, we don't know what they're up to which scares hell out of me."

Rowe was about to snap something about making it a priority to know why SOSUS missed *Triumph* when Sun spoke.

"Sean found a suspect."

Rowe didn't hide his surprise. "How does a California teen find a suspect in a sub hijacking? Is that why you called yesterday?"

"Yes," and Sun explained how Sean's spycams led to Mohammed who Sean had reason to suspect was involved in the hijacking. As he spoke, he loaded a grainy snapshot of a gracile male, mid-twenties, with dark curly hair and a tentative smile.

"Meet Ankour Mohammed. He looks Korean, his passport is Iranian, his culture Muslim, and he's a doctor of nuclear physics. He's currently traveling the US on a student visa to understand how capitalism and democracy promote national prosperity so he can replicate it at home. Problem is, he's only touring Navy bases."

Rowe's shoulders tightened as he studied the man who might have killed George. He had a flat face unmarked by emotion, a predator's eyes that even from the murkiness of a low-res jpg chilled Rowe.

"Is there any connection between him and Pakistan Taliban?"

"No, but I uncovered an interesting fact: He was a friend of the late Salah Mahmud al-Zahrawi."

James stopped pacing. "Maybe he wants revenge."

Rowe's stomach boiled. "Anger is a weakness we can exploit."

Sun brought up a second picture, a stunning woman in the uniform of a naval officer. She had glistening dark hair pulled back in a chignon, clear intelligent eyes, an aquiline nose, and a friendly almost impish smile shaped by generous lips.

"Is she also a suspect?"

"No. Her name's LT Paloma Chacone, Mohammed's girlfriend, though I think he's using her for access to the base or her ship. She comes from a middle-class American family with no history of dissidence. She piled up awards like cordwood in high school and was accepted into Notre Dame, Stanford and USNA. She graduated tenth in her class two years ago and service selected the cruiser, *USS Bunker Hill*. She receives excellent fitness reports and is consistently ranked #1 among junior officers."

Sun opened a third picture, this of a stocky, broad-faced woman in her early twenties. Her blouse exposed the top of ample breasts. Her stretch pants were tight when she was ten pounds lighter. She hugged a miserable Mohammed.

"This is an Ensign on another San Diego cruiser, *Princeton*. She appears to be another of Mohammed's girlfriends."

He dated two women from the same tight community. "Does he need both, or doesn't know which?"

Sun tapped the Ensign. "This one's missing. At least, failed to show up for her watch and her chain of command couldn't reach her." Sun pointed to a post-it note. "Sean also pulled three numbers from his surveillance—38 44 90—"

Rowe jerked. "What?"

Sun turned to Rowe. "I reacted as you did."

When neither Sun nor Rowe explained, James threw up his hands. "Well?"

What Rowe knew about these numbers was classified top secret and need to know. James had the clearance, but did he have the need to know? Rowe decided he did.

"38-44-90—just south of Wonsan North Korea. It must be the satellite's launch site."

James whistled. "We're set up at Musudan-ri. No wonder nothing is happening there."

Rowe scratched the back of his head. "So they're hiding from our Eye in the Sky because the comm satellite is something else, but why's Mohammed have the coordinates?"

Chapter Eighteen

Day Six, Saturday, August 12th
London, England, Lab of Dr. Penbury

By the time the firemen cleared Imperial College's Blackett Lab, students were arriving for morning classes. Oliver Najafian trudged home, trying to invent an excuse to be in the lab a second night. Allah provided. Dr. Penbury had an out of town commitment and asked Najafian to monitor an experiment for him.
Alhamdulillah.

Ten p.m. Najafian locked the lab and typed the password into Penbury's computer.
"Access denied."
What? That was not possible. Penbury had provided him the computer's password to facilitate monitoring the experiment. Najafian tried again.
"Access denied."
Perspiration beaded his forehead. He had one more chance before the system shut him out. He stared at the keyboard, eyes like saucers.

And saw the caps lock on. Of course. He took a shallow breath and tried again.

Allah smiled on him.

It took only minutes to find the file.

When the man named Salah first asked for help, Najafian refused. Sure, metamaterials could hide objects, but Najafian rejected the premise his long-time friend would use it to shield submarines. Salah insisted Penbury changed when his wife became 'collateral damage' to a peacenik protest. TV stations broadcast the protestors cheering as she bled out, the ambulance unable to reach her through the mob. Who wouldn't change, Salah asked? If Penbury figured out how to shield subs from detection using metamaterials, shouldn't the Muslim world be entitled to this device? Peace required protection.

In the end, Najafian agreed, not to serve Allah but to find out if the Penbury he knew was a fraud.

Najafian dug through a mountain of files before hitting pay dirt, a communiqué from the Royal Navy. They were eager to paint *HMS Triumph* with the sonar shield and required Penbury's delivery date. Najafian's brain stumbled. *Triumph* had been hijacked. Was there a connection?

His phone pinged. Time to collect the experiment data.

Thirty minutes later, measurements done, he located Penbury's formula. He knew as much about this science as Penbury and spent the next four hours running it through his own highly technical brain, looking for flaws, mistakes, inconsistencies, but found nothing that would prevent its stated purpose of shielding a submarine from sonar. He copied the formula to his flashdrive so he could send it to Salah. If everyone had it, no one would benefit and peace would prevail.

Before leaving, he browsed Penbury's deleted emails and found another 'metamaterials' thread, this one with the Americans. They wanted to test the shield on the fast attack submarine, *USS Virginia*.

Najafian's stomach heaved. His brother served on *Virginia*.

That changed everything. Najafian wasn't a brave man, but he loved his younger brother fiercely. Najafian would be in an Iranian prison except for a timely warning from his sibling. If Salah was behind hijacking *Triumph*, he would go after *Virginia* next. Najafian had to stop him.

The sun's first morning glow peeked over the horizon of blocky rooftops as Najafian walked home, lost in thought, the kernel of an idea percolating in his prodigious brain, vaguely aware of footsteps that mimicked his own. In Iran, scientists were always watched. Still, he was only a lab assistant. They would see they were wasting their time.

Chapter Nineteen

Day Seven, Sunday, August 13th, early morning
City College of New York

7 am and already the heat plastered Kali's shirt to her chest as she sprinted the last hundred meters. A smattering of applause erupted as she pulled up panting, head hanging, every part of her sweating, even her fingernails. Six miles at a six-minute pace—she too wanted to applaud.

She trudged to Convent Street and gasped when she got inside Zeke's Benz. It must be a hundred in the car. She cranked up the air, breathed in the maleness that made her heart stutter, and flew out of the parking lot. Zeke had offered his car to take Sean to the airport and Kali forgot to return the key when her son canceled. The man owed her.

Twenty minutes later, she showered in the faculty lounge, changed into a flowered sundress and sandals, pulled her damp hair into a low ponytail, bought coffee and soda for breakfast, and collapsed behind her desk.

"Hello, Kali. I thought you were staying home today. I'm glad you stopped by."

Kali eyed Otto. "How are you?" Otto had a self-diagnosis module so this wasn't an idle question. A mistake she'd made in yesterday's upload had caused his meltdown. It took six hours to fix, but he forgave her faster than she forgave herself.

Otto trundled closer. "Thank you for your assistance in repairing my algorithms. I visited Second Life after you left, but your world is more exciting. Did you enjoy your evening?" He adjusted his squat body and waited.

Kali smiled. Eight-thirty on a Sunday morning, and she was chatting with an AI who, to be honest, she liked better than most people she knew. She started to explain how she spent the evening pouting, but settled for, "It was ducky."

"Ducky? Like Zeke's friend, Mr. Duck Peters?"

Kali shook her head and Otto's drives whirred. "So this is 'sarcasm'?"

"Yes. 'Ducky' was a goal for last night, but not the reality."

She might as well work on her dissertation. She pulled the keyboard into her lap and for four hours, lost herself in a world of tables and footnotes and pedanticism. By the time she stopped for a break, she'd completed the introduction, methodology, a summary of steps, and timeline for completion. The Dean would be happy.

She stretched and padded to the vending machine. This time of the weekend, little remained so she settled for peanuts. When she got back to her office, Zeke was there, sandals on her desk, tank top tight over his muscular chest, hair tousled as though he just got out of bed.

"Zeke. What a ... surprise."

Without another word, Kali plopped into her desk chair and pretended to study her email which was a hopeless task with Zeke sitting three feet away. God, he looked good. Her heart quickened and she tamped down the smile that pulled at her mouth. She still wouldn't forgive and forget. She dropped the peanuts in the trash and tossed him his car keys. "Thanks."

James popped up behind the bookshelf dressed in a Polo and Houndstooth pleated trousers, hair perfectly combed. He grunted a greeting as he ran a wand over her shelves, desks, drawers, and any spot that could hide a wireless snoop.

She ate two Advil.

Zeke sighed. "Before Bobby starts, how's Otto?"

Otto awoke at the sound of his name and rolled over to Zeke. "I am at 100%. I reworked my scripts to prevent this problem in the future."

He proceeded to explain in excruciating detail what had happened while Kali read her email. Someone wanted to put her in *Who's Who*. Someone else promised her the perfect date. Several people worried about her sexual satisfaction. Trash trash and trash.

James's phone rang and he left the room hissing, "I'm about to," nearly ramming Sun. The scientist scuttled away, a quizzical expression on his face.

Otto churbled and rolled in a circle until he faced Eitan. "Hello, Dr. Sun. I understand clothes are kept in houses, though I've never been to one. Did you not go home last night?"

Sun offered a thin smile. "Like you, dear Otto, when I run out of energy, I fall asleep. In this case, it happened in my lab," and he wrapped one leg over the corner of the second desk in the office, which would forever belong to Cat, Kali's brilliant best friend currently on medical leave. Only friends could use her desk.

Sun's gaze flicked to the trash can, to Kali, around the room, and back to the trash.

Otto said, "I believe you can eat those. Peanuts give Kali headaches."

Sun fished the bag out, dumped the remnants into his mouth and said between chews, "I assume Bobby explained Sean's involvement with *Triumph*. I come to offer assistance."

Kali scrunched her brow. "What triumph?"

Zeke started flipping a pencil. "Oh, I thought… They didn't…"

Kali's headache flared. She rubbed her temples. "This is why everyone said they needed to talk to me yesterday and why you're all here today." She wanted to throw something, but at whom? "I repeat: What triumph?"

Zeke gave her the broad strokes, concluding with "Bobby re-activated your clearance which he'll explain when he brings his chicken butt back in here."

That seemed to be James's cue.

Kali looked away. "Sean told me everything was fine," which she believed because she wanted to. She sniffed. "Please, Eitan, what's going on?"

James nodded to Sun and found a wall to lean against.

Sun opened his laptop and petted the keys. "Sean has been obsessed with security since moving to San Diego. The past month, he picked up chatter involving slain submariners from a missing British sub—"

"*Triumph*. I saw that on the news."

"LT Paloma Chacone, a lieutenant on a Navy cruiser, and her boyfriend Mohammed, a..." He struggled to find the right word.

"Tourist," offered James.

"Liar," from Zeke.

"Stranger," Sun settled for.

While Kali's brain might be her greatest asset, emotions were her worst. She forced herself to take calm, measured breaths even though she wanted to scream, shake them for not telling her sooner, and … do something… to fix it for her son.

"Chacone looks fine. Mohammed worries us," and Rowe explained what Sean's cams had picked up.

"They're after my son because of what he heard or saw?"

"There's no evidence they know about Sean. No. He's convinced LT Chacone is in trouble and insists on helping her."

Kali's stomach lurched and she focused on Zeke. "But he's in San Diego. The hijacking occurred in Britain."

Zeke looked away. "We also have a missing American sub—*Virginia*."

"A continent away," but judging by the circle of faces around her, no one thought that made a difference. Kali took more deep breaths as Otto churbled and Sun started bouncing.

Zeke took Kali's hands. "This is likely nothing, Kali, but the timing is odd, and 'odd' is what we look for."

'We'—Zeke admitted to working with James, and it would appear, so did Sun.

Kali wanted to cover her ears. This was why she had to break it off with Zeke. At any given moment, she could wake up in an erupting volcano. Her eyes burned and chest tightened.

"This is your fault, Zeke. If not for your stories." She turned away, but not before she saw the hurt in Zeke's eyes.

And immediately wanted to take it back. Where her security and Sean's were concerned, Zeke would do anything. He took the street side of a sidewalk. He sat with his back to a wall in restaurants to have a view of the entrance. He knew where the best escape would be if the front door proved unavailable. She hated his past, but it also defined why she trusted him.

Dammit. If Sean had gotten himself involved, she would too. "Give me Sean's data. I'll see what Otto comes up with."

Zeke's voice came out soft. "It's more than that, Kali. No matter what Otto finds, Sean will never stop until this Paloma Chacone is safe, which won't happen until the hijackers are arrested."

James's phone rang. "James... Yes, sir, she's right here. No, sir, not yet... Yes, sir." He pushed speaker. "This is FBI Director Gen. Inman. He'd like to talk with Kali."

A deep authoritative voice boomed from the cell phone. "Hello, Dr. Sun, Dr. Rowe, Ms. Delamagente." Everyone greeted him. "Let me start by apologizing, Ms. Delamagente. When I made that deal last year," promising never again to request she put her family on the firing line, "Who would imagine you'd once more be smack in the middle of a world crisis. I should have said, *I promise unless the fate of the world hangs in the balance and you are our only solution.* I'm asking you as an American to step into the breach once more for us."

Kali stammered, "General Inman, sir, how can I be the only one who can help?"

"As our Muslim friends are so fond of saying, God's will, Ms. Delamagente. Bobby?"

"Yes, sir."

"SA Haster is on his way over. He'll explain more," and Inman hung up.

"Something happened." He turned to Kali. "Everything you hear is classified, ears only for Task Force members."

"I didn't agree to be on your Task Force."

"Then leave," James retorted. "There's no middle ground, Kali. You're with us or not."

Kali stayed, exactly where she must be until Sean was out of danger.

Chapter Twenty

Day Seven, Sunday, August 13th, early afternoon
Columbia Office of Kali Delamagente

A ping startled everyone. Sun adjusted his glasses and squinted at the screen.

"Ankour Mohammed is connected to a group at NYU Abu Dhabi directed by a Dr. Nasr Al-alah. The FBI considers it cover for a terrorist cell."

Kali's throat tightened. "The Ankour Mohammed Sean is tracking in San Diego?"

Sun nodded and continued reading the background material. "What sets them apart from other terrorist cells is the members are all superior problem solvers and excellent at connecting dots. Ankour Mohammed graduated in the top ten of his class with a major in nuclear physics. These kids are definitely smart enough to operate a submarine. To top it off, they're trained in social skills which means if you met them, you'd like them."

Zeke started pacing. "How does Al-alah run a terrorist cell on an American campus?"

Someone cleared their throat. Kali turned to see a man staring at her, tall and stick-thin from his knobby shoulders to his spindly wrists, with shaggy hair framing a pale effeminate face. He wore a dark worsted suit with a splash of blinding white at the collar and French cuffs.

James summoned him forward. "May I introduce SA Haster with MI-6?"

The British agent shook hands with James and Sun, and stopped at Kali.

"Splendid to meet you, Ms. Delamagente."

Kali recognized the whistling s. "You're the man who called me eleven times in three days? Not nice to meet you."

SA Haster colored.

Sun tucked his laptop under his arm and stumbled to his feet. "I'll see what else I can find. Waves," and left. Zeke limped after him.

"Please don't leave Mr. Rowe," SA Haster spluttered, but Zeke disappeared. "Well, let's wait for Dr. Rowe, shall we?"

Kali ignored Haster while James typed into his Blackberry and the MI-6 agent rambled through her office appraising her jumbled collection of books. When he started to sit in the chair Zeke had vacated, Kali shook her head, so he leaned against the wall. Zeke returned and whispered to James. His friend paled, but said nothing.

Haster extended a hand to Zeke. "You must be Dr. Rowe. I'm Special Agent Haster."

Zeke sat down, ignoring Haster, arm out, a nervous smile withering on his wan face. Zeke always read people right, so Kali determined to pay attention to the Brit's every move.

James circled *Hurry up* with his hand. "Everyone here has clearance so you may speak openly, SA Haster."

"Alright. Three hours ago, *Triumph* attacked an Iranian *Kilo*-class sub."

Kali felt a dangerous stillness pass through the room. A baseless attack by a Western warship represented a paradigm shift in world politics. Her phone rang and she silenced it. Probably the Dean about her draft which seemed woefully insignificant in light of Haster's news.

Zeke asked, "Where?"

"Off the coast of Spain. Our Gibraltar listening post caught *Triumph's* torpedo doors open followed by an explosion and break-up noises, hull-popping, and the *Kilo*-class blowing air as it tried to surface. The listening post lost *Triumph* when it dove."

Zeke pulled a pencil from his pocket and flipped it. "Why attack the Iranians?"

Haster turned to Zeke, face grave. "Western nations have long held we are the only ones responsible enough to possess such world-ending devices. Now, we seem unable to control them. The UN will table the vote condemning North Korea's August 30th launch. They consider a rogue nuclear sub a greater threat than the North Korean speculative threat to weaponize space.

"Nuclear subs, a ballistic missile in space, and the will to kill innocents—the terrorist's trifecta."

Haster nodded once, eyes down. "I wish it ended there. Iran demanded Britain release ten terrorists being held, as retribution. We are considering it."

Zeke cracked his pencil in half. "Don't. It will buy you nothing."

"SIGINT," data from cell phones, satellite phones, email and anything with a signal, "indicates this attack is merely the first step."

Zeke asked James, "Does the DNI," Director of National Intelligence, "agree?"

James and Haster both nodded. Haster added, "Surprisingly, it seems nabbing a sub with British royalty aboard was dumb luck."

Kali blinked. British royalty? One look at Zeke and she knew. "Oh my god."

Haster's head bobbed between Zeke and Kali. "Ah. You didn't know. Sir George Linley believed the sub community's closeness provided an opportunity to build bridges with Muslim shipmates, and through them, break down Britain's perceived Islamophobia."

Zeke's mouth turned down. "How could Britain allow him to serve on a sub?"

"He insisted, so was placed on the safest sub in the fleet."

That got Kali's attention. "Why *Triumph*?"

Haster looked away. "I meant the most modern, didn't I?"

Otto churbled. It didn't take a body language module to see Haster was hiding something.

Haster grinned. "Ah, the infamous Otto. Splendid to meet you."

Otto rolled over to position himself directly in front of the British agent. "You're SA Haster from MI-6, residing at 4 Hightower Place with your mother—"

"That's enough, Otto." From Kali.

Haster colored. "So I do, yes. Why the name Otto?"

"My name is a palindrome because the world is often engaged in puzzles and I am brilliant at solving these."

"Well, Mr. Otto. I have a puzzle that requires your assistance. I believe you are the only one in the world who can find the submarine we have been discussing." Otto had the unique ability to locate even minor disruptions in the magnetic fluxes circling the globe. Once found, he could match the disruption to a specific submarine if provided with its profile.

Zeke moved toward Kali and James's eye twitched. Kali had been prepared to refuse until George's name came up.

Otto turned to Kali and she turned to Zeke. "What will you do once I find it?"

"We'll try to stop it without further loss of life. Failing that, all options are on the table."

Kali fidgeted. "I could be responsible for the death of hundreds."

She wanted to ask if the pain of killing another human ever went away, but it didn't matter if she had to carry that weight for the rest of her life, if it helped Zeke find his friend's executioner and protected Sean.

"Yes, and you'll never forget those men or your part in their end." She lost herself in his eyes until the room held nothing but the two of them. "Consider this: We think the terrorist's purpose is to ensure North Korea can launch a space-based nuclear weapon. If the hijackers were willing to destroy a sub-full of innocent boys, without a doubt they will kill anyone who gets in their way."

Kali tried to think logically. "The media calls it a communications satellite."

"Intel fails to support that conclusion. First, they're using a different booster than they have in the past for a communications satellite, which means the payload must be different. Second, they're hiding the launch site, but why? Third, my gut."

Kali forced her hands to relax, ignoring the throb of her headache. She felt Zeke's eyes on her, but refused to hurry. No matter how she looked at this, whether she did or didn't help, someone died. With a sigh, she asked, "How can I help?"

"Find *Triumph* before it launches the next bloody missile."

"Otto can only find subs that aren't degaussed."

"For a lot of complicated reasons, that won't be a problem."

Kali pulled the keyboard into her lap to create the script. Haster handed Kali a paper with *Triumph's* magnetic signature—the summation of the delta in the magnetic fluxes created by the movement of matter with the mass and shape of a *Trafalgar*-class sub. Because every other sub in this class was degaussed, only *Triumph* would appear when Otto trolled the Earth's magnetosphere.

"He also needs a satellite with global magnetic data to affect the comparison."

"Use this one," and Zeke gave her a paper with a series of numbers. Otto and the satellite confirmed each other's identities allowing the AI to upload *Triumph's* magnetic properties. Then, Otto went on a simple search for that profile throughout the satellite's global view.

"After you find *Triumph*, would you plug in *Virginia's* profile?" James handed a paper to Kali. "We want to be ready if the crew manages to turn off the degaussing coil," the device that kept the sub invisible in the magnetosphere.

Kali plugged it into Otto. "He'll alert us if it shows up."

As Otto worked, he chatted with Special Agent Haster about MI-6, Haster's background and family, and what life in Britain was like. When Haster finished a particularly long diatribe about the joys of British Royal society, Otto requested access to a high-level MI-6 account which he insisted was critical for his quest. Haster dutifully provided it.

Sixty minutes later, Otto found *Triumph*. "It is in the Mediterranean."

James pulled his phone off his belt and dialed. "Send me the coordinates."

Otto brought up a global map with a blinking light between Italy and Egypt.

"SECDEF, please. … This is SA James... Sir, we have it, latitude 35°17'26.21"N, longitude 18°43'12.35"E... Yes, Sir, Otto will see if they move and I'll let you know… Yes, Sir, I'll stay on the line."

The Secretary of Defense called the CNO who called the Third Fleet Commander and the Carrier Strike

Group One Commander, the man in charge of the Mediterranean region, who admitted to no warships in the area.

Zeke traced a path with his finger. "*Triumph* passed right by an American destroyer in the Med. How did they miss it?"

After a moment of silence, Otto said, "It is trying to jam me. I must re-evaluate the variance in the magnetic field every few seconds."

"Find out why, Otto." From Kali.

Haster popped out of his chair. "I must take this to JTAC," the Joint Terrorism Analysis Centre, and he left.

James listened as the footsteps disappeared down the hall. "Maybe he grows on you."

"Like mold."

James's mouth tugged upward. "Now he's gone, let's you and I figure out how to break into a nuclear submarine before our Brit friends get trigger happy."

For seven hours, Kali and Otto tried to determine the cause of the jamming while Rowe and James talked to experts about breaking into a *Trafalgar*-class sub. They all agreed it must be done through the hatch, from the inside. The only other ingress would be to blow a hole in the side with a torpedo.

James ordered pizza. Kali asked Mr. Winters to keep an eye on Sandy until she got home. He was thrilled.

And then Kali got an idea.

"I think I know what's jamming *Triumph*. The maintenance logs show *Triumph* was painted earlier than its scheduled time. This paint came from a different supplier, one at a significantly higher price because MI-6 wanted a chemical added to the formula. I think that's what's jamming us. I've seen that formula or close to it," but she couldn't put her finger on where.

James's phone vibrated. "Yes, sir.... yes, the same position. Will do," and hung up.

"What's up, Bobby?"

"The Royal Navy established a perimeter around the sub's position, but can't find it on sonar. SAS divers are waiting to infiltrate if they can figure out how. British warships are approved to destroy *Triumph* if it becomes a threat. Directly above its position is an American *Arleigh Burke*-class destroyer, *USS Bainbridge*, in case everything goes to hell. The Brits opened satellite communication with the sub and instructed the hijackers to surface."

Otto added, "The hijackers want to trade *Triumph* for prisoners. They directed they be delivered to the Riyan Airport in Yemen. They'll drive *Triumph* through the Suez Canal, down the Red Sea, out the Gulf of Aiden, to the coast of Yemen where they'll make the swap."

James turned to Otto. "How do you know?"

"SA Haster gave me access codes to his phone when we were chatting. I see what he sees."

Kali fought back a smile. "Haster didn't do his homework."

James sighed. "I love cooperation."

Otto whirred. "The Brits want to talk to *Triumph's* Captain... One of the hijackers—a man named Obeid—says the captain's dead."

Zeke turned to James. "The hijackers were as silent as the French in Algiers until the Royal Navy surrounded them. Now, they want to negotiate. They think we found them by damn luck. All they want to do is get to open waters and escape."

James called Haster, put him on speaker and made Zeke repeat what he'd said. Haster's response was to snort. "Our people are pleased they're talking."

"Muslims don't negotiate, SA Haster. Islam is clear. The truth is one and cannot be divided. If it is not the truth, it must be falsehood—*jahiliyyah*, or *ignorance of divine guidance.* The coexistence of truth and *jahiliyyah*—what results from compromise—is impossible."

"There is some truth to the hijacker's claim Britain holds no jurisdictional right over Muslims. Islam follows Sharia Law," Otto added.

"International standards give legal authority to where the infraction occurred, but this is their goal—gain time by tying us up in a philosophic debate. Tell Britain not to do it."

Haster sighed. "Britain agreed in concept."

Zeke balled his hands. "Keep it secret we can track them. That's our ace in the hole.

James spoke into the phone. "Haster, you hear Zeke?"

"We shared that detail already to prevent them from doing anything dodgy."

"You call yourselves negotiators? They now know escape is impossible. What reason is there to NOT attack?" Zeke was disgusted. "Otto. Let me know if the sub ascends. It must be close to the surface to launch missiles."

He waited, knowing what was coming.

Ten minutes later, a voice came over the phone, "This is *USS Bainbridge.* Our helo picked up ballast bubbles. The sub is ascending. Request permission to drop depth charges."

Moments later, a British-accented voice came over the speaker, calm and modulated. "*Triumph.* We will not allow you to surface."

A high-pitched, frantic voice shouted, "I am trying, sir! The Navigator and helmsman are both dead. Please help me or they will kill me, too!"

"What is your name, sir?"

"Eyad Obeid. I am a nuclear physicist. I have managed to lock the hijackers out of the communications area, but they have the rest of the sub. What can I do? Please help!"

From the phone, "Calm down, Mr. Obeid. Ask one of the British crew how to stop the boat's ascent. We would like to avoid taking action. Do you understand?"

"I am alone. I do not know how to reach the rest of the crew."

Suddenly a new voice yelled, "This is *HMS Daring*. We have sounds of torpedo doors opening. I repeat, *Triumph* has opened torpedo doors!"

Another voice: "General quarters!" "Do we have permission to fire?" "No—hold fire!"

The British negotiator, his voice a notch higher, asked, "Mr. Obeid. Why are you opening torpedo doors?"

Another voice: "*Triumph* launched a Tomahawk TLAM! Permission to fire!"

"Please sir, do not kill me!"

HMS Astute: "We have the OK to attack. Fire at will!"

A flurry of commands filled the airwaves: "Prepare to fire!" "Flooding tubes!" "Outer torpedo tube doors open" "Check firing solution—all OK." "Fire one! Fire two!" Two more British subs repeated the same.

"Torpedo one a direct hit! Torpedo two a direct hit. I have break-up noises."

No one cheered the end of the British submarine. There wasn't time with a Tomahawk still headed for an unknown target.

A voice came over the phone. "*USS Stockdale*. This is Commander 6th Fleet Actual. Put your Captain on the line."

"This is *Stockdale* Actual. Roger, over, Sir."

"A Tomahawk is on a flight path over your unit. Prepare for orders to shoot it down."

"TAO. Captain. All hands on deck. Prepare to fire SM-2." "OOD. General Quarters."

"Captain. TAO. Yes sir, bearing one-nine-five. Tracking it. Current trajectory lands it in Khaled bin Walid Stadium."

Kali's throat tightened. "35,000 people are at a national football match there today."

James ran his fingers through his hair. "We need approval from Greece, Cyprus, Lebanon, the Syrians and anyone else that damn missile flies over to shoot it down."

A din of voices filled the airwaves. *Stockdale's* captain kept requesting permission, saying he had a fire solution, he could bring it down in ninety seconds, then sixty seconds. His voice got tenser with each request. Rowe sat numb, listening, waiting, until with only forty-two seconds remaining, Admiral Cyrus Xibon, Assistant to the CNO, came on, his voice calm. Only Rowe heard the tension.

"*Stockdale*. This is Admiral Xibon. From the CNO. Shoot down that Tomahawk."

"Roger, Admiral. Fire!"

Stockdale's SM-2 lifted off. Cruising at just over 1.0 Mach, it would be close. Rowe held his breath. The hijackers hoped the Navy with their political bosses couldn't react fast enough. Rowe hoped they were wrong.

"Captain. TAO. Tomahawk destroyed."

Kali threw her arms around Zeke and crushed him to her chest.

"Kali, you saved lives today and kept Sean safe."

Even he heard the wobble in his voice. Kali put her hands on his chest and tilted her head up until she looked directly into his eyes.

"But we lost one who will forever be sorely missed."

Kali walked home, instructing Otto to find everything on the paint's formula. Rowe promised to come over after he and James wrapped things up, but he wouldn't, His still needed to bring *Virginia's* crew home.

As Kali turned into the alley behind her apartment, a hand wrapped over her mouth. She tried to remember what she learned long ago in a self-defense class and ended up scratching the mugger's covered arms and face and stomping on his foot, none of which bothered him.

"Do not scream. I will not hurt you. I am here to make a deal." The voice was soft and cultured, and uncomfortably familiar. "Suspend your assistance to the FBI and MI-6. Do anything else and you will cause not only the demise of your son, but two hundred submariners. Do not tell anyone about my visit." He slammed her into the wall and left.

Her head exploded, stars dancing where sight should be. She tried to focus, staring in the direction of footsteps, not believing what had to be true. The man who owned that voice was dead. All she could make out was a medium height figure sheathed in black from head to toe. He glanced back once, but sunglasses hid his eyes. His cheek was red and mottled even in the dim alley light, like the man who knocked her purse out of her hands on campus and dropped in on Mr. Winters. Then nausea overtook her and she retched. By the time she recovered, he had turned the corner.

She stumbled into her apartment, petted Sandy because he would not leave her alone, washed the blood off her scalp, and collapsed on the couch, an ice pack over her throbbing head.

Al-Zahrawi lived. Kali shivered. She saw Zeke kill him.

She popped three Advil and climbed into bed, exhausted and hurting. Sandy leaped up with her, circled three times, and plopped against her legs. Within minutes, he was asleep on his back, paws dangling, chest moving softly up and down, yipping as he chased some dreamland prey, knowing as only children and dogs know, their parents will protect them. Kali, though, didn't sleep. Every time she drifted off, her brain reran the evening. Something bothered her. Sure, al-Zahrawi knew Otto could find the submarines, but how did he know where she was? After rejecting every idea she came up with, she dumped her purse over and found a flat shiny disk the size of a quarter. A tracker, but closer inspection revealed a tiny microphone. The man who must be al-Zahrawi had heard everything from the moment he dropped it in her purse. She went outside and threw it, not caring if he knew. At 4 am, Kali took another half Imitrex for the headache that threatened to blow the top off her skull, and fell into a dreamless sleep.

Chapter Twenty-one

Day Eight, Monday morning, August 14th
New York, New York, Kali's Apartment

A paw nudged Kali though darkness still shrouded the room. She ignored him. Undeterred, Sandy bounced off the bed and out of the room. She groaned, swung her legs over the side of the bed, paused to let her body adjust, and then shuffled blindly to the kitchen.

"It's 5 am, you crazy mutt."

Her head ached. She touched the Band-Aid and remembered last night. In the warmth of a new day, she doubted al-Zahrawi had risen from the dead to again hunt her. She poured Sandy's breakfast feeling strangely content, and then turned on the morning news. One talking head after another blamed Britain for not only the loss of two hundred submariners, but the near-death of thousands in Syria. Kali sighed. A nuclear threat had been averted and all the media could do was whine about blame.

She poured a cup of coffee and got dressed. Truth, the man who might be al-Zahrawi would have no reason to object to her actions because she was finished helping Bobby and Haster. Otto would be no assistance finding a sub that had been degaussed. Besides, now that she had destroyed the surveillance disk, he couldn't track her.

She called Zeke and invited him to lunch, put a Band-Aid over the gash in her forehead, downed two Advil, dressed in freshly-pressed crop pants, a stretch white blouse with cap sleeves, and open-toe woven sandals she bought on sale from Nordstrom. As she splashed cologne on the inside of her wrists and behind her ears, Sandy snuffled and lay down.

"Ready for an after-the-nap nap, Pup?"

Coffee in one hand and instant oatmeal in the other, Kali stopped to tell Mr. Winters she had seen a stranger last night and would he keep an eye on Sandy.

The sun beat down and the windless heat left a glistening sheen on her neck and forehead. The Sheltering Arms, one of the area's free swimming pools, would be busy today. She took Sean there until he got to high school and started using the school's pool. She ate her oatmeal as she walked, working out how to explain to the Dean why Otto lost Saturday. Fifteen minutes later, she was working on her dissertation. By ten, she emailed an update to the Dean.

"Done."

"Are you talking to me, Kali?"

"No, Otto. To myself."

Otto churbled. "Humans do that. I may have to incorporate it into my processes. I have some information on the paint."

"Paint?"

"You asked me to investigate the new coat of paint applied to *Triumph*. Two submarines were repainted as a joint experiment—their words, not mine—between the British Navy and DARPA—the research arm of the United States military."

Triumph and *Virginia*?

As though he read her thoughts, which Otto could do in a manner of speaking, he continued, "Logic dictates the second sub is *Virginia*. I also found information on the prisoner list."

Her phone buzzed. Instead of Zeke, Otto announced Special Agent Haster. "I see his outgoing call."

He started without waiting for Kali's greeting. "Please, Ms. Delamagente, ask Otto to stop. I provided him with top-level passwords to show good faith and will be in frightful trouble if anyone finds out he's reading my email."

Kali fluttered her hand. "Oh, that. No one around here falls for it anymore."

Haster squeaked, "What does that mean?"

Before Kali could answer, Zeke arrived. Today he wore work clothes—light-weight sweat pants with a cut off pullover and sandals. He pointed to her head and arched an eyebrow. She shrugged—*Nothing important*. His eyes were dark and brooding and tension had etched new lines in his face. He kissed her and she mouthed, *Haster*.

She finished quickly and asked, "What's wrong?"

"First, what happened? And he gently moved her bangs aside to look closer at her head.

"Nothing. I banged into something in the dark, walking Sandy… Let me ask you something." Her mind bounced back to the man she thought was al-Zahrawi and his threat last night. "Do you have any thoughts on who is behind this?"

Zeke paced, slowly. A handful of steps covered the available space in her office and then he pivoted. "Someone who is a lot smarter than the average terrorist."

Kali dug through a stack of papers on her desk. "Like who?"

"Someone like Salah Al-Zahrawi. If he weren't dead, he'd be at the top of my list."

Kali felt the color drain from her face. She turned quickly so Zeke wouldn't notice and then changed the subject.

"Otto found something—things," and she deferred to Otto.

The AI whirred into position between the two. "The coordinates you gave me appear to be a rock wall in the vicinity of Wonsan. Second, Wonsan does show an interesting level of activity customarily associated with the launch of a rocket. Soldiers staff the Main Gate. The graded dirt path leading to the facility is clogged with jeeps. The trails that cut the back country behind it have been widened. A variety of machinery surrounds the rocket engine Test Pad, the High Bay Processing Building, and the Horizontal Processing Building.

"As for the prisoners *Triumph* requested be released," he whirred as though paging through a reef of documents, "here is some background: Abu Doha, rumored to be al Qaeda's main recruiter in Europe and wanted in America for his alleged role in the 2000 plot to blow up Los Angeles airport; Abu Hamza, called the 'preacher of hate' and convicted in 2006 of inciting racial hatred as imam of Finsbury Park mosque in north London; Rachid Ramda, the Algerian leader of the Paris Métro bomb plot; Adel Abdel Bary, leader of the UK branch of the Egyptian Islamic Jihad; Dhiren Barot, leader of the so-called "dirty bomb" plot—"

"Dirty bomb? What d'you have on that?"

"He tried but failed to turn one of Britain's nuclear subs into a dirty bomb."

Kali knew the term referred to nuclear, but nothing else. "What's a dirty bomb, Zeke?"

"It combines radioactive material with conventional explosives. Its purpose is to contaminate the area around the explosion."

"You think they want him released so they can use his plan?"

"No. He probably agreed to trade the information for his release."

"So why not lead with the prisoner swap?"

Zeke paced in the small room. "Can I take a rain check on lunch?"

Without waiting, he kissed Kali, promised to be back shortly, and left.

"No problem. I wasn't hungry anyway," Kali muttered to herself. "Otto. Find anything you can about Salah al-Zahrawi. Develop a model for his methodology and match it to whatever terrorist actions or intel you can find. If he's out there, I want to know. And confirm the name of the second sub painted with the chemical paint.

"Oh, also locate Barot's dirty bomb-from-submarine plans."

At 5 pm, Kali left. The day's heat had faded to tolerable, so she changed into shorts and a tank top, looped a collar around Sandy's neck, and jogged the perimeter of Riverside Park, avoiding the families barbecuing, students hanging out after classes, and dogs barking. Forty-five minutes later, she stopped to invite Mr. Winters to share a pizza. He declined.

"I have a date."

Kali did a double take. "I've never known you to go on a date."

"Doesn't mean I can't. Eighty-five's the new sixty."

"Soon you'll be younger than me," and she went in to change.

Around 10 pm, Kali could stand it no longer. If things were OK, Zeke would have come over. Sean answered on the first ring.

"Sean. I know what you're doing."

Finally, Sean said, "Paloma's in more danger than she knows. Someone needs to help her."

Kali smiled. "It's over, Sean. The sub Mohammed targeted was destroyed last night. He failed."

"Then why is Mohammed still following Paloma? And I think he killed the other woman. This thing's not over, Mom, and Paloma has no idea how dangerous her ex-boyfriend is."

Kali was stunned. "Then you're in danger, too. You have to leave this for the police!"

"You taught me, Mom, to look after each other. It finally made sense last year when Cat almost died trying to help me, Sandy almost got killed following me, that Detective risked his life saving mine, and Zeke and you rescued me. Then I got it. We do what we have to do."

She was hit by one of those tidal waves that sneak up on parents and make them want to wrap their children in protection and never let go. God, she loved her son.

Kali coughed, her voice hoarse. "Be careful. Please."

Sean's attitude made it easier to do what she had to do.

Monday evening
San Diego, CA, Sean Delamagente's apartment

Sean believed everyone must look after each other. Paloma never talked about family or received calls from friends. She was alone.

He finished his ice cream and gulped down a cola, for the caffeine. Yeah. To unravel this mystery, he had to tell Paloma the truth and ask for her help. He knew how to make that happen.

Chapter Twenty-two

Day Eight, Monday evening, August 14th
San Diego, CA, **USS Bunker Hill**

Paloma felt like the only fire hydrant at the San Diego Dog Show as she fielded questions from fifty sailors about the upcoming Tiger Cruise. For many, this would be their first experience with this Open House-like event, where invited friends and family toured the warship, went out to sea, took part in a weapons test, and asked questions. In short, experienced the world their loved ones inhabited every day.

"We're finished, Ma'am."

She breathed out. "Good job."

She tried to cancel her date with Anchor, but he insisted. Every day since they met, he made an excuse to see her. Yesterday, he was lurking in the produce aisle of her grocery store without a cart. She ignored him. Was it supposed to flatter her?

Tonight, she would end it.

"Ma'am, can I ask you a question?"

His coveralls said, *Shaw*. Paloma couldn't come up with his first name, only that he arrived onboard three days ago. She forced the weariness from her voice. "Absolutely."

"What will I do at the Tiger Cruise, Ma-am?"

Why hadn't his Chief explained this? She disregarded her aching feet and the buzz of fatigue that threatened to engulf her mind. "Is your family coming?"

She wished. Anchor had invited himself.

"Oh, sure, ma'am," he grinned proudly, then tilted his head up, letting the rain splash onto his broad farm boy face.

"Your job is to ensure they have a great time."

"What do we do if it rains?"

Paloma laughed, remembering the first time she thought rain affected the Navy's plans. It was the summer before her senior year in high school. The Naval Academy invited her to spend a week with them to see if she liked military life. It poured the day she arrived. The schedule called for a jog around campus and she asked one of the Cadre—a Midshipman responsible for training—what they would do instead. He chuckled. "We plan all our wars for sunny days!"

"We get wet. Go check in with your Chief, see if you're done for the day."

By the time she left the ship, only an annoying drizzle splattered the streets. Ten minutes later she was home, ran a blow dryer over her damp hair, and wriggled into her little black dress and pumps.

"Trisha! You coming?"

"You're meeting Anchor? Nah. I'll read my book, go to bed early. You kids have fun."

"Trish—please! I need someone there."

Trisha was deaf to her plea. "You'll do fine, girlfriend."

Paloma took the elevator down to the lobby, turned left at G Street and wended her way toward a downtown rooftop bar Anchor had suggested. She had to be back aboard at oh-six-hundred, which gave her an excuse for limiting this to a quick drink.

Why did she need an excuse? Just tell him.

"Hey! You made it." Anchor handed her a beer and pecked her cheek.

He looked great in Citizen jeans, a tailored embellished button-down that set off his dark skin. When he smiled, it lit up the room. Several girls sighed as he guided her through the crowd.

"Come back tomorrow night. He'll be available," she mumbled under her breath."

They found a small table in the back.

"Tell me about your day, Kali. You look tired."

Between sips of beer and handfuls of peanuts, she told him about preparations for the Tiger Cruise. He soaked it up, asking questions, curious about all the details, letting her blather on. Before she knew it, she told him her concerns about Taggert talking out of school.

"That is not acceptable, is it?"

Paloma laughed. "To put it mildly!"

Anchor took her hand and wrapped it between his warm palms. "You must turn him in."

She fidgeted. "He might get thrown off the ship. I want to be sure first."

Anchor smiled. "You, Paloma Chacone, are a caring person."

She forced a smile. Another reason she was tired of Anchor, she always had to talk about herself. She knew nothing about him. When she asked, he deflected. What was he hiding?

"And you are a great listener. You never talk about your job."

"I live vicariously through you and your *Bunker Hill.*"

She tried again. "Why's an Air Force guy so interested in cruisers?"

"My great grandpa's friend served on the *HMS Invincible*. 17,373 tons with eight 12-inch guns in four twin-gunned turrets. One of the first battle Cruisers in the world. At top speed, it went a blistering twenty-five knots. The German's sank it in WWI at the Battle of Jutland."

Anchor started to say more when a news alert flashed across the TV about *Triumph* attacking an Iranian sub. He nodded toward the screen. "What do you think?" He sounded upset.

"Do you have friends on that sub?"

He shrugged, eyes on her. "I bet you Americans believe a hijacking could never happen here."

She bristled. "Damn right." She remembered the 9/11 terrorists who planned to fly Flight 93 into the White House only to be stopped by a passenger uprising. "God help the terrorists who try to take an American sub from its crew."

"How do you think this happened? Are the British worse sailors than Americans?"

Paloma took a swallow of beer. "My friends on a *Virginia*-class sub say there'd have to be an insider. Maybe *Triumph* had a mole."

Anchor let out a violent cough, spitting beer over the table. "Sorry. I swallowed wrong." He wiped up the table, and then fiddled with his drink before continuing. "Or the Brits made it up as a ploy to attack my homeland with impunity."

The remark came out of left field and she stared at him, aghast. Until now, she had never considered Anchor's nationality. She tried to put herself in his position.

"Don't think that, Anchor. The West is committed to finding a middle ground with your leaders so all people can live together in peace."

Anchor's smile looked forced, his face impassive. "I know what you are thinking, Paloma. What does it mean Anchor is Muslim?"

Paloma's ire rose. In fact, she cared nothing about Anchor's religion. Why should she?

He continued talking. "Muslims put religion over country. The Qur'an is not only our religious guide, but tells us how to live our lives. Those," and he gestured at the TV, "are the opinions of frightened people."

He made it sound like she was close-minded. She should respond, but the deadness in his eyes made her doubt he'd listen. More reason to end it. She looked at her watch. "I'm sorry, I have to go. I enjoyed this."

They made their way outside and Kali was relieved when a stranger blocked their path. Anchor pulled her closer, or pushed her in front, but the stranger didn't seem dangerous. In fact, she'd describe him as frail, like a strong wind would knock him over. His shoulders were slumped. He wore a t-shirt too small for his lanky frame, feet shod in tattered tennis shoes.

"Excuse us." She started to brush him aside, but the intensity in his eyes stopped her, as though he recognized her. Or Anchor. "Do I know you?"

He blushed. "My name is Sean—Delamagente." He stuck his hand out to Paloma first and then Anchor. "I-I know you. Ankour Mohammed? From my apartment building?"

Anchor blinked and looked away. "I don't think so," but something made her think he did indeed know Sean.

Sean grinned. "Oh. Sorry, man. Do we work together?"

"I'm in sales. I know everyone at my company. You're, uh, not one of them." H returned his attention to Paloma. "I must leave. I'll see you Wednesday."

Paloma let him go. Dumping him could come later.

The boy waited until Anchor left and then turned to Paloma. "I need to talk to you."

Paloma looked him up and down, figured she could outrun him if her Black Belt in karate failed her. "OK, Sean Delamagente. You look harmless enough. Walk me home."

Sean fell in beside her. "I have no idea how to explain this to you, so I'll just say it. Yeah. I feel like I know you because Ankour follows you and I follow him. He dated some officer on the *Princeton* who has disappeared. He shadows you from your apartment to the Naval Base. Evenings he's not with you, he's close by. Yeah. He's obsessed with you."

Paloma was appalled he knew so much about Anchor, and then realized the boy must be an undercover policeman or some other security sort. His youthful looks probably made people feel less threatened. She started to bluster a response, but he put his hand up.

"Here's what else I know: Ankour is dating you for your access to the Navy."

She had enough. "That's ridiculous. Why wouldn't he date me for me?"

Sean looked flustered and stammered out, "Oh, no, you're beautiful, one of the most… Yeah, I said that wrong," and he pulled a fist-sized black cube out of his pocket. "Lying stresses people and stress causes voice changes that can be detected by this device. I made it, but similar ones are used by police all over America."

Paloma knew about these. "How does someone your age know how to build this?"

Sean turned it over and over as though seeing it for the first time. "Anyone can make one. Yeah. It's pretty intuitive." The read had a lot of spikes and bumps. "Anchor lied about where he lives and works. Why?"

Paloma felt her face flush. "I don't believe you."

"What do you know about him?" Sean's voice was calm and reasonable. Then he waited, kind eyes hopeful like he wanted to be wrong.

Paloma thought through what she knew. "Well, he went to the USAFA."

"How do you know?"

Paloma thought back. "We talked about how he dropped out to help his family."

Sean tapped away on his phone in silence. "No one named Anchor or Ankour or any other derivation graduated or dropped out of USAFA. Nor do I find an Air Force member with that name. Do you know where he works?"

Paloma mulled that over and came up blank. "He's in sales, drives a company car."

"His car is leased by a shell company that traces back to a man in the United Arab Emirates. I checked his phone records—"

"How are you finding this out?" Even as she asked, she realized it would be easy if Sean was police. He smiled as though reading her mind. "I'll show you how when we know each other better. Trust me when I tell you no phones are registered in his name. He's using a throwaway, the type people buy to hide calls."

Paloma stared at him. "I'm not going to listen anymore unless you explain yourself."

Sean's eyes remained steady, unwavering, as he came to a decision. "Here's what I can tell you."

For the next thirty minutes, he told an amazing tale about submarines and warships and nuclear warheads, terrorists and hijackers and his suspicion that it all revolved around Ankour Mohammed, then asked her to keep it to herself.

By now, they reached her building. She stared at this boy with the incredible story that had enough details she recognized to ring true. "How can you know all this?"

"Paloma. I'm a problem solver. I had stuff in my past, my mom and I, and they left me unable to stand by when trouble happens to anyone. Like you." He scuffed his shoe on the ground, stuck his hands in his pockets. "Look. I need to find the truth. Believe me when I tell you, I would prefer an innocent Anchor to a guilty terrorist."

She chewed her lip. It cost her nothing to give this boy—man—a chance. "We have a ten-hour Tiger Cruise Wednesday. You can join Anchor and me. That should be enough time to see if he's innocent or I've been duped. I'll add your name to the list at the gate," and went inside her building.

Chapter Twenty-three

Day Nine, Tuesday, August 15th, evening
Columbia University, Zeke's office

Rowe sat in his Columbia office, feet propped up on a wastepaper can, flipping his pencil. Kali had been shocked when he mentioned al-Zahrawi and lied about her injury. Why?

He rubbed his hand down his face and yawned. There still were no signs of *Virginia*, nor any virtual footprints explaining Mohammed's purpose in San Diego. It couldn't be to kill Parishers. Maybe to meet LT Chacone, but was it for her Navy connections? Her ship?

James would get a sample of the paint tomorrow. That would confirm *Triumph* could hide from sonar which would explain how it escaped after attacking the Iranian boat, how the American ships failed to find it in the Med, and why the terrorists thought they could passage fourteen hours through the Suez Canal without being stopped: Egypt, who owned the Canal, now knew the terrorists were not afraid to use the sub's weapons.

He flipped his pencil, ideas bumping around, but nothing bubbled to the surface. His gut said *Triumph* and

Virginia were redundancies. As long as one survived, the plan survived. And Haster slipped when he called *Triumph* the 'safest sub'. Not degaussing *Triumph* during the wargames meant Britain could test the paint. It worked perfectly. Rowe would see Haster at George's funeral tomorrow. If Haster didn't level with him by then, he was going to shake the man until he gave it up.

His phone jangled. James. "Turn on the TV. North Korea is making an announcement."

Rowe flipped it on to Fox and found a news conference with the North Korean ambassador:

> *This latest attack by the West makes it imperative we continue to use any and all means to protect our nation, our sovereignty, and our people. We will consider any attempts to deter or end our efforts an Act of War subject to a response of our choosing.*

"You get that? No denial anymore. This is their excuse to launch a nuclear warhead into space. Japan is scared out of its rising sun. They want us on site armed to the teeth, but the President says and I quote, 'the international community won't support our interference in another nation's exercise unless it endangers us.' All he'll authorize is one of our cruisers be on site to destroy the missile if necessary."

A chill went up Rowe's spine. "Mohammed is still there because that warship will come out of San Diego," and LT Chacone was an officer on it.

"Yeah, but here's what confuses me. How do they think they can prevent *Bunker Hill* from stopping them when it is backed by the 7th Fleet? Zeke, what's going on?"

Tuesday, August 15th, 9 pm
Kali's apartment

Sandy curled on her foot, Kali waiting for sleep to claim her, but images of Dr. Zeke Rowe, a youthful professor lecturing in a high-ceiled nineteenth-century classroom, eyes aglow as his students listened, headlined as 'Youngest Professor in University History wins Gandhi award'. Today's Zeke Rowe was Steven Siegel in *Under Siege,* violence simmering just below the surface, this time eyes aglow as he brought justice to the downtrodden.

Once last summer as they fought to stop Salah al-Zahrawi from decimating the US Navy, James opened up to her.

"Zeke has always been aloof to his women friends no matter their kindness, intellect, or feelings for him. You though, Kali, are the oil in his gun, the passion in his fight, the hydrogen in his H2O. In a world without terrorists, you two would be deliriously happy.

"But in this world," and James waved his arm slowly in front of them, "America needs him. His genius is unrivaled by anyone I've ever met. Zeke turns fragments of raw intelligence into a picture of enemy intentions. I can't count the times, if not for Zeke, lives would have been lost, plans collapsed, the future changed. I know the toll it takes on him, but I thank God every time he returns my call."

His affection for Zeke was as much for his service to America as the man himself. Kali liked James a little more because they both cared for Zeke.

Zeke let himself into Kali's apartment, double locked the door, popped a beer can, and then tiptoed into her room. She watched him undress through slotted eyes, toss his clothes in a heap, down the last of the beer, and crawl in next to her. He curled around her body. She wanted to lose herself in the moment.

But no warm body or tingle of contentment would stop her tonight. To protect Zeke from the man who must be al-Zahrawi, she must make him think she no longer cared.

"Zeke. I-I can't handle your life anymore." She faced him, running through the reasons she had to break it off. "You carry a gun and are not afraid to use it. You work alone. You have no safety net. Worst of all, you like it. What if we had children?"

When Zeke's eyes met hers, the mask disappeared. She had the power to destroy this man who had saved her life and her son's, who had suffered more than anyone she knew and still believed a better world existed out there.

She struggled to continue, tears filling her eyes. "Give me one reason," *Please*, "to continue, Zeke."

A minute passed and another before Zeke responded. "Because I can't do it without you. You are my barometer. You keep me centered. You give my work heart."

Kali pulled him to her and stroked his hair, tears rolling down her face. "Playing the vulnerable hero card, hunh. That's dirty."

Zeke looked at her, fingers caressing the Band-Aid on her forehead. "This is about you getting hurt." He spoke softly, but he didn't need her to explain.

For the next hour, she forgot about submarines and dead sailors and international terrorists and anything other than how much she cared for Zeke. When they finished, her headache was gone. They lay in the dark, her face against the hollow of his neck, his arms wrapped gently around her body, a radio down the street playing an old love song. She was nearly asleep when he whispered, "I wanted to keep my promise, Kali. I felt so sure this time, nothing would derail our plans, but I can't—not with Sean to think about, and George's butchers free." A fat tear dropped from his cheek to hers.

And Sandy banged against the bedroom door

Kali giggled. "Sandy needs to go out."

Zeke grinned. "Me, too."

They threw on clothes, put a leash on Sandy, and walked 122nd to Riverside Drive and looped around the park. In the thin night air, she smelled the river mingled with the park's American Yellow Wood and the exotic aroma of Chinese Ginkgoes and Japanese Cherries. They passed Grant's Tomb, the largest mausoleum in the world, and then the understated Amiable Child Monument. Sandy huffed, prancing along the stone path, hurrying back to Kali's side whenever an unfamiliar noise popped up. No one would call him the bravest dog on three legs, but he was the happiest.

They walked in silence, each in their own thoughts, comfortable with the quiet. Time to bring up the elephant in the park.

"Zeke. It's not your fault George died."

"I know, but someone must pay. I'm taking time off teaching until they're stopped. If I did that sooner, we might have saved George and *Triumph*. I'm damn sure going to find *Virginia* before someone else's best friend doesn't come home for dinner."

Zeke looked away. "After George's funeral tomorrow, I'm going to San Diego. I think Mohammed is the key."

Kali smiled. "Please convince Sean to stay out of this."

"If he's set on protecting this Chacone, I'll do it." His voice was thick with conviction. "Knowing Mohammed's interest in her will go a long way toward understanding what he's after."

"Kali?" Otto's voice came out of her phone as Zeke's rang. "I found *Virginia*."

Beside her, Zeke stiffened. "A submarine tried to sink a Chinese carrier. Luckily, they didn't set the shot up well. There are massive casualties, but it looks limp back to port. Our folks are pretty sure it's the *Virginia*—and so are the Chinese. In fact, they blamed America in a press release.

"I have to go."

Tuesday, August 15th, night
Dr. Penbury's lab

Oliver Najafian no longer doubted he was being followed. Yesterday, he reversed quickly and someone ducked out of sight. Still, he wasn't truly in danger until they no longer hid.

He checked his watch. Ten minutes. He patted his pocket, confirming he still had the paper with the phone number. He had to make the call this evening.

When he confronted al-Zahrawi about hijacking *Triumph*, al-Zahrawi confirmed his part but insisted sinking the Iranian sub was unintended. He had no such defense for *Virginia's* attack on the Chinese carrier, reportedly on a goodwill mission to draught-torn Morocco. China didn't believe the sub had been hijacked. They thought it was intentional.

Najafian believed it was all part of al-Zahrawi's plot to discredit the West and sell the sonar shield to anyone with a fleet. Najafian had to save his brother's life.

Najafian locked the door and was about to place the phone call when a noise stopped him. No one should be here. He walked the confines of the lab, found nothing but still called the guard desk. They promised to check, and then asked why he was in Penbury's office. He said he was probably hearing things.

His phone call got no further than the FBI switchboard. A shuffle, a slash and something wet on his chest. A female voice asked, *May I help you*? as pain exploded. Najafian reached up, meaning to staunch the blood flowing freely from his neck, but within moments he no longer cared. Darkness crept in, bringing a calm he last felt as a child. Everything would soon be fine.

Chapter Twenty-four

Day Ten, Wednesday, August 16, morning
Naval Base San Diego

Sean bathed, dressed in nondescript jeans, a patriotic t-shirt, and flip flops. He'd buy a *Bunker Hill* cap when he got there.

He hated driving, but California's public transportation sucked, so he jumped in his apartment manager's beat-up Toyota, almost bumping another car as he edged out of the underground parking lot. He had five miles to travel and gave himself thirty minutes. Yeah. What if he got lost? He managed to merge onto the 5 Freeway south and exit at 8th street with no mishaps, and then wended his way toward Naval Base San Diego where he would meet Paloma.

For her sake, Sean hoped Anchor was innocent, but had no doubt how the day would end.

The sky glowed azure, spotted with fluffy whimsical clouds. A soft breeze carried a hint of salt water. What a perfect day for a cruise. He stopped at the entrance to the Naval Base, the marquis announcing, *Naval Surface Forces*. The guard looked up his name, compared Sean's student ID with his face, and pointed down Cummings Road.

"It turns into Mole Road. Proceed to the lot by Pier 9. You'll see a crowd of civilians."

Five minutes later, Sean parked near the *USS Bunker Hill*, Sword of the Fleet, sporting six massive E's on its hull.

"You see those."

Sean glanced at the wizened old man off his right side. The septuagenarian hobbled forward, one arm pumping, body rocking side to side as he leaned into a stout cane. He wore a *Bunker Hill* cap, t-shirt, and precisely creased tan pants held up with a thick brown belt adorned by a heavy aluminum Navy buckle.

"The E's? Uh, yeah. What're they for?"

The man had to squint up at Sean. "Departmental Efficiency Awards. Each E signifies the ship's high level of overall readiness to carry out its assigned wartime tasks. Competition for that award is keen. CG52 is one of the best ships in the fleet."

Sean had to hurry to keep up. "How do they get an E?"

The old man raised the forefinger of his right hand, the other hand still gripping the wood cane. "To qualify for Battle E consideration, a ship's gotta win eighty percent of the Command Excellence awards. Things like," and he ticked them off on thick, bent fingers, "Maritime Warfare, Engineering/Survivability, Command and Control, Logistics Management. The cruiser must be nominated by," he stopped dead in his tracks, head down, and then started up again, cane thumping out his pace, boney body rocking side to side.

"Doesn't matter." He nodded, agreeing with himself.

Sean figured as much as this guy knew, he must have served. "Did you win one, you know, when you served?"

"Hell no. I never cared enough and no one could change my mind. My grandson, though, there's a sailor to be proud of. Petty Officer 3rd Class Drew Collins" and he pointed his cane toward the *Bunker Hill*. "The US Navy is lucky to have him."

The old man ambled toward the hulking superstructure in front of them. Sean would have liked to talk with him longer. He knew a lot.

Sean headed toward the cheerful group of friends and family, dressed casually, all-weather jackets slung over their arms. Some carried chairs and blankets. Many had slathered on sunscreen. All were excited to see an American warship at work.

He found Anchor in the sign-in line dressed like a model from a sailing magazine—white cargo pants, blue polo, white ball cap, fake Rolex, and a gold chain around his neck. Paloma stood beside him, elegant in summer whites, hat—cover, they called it—perched atop a tidily combed bun, and a light touch of make-up. She was more beautiful than anyone Sean had ever seen.

"Hey, Anchor. Thanks for inviting me, Paloma. This is my dream, yeah, touring a warship."

Paloma popped a *Bunker Hill* cap on his head. "You'll be happy to have this later." She smiled as she spoke which made him feel queasy and warm inside. His mouth hung open and he slammed it shut. He stepped back and made a circling motion with his hand.

"Let's get a group snapshot," and flipped open his phone. It looked normal enough, but Sean had enhanced it to take hi-res digital photos that immediately uploaded to his DropBox account. Anchor smiled woodenly. Done, Sean pretended to study it while uploading it to his cloud account.

"Can I watch them throw the ropes off, when the ship leaves the dock?"

Paloma gave him a funny look, "Sea and Anchor duty. Sure." Once on deck, Paloma began an informal tour.

"The crest of *Bunker Hill* honors our roots. Colonists were formidable opponents at *Bunker Hill*. The redoubts they built are symbolized by the scarlet hill and battlements. The muskets with bayonets recall their weapons and the powder horn refers to the New Englander's dogged stand against superior forces, never capitulating even when ammunition ran out. The anchor is symbolic of maritime traditions and excellence of achievement."

"Wow." Sean felt awed. Anchor looked bored.

Paloma continued, "Cruisers have been around longer than any other class of warship save battleships. Today, their primary duty is to protect the carrier and bombard shore armaments."

Anchor perked up. "So, uh, tell me about her insides." Finding out about *Bunker Hill's* capabilities might explain Anchor's interest.

Paloma smiled. "For an affordable $1 billion, *Bunker Hill* provides more bang for the buck than any other warship. To start with, it has four GE LM2500 Gas Turbine engines that kick out 80,000 horsepower."

"Crummy mileage, huh?" Sean joked.

Paloma laughed. "But we can go six thousand nautical miles on a tank of fuel."

"I heard a cruiser can go thirty knots per hour," Anchor said.

Paloma's eyes narrowed. "That is the speed we admit to."

The man grinned as though Paloma had told a joke. "Do you keep guns onboard?"

"Do you mean are our sailors armed?" She shook her head. "Navy regs prohibit the carrying of firearms while onboard except by watchstanders, but we have well-stocked weapons stations and an armory. All 360 crew members are trained to use them."

Paloma's face said she caught the same thing. No man so proud of his military background would say *thirty knots per hour*. Knots were a unit of speed per hour, making *thirty knots* sufficient. And he should know ropes were called lines, and guns weapons.

As she continued the tour, the ship cast off and moved out of the dock. "Fore and aft we have VLS tubes, Vertical Launch Systems. They are a firing solution for anti-aircraft/anti-ship missiles, Tomahawks, and rocket-assisted torpedoes."

"What's loaded now?" Anchor asked, fumbling with his smartphone.

Paloma seemed to consider her reply. "Only the captain and WEPS know the exact loadout. Let's go to the Bridge as the ship moves out to sea."

As they passed through the Bridge doors, they heard, 'Very well... Very well..."

"That's the Conning Officer confirming course instructions with Nav—the Navigator."

"Officer of the Deck based upon an excellent visual fix at time 0900, Navigation holds you fifteen yards right of track and correcting. Nearest aid to navigation is buoy seven fifty yards off the starboard bow. Nearest hazard to navigation is shoal water fifty yards off the port beam. Fathom reads forty feet beneath the keel which concurs with charted depth. Navigation recommends marking turn, next course 230."

"OOD."

"Left full rudder, steady course 230."

Helm: "Left full rudder, steady course 230, aye, sir."

"My rudder is left 30 degrees, coming to course 230."

Conn: "Very well."

Helm: "Conning officer, steady on course 230; checking course 218, sir."

"Very well."

Sean said, "All that to complete a turn? Wow."

As *Bunker Hill* approached the National Cemetery on the starboard side, the ship slowed and a whistle blew. Every sailor on deck snapped to formation.

Paloma murmured, "We venerate those who gave everything for the country." She pointed to a group of three headstones. "Those honor the three tin cans—destroyers—that held off the Japanese Navy during the WWII Battle of Surinam. What those sailors did remains the Navy's definition of heroism."

Sean smiled. "I read about them in *Last Stand of the Tin Can Sailors*. Yeah. Great book."

Anchor glared at Sean and scooted closer to Paloma. "You are so smart, sweetheart." He put an arm around Paloma which she shrugged off.

"No PDA on the Bridge, civilian."

"Oh. Anyway, how's the cruiser defend a carrier?"

"With what's called the Aegis Weapons System, the most sophisticated defensive and offensive system in the world."

Sean had spent hours reading the Navy background material on Aegis and visiting the manufacturer's— Lockheed Martin's—website. Anchor apparently hadn't.

"What's Aegis?"

"Aegis enables synchronized defense against air, land, and sea attacks. *Bunker Hill's* hull-mounted SPY Phased Array provides 360-degree coverage at all times. It can track 256 objects simultaneously."

"256!" Anchor stuck his hand in his phone pocket. "Say you're attacked by dozens of planes, each with dozens of bombs. How does Aegis stop that much fire power?"

Paloma blinked. "I'll show you."

She led her group down a flight of stairs Sean calculated at a steep seventy degrees and toward a hatch aft and right. "We're headed for CIC—Combat Information Center, but Combat for short—the heart of our defensive and offensive capabilities. There, you'll get an idea of Aegis' power which should resolve your question. We scrubbed it, but still no cameras, cell phones, or recording devices are allowed."

Sean stepped carefully over the four-inch raised hatchway into a room stuffed wall-to-wall with computers, each manned by a serious-looking watchstander. As Sean gaped in awe, Anchor shrieked and landed face down on the deck. Sean helped the red-faced man to his feet.

Paloma stifled a laugh. "No embarrassment, Anchor. Kneeknockers—the bottom of the watertight doorframe—face plant us all at least once." She gestured across the room and grinned at Sean. "A geek's dream, huh?"

Sean bobbed his head. "It makes me want to join the Navy."

As Paloma explained the room's activity, Anchor swiveled in a circle to take in all the consoles. Sean was alarmed, but Paloma merely continued her tour.

"These watchstanders process the tactical representation. That group over there," and she pointed to the row furthest from Combat's entrance, "is called Air Alley. They identify air traffic within range of the ship and combat airborne threats." She beckoned one the watchstanders. "This is Petty Officer Williams, the man responsible for Air Alley."

As Williams explained procedures to a rapt Anchor, Sean sidled up to Paloma. "You see him taking pictures?"

She smiled. "Who could miss it? No worries. Nothing electronic works in this room except our stuff. Same with the ones he tried to take on the Bridge."

When Williams finished up, Paloma said, "Let's get coffee in the wardroom?"

They thanked the watchstanders and descended another cramped set of stairs, through more doglegged pways, to a narrow, rectangular room, walls lined with counters, center a Formica cafeteria table. Paloma motioned them to sit while she poured coffee.

"This is officer country. No enlisted allowed. Here, we let our hair down."

The Captain greeted Paloma and introduced himself to Anchor and Sean. His bearing radiated a fierce, uncompromising intelligence weathered by the confidence that came from making the right decisions often. He made small talk for a few minutes, glanced at Sean and left.

"What'd I do?"

Paloma laughed. "You're in his chair." She pointed to the inscription on the back.

Sean leaped to his feet. "You should have told me!"

"Sit. It's not a big deal or he would have said something. He's not shy."

Before Sean could say more, Anchor started. "I do not believe you can accurately target two hundred bad guys from that small room. You say that to scare your enemies."

Paloma flushed, but smiled sweetly, "We're variously tasked with launching missile attacks, stalking submarines, protecting aircraft carriers, stopping drug traffickers, and carrying out relief missions. If required, we can shoot a cruise missile through the porthole of a ship." To Anchor's gaping mouth, she nodded. "Yeah, we're that good."

Anchor's fists balled and his face turned red. "You think you are gods, your strength inviolable." His voice had become strident. Several officers glared and left.

Paloma's eyes flattened. She forced a smile, "No Cruiser has been in battle since WWII so the effectiveness of these weapons is theoretic."

A lone, slow applause echoed from an alcove of overstuffed chairs. "That's the way to do it, Chacone," in the same tone he might say, 'I found a dead rat in the kitchen'.

Sean jerked. He recognized that voice from the tapes as the man who had been talking to Mohammed. He glanced at the name tag. *Kevin Taggert, Executive Officer.* His posture, confrontational stance, and scowl said he grabbed respect rather than earned it. Beside him stood a woman who might have stepped off the pages of Penthouse. She wore tight beige cotton pants no panty line and a loose cotton top striped with shades of blue and red. She had a long, alabaster neck, skin like porcelain, and blue eyes big enough to fall into.

Paloma blushed. "XO, Sir. These are my friends, Anchor Mohammed," Anchor bumped his chin up, eyes on Taggert's date, "and Sean Delamagente." Sean nodded, shoulders hunched, hands deep in his pockets, and wondered why Anchor and Taggert pretended not to know each other.

"This is my fiancée, Shalimar. She's a writer," and Taggert wrapped a beefy arm around her slender bronzed shoulders. She tilted into his shoulder, eyes on Sean. Taggert smirked. Testosterone oozed from him like body odor, or—Sean sniffed shallowly—it was body odor.

"Come on, baby." He pulled Shalimar closer and they sauntered off.

"XO Kevin Taggert. He never misses an opportunity to call me out in public, always trying to prove he's better, smarter, and handsomer than everyone around him. Let's go or we'll miss the Steel Beach picnic."

The Steel Beach picnic turned out to be a buffet lunch on deck complete with barbecued hamburgers, chips, beans, potato salad, brownies, chocolate chip cookies, canned music and good cheer as everyone chatted and basked in the warm California sun. Sean collected his meal and joined Paloma at the only three seats left—the stationary bikes. They balanced their plates on the screens, tucked drinks into the curve of the arm rests, and ate as they talked to the family of the old man Sean met when he arrived. When he asked how a stationary bike worked, Sean pretended to reach across Anchor to point and knocked Anchor's phone over.

"Oh, man, sorry," and he leaped down, retrieved the phone, and sneaked a peek at the number. "An iPhone. Yeah. I wish I could afford one. Is it from your company?"

Before Anchor could snap back an answer, his phone rang, the number popping up on the screen with the international prefix 850.

North Korea.

"Give me my phone," and he yanked it away before Sean could memorize the rest of the number. "Father!... Yes, our friend will arrive on schedule.... No, I was unable to. … Oh, thank you for arranging the ride. I am looking forward to it... Soon, yes. Excuse me?" Anchor's gaze hopped to Sean. "Yes, I do... Thank you."

After lunch, *Bunker Hill* demo'd the deck guns. The five-inch 54 cal boomed with delicious authority, but the 50 cal shoot was canceled for what XO called 'technical difficulties'.

Anchor snickered. "I guess the volunteer army needs new volunteers."

Paloma retorted, "We're about to dock. Anything either of you would like to see before we wrap it up?"

"I have a few places." Anchor proffered a list and Sean's photographic memory took a snapshot. Sean would run it by Eitan.

Paloma's forehead wrinkled. "XO has the same list. Did you get it from him?"

"Never mind. We should go." His voice trailed off.

As Sean drove home, he mulled over the day. The tension between Anchor and Paloma finally boiled over as they pulled into the dock. Paloma accused him of hiding something and he told her to mind her own business. Sean's car was blocked by several other families, so he didn't get to follow Anchor as he'd planned. Instead, he stopped to pick up snacks at the corner store, parked the car back in the manager's spot, and sprinted to his apartment, eager to get Eitan's take on everything.

His door was open. He flipped the light switch, but nothing happened so he stepped in slowly and let his eyes adjust to the dim.

"Man."

Every piece of electronic equipment was smashed, furniture turned over, food dumped randomly. Only the eel remained unaffected. The three-foot baby swam serenely back and forth in its massive tank.

"I got lucky." He pressed his face against the glass tank. "Hey, Itui. Everything's OK."

The fish latched onto him with her luminous unblinking eye. Sean smiled. The most important piece in the apartment and the thieves missed it.

Sean didn't care about the equipment and his computer's nine-digit encryption made it unhackable in the ten hours he'd been gone. He sent a command to wipe the drives. Anything of importance was stored online. What bothered him was the empty desk drawer. After ten minutes kicking through the detritus of what had been his apartment, he had to admit the only paper file he owned was missing. Why would someone want it?

His thoughts were interrupted when pain knifed through his head. As he lost consciousness, his brain went on autopilot. He connected Anchor's call from his father to another conversation… Taggert's voice… His mind flipped everything into place until Sean knew why Anchor needed those six locations. *I have to call Eitan...* And he passed out.

Chapter Twenty-five

Day Ten, Wednesday, August 16th, 1 am
Columbia University Office of Kali Delamagente

After Zeke rushed off, Kali gave up sleep and went to her office. Since the funeral was today, she wouldn't see him most of the morning.

"Otto, how did you find *Virginia*?"

"When *Virginia* launched torpedoes, my sensors tracked the variance in acoustics."

No matter how silent *Virginia's* passage, Otto would pick up the difference between the ocean with a sub and without. Kali started at *Virginia's* last known location—the Caribbean—and extended out. Any sounds, Otto would compare to an immense database of audio files identified as typical to a *Virginia*-class submarine. Since nothing in nature compared to the mechanical sound of torpedo doors opening or weapons launching, the ID was easy.

Kali had a hunch. "Would you compare time-frame of data to what it should sound like without a submarine and identify discrepancies."

Otto hummed through data for three minutes. "There is a disruption in the surrounding magnetic fluxes that, although does not negate the degaussing, provides an obvious sensory digital image. It is unusual. I wouldn't expect it to accompany a submarine."

"Find the change in the data for the area." Otto would use the same model astrologists use to find new planets, by noting deviations in gravitation pull. If America's warships could find the variances Otto identified, they could find *Virginia*.

"Can you identify what is causing it?"

Otto churbled. "I will require more information."

"It must be the paint. They didn't apply it to the inside of the torpedo tubes. Why would they? A torpedo pretty well gives their location away."

"Hey, babe." Fatigue shrouded Zeke's voice.

"You look tired," despite a new black pinstripe suit, paisley tie, white silk shirt, shining patent wingtips. "And…un-Zekelike."

"You look gorgeous."

"I have news—" Before she could continue, James marched in.

"I brought lunch," and he dropped a pink donut box on the table. His clothing was impeccable, but a deep dent scarred his forehead. Kali helped herself to a Styrofoam cup of donut holes. Zeke and James each took frosted buttermilk. Donuts had been Zeke and Kali's first commonality, a year ago when they hated each other.

"*USS Chancellorsville* has two SH ASW 60Bs— anti-submarine warfare helos searching from *Virginia's* last known position." James's voice sounded as defeated as Kali had ever heard.

"Thanks for inviting me, SA James."

Kali and Zeke both jerked toward the door and then to James. "Special Agent Haster," they said together.

"I didn't expect you," from Zeke.

"Didn't want you, either," Kali muttered under her breath.

Haster's funeral dress included rolled up sleeves and a tie stuffed into his pocket. "Oliver Najafian, a man we believe connected to the hijackings, died last night. He was a lab assistant for Dr. Penbury at Imperial College London."

Kali blanched. "Dr. John Penbury?"

"You're a friend of his." Not a question. "How close?"

She forced a calm she didn't feel. "We share our notes. He's a brilliant theoretician."

"A while ago, Penbury came to the attention of MI-6 because of his groundbreaking work in metamaterials. He began assisting us with a top secret project. This morning, we found his work had been copied and Najafian had received a large deposit yesterday."

Kali's insides went cold, but she said nothing.

"You knew Dr. Penbury well. Lovers?" Haster's voice had taken on an edge.

Kali shook her head slowly. The first hoofbeats of a headache rattled across the base of her skull.

James looked from Haster to Kali and back. "What are you talking about, Haster?"

The MI-6 agent crossed the room, eyes glued to Kali. "When Penbury accepted the contract, he understood the project fell under the International Traffic in Arms Regulation."

"ITAR regulates defense-related materials and research. That's not what this was."

Haster put his hand up like a stop sign. "Dr. Penbury developed a revolutionary method of making submarines invisible to sonar. When costs far exceeded our expectations, we involved your DARPA—"

Zeke interrupted. "He finished it?"

Haster moved his handmade stop sign Zeke's direction, his voice a notch higher. "In a manner of speaking. MI-6 tested it on *Triumph* and DARPA on *Virginia*. My point is—"

He never got to finish. Zeke turned a frightening shade of red and levitated out of his seat. "You should have told us. We could have saved George—*Triumph*—kept *Virginia* from the hijackers? What were you thinking?" Zeke gripped Haster's lapels, face an inch from his nose.

A light bulb popped in Kali's head. Metamaterials' properties were suspected of interfering with magnetics though no one had proved it. That's why Otto had difficulty locking onto *Triumph*.

A choking sound from Haster brought Kali back to reality. "Zeke—stop! You're hurting him!"

Haster shrank into the bookshelves, knees shaking, hands thrashing. He yanked a book out by the spine and battered it against Zeke's shoulders to no avail.

"SA James! Stop this man!" His voice dripped fear.

James pulled a penknife out and started cleaning his nails. "I wish I'd stopped you from lying to us."

Haster flailed a boney hand Kali's direction. "*She's* why hundreds lost their lives on *Triumph* and hundreds more are in jeopardy on your *Virginia*. She was desperate to crawl out of the financial hole grad school put her in so befriended the unmarried Penbury, asked for a copy of his formula and sold it. Seeing her, I understand why he obliged. When *Triumph's* disappearance hit the news, she paid off Najafian."

Kali gasped. "You're wrong," but Haster wasn't listening.

"A-as we speak, we're checking your accounts so you might as well level with me. Your future is in my hands," he concluded with as gracious a smile as possible considering his head was wedged between Darwin's *Origin of the Species* and Margaret Mead's *Notes from the Field*.

"Knock it off," James snarled, returning the knife to his pocket. "Both of you."

Kali lifted her chin. "Zeke, I can defend myself." Her voice came out calm with no room for argument.

Zeke elbowed the MI-6 agent as he turned away. "You're disgusting. I should stuff you in a grenade launcher and send you back to Britain."

James turned to Haster. "You're way off base. Put your detective pants back on and find some real clues."

Haster rubbed his jaw, smoothed his coat and pulled a notebook from the pocket. "You can clear this up, Ms. Delamagente. We know you received a copy of Dr. Penbury's formula. How does it apply to you?" He fluttered his hands as though confused.

Kali approached the wall-mounted monitor that had once been Otto's entire view on the world. She kept her voice soft, biting back a snarl.

"Please direct your attention here." When all eyes focused on the screen, she flipped a switch and it disappeared, replaced by a Degas reproduction.

"What—Where..." Haster approached with halting steps and stabbed a finger at the artwork. Otto squealed. Haster jumped and glared at the AI.

"The screen disappears, thanks to Penbury's formula. It deflects light around the object to what's behind it, which is my painting. After last year's problems, I wanted Otto hidden if necessary. Penbury offered his assistance.

"John also wanted my help. His program didn't work with sonar. Not much use to a sub, is it?"

James glared at Haster. "MI-6 fixed the formula?"

"Penbury must have sussed it out himself. The one we received worked like magic on *Triumph*." He turned to Kali. "Ms. Delamagente. It seems we've gotten off on the wrong foot."

Kali couldn't stop herself. "Because it was in your mouth."

"You three chat among yourselves while I update the ACNO," and James slipped into the hall.

Kali shuffled over to the tiny window in the corner of her office. Lights twinkled in the Mudd Building and laughter floated up from the Engineering Terrace. At least somewhere, life went on without fear of nuclear attacks and terrorists. She preferred to spit on Haster, but decided to try honey.

She smiled pleasantly. "SA Haster, would you please forward me a copy of the revised formula? I'll see what John changed and if I can defuse it."

Haster bobbed his head and left.

"I gave Admiral Xibon everything, but the President wants more," James announced as he returned. He loosened his tie and turned to Kali. "I want you to head a group of scientists. We've got a paint sample on its way and Haster is sending the formula. Figure out how to defeat that paint."

Kali thought about al-Zahrawi's threat. If she stayed here, everything business as usual, how would al-Zahrawi know?

"As long as I can start with a nap. I'm beat." She kissed Zeke on the cheek, collected her briefcase, and left.

Chapter Twenty-six

Day Ten, Wednesday August 17th, evening
Kali's apartment

By the time Kali got home, a throbbing headache battered her neck and shoulders. Even Sandy's happy snorts and furious tail-wagging did little to take her mind off the pain. More aspirin would destroy her stomach. She needed something stronger, but would call John first.

She ended up leaving a message and then let her thoughts rattle around as Sandy sprawled across her lap, nose mashed against the arm of the sofa in the most peculiar position.

"Sandy. That cannot be comfortable."

He snored.

She called John Penbury again.

"Hello?"

"John. This is Kali."

"Who?"

"Kali Delamagente... from Columbia University."

"Kali. Good to hear from you. What's on your mind?"

He sounded not at all like it was good to hear from her. She hesitated a beat. "I heard one of your lab workers died."

He sucked in a breath. "They talked to you? Oh, God. This is frightful. Someone penetrated my firewall, Kali. You warned me. Now, I'm too late."

"Yes, but they understand—"

"Bollocks. I worked for the benefit of mankind my whole life, haven't I? I wanted to protect our boys, not arm the enemy." He paused, his voice wet, and took a deep, trembling breath. "MI-6 accused me of betraying my country. I would no sooner turn on Britain than become American." His voice was thick with outrage.

Kali felt for her friend. "I had no idea you made such progress on the sonar shield."

"That's just it—I never tested it on anything the size of a sub, did I. They painted *Triumph* without my approval. I heard about it through the tele." Penbury breathed heavily as he thudded around his apartment. She tried to think of something to say, but came up empty.

"I'm leaving for a prolonged holiday. I don't know who to trust, Kali, I trusted Oliver as much as anyone I know and he stole my formula."

"John. Send it to me. I'll find a hole in it so we can locate *Virginia*. I'll clear your name."

A buzz announced an email arriving. "Take it. I-I must go."

Kali held the empty phone for a long minute, took four Tylenol, asked Mr. Winters to watch Sandy, and returned to her office. Every time something rustled, she walked faster until she was running.

Ten minutes and she was locked inside her office. She shrugged out of her jacket as Otto swiveled his pudgy body toward her. "Hello, Kali. How nice to see you."

"No time to chat, Otto." Her fingers flew over the keyboard. "I uploaded a formula for you. See if it accounts for the changes you saw around *Virginia*."

Otto whirred, eyes glowing, zeros and ones flowing down his chest. Ten minutes later, he replied, "Yes, in theory."

"Now run a sim to see if the formula explains the sub's invisibility to sonar."

More silence as Otto worked. Twenty minutes passed and then Otto turned to Kali.

"Yes. Again, in theory."

Kali grinned. "We now know why *Triumph* and *Virginia* are invisible. Can you find the disruption caused to the surrounding magnetic fluxes by the formula?"

Otto churbled. "Yes."

Kali wanted to cheer. "How long, Otto?"

He burbled. "I stopped the calculation at fifteen days because in that amount of time, the submarine could return to a tested part and negate our effort."

So, if they locate the sub when its torpedo tubes opened, Otto could attempt—in theory--to track it by following the difference between what should be and what actually was in the surrounding environ.

They had to wait for the next attack.

"Let's look into Dr. Najafian and Dr. Penbury."

John had been a loyal friend to her last year. Now was the time to repay him. She started with why the world's two top metamaterials experts ended up in the same lab. Maybe Najafian used his friendship with Penbury to obtain the spot, but the scientist in Kali forced her to consider all possibilities. Possibly, in Najafian's eagerness to leave Iran, someone made Penbury's lab the path of least resistance and then tricked the immigrant into helping the *jihad*.

Otto chirruped. "Dr. Oliver Najafian received doctorates in theoretical physics and practical physics from NYU Abu Dhabi in the United Arab Emirates."

NYU again. "Any evidence of involvement with Nasr Al-alah's group?

"I see none. After graduation, he taught at the prestigious Iran University of Science and Technology for several years until asked to leave for promoting Islamophobic beliefs. That's when he immigrated to Britain and became a lab assistant."

"Why not teach?"

Otto made riffling sounds. "His degrees from NYUAD were not accepted in Britain. He was appealing the decision."

Had someone deliberately held the approvals up? "Why Dr. Penbury's lab?"

"Dr. Penbury is his sponsor, as is Nasr Al-alah."

"Penbury and Al-alah knew each other?"

Oliver made a riffling noise. "There is no evidence of that, nor that Najafian and Al-alah were friends. I see several philosophical confrontations between them on a popular Muslim chatboard. Najafian was a pacifist and Al-alah contended the Qur'an supported war against the infidel."

Kali paced. Did Al-alah sponsor the man who was his philosophic opposite and then hold up Najafian's approval to force him to work for Penbury? There had to be a different reason.

"Are there any connections between DARPA or MI-6 and Najafian or Al-alah?"

"No."

Kali paced some more. Penbury denied completing the formula, so who had? "What can you find on DARPA and any paint or submarines they're involved with?"

A moment passed. "DARPA contracted with Acentech to provide services to submarines. Would you like me to read the news article?"

"Quickly."

> *DARPA awarded funding to Acentech's*
> *RH Lyon Division, one of the most*
> *experienced noise and sound specialists*
> *in the U.S., for a top secret project to*
> *create a paint that will make tanks,*
> *trucks, and even submarines invisible.*
>
> *"This is the most interesting concept in*
> *military defense since sonar," states Dr.*
> *Steven Africk, Supervisory Consultant*
> *and principal investigator at Acentech.*

RH Lyon must have completed the formula. She went to DARPA's database with her renewed Top Secret clearance and spent two hours drilling through the layers of data. She found a reference to *Triumph* and *Virginia* as candidates for the sonar-shielding paint, as well as an interview with a submariner named Najafian about how subs evade sonar.

"That's an odd coincidence."

She called Zeke and gave him an update. He offered to come over—did no one sleep anymore?—but she said she wanted to go to bed. Instead, she sat quietly, body motionless but mind burning through scenario after scenario, trying to find a way to neutralize the cloak.

Finally, she came at it from a different direction: Find a chink in Penbury's formula. Two hours later, she took a break, got a soda from the machine down the hall, and drank most of it as Riverside Church tolled two a.m. She stretched and settled in to start again when her phone rang. It must be Zeke. Who else knew she was here?

"I don't have—"

"I warned you of the consequences." The voice was muffled and raspy. "Now, I'll provide proof," and the line went dead.

Her hands shook so, it took three attempts to stab Sean's number into the keypad. "Come on, Sean!" She gave up after eleven rings.

"Otto, where is Sean's phone?"

Last year, when she helped the FBI, James loaned her GPS tracking software. He never asked for it back and she didn't offer.

"In his apartment, Kali. Shall I call it?"

"No. I tried already."

He took a day trip—somewhere. Did he leave his phone home?

A heaviness descended upon her. How stupid to think it would be OK this time. She sat, shoulders slumped, head in her hands, as she tried to figure out what to do.

Chapter Twenty-seven

USS Virginia
Somewhere in the world

The moment the hatch opened to the crippled ASDS, Joey Najafian knew they were in trouble. No submariner he knew had a tan or, for that matter, the demented look of a kid with a Disneyland season pass. The clincher was their watches were set to EU time. American subs followed Zulu.

Damn these religious nuts and their crazy definition of Islam. Joey believed Allah to be kind and caring, nothing like the god these radicals worshiped.

But Joey was no fool. When they killed the Chief of Boat for no reason but he stood up to them, Joey greeted the next thug he ran into with folded hands, a slight bow and the required *Assalaamu Álaykum*. The man pinned Joey to the bulkhead with a massive muscled hand, and asked, "What right have you to offer the traditional Muslim greeting?"

Without hesitation, Joey responded, *Allahu Akbar. Astaghfirullah.* I seek refuge in God."

The man tightened his grip until Joey almost passed out, and then asked why a loyal Muslim would serve the infidel. Joey blurted out the first thing that came to mind.

"I am a sleeper. I have awaited this day. Praise be to Allah and his messenger you have arrived and we can reclaim our destiny. I offer you my services."

"What exactly do you do on this ship?"

Boat, you lout, but Joey answered modestly, "Fire Control Technician. If you intend to use the weapons, I can help."

The Kenyan stared without a word. Najafian sweated, fearing he'd gone too far until the terrorist hugged him, kissing both cheeks. "Welcome. We were told we might be blessed with a True Believer."

It turned out they needed Joey badly. They knew little about how a nuclear submarine operated. Najafian told them he could do anything on the sub, parallel park it if they needed, which they took literally. Soon, they gave him free reign, took his advice on operations and strategy, albeit warning him treachery would be punished by death.

But Joey had bigger fears, like finding the real sleeper? Worry worked on his nerves like cook's morning coffee. He found himself staring at every Tom, Dick, and Farha on the crew, wondering which was the terrorist.

Those he trusted, he warned to remain calm, keep their ears open, pass him anything they overheard and he'd get it to the Captain.

Within a day, he knew something big would happen August 30th.

"That's two weeks," was the Captain's stunned reaction. "We have to alert Command."

He gave Joey his personal comm code, but Joey couldn't get past the hijackers. He tried to tell the Captain, but one of the Kenyan's kept him busy trying to crack the nuclear weapons' PAL codes. That would never happen, but Joey happily wasted time.

Then *Virginia* attacked the Chinese Carrier and everything changed.

The next time Joey saw the Captain, he was bleeding from a four-inch gash in his arm.

"Joey," he wheezed. "Stop this bleeding."

Joey found the first aid kit and bent over the gaping wound.

As Joey worked, he whispered, "We must prevent them from using *Virginia* to terrorize the world."

The FCO's throat tightened and his hands shook as he said what he must say. "Sir, what if I sabotage the MRG?" The main reduction gears. *USS Georgia* had been sidelined three months because one loose bolt rolled into the MRG. "Everyone will hear the rumble and know we have to surface and lock the shaft."

"They took the key." The MRG was secured for the very reasons Joey just explained.

Joey wrapped gauze around the Captain's arm, his hands clumsy with fear. "Damage the turbine." Engineers joked if you wanted the sub back in port, throw something into the turbine.

"Except they're guarding the door." The Captain lowered his voice even more. "Tell the crew to do everything possible to destroy the weapons' usability. Damage the torpedo doors, the VLS tubes, the firing mechanisms—anything they can think."

He paused and began again. "Then disable the check valve from the carbon dioxide scrubber's discharge pipe," prevent it from sending the CO_2 out to the ocean. "Next—and this is the big one: Figure out a reason to go to the degaussing station. Turn one of the coils to 0. We'll show up on sonar like red paint on the White House."

Joey bobbed his head, but that worried him. "They'll see that from the Bridge—:

"Only if they're looking. We get lucky and there's an American sub close by, a few seconds could be all we need." He winced. The white gauze bandage was already pink. "Failing that, break the RO," the reverse osmosis, responsible for turning seawater into drinking water.

"Captain, that's suicide!"

The CO's eyes hardened. "We're not letting them use our sub to attack the country we love, Joey. We may all die, but when those damn alarms go off, I'll salute the shipmate who made it happen."

Joey gulped. "Yes, Sir."

The Captain patted his shoulder. "I know the crew has a sleeper. I'm trying to figure out who it is, but until I do, be careful. You're a brave man, FCO. Can you make this happen, son?"

Joey bobbed his head again, not at all sure he told the truth.

Chapter Twenty-eight

Day Eleven, Thursday August 17, 2 am
Columbia University, lab of Dr. Eitan Sun

Sean didn't return Sun's call.

Sun swallowed half a can of Fanta cherry soda, tucked his feet underneath his body and bounced in his chair. Worry. Sun had asked Sean to stay away from Mohammed and Chacone until Zeke Rowe got there, but Sean didn't take orders well.

The scientist bounced again. Sean's silence, a Muslim North Korean, a Navy cruiser, *Triumph* attacking Syria, and *Virginia* attacking China. Not good. Not good.

He poured red M&M's into his mouth and petted his wife's image. She would bring him food if he worked late, a change of clothes, tell him funny stories about her day, and they would giggle together. He stuffed those thoughts into a dark room and locked the door, dropping the key down a mental manhole.

Where was Sean? He tapped into the boy's webcam, but it was off. A ping announced an invitation from Sean to view files. He entered the password and opened the file. They were from a Tiger Cruise Sean had taken with LT Chacone. Mohammed had also attended... His call from a man he called Father... The list of places Mohammed wanted to visit... an audio file of Sean asking Sun to compare Anchor's questions to what most people asked on Tiger Cruises. Something about those locations bothered Sean.

Five minutes later, Sun had a report. Anchor varied on weapons locations, vulnerable spots on the ship, crew routines, and details about how borders were repelled. Sun put that together with everything floating around his brain. With time, the like parts would align until the image became a landscape Sun could read.

As he sat, enjoying the cerebral flow, a question popped up. Al-alah had a stellar reputation as an educator until two years ago, the same time Ankour Mohammed joined his mentoring group. Did Al-alah recognize an opportunity in a boy with his multi-cultural background and connections to North Korea? Rowe thought Mohammed might be the fulcrum. The CIA thought a strategic alliance between Iran and North Korea wasn't actionable. Their political philosophies—North Korea ruled by the military and Iran by theocracy—prevented substantive collaboration.

Sun considered Rowe's analysis in view of what Mohammed had done the past week. He befriended officers likely to be part of the Task Force on scene during the North Korean missile launch. The Parisher trainees perished to enable Islamic jihadists to hijack *Triumph*.

He played the Tiger Cruise videos again. And again. The fifth time, he saw it. A look passed between Taggert and Mohammed. They knew each other. Sun ran an audio match of Sean's files and got one. The words were garbled, but the voice could only be Taggert. Sun plugged both men's visages into a web crawler to track their movements after the Tiger Cruise. Taggert went home with his girlfriend, someone called Shalimar.

Anchor took a taxi.

Sun called James while he pinned down the taxi's destination.

A groggy voice answered on the seventh ring. "What?" Something crashed. "God damn clock!" A female voice slurred in the background.

Sun didn't apologize. "Anchor's leaving town. He's moving to the next phase."

James coughed and sheets rustled. "How d'you know?"

He told James everything while tracking Mohammed. "He left out of Ontario Airport—"

"You know this how?"

"I hacked—"

"Never mind. What else?"

"I lost him inside the terminal. I checked all evening departures, but no 'Ankour Mohammed'. He used a fake name."

"Hold on." James entered a number on his FBI phone. "This is Special Agent Bobby James. I want the picture I sent in front of every gate agent at Ontario Airport. Find where this man went and catch him at the other end. Eitan, you still there? Let me know when you hear from Sean."

Sun replayed the Tiger Cruise tape, hoping to catch something else. He liked Paloma Chacone's voice. She was authoritative, knowledgeable, and cared about her job.

Another invite to view Sean's DropBox pinged. It would have to wait. Decrypting Dhiren Barot's dirty bomb plans had risen to the top of his to do list.

Chapter Twenty-nine

Day Eleven, Thursday, August 17th, 8 am
Somewhere over the United States

No one suspected a man would be under the traditional female *burqa* with *niqab*—full face veil. No wonder parts of Europe outlawed them.

Mohammed had planned to dispose of Chacone now that Shalimar had built a trail of payments to Taggert's account as well as incriminating photos. Unfortunately, Nasr instructed he leave immediately. He said Mohammed's cover was blown.

Not likely. Mohammed had been careful, but he did not argue, not with the end so near.

Mohammed stretched his legs, edging away from the female who sat too close. Typically, people honored the need of Muslim women for privacy. This American female, if anything, seemed drawn to him.

"I love your robe—what's it called?"

"A burqa."

"Burqa! Of course. Where would I buy one? It must be nice not to have to do your hair or makeup when you go out. Look!" She thrust her face so close to Mohammed, he could see the pores. He jerked back, but she was oblivious. "It takes an hour to fix this every morning." She winked their mutual understanding. He rubbed his nose at the stench of her foul breath.

"You're Islam, right? Or Muslim. I get confused. There are so many of you around. Oh, my. I'm so impressed with the Qur'an. That's your Bible, right?"

"Yes, praise be to Allah." He tried to keep his voice high-pitched and feminine.

"*Allahu Akhbar*! Did I say that right?" She continued without waiting, "I don't know why the world blames you-all for those horrible terrorists. You're peaceful. I have a Muslim friend—"

Mohammed snapped. "We are peaceful unless faced with rude, superior Westerners. You are degenerate with your nakedness and damned by your lewdness. You deserve Allah's wrath. "

She gasped and pulled back as though burned. "I never!" Then she rang her bell until the steward moved her.

What arrogant fools these Americans! With her gone, Mohammed called Nasr.

"*Assalaamu Álaykum.*"

"*Wa alaykumus salaam.*"

"May I have directions to your new location?"

"Check your phone. If you're finished…"

Mohammed wanted to talk. He had succeeded in everything and wanted—expected—Nasr's praise. "Nasr. I—"

Nasr shouted, "Never say my name! These lines are not secure. Meet me online."

Mohammed bit back a sharp response, opened his computer, plugged the flash drive in that allowed it to boot, and wended his way to the virtual chat room.

"Why not eliminate the female?"

Nasr's anger came through the typed words. "There were two—two! They both live?"

Mohammed lied, "Yes, mentor, but Paloma Chacone is an affront to Allah. She hugged and kissed other males in my presence. She must be taught a lesson."

"She is an infidel. Allah expects nothing of the unbeliever. BRB."

But Mohammed could not dismiss her. They were to go out after the Tiger Cruise, but she canceled, said she wanted nothing more to do with him. Now, she invaded his every thought. He had even asked his father's advice. "Bend her to your will, my son, and then destroy her. A family cannot be ruled by two."

My son—he had called the boy he once considered an outcast 'my son'! Here, finally, was the caring, paternal figure who would guide Mohammed through life's landmines. With his father back in his life, Mohammed no longer needed Nasr.

A ping intruded on Mohammed's thoughts. "Salah Al-Zahrawi wishes to know how you connected with Kalian Delamagente. He found her name in the file you stole from the boy's apartment."

Mohammed's voice burst with pride as he explained how he killed the boy, tossed his apartment to make it look like a burglary, and stumbled upon the file of contact information.

"Sean Delamagente is dead?"

"He was the one following me. You instructed I take care of him. He-he also figured out my plan." He heard the whine in his voice. Mohammed clenched his hands until his fingernails cut into his palms, dropped his tone a notch. "He had spy devices in my apartment too," he lied. The last came out forceful. That was better. "How is the jihad progressing, mentor?"

Nasr did not respond for so long, Mohammed thought he left the room. Finally, his mentor responded. "Britain and the Great Satan's reputations are damaged,

Allah be praised. The world will seek new protectors and we will respond with ships no enemy can find."

"*Aameen*." May it be so, Mohammed responded automatically.

"*Allahu Akhbar*. I will see you when you land," and Al-alah left the chatroom.

Mohammed logged onto the Usenet newsgroup *microsoft.public.de.internetexplorer* and scanned for a posting from 'Nivek.Treggat'—*Kevin Taggert* in reverse. To any who read the posts, it came across like a writer chatting with a confidential source, but into the files, Mohammed embedded the incriminating data Shalimar had collected against Taggert.

Mohammed clicked and smiled. Taggert cashed the $5000, payment for allowing Shalimar to take snapshots on the Tiger Cruise. Soon, Mohammed would give the fat man a choice—help Allah or have his duplicity unveiled. Taggert, of course, would do anything to save his name, at which point, Mohammed would anonymously direct the FBI to this Usenet group with its proof *Bunker Hill's* XO was the mastermind behind everything.

Mohammed rang his service bell and asked for a place to pray. The attendant pasted on a smile, conferred with her team, and offered the galley. Fifteen minutes later, Mohammed squeezed back into his seat, dark robe swishing around his feet, and peered out into the cold night.

Chapter Thirty

Day Eleven, Thursday, August 17th, morning
New York, New York, Zeke's apartment

At 5 am, Rowe flipped on the TV to find the talking heads shouting about terrorists controlling a nuclear sub and hundreds injured.

You don't know the half of it.

How do you find a submarine invisible to sonar?

Rowe threw on navy blue shorts, Nike running shoes, and a sleeveless gray sweatshirt, turned on the coffee maker, and stepped out onto his back patio. The nighttime chill still clung to the air and the last stars sparkled in the pre-dawn sky. He stretched and then took a trail that would take him as far from civilization as possible and still be in New York City. He hugged a series of slopes and terraces that separated the upper middle-class neighborhood from Flatrock Brook, then paralleled the water for a short distance before swinging back through the expensive tree-shrouded homes of west Englewood. He sprinted the last quarter mile and then stumbled through the sliding glass door into his living room. He took a cup of freshly-brewed coffee to the bathroom, downed it in the shower, brushed his teeth, pulled on comfortable clothing—dark Chinos, black polo, grey tennis shoes—downed a power bar and breakfast drink, and left.

His phone rang. "Hey, Kali. It's 3 am over there. Everything OK?"

"I'm fine. Couldn't sleep."

"Anything new on the formula?"

"We're trying to figure out why it works. Metamaterials have been effective, but not against sonar and not on such a large scale." She went into an involved explanation about the difference between salt and regular water and how pressure and temperature affect paint. Rowe figured he should say something, but most of what he was hearing made no sense so settled for an interested, "Hunh," or the occasional, "How 'bout that."

"Here's why I called. Last night, someone threatened me if I continued to help you."

"What?" Rage exploded deep in Rowe's gut.

Her voice hardened. "The first time, he said if I told anyone, he'd hurt someone I loved." Her voice broke. "Now, Eitan can't reach Sean. Zeke, I'm afraid."

"What—there was a first time."

"I thought I'd solved it, and besides, if my sixteen-year-old son refuses to quit, how can I? I got the caller's address."

"How'd you get that?"

"Reverse look-up on his phone," and she hung up.

That was too easy. They wanted to be found. He stabbed the address into his car's GPS and left. On the way, he called a detective buddy in Los Angeles who gave him the name of a friend on the San Diego PD, a Detective Charlie Ruiz. After a few minutes of establishing their bona fides, Rowe gave Ruiz Sean's address and asked him to check.

"I remember something about that location. Yeah. Here it is. Landlord said the renter was out of town, but thought someone had broken in. He wanted us to check. We have two murders going, one a high-priced call girl and the other an officer on a Navy cruiser docked here."

Rowe had a bad feeling. "*Princeton?*"

"Yeah. How'd you know?"

"Lucky guess."

"Right. We think those might be tied to eight other homicides a couple weeks ago."

"British submariners."

There was a sigh and a grunt. "I left the LAPD to get away from this craziness. You think this burglary is tied in? We'll get to it soon as possible."

Rowe swerved around a puttering 1977 Cadillac, barely stopping short of honking at a teenager, frightened eyes on the road, hands at ten and two. He called James. "I'm going to check an address," and he rattled it off.

"Hold on." Paper riffled. "That's half a mile as the crow flies from a phone number Sean got off Mohammed on the Tiger Cruise. Find something, I'll get a warrant."

Rowe wended his way to I-95 S. The terrorists were too smart to use a traceable land line. He hoped this was a trap so he could ask a few questions.

Rowe exited 9-S at Smith, turned right onto Elm, puttered past a greenbelt between Hilo Fish Market and Preferred Freezer Services, took a right onto an access road that led to the Fish Market's docks, and parked about a hundred yards from where the map said the call originated. To his right was a warehouse and a row of beat-up cars; to his left, a flat reedy area that separated the Fish Market from its closest neighbor a quarter mile away.

Rowe got out, senses in overdrive. Eighteen wheelers lined up along the docks, two soft sides, and an open warehouse door. An employee out for a smoke took a look at Rowe and disappeared inside. Moments later, five men hopped down from the dock and approached Rowe, each an arm's length apart, hands at their sides, burly shoulders straining under t-shirts, hair buzzed to bald. Rowe took the measure of his opponents and liked what he saw.

"Follow me." The speaker stood half a head shorter than the others, nose squashed like it had been broken too often, no neck, and ledge-like shoulders. Rowe recognized a man whose life had been distinguished by nothing but brute force.

Rowe smiled, took one step forward, and then charged. The speaker threw up his forearms like an offensive lineman blocking a defensive back, but Rowe slipped to the side, slapped the man's elbow down and away, clamped onto his head and rolled him to the asphalt. His head bounced, eyes glazed over, but Rowe already focused on the next man. He reached behind his back no doubt for a gun. Rowe closed the distance, pulled him backward and down. He snatched the gun as the man slammed to the ground next to his buddy still sitting in a dazed heap.

The next man slammed forward, trying to take advantage of Rowe's busi-ness, but Rowe head butted him, breaking his nose, and then kneed him in the crotch so hard, it lifted him off the ground. He dropped to the ground where he curled into a painful pile.

The remaining two wanted no part of him and ran. The leader recovered enough to try to run, but Rowe jabbed the abandoned gun into the man's temple.

"Who d'you work for?"

"You might as well kill me. I cross him, I'm dead."

"I believe you," and he shot him in the knee. The man howled. Rowe waited for him to stop. "Tell your boss to back off or he won't be so lucky."

Before the man hobbled away, he pulled a manila folder from his shirt. "A present."

Rowe flipped the cover open to find Sean's apartment lease with Kali's phone number, address, and email as an emergency contact. One call to James and an officer was assigned to Kali's location. Rowe got back in his car, grunted from where the leader tagged him with a wild punch, and headed for the Kearny Ave address James gave him. His hands balled into fists as he forced himself to calm. Whoever this was had come dangerously close to pushing a button most people didn't know existed. Rowe took a deep breath. He was worthless angry.

He turned onto a wide tree-lined street of older houses and parked two doors down from the house that might hold the key to the case. There, he sat, listening to the engine tick while he blotted blood from his knuckles and took four aspirins.

176 Kearny was a one-story older home desperately in need of paint. The front yard was a weed patch. A rickety fence hid the backyard. The splintered steps led to a tattered screen door. After thirty minutes and no evidence anyone was there, Rowe donned a blue short sleeved shirt with 'Ralph' stitched over the pocket, pulled a clipboard from a duffel bag he always kept in the trunk, tucked a cap over his hair and ambled down the street. No one looked twice. Utility guys were invisible.

He approached the door, making a point of comparing the address against his clipboard, and knocked efficiently. No response so he peered in the window while attaching a dime-sized cam to the front sill and then trotted to the backyard as though to check the meter. Once in the relative privacy of the fenced rear, he planted cams and mics on windows, in trees, over bushes, and under the eaves. When he returned to his car, he activated the surveillance and waited.

Two hours later, he pulled out a sack lunch, wolfed it down, and then poked around inside the bag, hoping he'd missed something. Sitting made him hungry and hungry made him irritable. He focused his hindbrain on surveilling and let his intel brain lose to play. The more he got into this case, the more convinced he was Salah Mahmud al-Zahrawi, the international terrorist whose goal was to destroy America, lived. Kali had stopped him last year. For that, al-Zahrawi hated her.

The last time Rowe and al-Zahrawi faced off, the terrorist had out-thought him every step of the way except the last where Rowe had the distinct pleasure of watching him die.

No, he corrected, he blew the man's chopper out of the sky. He corrected again—he saw a puff of smoke he took to be the helo exploding.

That meant the most brilliant criminal Rowe had ever faced could be alive. Nothing else made sense. Neither the youngster Ankour Mohammed nor his mentor, Nasr Al-alah, seemed smart enough to hijack two submarines, but al-Zahrawi was, not to mention he had the worldwide network to carry it off. When Rowe reframed everything with al-Zahrawi in the driver's seat, it all popped into place.

While Rowe waited for James to come to the phone, a dachshund raced into the street, tail wagging, feet flying, ears flapping in joyous abandon. Rowe flashed on Survivor and his damned positive outlook even as his world collapsed around him. A barefoot matron in an apron chased after the dachshund, raw hamburger patty in one hand, yelling, "Babe! Get back here!" Rowe tried not to chuckle at another unfortunate victim of the pig movie's popularity.

The dog pulled to a halt, legs wide under his squat body, and then sprinted toward the woman. She slipped a collar around Babe's neck while he chomped through a hamburger.

"Zeke, what d'you have?"

He told James his suspicions. The agent grunted his disbelief, but listened because it came from Rowe.

By now, the matron was dragging Babe back to the house, hissing and shaking her finger while Babe's tail wagged furiously. He veered toward Rowe, but his owner yanked him so cruelly, he yipped in pain, making Rowe wince.

"By the way, CIA got pictures of the missile. It looks to everyone who would know like the delivery system for a nuclear warhead. The problem is the President insists a cruiser can stop it, despite the danger *Virginia* poses. Guys got his head up his sand."

Rowe clenched his teeth rather than point out James had butchered the ostrich metaphor. Instead, he switched topics. "Kali needs more protection than someone walking her home," and he explained his worries about al-Zahrawi.

"Offered and refused. You want me to tell her your suspicion?"

"No. Let's wait until we're sure."

"Anything going on there?"

"Just staring at an empty house."

He let his mind go blank, ideas floating anywhere. One drifted to the top, North Korea and Iran. He called James again.

"Maybe this is a quid pro quo, North Korea and Iran helping each other."

"I got something on that. North Korea will use the Taepodong-2 expendable carrier rocket to launch the Kwangmyongsong-2 communications satellite. The size, clustered engines, and dimensions are nearly the same as the Iranian Unha-2. Pretty expensive for a country that can't feed its citizenry."

"Madmen controlling outer space and the seas is not the world I want to live in."

Rowe disconnected and squirmed, but could find no comfortable position after four hours in a car. When the postman dropped off the mail, Rowe jumped out, clipboard in hand. He knocked, wrote a note, and pretended to slip it into the mailbox while he peeked at the name on an envelope. *Nasr Al-alah*. Bingo.

He called James on his way back to his car. "Get a warrant."

"Not with what you have, Zeke. We need visual or oral confirmation."

At 5:05, a middle-aged man with glasses and a neatly trimmed goatee drove in. When he got out of the car, Rowe saw a body type that fit Al-alah—average height, slender frame, salt-and-pepper hair cropped short. He wore a rumpled suit and despite the heat, skin-tight gloves. Rowe snapped his picture as he approached the front door and ran it through facial recognition.

The man Rowe assumed to be Nasr Al-alah tossed his briefcase on a couch and got a glass of water. The gloves remained on. Skin problem? Rowe's laptop beeped. Facial recognition was inconclusive. Rowe would need a voice match or fingerprints. Since Al-alah kept his gloves on, Rowe would have to wait for the spycams to pick up his voice.

The man listened to phone messages—one made him smile—and then disappeared into the back. Five minutes later, he was barefoot wearing the traditional *salwar kameez* of Islamic men—a long, cotton tunic over loose-fitting trousers that stopped above the ankles—and a *kufi*, the Islamic skull cap. He turned on a tinny radio, heated something in the microwave, and worked at his computer while he ate. Rowe checked the camera opposite the office window, but the monitor blocked the man's face.

When Al-alah's cell rang, he walked outside and stood right next to one of Rowe's microphones.

"Gotcha." Rowe emailed the .mp3 to Kali with a note, "Is this your caller?" then called James. "He's our guy. I'll wait here for the warrant."

Al-alah finished his call and went inside. Five minutes later, he left in street clothes, gloves still on, briefcase in hand, a look on his face equal measures fury and fear. He jumped into his car and drove off, Rowe two car lengths behind.

He called James. "Al-alah got a phone call and left in a hurry. I need that warrant."

"I'm getting it fast as I can."

Rowe took a left onto Gordon. "I have a flight to San Diego in an hour. Have your guys pick up the tail until you get paperwork."

James' agent had just taken over the chase when Kali called.

"Zeke! Sean's hurt! I have to go—oh, Zeke!" and her phone shut off.

In a blink, Rowe was back to the tiny Parisian apartment he shared a lifetime ago with his fiancée, Paulette. He'd begun the teaching career he'd dreamt of since grade school and the woman he didn't deserve had agreed to marry him. When rioting closed the University for only the second time since 1229, Rowe sided with the idealism of the angry students, believing compromise held the key to peaceful coexistence. They were walking home from class, comparing the marches around them to other historic socialist boycotts. He nodded to a band of tough looking students, telling them to keep up the good fight, when two of them grabbed his arms, easily immobilizing him, while three others attacked Paulette. When Rowe tried to help Paulette, someone hit him with a brick and everything went black. When he came to, Paulette lay dead in a bloody heap.

Fifty-eight minutes after Kali's phone call, Rowe crashed through her front door, breathing heavily from a three-block sprint on hobbled knees. Kali's face was tear-stained, but with a hardness that broke his heart. He reached to hug her, but she brushed him away.

"I'm fine, Zeke, but Sean's in a hospital."

She wasn't fine. Her face looked ashen, eyes glassy, and one arm trembled as she moved from dresser to closet to kitchen and back. Otto tried to follow, but tipped over, flailing his chubby arms. Rowe righted the bot, patted his metal head and received a muted churble in thanks.

"Eitan got a notification from Sean's online storage. It included a link to a video showing someone trashing Sean's apartment." She choked back a sob as she threw clothes into a duffel bag. "Th-the police went to check—the manager called in a robbery." Rowe trailed her into the bathroom where she tossed toothpaste, floss, shampoo, and anything close by into a make-up case. "They f-found Sean on the floor." She printed her boarding pass.

"I'll drive, Kali. I'm going anyway."

Kali shook her head as Eitan arrived, hair wet from a shower, dressed in newly-pressed dark pants, a starched flowered shirt and a navy blazer. Only sandals over white socks gave him away. He carried a ticket in one hand, a carry-on bag in the other and his laptop across his back. Around his neck were sunglasses, three flash drives, and a variety of digital jewelry Rowe didn't recognize. He looked pale.

"You hate flying, Eitan," from Kali. "I'll be OK."

"This is my fault. I taught Sean how to surveil his surroundings—"

"It's my fault. Haster must have let it slip Otto found the sub." Her eyes glistened as she tried to close her suitcase. Rowe gently nudged her away and latched it. "The voice print, Zeke—he called last night."

Rowe turned to Eitan. "Nasr Al-alah, Mohammed's handler. Bobby's going to pick him up." He turned to Kali, "I'm coming with you."

"Mohammed's on his way here, Zeke" and Eitan explained how he tracked Mohammed after the Tiger Cruise. "Kali's safer in California than New York."

A car honked.

"It's my taxi. Mr. Winters will take Sandy. Would you get Otto back to Columbia?" And she left, heels clicking on the sidewalk, not waiting for a response. Eitan scuttled after her.

Chapter Thirty-one

Day Eleven, Thursday, August 17th, evening
New York, New York, Kali's apartment

Rowe stood, silent and unmoving, as the taxi faded into the distance. Sandy nuzzled his leg. Otto whirred in slow methodical circles in front of him. Soon, the clicking and chirring of insects replaced the birdsong. The shadows deepened into blue and purple and the ragged silhouette of the city darkened against the early evening sky.

Rowe forgot some of the lessons from military life, but not how to slow the world down when everything happened at once. If a SEAL's position took a grenade, he covered his buddies and attacked. Having time to think was a luxury. Knowing how to act saved lives.

The time had arrived to act.

He stooped over Sandy. "Nothing to worry about, boy. I know you like order to your days, the sureness your master runs your world. We'll fix things. First, let's go for a walk."

Sandy trotted gravely at Rowe's side, never stopping to play, romp with other dogs, or investigate the intriguing odors floating from the urban greenbelt, but by the time they got home, his tail was wagging.

Next, Rowe knocked on Mr. Winters's back door. "Hello, Gunny."

"Hey, Zeke." He banged out the door wrapped in a bathrobe and wearing Ugg boots despite the heat. "Haven't seen you in a while."

"Kali's going to see Sean in California. She said you'll babysit Sandy while she's gone. If it takes too long, I'd be happy to share responsibilities."

"Could never be too long with my buddy here." He ruffed the thick fur on Sandy's neck.

"Is your hip OK?"

"Oh, sure. Never better. Sorry I missed the contest, but Kali gave me a C-D of it."

It took a moment for Rowe to realize Mr. Winters was staring at him. "What did I miss?"

"I hoped things would be better, what with Sean in college, Kali getting her PhD. Guess it's like the Marines, normal is SNAFU. You know what I mean."

Situation Normal. All Fucked Up. Rowe couldn't help but smile. "I think these guys are as dangerous as the ones you never met last year. May even be the same."

Mr. Winters led Sandy into his unit. "No one picks a fight with an old man because we'll just kill him."

Rowe loaded Otto into his car, drove to Columbia and then trundled to Kali's office. He dropped his briefcase on the floor, canceled his San Diego flight, and then slumped behind Cat's desk. He expected the terrorists to go after Kali, but not Sean. Was Mohammed jealous of Sean—a love triangle with Chacone? Rowe had trouble thinking of Sean in those terms, but he needed to consider it.

Something bumped his leg. He looked down into Otto's upturned face. His eyes glittered, but less than usual. Odd.

"Zeke." His voice dragged. Could Otto stutter? "Kali forgot to recharge me. My battery is down to 5%." His head flagged. "I'm having difficulty... focusing. Would you... plug me in?"

"Uh," Rowe felt around Otto's head, neck, and trunk and found a port on the rear panel. "Where's the cord?"

"Cord... cord... Otto stammered and took halting steps toward Kali's desk. "My battery is down to 4%. My files show she ... puts it ... in her desk drawer."

Otto's head bounced off his chest. Rowe found the cord and connected Otto to the wall outlet. The bot perked up instantly.

"That is much better. Thank you, Zeke."

"Why were you at Kali's house, Otto?"

"I wanted to see what she called a home so I understand the difference from an office. Did I do something wrong?" The AI clung to Rowe's side, arms wrapped around Rowe's legs, his glowing eyes innocent, trusting. Rowe explained as much as he understood, though it felt odd comforting a robot.

Otto rolled back and forth as though he wanted to say something.

"What's on your mind?"

"Your briefcase holds a data device with an infrared port. I peeked."

"I collected data on the man responsible for Kali's problems."

"Do you mind?" Rowe nodded and then data flew, stopping at an image of Al-alah sitting at his computer.

"You have quite a bit of information here. I can see everything he's reading as a reflection off his glasses. When his eyes are on the monitor, I can read his emails and documents. When he looks at his hands, I get keystrokes."

Rowe zoomed in on Al-alah's glasses. There, as Otto said, was a warped image of the terrorist's computer. "The image is too bent, Otto. And blurry."

"The bend is from the lens of the glasses and the blur is from the eyeball's movement. They're both predictable so I can adapt for them. May I?"

Rowe sat back and put his hands behind his head. "Why not."

"Hmmm. This email is from 'Ankour'. I'm familiar with the name."

Rowe sat up. "Can you trace the address?"

Otto chirruped. "It bounces through six different countries and dead ends at an anonymizer. Ankour did not want to be found."

"Anything else?"

"An email to 'Gil-dong', no family name. I am unable to track who forwarded it."

"Can you find Gil-dong's identity?"

"With difficulty. It is like John Doe in Korean."

North Korea again. It gave Rowe an idea. "Focus on anyone related to the upcoming missile test program and, uh, turn yourself off when you're done."

Rowe phoned James and told him about the positive tie-in between Mohammed and Al-alah, then asked where the terrorist ended up.

"My agent lost him. One instant, we were following him, the next, three cars all driven by Middle Eastern males in the same shirt appeared. We tailed the wrong one. I put a BOLO out. As soon as I get a warrant, the team will ransack the house."

Rowe bit back a string of profanities settling for, "I'm going to sit on it in case he returns."

Forty-five minutes later, he shoehorned himself into the last spot on Al-alah's street. The lights were out in the house and the driveway empty. Rowe rang the bell and wiggled the knob. It opened. He debated going in, but it could be a booby trap. Instead, he snuck around outside removing his spycams and peering in windows.

As he walked back to the car, his phone rang.

"Duck." Rowe breathed a sigh of relief. "Where the hell are you?"

"On my way to San Diego. James gave me an update."

"Talk to Detective Charlie Ruiz." The phone went dead in his ear.

Rowe knew Al-alah had left for good but hoped his contacts didn't, so sat in his car, stomach in a knot, staring at the house. Al-alah had been activated for this jihad after being asleep for a decade. He came to America under his own name. After all that, what in a phone call drove him away?

The night was warm, the sky a dull black, the stars remote pinpricks and the moon a pale blue-white half-disk high overhead. Cooking fragrances wafted by his car, as did the drone of TVs playing sitcoms and reality shows. Here and there, music played.

Just as he decided this was a waste of time, Babe came out for a constitutional. He must have recognized Rowe's scent and wanted to visit. He tugged so hard, he broke loose from the leash. The dog froze a moment, surprised by his freedom, then took off for Rowe's car, ears flying, mouth open, rushing forward in blissful abandon.

Oblivious to the car hurtling down the street. It would never see Babe in the gloom.

"Damn." Rowe jumped out of the car and into the street. Shocked eyes jerked left and zipped past. No brakes, but he had time to fling a finger at Rowe.

Rowe scooped the canine out of the air as he leaped to greet Zeke and crushed him to his chest. "Hello, boy, aren't you a wonderful pup. Come over to say hi, did you?" His chest heaved as the dog struggled in his grasp. "I ran out of bones, but I can pat your belly." He turned the dog over in the crook of his arm and vigorously rubbed his tummy. Babe's legs squirmed, chest pumped up and down, and if he could, Rowe figured he would have laughed.

"Hey!" A strident voice broke their play. "That's my dog."

"Just saying hi, ma'am" and he gently placed Babe back on the ground with a head pat. "He's a cute dog." Babe wagged his entire body in a spasm of greeting.

The woman glared at Rowe in response, circled the collar around Babe's neck, and yanked the poor thing viciously. Babe's ears went flat and he whimpered.

Rowe recoiled. "He'll go easier if you're friendly," but the woman stomped away. Rowe wished he had the ASPCA on speed dial.

Ten minutes later, he was picking out constellations, starting with the Big Dipper, when a voice came out of his phone.

"Zeke?"

"Hello?"

"I have the images from Mr. Al-alah's house cleaned up."

"Otto? How'd you call me?"

"I tapped into your phone. If you're occupied, I wait until you are free. I find that efficient. Al-alah emailed a 'Norman Krakhower' at Northrop Grumman. Told him he—Al-alah—wanted to arrange a meeting to give Krakhower a bonus."

Bonus? "What's Krakhower do for Northrop Grumman?"

"Their directory lists his job as 'Purchasing'."

Rowe drummed his fingers on his leg. "I guess I need to pay him a visit. Thanks, Otto."

Otto made a riffling sound. "Al-alah was reviewing a tour he took of the Chesapeake Bay when he got the last phone call."

"The Chesapeake has great rockfish."

"These were not fishing tours. He went the length of the Bay, took pictures of the beaches, and collected depth data."

"Thanks, Otto. Uh, how do I disconnect you," but an empty line greeted him.

The phone rang in his hand. James.

"Get out of there, Zeke. Some lady called the police. Said you tried to steal her dog. You know anything about that? Never mind, just leave. I'd have a hard time explaining why you're surveilling an innocent member of the Muslim community."

"Have your guys go through Al-alah's house. The door's unlocked, so they should be careful," and Rowe sped off.

By the time he got home, it was too late to call Kali. He took a beer from the refrigerator and headed through the nature preserve until he came to a small clearing and a tree stump big enough for two. He drank the beer, glancing occasionally to his left. If Kali were here, they'd talk about anthropology and how Sean was doing in school while Sandy roamed through the clearing, making those happy woofing sounds of a dog discovering hidden treasures.

He ran everything through his brain, but too many pieces didn't fit. He went home. The pictures in the living room were exactly as he'd left them. The office door stood open at a forty-five-degree angle and his bedroom door at twenty. Every day, he changed it.

He showered away the sweat, first hot water and then cold, rubbing it into his face, over his shoulders, and across his chest. As he toweled off, he considered working out, but instead checked that the five-lumin flashlight by his bedside worked and dozed off.

Chapter Thirty-two

Day Twelve, Friday morning, August 18th
Englewood, New Jersey, Zeke Rowe's house

Rowe woke after a fitful sleep, rushed through his morning workout, and dressed comfortably in jeans, a polo shirt, and boat shoes, not knowing what the day would bring. He had an empty text from Duck, the SEAL way of saying everything was fine, nothing to tell. He called Mr. Winters to check on Sandy. The dog had made a new friend at the park. Mr. Winters made friends with the dog's owner. Everyone seemed happy.

Rowe ate a quick breakfast and returned to Al-alah's house. He checked the door for booby traps before entering. The tempting herbal aroma of Al-alah's final meal tugged at him. The rooms were clean, counters scrubbed, closets and cupboards empty, toiletries gone from the bathroom, prayer rug absent.

He called James. "Al-alah's handlers cleared the house out last night."

"My guys should be there any moment with the warrant."

Within moments, Rowe limped outside to greet James's crew. A tall thirty-something man with spike-straight hair and a pinched face eyed Rowe suspiciously.

"Who are you?"

"Zeke Rowe. Bobby probably mentioned me." He stuck his hand out. After a moment, the man took it. "Agent Scorty. What are we looking for?"

Rowe shrugged. "Anything would help. We're kinda desperate," and he left to chat with the neighbors. No one seemed suspicion of Al-alah or his visitors or knew where he worked. One old man peered at Rowe out of eyes no more than slits.

"I saw you yesterday, din I? In Mr. Alah's backyard? I din have my glasses on." He shuffled inside as he talked. "Mr. Alah don' get white visitors. All Middle Eastern. Seem nice." He donned a pair of thick glasses and gasped. "Woah! You look like one of those SEALs. The guy I saw din have so many sharp… edges."

"Anything suspicious go on in Mr. Al-alah's house?"

"Nope, and I'd know 'cause I'm Neighborhood Watch. If you're police, get the witch across the street to treat her dog better. She's awful to him." He closed the door, muttering.

Rowe stopped in on Agent Scorty, hoping he had something, but he said the place was scrubbed clean. On the way to James's office, Duck called. "They're delayed in Dallas by thunderstorms. Sean's still in a coma. They won't tell me more because I'm not family." Duck sounded disgusted.

Rowe breathed a sigh.

"Now, what's going on with you and Kali? If she had a sister, I'd stow my Navy career behind a white picket fence and make babies."

Rowe winced. "Sean's been sleuthing and Kali blames my influence."

"Let's refocus Sean, throw that satellite phone away Bobby calls you on, and fix things." He beeped at someone, suggested they have a nice day in another lane of the freeway, and continued. "Sean's landlord calls him the best kid to ever walk through his door. Says Sean identified all sorts of problems. Thanks to the boy, he could charge more for units. He wanted to know when Sean would be back."

"Does he know what happened to Sean?"

"Nope. I met with that Detective you put me in touch with. He's in charge of the case. I'll give him the tapes from Sean's DropBox. The CSI team took fingerprints, but it looks like the intruder wore gloves. We found hairs, darker than Sean's. They cleared all the tenants that were home. According to the manager, Sean never had visitors, so any trace was the attacker. The police lab has a lot of the equipment you used at ONI," Office of Navy Intelligence, "microspec—" Duck tried to fish the name out of his memory.

"Microspectrophotometry, a polarized light microscope. High end."

"Don't worry about us, bud. Find that sub."

Rowe pulled into James's building, passed through security, got two coffees from the ground floor Starbuck's, and went up to the third floor. James met him at the elevator. His clothes were fresh, trousers creased, light blue shirt starched, but dark circles bruised the space under his eyes and a stillness about him worried Rowe.

That reminded him where James was this morning. "How'd your Skype with the Congressional Oversight Committee go?"

Anger sparked through the Special Agent's eyes. "They want the SecDef to resign, called him 'incompetent,' 'uncaring' and 'incoherent'. Britain's Commander-in-Chief Fleet Admiral Trevor Baldwin, apologized for hiding the sonar shield from us, but insists no one knew which subs had it. I agree, unless they read Penbury's unencrypted email."

James snorted. "Penbury is the only one who can neutralize the sonar shield and he disappeared. I'm crossing my fingers Kali can."

As they talked, they zagged through the cubicle farm that housed a score of agents. Rowe pulled a tooth out of his pocket and dropped it onto the desk outside James's office. A matronly fiftyish woman with tightly curled shoulder-length hair, light makeup, a classic box suit with a bow blouse, rose and hugged him.

"How could you remember with all that's goin' on?"

Rowe smiled. Tess's son Jason was a bright, happy, twelve-year-old interested in paleontology and had called Rowe when he discovered his mom knew the famed Columbia paleo. Rowe took him on a tour of his lab and demonstrated how to synthesize aDNA—ancient DNA—from old bones. Rowe had as much fun as Jason.

"Tell him it's from an 800,000-year old hippo who wandered the Dmanisi wetlands. He got a lot of use out of this tooth."

As he turned to follow James into his office, Tess grabbed his arm. "Cheer 'm up. He acts like he's responsible for *Virginia's* disappearance. Like he has that kind of power."

Other than a few pictures, James's office contained only the standard desk, chair, bookshelves, phone, and six TV's, one playing a news conference.

"The UN's considering a sanction of the US and Britain. They contend we've lost control of one of the planet's most dangerous weapons and want to know the name of the missing sub and supervise our efforts to find it. The only one likely to vote with us is Israel." James shut the website in disgust. "Days like today, the UN is as useful as a chocolate teapot."

"I need some good news, Bobby. Anything from *Virginia's* Blue crew?"

"They say the Gold crew would never freak out or mutiny. And no visitors are aboard. If there's a traitor, he's hidden deep."

Tess stuck her head in. "You have a call from the head of MI-6."

James sighed and turned on speaker so Rowe could hear. "Thank you for returning my call, Sir. Someone reached out to us Tuesday evening from Imperial College, but left no message. Can you check for us?"

"We'll get back to you," and the line went dead.

"Let's get out of here. I'm hungry."

They went to the cafeteria, a cheery yellow brightly-lit room overflowing with the aroma of warm chocolate chip cookies. The floors were polished stone and the small round tables ceramic. Rowe selected a club sandwich, potato chips, cherry pie, coffee, and a soda. James settled for a tired looking chicken salad and coffee. Both ate most of their food without a word. Rowe had never seen his friend uneasy, let alone floundering. It left him tongue-tied.

Finally, James leaned back, coffee on the edge of the table with both hands wrapped around it.

"I need Kali to find a hole in that paint, Zeke. Fast. We need to find *Virginia*."

"She's close, but is thinking about Sean."

"One of our Destroyers found *Virginia's* signal buoy. We think the crew hid it in the garbage."

"Our boys can think on their feet."

James turned his phone to Rowe so he could read the message: *Sub hijacked. Will try to change polarity.* "If they can turn off the degaussing coils, Otto will find them."

"Can they do it without revealing themselves?"

Rowe shrugged. "A light will blink on the Bridge. They'll have a few minutes—if the hijackers even know how to fix it."

A deep groove cut between James's worried eyes. "Those boys will not stop until *Virginia* is back in American hands. We have to find it before the crew gets themselves killed."

A server came to refill coffee, but James said, "Let's go. I'm expecting an email."

At James's office, all eyes were glued to the TV. Greenpeace was picketing.

The very existence of a nuclear submarine exposes world citizens to the danger of a nuclear catastrophe. Nuclear powered warships and submarines are ticking time bombs.

Someone muttered, "They forgot those 'ticking time bombs' pulled the planet from the brink of nuclear war during the USSR's heyday."

"Boss, you got a message." Urgency saturated Tess's tone.

James rounded his desk to his computer. "We know how the hijackers boarded *Virginia*. It received a Comm burst from Command, right after it left port. No one admitted to sending it so we kept digging. One of the radio operators cracked, said they were going to kill his family unless *Virginia* helped a stranded ASDS."

"An Advanced SEAL Delivery System—a midget sub. It's designed to deliver up to sixteen SEALs and supplies for covert operations. It rides piggyback on a sub's afterdeck. You get in and out through a spherical air lock. *Virginia*-class subs are designed for them."

"Man's name is Chou. They killed his daughter after raping her with a broom, threatened to do the same to his wife and son unless he sent the message. They lied and he killed himself after talking to us."

James plunked at his keyboard. "ONI pulled images from *Virginia's* last known location, complements of our Keyhole satellite, hoping to locate the ASDS. If the water's clear, you can see all sorts of things."

James turned his monitor toward Rowe to show a video of a squatty, rusted out tub of a boat, floating aimlessly. They fast-forwarded through two hours until it chugged off. Rowe replayed and leaned forward as the jerky compressed time scenes slipped by.

"What's it doing there for so long?"

James scrolled through an attached memo. "No record of the boat's numbers anywhere."

Rowe played it a fourth time, not knowing what he was looking for but hoping to catch something, and bolted upright.

"There." He stabbed a finger to pause the video, rewound, played and paused again. "See the shadow to the side, just about out of range."

"A whale maybe."

"Or an ASDS blurred through twelve feet of water."

Rowe stared into the distance, pencil flipping. "All they needed were seven or eight men to run the ship— maneuvering, sonar, control room, the Helmsman, a planes man, security.

"*Virginia* knew about *Triumph*, but with the 'authentic' message—and the ASDS probably presented as in distress. Any nearby vessel would be required to help. Once aboard, it'd be easy to incapacitate an unsuspecting crew and threaten the Captain."

"How'd they get ahold of an ASDS? They're not exactly sold on eBay."

"The manufacturer is forbidden by law from selling it privately." His voice trailed off, his eyes looking inward and a piece of the puzzle slipped into place. "Last night, Al-

alah emailed someone at Northrop Grumman. I bet they built the ASDS."

James told Tess to find out who had the minisub contract while Rowe got on his phone.

"Duck? Yeah, how's Sean? ... In and out of consciousness... Concussion, brain swollen... They beat him, broke a cheekbone, fractured his jaw and clavicle, stomped on his hands, and ruptured the spleen. I thought the medical folks shut you out? ... You changed their minds...."

James pushed speaker as Duck said, "I doubt the attack is related to Sean's academic or social life. He rarely went to school and had no friends. The only change in his life is Chacone and Mohammed. No one I can find knows anything about Mohammed."

James moved his hand in a circle saying, *Get to the ASDS.*

"Duck, we have satellite footage of *Virginia's* hijackers. I want to know if you see what I do."

"Email it to me."

Done, Rowe and James sat in silence, broken only by the rumble of voices from the bullpen, printers churning, and phones ringing. Rowe needed to do something.

He stood to leave just as his phone rang. Duck didn't wait for hello.

"An electrical fire demolished the ASDS in that video."

James asked, "Wouldn't *Virginia* know?"

"Do you think the Navy notifies people when they destroy a half-billion-dollar piece of equipment?" Duck's voice was tight. "I'll call if I see anything else."

Rowe sat. "In property destruction cases caused by faulty equipment, Northrop Grumman gets paid nothing. An electrical fire would be pinned right on Northrop's financial chest. Their contract required they destroy it so no top secret parts, blueprints, materials get into the wrong hands. At completion, they had to file a verification of destruction with DRMO—Defense Reutilization and Marketing Service."

"Tess. Get proof of destruction from DRMO on the ASDS. Next, ask USSOCOM if the picture matches the ASDS that burned up. And where's the minisub contractor contact?"

Two minutes later, a woman handed him a fax. James craned his neck. "Where's Tess?"

The woman smiled. "She said to tell you she's busy."

"Who're you?"

"Tess's assistant," and left.

"When did I authorize an assistant for Tess?" He pivoted the page toward Rowe. "Here's our proof—bailed refuse with numbers and authorizations on it. Tess! Get in here and not a damn assistant! What dumb shit accepted this?"

Rowe zeroed in on the signature: *Norman Krakhower.* "Al-alah called him before disappearing. They're cleaning up loose ends."

"Someone bought a burned out tin can of an ASDS from a vetted government bidder, repaired it enough to be seaworthy, and used it to hijack *Virginia*. That's clever, make the outside look legit, and get the engine and the coupler working."

Rowe got up. "I'll chat with Krakhower, if he's not already dead."

Chapter Thirty-three

Day Twelve, Friday, August 18th, Midday
Northrup Grumman Campus

Four hours later, Rowe arrived at Northrop Grumman. He flashed his pass at the gate guard, parked in a handicap slot, and limped inside to reception. There was a time when Rowe could charm the most tight-lipped administrator, but then he met Kali and his bon vivant charisma rusted.

The twenty-something receptionist was on the phone, but her brown eyes danced over his face and she held a finger up. She wore a short-sleeved sweater hugging a narrow bosom, a pearl necklace around her smooth throat complimented by pearl earrings. When she turned her attention to Rowe, she had a smile as warm and honest as a country-western ballad.

"Hi. My name is Dr. Zeke Rowe. I'm looking for Norman Krakhower."

"Yes, Dr. Rowe. SA James called ahead. Regrettably, Mr. Krakhower went home for an emergency. I let him know you were on your way. Can I offer you coffee while you wait?"

It was Rowe's bad luck the receptionist was a monument to efficiency. "No problem. I'll meet him at home, save him the return trip."

She took her time matching his face to his ID and then passed him a note with Krakhower's address. "You'll be there in fifteen minutes."

Rowe jumped in his car, swerved through a maze of turns until he found the right street and the right house, then parked across the end of the driveway to block Krakhower.

The purchasing agent lived in a blocky two-story dwelling built from red Lyons sandstone with the most god-awful bright green picket fence Rowe had ever seen. A boy's bike lay abandoned on the manicured lawn and a basketball hoop drooped by the garage door. Rowe slipped the Colt into his waistband as a man came into view, arms overflowing with books, binders, and clutter. He matched the company photo on Rowe's phone though ten pounds heavier, hair four shades darker, and face considerably more stressed than the carefree employee who promised to go out of his way to help you.

"Mr. Krakhower?"

Krakhower's mouth formed an O and he hurried toward a late model Mercedes, already stuffed full with boxes, clothes, books, photos and other bits and pieces Krakhower must consider essential to a new life.

"We need to talk."

"Uh, I'm busy. Can you make an appointment?"

He wore jeans, a collared Polo, tasseled loafers, and no socks. His hair was mussed and his face red with a sheen of sweat.

"It's too late for appointments. You're in trouble."

Krakhower tried a smile. "I'm always in trouble. Why should today be different?"

Rowe tossed the top box from the pile aside. Something inside shattered. "You want to do this in view of your neighbors, fine with me. Let's start with your wife. Is she involved?"

Something rustled to his left. Rowe drew on it and Krakhower squealed. "That's Fluffy!"

It was a cat.

Rowe holstered his weapon in the waistband of his pants and dragged Krakhower inside the house, scattering boxes like breadcrumbs along the path. Rowe instructed the traitor to sit while he cleared the structure. The noxious aroma of bleach and Lysol assaulted him as though the family never took enough time to clean. Krakhower had been burning something plastic in the fireplace which added to the foul bouquet. Atop the mantle where most Dads put photos of their kids were Krakhower's Karate trophies.

"You a martial artist, Norman? I can call you Norman, can't I?" Rowe asked as he checked the downstairs.

"Y-yes. I'm a bl-black belt." A hint of pride crept into his voice. "Once I was out to—"

"Whatever you did won't help, Norman." Rowe slammed his hand onto the coffee table to get the man's attention. "I'm a professional thug. Who do you think will win?"

Krakhower nodded so emphatically, Rowe thought he'd get whiplash. "I don't want to fight you—whoever you are." The man sniffled.

"Anyone upstairs?"

"Oh—no! I need to leave before they get here."

Rowe pointed his Colt at Krakhower. "I'm going to check. Move and I shoot you." He got two steps and the cat yowled. He turned to see it sprint under the couch as Krakhower fall face first onto the tile entryway. Rowe yanked him up by the back of his shirt, spun him around by his shoulders, and slapped him open-handed across the face.

"Don't do that!" He leaned in so spittle sprayed the purchasing agent's face. "I have a hair-trigger temper." The man started shaking.

"Come with me," and Rowe shoved him forward as he methodically cleared each upstairs room. He hoped to discover Mohammed or Al-alah holed up in the spare room, but all he found was trash, unmade beds, and wrinkled clothes piled in heaps.

"You-all should pick up in the mornings. This is no way to raise kids." Rowe propelled him downstairs and onto the living room sofa. "Keep your hands up."

"Wha-what d'you w-want?" Sweat prickled on Krakhower's face. His mouth hung open.

"You're crummy at this spy stuff, Norman, which makes you perfect. As Jerry Garcia says, you been set up like a bowling pin." He dropped onto a flowered monstrosity of a couch with overstuffed pillows. "I'll ask simple questions. I want honest answers. Maybe I save your life. Ready?"

"Y-yes." He started to lower his hands so Rowe slapped him across his cheeks.

"Did I tell you to move?"

Krakhower yelped and thrust his hands back in the air. "Please stop! I'll help! Stop hurting me!" Tears ran down his cheeks.

Rowe hated hitting a crying man, but *Virginia's* crew had no time. He peered at the details from James about Krakhower's family.

"Your wife works as a paralegal for Libbey and Anderson. She's beautiful, by the way." He turned his phone to show Krakhower a snapshot of his wife taken this morning, ignorant that someone was observing her. "They like her, but wouldn't if they knew her husband's a traitor. He brought up another picture. "Your children go to a prestigious private school. Their teachers say they have leadership potential. They were supposed to spend the weekend with friends, but are first getting ice cream with my associate. What happens next is up to you." Not true, but Krakhower didn't look like he took chances. "Here, talk to Bobby. He's with your children. I'd let you talk with them, but you'll scare them with your hyperventilating."

Krakhower's hands were glued to the chair so tightly, his knuckles went white. "Leave them alone. Please?"

Rowe stood over Krakhower. The man craned his neck back to keep his bloodshot eyes on Rowe. "You can put your hands down, Norman."

As Krakhower lowered his arms, Rowe said, "That ASDS you sold instead of scrapping is responsible for the murder of two thousand sailors on a Chinese carrier and may be the catalyst for World War III. That makes you a traitor besides an international criminal. Tell me what happened—and tell the truth. It's easier to remember."

Krakhower couldn't talk fast enough. "Hold on, cowboy. I have to tape this." He put his phone on the table between them and started the recording. "I'm with Norman Krakhower of Northrop Grumman. He volunteered to share his knowledge of the missing ASDS."

Krakhower talked for thirty minutes, words tumbling over each other in his rush. "I have money problems. My kids, private school—and my wife's social group. It's all about appearances—wearing the right clothes, going to the right restaurants. It costs so much. I'm drowning. Then, like a gift, this man wants to buy the ASDS scrap. I was to notify him when the bid opened. He said he needed it for his father's birthday—would reimburse me for helping him out. He said all purchasing agents took kickbacks—someone always won the bid, right? See, I'm new to this job. The last guy—he got fired. Anyway, he ended up giving me $5000 in cash simply for listening! I deposited it, took my wife to a fancy restaurant, and bought her a new dress. I decided to take the money but you know, not help him. Well, I got a second visit, this one less friendly. He thanked me for agreeing to help, played a tape of us talking and had screenshots of the money in my account. I decided to do what he wanted and get it over with."

Rowe showed him three photos. "Which one did you deal with?" Krakhower pointed at Salah Mahmud al-Zahrawi. "What did he say?"

"He's South Korean and his dad always wanted his own sub." A wistful smile crossed Krakhower's face.

"This 'son' you're getting misty eyed over is an international terrorist who wants nothing so much as to destroy America. You just gave him the weapon."

Krakhower started to cry again. "I needed money for my kid's college. Damn government takes so much, how am I supposed to make ends meet?"

Rowe turned away in disgust. "Did he say anything about an American cruiser or the *USS Bunker Hill*?"

"No! I'm trying to tell you—I know nothing else."

By now, Krakhower was crying so hard, he hiccupped. Rowe was sick of the man. How'd he survive life so afraid of everything?

"I have some friends who want to chat with you."

Rowe checked that no one lay in wait outside, and then handcuffed Krakhower to the back seat of his car. When he got back to Northrup Grumman, he left his prisoner to ponder the error of his ways and met James outside the lobby.

"He peed in my car, Bobby. I have to get it cleaned. Here's the photo he identified."

"Impossible."

"What's that saying about impossible and improbable," and told Krakhower's story while two FBI agents handcuffed the former purchasing agent and marched him across the parking lot in front of his former colleagues. Krakhower completely broke down, sobbing, nose running, and chest heaving as he gasped for breath.

Something glinted behind Krakhower, followed by a whisper of movement.

"Get down!" Rowe screamed, but was drowned out by a crack and Krakhower's head disintegrated into a spray of blood and tissue. The two agents dove for cover, dragging Krakhower's headless body with them.

Less than two weeks to go and they had lost their best lead.

Chapter Thirty-four

Friday, August 18th, late afternoon
UCSD Medical Center, Sean Delamagente's room

Kali and Eitan stepped off the elevator at the sixth floor and followed signs to UC San Diego Medical Center's intensive care unit. There'd been delays on every stage of the flight, even switching planes after a six-hour wait. Each hour cost Kali years.

Nurses in white uniforms and leather-soled shoes hurried by. Families huddled in groups, whispering. In one corner, a harried woman sat alone, head in her hands, tears leaking through her fingers. The speaker shouted calls for doctors needed in some corner of the hospital. Kali stifled her fear and forced one foot in front of another.

A six-foot-wide double door blocked her entrance. Kali pulled, but nothing moved.

"How are we supposed to get in if the door is locked?" Her eyes burned. She never cried, but today, couldn't stop.

Eitan touched her arm. "Push the call button," and indicated a palm-sized red disc.

Kali waited an eternity before a voice asked who she wanted to see.

"Sean Delamagente." She tensed, worried they'd forbid her entry which was ridiculous.

The doors popped open. Kali stepped inside the ward and juddered her head side to side, looking for reception.

"Ms. Delamagente?" Kali pivoted. A young woman in a uniform smiled at her. Kali tried to focus, but failed. Eitan brushed past her.

"Hello, LT Chacone. My name is Dr. Eitan Sun. We talked earlier." He extended his hand, a smile filling his face.

"Yes, Dr. Sun. Please call me Paloma. I decided to meet you here so you have a familiar voice." Paloma shook hands with Eitan and turned to Kali. Dimples dotted her sculpted cheeks when she smiled and her eyes sparkled with youth and life. Her hair was pulled back in a chignon, hat in the crook of her elbow, white uniform spotless. Kali smoothed her clothing, rumpled from the long flight. Her headache sent hot spikes into her left eye. It took all her strength to focus on the young officer.

"Ms.—er, LT—Chacone, do you know where Sean is?" Her voice cracked.

"You must be his mother." She spoke in quiet, confident tones. "Please, I'm Paloma. I'm...a friend... of Sean's. Well, a new friend." This seemed to confuse her, but she barreled forward. "They moved him. I'll show you."

They headed for the elevator, away from intensive care. Eitan took Kali's arm. "That's good. He's getting better." He nodded to himself as they descended a floor, went down another antiseptic hall, past open doors and quiet whispers, until they reached Sean's room. It felt calm and peaceful after the buzz of noise and blur of activity in the rest of the ward.

Paloma smiled. "A call from the Assistant CNO got my Captain's attention. He told me to take what time I needed to assist you. I didn't know Sean well, but he seems a wonderful, serious person." She turned toward Kali. "I am so sorry about this."

Kali ached. She wanted to talk to this gracious young woman who could be the last person to see Sean healthy. Instead, she mumbled *Thank you* and slipped past to Sean's bedside.

Her son's face was pale and drawn. White gauze swathed his head and tubes ran from his mouth and nose. His bones were etched against the thin material of the hospital gown as though he never ate, his chest gently rising and falling, the fingers he always took such care of now bandaged and thick.

Kali collapsed. Hands guided her to a chair. Eitan cheerily thanked Paloma for her assistance, asked how she knew Sean and inquired about her time on *Bunker Hill*. His face was animated, hands flying, and Paloma seemed entirely engaged. This Eitan Kali had never before seen.

When she convinced herself Sean would live another five minutes, she approached Paloma and took her hand. Kali tried to speak, but her voice stuck in her throat.

Paloma smiled, eyes soft and gentle. "Have you talked to a doctor?"

Kali coughed. "I'll have to find one..." It came out a whisper, but Paloma put her hand up.

"Stay here. I know where to find him, and my uniform tends to inspire action."

Another voice, this one Eitan. "I'll go, too," As the pair disappeared down the hall, Paloma asked, "Your t-shirt, Dr. Sun, is Maxwell's Equation, isn't it?"

Kali smiled, knowing how happy that would make Eitan, and tucked the chair closer to Sean's bedside. "Sean, everything's going to be OK. I'm here—Eitan, too. We're going to find out what happened and get you better."

He lay there, unmoving. Kali sucked in a breath, squeezed her eyes to keep them from overflowing and waited until she regained a measure of composure. "I'll be here until you wake up. Whenever you're ready." She rubbed his hand between hers.

There she sat, brain spinning in neutral, too exhausted to think past breathing and pumping blood through her battered body. Last night's call echoed in her brain, '*I warned you...*'

But they made a mistake attacking her son. Now, she had but one goal. Find the sub and find who hurt Sean. She'd sent a set of blueprints to a Columbia friend and run a simulation in Second Life. It was just a question of time.

"Mrs. Delamagente. I'm Dr. Jorge Medallon."

Kali jerked her head up and found a set of kind eyes behind stylish glasses. The doctor's shoulders were bent, hair thin, face mapped with the worry incumbent upon a surgeon, but intelligence spilled from him like sunlight on a winter landscape. Her mind flooded with questions, but she started with one, "How is Sean?"

"He's been unconscious since he arrived. He was bleeding internally when they brought him in, but surgery corrected that. He could awaken at any moment—this evening or next week. His body is resting. Nothing worries us particularly except..." and he paused, as though unable to find the right words.

Fear welled up in the back of her throat. Her eyes teared, but she gritted her teeth. "Just tell me, Doctor. I almost lost Sean last year. Whatever you're not saying, I can handle."

Dr. Medallon shot a look at her over his glasses. "Whoever attacked him tried to smother him, but stopped short of killing him." He shrugged a timeless communication that greater forces ruled.

She shuddered. "You're afraid of brain damage."

Dr. Medallon nodded. "Let me know the moment he awakes," and left.

"Are you alright?" Eitan stepped into the room.

"Yes, of course. If I survived Africa—if Sean did, we'll get through this. Go eat something." For a man who nibbled all day, he must be starving. "I'll stay with Sean."

"A vending machine is down the hall, Dr. Sun." Chacone smiled at him.

"Call me Eitan, please."

As the two left, Kali turned to her son, wondering what occupied a brain in a coma.

A gentle voice broke her reverie. "Kali."

"Duck!" She leaped to her feet, hugging the man she loved almost as much as Zeke. He might have stepped right off a battlefield—khaki colored uniform, muscles bulging against tight sleeves, thick black lace-up ankle-high boots. The room filled with his strength and energy.

"Zeke called you?"

"I called him. I know when he's upset." I came out *Ah*, and him came out *heim*. Duck's southern twang increased with stress.

Kali started to cry. "Duck, they hurt my baby..."

Duck held her. "Whoever did this will pay, Kali. No one hurts someone I care for.

Sun and Chacone bought a variety of crackers, cookies, chips and sodas, and hurried back to Sean's room to find Duck regaling Kali with a story that made her howl with laughter.

They dropped the snacks on Sean's bedside table and Duck turned to Chacone with a wink. "They sure don't make 'em this perty where I work."

Chacone took in Duck's uniform, his bearing, and the intensity of his gaze. "When I interviewed for my Service Selection, the Captain asked me where my sidearm was—as if to say I wasn't prepared. I responded, 'Sir. If I expected trouble, I'd bring my M16.'"

Duck laughed until his eyes watered.

Sun wilted.

Within minutes, Chacone was telling Duck how Anchor got his nickname, how sweet he seemed and interested in her, and how lonely she was. Her face lit up and shoulders relaxed as the tension she carried from guilt and worry evaporated. How did Duck do that? Somehow, despite his massive size, women felt secure with him.

Okay, Sun thought, *you're here for Kali.* If Paloma fell for Duck's chiseled face, sexy grin, mischievous eyes, and muscular…everything…how could a chubby, pear-shaped, albeit kind and sincere scientist compete? But it made him wish he worked out more than his brain the last twenty-five years.

Chacone turned to Sun with wet eyes. "Sean's here because of me. He warned me about Anchor. If only I'd listened..."

Sun put his hand on her arm and felt a jolt. His vision glazed over for an instant before he recovered. "This isn't your fault, Paloma. Sean's a scientist. He needed to test his theory."

"It's not your fault either, Eitan." Duck added.

Sun bowed his head. That, he didn't believe.

Duck clapped him on the back. "So let's find the bad guys. You two see what you can find at Sean's apartment while I chat with a few folks."

Sun smiled. "I'll drive."

Duck whispered into his ear. "Don'chu worry 'bout Paloma, Eitan. I wanted to make sure she's part of the solution and not the precipitate as you scientists say."

Sun led Paloma to his rental, plugged Sean's address into GPS and lurched into traffic.

"Oh, Eitan, you'll love— love San— Ahh!"

Sun glanced over to see what frightened her. Her face was pallid. One hand grasped the handhold on the door and the other clung to the edge of her seat. Sun swerved, barely missing a parked car as he turned his attention back to the road. "What's wrong, Paloma?"

"Nothing. Uh, would you like me to drive? I know this area—Ahh! That was close."

"Wow. That car came out of nowhere."

"I can drive, Eitan. I know our motorists, and—"

Sun fluttered his hand. "You did enough, meeting us in the hospital like you did—Woah! Crowded around here, isn't it?"

Chacone jerked her head up and down. "I'll drive back."

She sounded frightened, but the odometer distracted him.

"Eitan!" Paloma screamed. He slammed the brakes, barely avoiding rear-ending a truck.

"Wow. Oh wow. The odometer reads 557 miles. Each digit is a prime. The entire number is a prime and if you add the 5, 5, and 7 together, you get another prime!"

Paloma's face had a green cast. "Do you use taxis in New York?"

"Of course. Why drive when you can't park once you get there?" Why was she giggling? He better explain. "New York is nothing like San Diego. Here, the streets are tree-lined. There's space between buildings. People smile at each other. Everyone should live here."

Paloma wiped tears from her eyes and stifled the last of her laughter. "It's all fake, Eitan. A couple of weeks and you'll yearn for the honest anger and contempt of New York."

Sun swerved into the curb and with a brilliant smile announced, "We're here." He jumped out and flung his arms over his head, and then spun a circle. Somewhere, a siren whined. Overhead, a jet screamed on its way to the Marine Corps Air Station.

Paloma turned to the building, then back to Sun, confused. "Eitan, this is Anchor's building. Why are we here?"

Eitan checked his phone for the address. Although he had an eidetic memory, Kali suggested he pretend to forget things when with a woman he cared about so she felt less mentally inferior. Right now, he wanted this woman to like him because of the feeling he got in his stomach that had disappeared with his wife. "I'll check."

He grinned, started bouncing, and forced himself to stop. "Excuse me while I make a quick call... Zeke! Anchor lives in the same building as Sean. ... I'm thinking the same. ... What? Al-Zahrawi's alive? ... Bye."

He fidgeted.

"Bad news?"

Sun opened his mouth to explain why a live al-Zahrawi was such bad news, but why worry her? "I wish Zeke was here. He's the intel guy. I'm tech." He tried to think what to do. "Will the manager be here this late?"

"I called ahead and told him to wait."

"He agreed?"

"When I told him we were Navy and FBI."

She was amazing. "Well, let's go inside."

The lobby was big and open and looked modern on the surface, but underneath, worn with frayed chairs and dinged tables.

"Go to the Rental Office," Paloma directed, "and I'll check the mailboxes."

She walked purposefully across the room and he approached the reception desk. A young man grinned at Sun.

"It's a beautiful sunny day in Southern California. My name is Philip. Can I help you find an apartment?"

Philip was short and thin and his voice whined when he spoke. He wore a long-sleeved striped dress shirt with a matching knit tie, maroon corduroy pants and Top-Siders without socks. Sun pasted an official frown on his face. "Your manager, please?"

"Uh, yes," and he fled through a door behind his chair. Two minutes later, they were greeted by a chunky, square-faced man with short, curly hair and a bald spot at the crown of his head. He wore off-white linen pants, a polo shirt, and a touch of mayo on his cheek. He rubbed his hands down his pants, face beaming as though Sun's visit was the highlight of his day.

"My name is Dr. Eitan Sun with the FBI. I'm here with my colleague," he pointed across the room, "LT Chacone with the US Navy."

"My name's Joe. Call me Joe." He tittered at his joke as stuck his hand out. Sun shook it and wished he hadn't. It felt gritty. He forced himself not to think why. "Sorry to hear about Sean. He did—does—he's going to be OK, right?"

"Joe," Sun tried the name out, "What happened the day Sean was attacked?"

Paloma appeared at Sun's side which made the manager nervous. "I stop in every morning to see what he found overnight, to save him from walking through the public areas. He's," Joe paused and then settled on, "You know gearheads." Sun bounced and Joe blinked. "I knocked, but no one answered so I called the police. You know the rest."

She smiled. "What do you know about Ankour Mohammed?"

"Ah. Very clean. Friendly. Did he have something to do with this?" Without waiting, he continued, "He joined our family a few weeks ago. I can give you a copy of his application." He snapped his fingers and Philip scuttled into the back room. "He paid six months in advance."

"May we see both apartments?" Sun hardened his voice, trying to make his question a demand. Joe nodded enthusiastically.

"Of course! You have permission, I'm sure. Between the Navy and the FBI, I'm seriously outgunned." He shot them with both index fingers, chuckled as he speed-walked to the elevator and pulled a key ring from his pocket.

Philip hurried up. "The rental app, Sir."

Joe passed the sheet to Eitan and turned to Philip. "Back to work. Rentals are money and money is your job."

As they ascended, he gave what must be the sales pitch. Sun breathed a sigh of relief when they reached the third floor.

"Here you are. Sean is one floor up and south." He pointed north. "Lock the door when you're done," and he scurried away.

Paloma stared after him through narrowed eyes. "Nervous guy, huh?"

Sun smiled. He liked Paloma. So calm, sure of herself. He liked how her hips swayed when she walked and bits of hair escaped the chignon. He liked her fragrance—musk and soap. In fact, he liked everything.

Mohammed's apartment was a three-hundred square foot bachelor unit with a single bed on the left and a closet to the right. Against the far wall stood a desk, a hardback chair, and a cheap slider with no drapes. As Sun expected, Mohammed had nothing personal. He uploaded photos to Zeke and they went to Sean's apartment.

The layout matched Mohammed's, but there the likeness ended. Scattered across the floor were broken CPU's, monitors, recorders, cameras, camcorders, and electronic circuit boards, most of which Sun had paid for. Sean backed everything up online so the intruders hadn't destroyed anything except hardware.

Paloma stood, mouth open. "He said he was some sort of surveillance expert." She scrunched her face. "What's with the fish?"

A massive aquarium covered the end wall. Inside, a beautiful eel swam lazily back and forth. It thrust out of the water, mouth gaping, lidless eye on Paloma, the message clear. She found some brown flakes that might be tasty to an eel and sprinkled them into the water.

"Look at this." She held up a wire running from the fish to an iPod. "I think his iPod runs off the eel's electricity. Hunh."

Sun cataloged that and moved on. He pulled his iPhone out and checked the time of the last backup to Sean's DropBox account. 2:30 pm. Today. It took a moment and then he had it.

"We need to get on the roof, Paloma."

"I'll get the key from the manager," and she disappeared. Sun made a mental list of the other offsite locations. He needed to visit them.

Paloma returned, waggling the key. "The manager happened to be outside on a resident call. He says he knows nothing about anything on the roof."

They walked down the hall, up four flights and a roof access ladder. Paloma led, her pace more trot than walk. Sun puffed to keep up, though he tried to hide it. Once on the roof, a panoramic view of San Diego spread before them, from the towering downtown skyscrapers to the great naval warships of America's fleet. Sun saw the curve of the Coronado Bridge, the stout old downtown buildings and the spikes of the big hotels by the water. There, to the south was the busy muscle of the naval installations that gave the city vigor.

He found a camcorder on each corner of the building with dishes to collect audio.

"I'll pack these tomorrow." He knew a CEO who owned a G550 and owed Eitan a favor. "Let's get to the ship before it's too late."

Chapter Thirty-five

Day Twelve, Friday, August 18th, early evening
USS Bunker Hill

"I've never been on a cruiser!"

Eitan knew he had only twelve days to stop the terrorists, but still felt like a kid on the set of *Star Trek*. He stared at *Bunker Hill's* superstructure, the aft- and fore-mounted guns, sailors hurrying here and there in crisp white uniforms all tan and muscular.

Paloma returned the salutes of watchstanders. Once inside the ship, she chatted with crewmembers, asked about their jobs and shared a few one-liners. Eitan huffed as they moved along. He lived at his computer since his wife's demise and vowed to change that. Everyone Paloma introduced him to focused on his oversized head. Usually, he giggled, saying it came from exercising his brain, but today he wished he wore a cap.

"I'll show you what Anchor wanted to see during the Tiger Cruise."

He tried to reply, but didn't have enough breath. Thankfully, she seemed oblivious to his struggles.

They went to the enlisted mess deck, the foreword engine room—Main Engine Room One—and five other locations Eitan recognized from Sean's list. They climbed stairs, hurried down pways, leaped over kneeknockers, and scooted around sailors hurrying to watches. Every time his lungs began to burn, she paused to explain how this or that worked or chat with sailors. Eitan liked meeting the crew, seeing how at ease they were with Paloma the Officer.

As they finished the last spot, a heavyset officer stopped in the pway, blocking the passage. Paloma stiffened and her step stuttered as the man grinned at her in between noisy slurps from a can of soda.

"Hello, Sir. This is Dr. Eitan Sun, an FBI consultant. Dr. Sun, this is Commander Taggert, our XO."

The XO raised his eyebrows in mock surprise, eyes traveling from Eitan's thick dark-rimmed glasses to the wisps of thinning hair to the slogan on his t-shirt.

"A nerd! Let me get my copy of 'How to Talk to a Geek'. Tell me Eitan, can you teach FCO to use computers?" Without waiting, he turned to Paloma. "How's the boyfriend?"

Taggert's face flushed. He knew something.

Eitan responded for her. "He's missing. Do you know where he is?"

"Know where he is?" Too fast, and Taggert's gaze slid away. "How would I know?" His voice rose a pitch and his hand tightened around the soda can.

Eitan stood still, the entirety of his formidable attention focused on Taggert. "The 'how' is a mystery, but clearly you know something."

Eitan said not another word. Irrational anger spread through his body for this insecure man, no doubt a traditional bully who got his way by force so never learned the power of words. His average intelligence would be intimidated by anyone with a brain. How he rose to the command position of XO amazed Eitan. The Navy deserved better.

While Taggert fumbled for a response, Eitan studied his clothing. Tailored, the ribbons professionally attached. His shoes were the kind James wore, so a thousand dollars, and the watch a real Rolex rather than the knockoff he probably claimed it was.

"All I know is FCO here fell for an... Air Force guy." Taggert rubbed the side of his nose with his forefinger, oblivious to his body's autonomic and blaring reaction to lying.

Eitan cocked his head. "I wonder why we make you nervous. Is it something to do with your visceral need to impress people? Ah, your eyes dilated. Not impress *people—person*. The author you're consulting with— Googling her found nothing. I know because I Googled her too, and then I checked social security, DMV, tax rolls, and six other lists legitimate people appear on and she didn't. You brushed it off because the money kept coming. You should have trusted your instincts. They are still there despite years of disuse."

Taggert looked as though he'd been slapped.

"You polished your shoes this morning which means you still have pride in your job despite whatever is going on. These people you're involved with have slain thousands. What you know will save lives, maybe your own." Eitan softened his voice as Zeke would, trying to sound non-threatening, even friendly. "How long were you on subs?"

Taggert squinted and his fingers clutched his soda can so tightly, the sides crumpled. Eitan never took his soft gaze off the rotting man in front of him.

Finally, Taggert tossed his soda into the trash and scuttled off.

Muted applause came from behind them. Eitan blushed and discreetly stuffed the discarded can into his pocket. Paloma broke into a grin. "So you dislike my XO—something else we have in common. I'll make sure I'm never on the wrong side of that remarkable brain."

With that, she led the way back through the endless winding pways to the gangplank. Eitan listened to her chatter while running Taggert's name through INSCOM—U.S. Army Intelligence and Security Command—then ONI, USCGI, and the Marine Corps version though he doubted Taggert could survive the Corps. They beat the whine out of you or tossed you out.

When he found nothing, he copied Taggert's fingerprint from the can into a mobile print device—part of the digital jewelry around his neck—and sent it to AFIS. It came back as Kevin Taggert, XO *Bunker Hill*, no arrests but a few warnings in his Navy file. Interesting.

Next, he tried NCIC and the Real-Time Collaborative Criminal Investigation and Analysis solution. Those came up empty so he checked the National Counterterrorism Center and TIDE. Still nothing. No surprise. The man wasn't smart enough to survive in that world. He moved to international agencies like the Joint Terrorism Task Force and the Interpol Terrorism Watch List. That came up with too many hits so he added 'Kevin' and 'USN', and then programmed a bot to find tie-ins to this Taggert's profile.

As they made their way back to Eitan's car, he wracked his brain for a conversational tidbit but small talk was as foreign to Eitan as which fork to use at a dinner party.

Paloma broke the silence. "Taggert changed when he hooked up with the author. He used to be friendly. We even shared dating horror stories. He knows my uniform turns guys off and I'm opinionated. Men want malleable, needy women, which I've never been." Her head dipped as they walked.

"I don't."

Paloma's pace stuttered, but she gave no other sign she heard him. He shouldn't have said that. Why would she like him? Sad. Sad.

They reached the car. "My vehicle's at my apartment. Would you drive me home?"

"My pleasure," and Eitan meant it.

As he put the car in gear, Paloma snugged her seatbelt and gripped the door handle.

Eitan searched for a neutral comment. "What kind of car did Anchor drive?"

"A Volvo, I think. We walked places or arrived separately."

"Do you remember the license plate?"

"Well, no, but he had a USAFA Alumni tag. He shared Doolie-year stories. That's like my Plebe year and freshman year in civilian colleges. It made me trust him—which apparently was his goal." She picked at a hangnail. "How stupid."

Eitan swerved around a truck and Paloma gasped. It was the first time. Good. "He lied, Paloma."

"Sean said so, too, the night before the Tiger Cruise."

"He graduated from NYU Abu Dhabi, one of ten students selected as much for their cultured bearing as their intelligence. Did he ever mention a mentor?"

Paloma shook her head. "Can we change the subject?"

"Oh! Yes. Of course. I'm sorry!" This spy stuff was harder than Zeke let on.

He parked in an Office Depot next to Paloma's building. They took the elevator in silence and walked down a winding featureless hallway until Paloma turned into a tiny alcove.

"Surface warfare officers deploy all the time, so everything here is second-hand."

They stood in a roomy living room with a postage-stamp-sized but spotless kitchen to the front. Two doors—probably bedrooms—split off to either side at the back. A small patio with a sliding glass door filled the space between the bedrooms. The living room was decorated tastefully with a cloth couch and matching chair, a boxy wood laminated coffee table, three Pier 1 faux walnut bar stools, and a squat table holding a too-small TV. He walked out onto the patio. It overlooked an internal quad and butted up to the neighbor's unit. There, a man barbecued hamburgers while refereeing two children arguing over which TV show to watch.

Eitan's stomach rumbled. Wow. When did he last eat?

"Are you hungry?" Paloma asked.

"I thought you might have orange juice," he commented while riffling through her cupboards. "These will do," and he swallowed a handful of Cheetos.

As he ate, he walked around humming, touching her books and knick-knacks. It calmed him.

"The *USS Wampanoag*, the nation's first cruiser, steam-driven, one-time flagship for the North American fleet. It's arguably the most famous cruiser in American history." He stuffed a massive handful of Cheetos into his mouth and chewed, making sure to close his mouth.

"I drew it in high school. My great-great—I don't know how many greats—granddad, Percy Lafoil, served on it." She moved to Eitan's side, her shoulder touching his. "Despite its 4,200 tons, it clocked seventeen knots which made it the fastest warship in the Civil War. No ship beat that in Navy Sea Trials for twenty-one years." The pride came through in her voice. "The British designed an entire class of ships around the *Wampanoag*.

"They say she 'worked technically and failed socially', a trait I can relate to."

Paloma stared at him for a moment and broke into laughter. It could be birdsong in the morning. Eitan chewed through another handful of Cheetos and peeked into both bedrooms.

"You and your roommate don't get along, do you? She's shallow and you're too honest not to say something."

When Paloma said nothing, Eitan thought he blew it again. Darn! He started to make an excuse to leave when she grabbed his face and planted a kiss on his mouth.

"Where have you been my whole life, Dr. Eitan Sun?"

Eitan was so shocked, he froze, eyes closed, mouth puckered, ready if she did it again, then tried to think of something—anything—to say, but this was uncharted territory. The line that worked on his wife at the Twelfth Conference on Calculus Variations in Vienna—'I wish I was a derivative so I could lay tangent to your curves'—seemed wrong tonight. Paloma finally looked away and latched onto one of her books.

"My dad's favorite naval battle was Manila Bay in the Spanish-American War. The flagship cruiser *Olympia* engineered the American victory."

"Unh huh."

"You remember the quote, *Fire when ready, Gridley*, 1 May 1898, Commander Dewey said to his executive officer."

"I wish to have no connection with any ship that does not sail fast for I intend to go in harm's way. Captain John Paul Jones, 16 November 1778."

"I can go one better. *A good Navy is not a provocation to war. It is the surest guaranty of peace.* President Theodore Roosevelt, 2 December 1902."

"Good, but I can do better. *'Praise the Lord and pass the ammunition*!" Lieutenant Howell Maurice Forgy, USN, serving on the heavy cruiser *USS New Orleans* Pearl Harbor on 7 December 1941"

They broke into gales of laughter.

When Eitan got back to Sean's hospital room, Duck had left and Kali was asleep. Eitan tiptoed into the hall and called Zeke, told him about the apartments and his tour of *Bunker Hill*.

"Taggert's involved, Zeke."

"I'll get Duck to check him."

As Eitan hung up, Kali yawned. "If you had a tail, you'd be wagging it. What'd you find?"

Eitan repeated what he told Zeke and then settled into a chair, eyes on Kali.

"The nurses bathe him, change his tubes, smooth his sheets, but no reaction." She wore a half-smile, as though it could protect her from pain.

Outside, the occasional after-hours visitor slipped down the hall and doctors updated patient instructions. The omnipresent stench of antiseptic and sickness flooded the air.

"What bad guys use their own names, Eitan?"

"Bad guys who expect to die, who are the leaders. We need the monster's head."

Kali nodded. "I better check us into the hotel," and she left.

Eitan opened his computer. His bots had uncovered hundreds of hits. He read through the first fifty to get a sense of Taggert, then delimited for pictures. He found dozens showing Taggert racing cars, rappelling down mountains, bungee jumping and hang gliding. It built a profile of Kevin Taggert, thrill seeker, adventurer, and big spender. On a hunch, Eitan added 'Las Vegas' and found Taggert often with scantily-clad women—the perk of chronic gamblers.

So where did he get that kind of money on a Navy salary? It took twenty minutes to find the PayPal account funding Taggert's gambling—under the name *Nivek*

Treggat. Six weeks ago, someone began regular deposits which Taggert quickly withdrew. To date, it amounted to $24,587.00. Whoever set it up made it easy to find, presumably so Taggert would take the fall for whatever happened. Eitan banged away for three hours, barely noticing Kali's return, trying to track back to the depositor with no luck.

He had to warn Paloma.

When he called her, she sounded wide awake. "Hey, would you like an early breakfast? I have a few more questions."

"Meet me downstairs."

When he got to the Lobby, Paloma was leaning against the wall, keys slapping against her hand. Her hair was pulled into a long tail that stopped midway down her back. She wore a tight sleeveless tunic over crop pants, a light sweater and sandals, and a smile. Eitan's heart raced. The room sparked with electricity.

"Do you always call women at this hour?"

He clasped his hands together and dropped them to his side. He bounced twice, but stopped and lowered to his heals. "Actually, well, I never call women."

She took a deep breath. "I'll drive."

They jumped into a well-maintained '67 Mustang and drove to Seaport Village, an upscale collection of eateries and shops that catered to tourists. Paloma parked and pointed. "We'll go over there."

Eitan squinted into the gloom and saw only the black expanse of ocean with the twinkling lights of boats moored off the coast. Overhead, a web of clouds, backlit by the full moon, hung like filigree over the water. Cool sea air enveloped him as a lone seagull called its mate.

"Have a seat. I'll get coffee."

Eitan found a few picnic tables and sat as Paloma pulled a thermos from her bag, poured two earthenware mugs, and placed a steaming cup in front of him.

"Great ambiance and no one bothers you about staying too long."

Eitan thought he might be falling in love.

As they started their second cup, Paloma asked, "So what's on your mind?"

Eitan avoided the topic of Anchor and asked about Taggert's career, his relationship with people on *Bunker Hill,* friends off the ship, girlfriends, and trips to Vegas. Paloma answered between sips of coffee, her voice calm and relaxed, gaze switching between Eitan and the first faint yellow sunlight creeping over the horizon.

"Did Taggert get along with Anchor?"

"Anchor asked lots of questions about XO." Paloma focused out to sea, face tense.

Before Eitan knew it, they were no longer talking about terrorists, but favorite books, college experiences, friends, and whatever else came to mind. He couldn't stop laughing when Paloma shared a Midshipman contest about swallowing goldfish and spitting them up — live. Eitan didn't want this to end.

But Paloma's phone rang. "Good morning, Sir... Yes, sir... Immediately, sir."

Eitan knew. "You're deploying to North Korea."

No one who knew that North Korea had weaponized the upcoming launch, that the President expected *Bunker Hill* to stop the missile, that the cruiser might also battle one of the most advanced subs in the world, would take this deployment lightly.

But Eitan had to keep those to himself.

"I have to report at 0600. We're part of a Surface Action Group monitoring the launch."

Eitan pivoted away, not wanting Paloma to see his sadness, or fear. The ocean lay before them, edged in light. Eitan heard the water rustle against the rocks. A thin line of pink rose from a distant horizon, offering a hint of the day to come. He stood, hands damp. He knew this time would come and still he wasn't ready.

"Why your ship?"

"Only two cruisers are in San Diego right now and *Princeton* is in the Yard. Even so, *Bunker Hill* is the logical choice because we're shifting homeports to Yokosuka."

Eitan choked. "Japan? Who knew you'd be moving homeports?"

She shrugged and started the car. "Everyone."

The entire drive back to the hospital, Eitan wanted to warn her, but doing so would breach national secrets. As he got out of the car, he settled for, "Be careful, Paloma. Something's off about Taggert."

She laughed. "Oh, Eitan, I'm sorry Sean's injured, but I'm so happy he brought you to me. Will you remember me when I return?" She gave him a long deep kiss and fled.

Two policemen approached him, flaps open on weapons, faces tense.

"Dr. Eitan Sun? Please come with us."

Chapter Thirty-six

Day Thirteen, Saturday, August 19th, early morning
UCSD Medical Center

Kali turned panicked eyes to Eitan. "Duck's been shot!"

Eitan froze, big brain unable to make sense of her words, when Duck shouted from somewhere, "I'm fine. Just a scratch. How'd someone get a gun in the hospital?"

Duck appeared in the doorway, a ragged hole in his left arm, blood dripping on the t-shirt that had started the night so pristine. His face was livid, cheeks ruddy. "Someone tried to get into Sean's room."

"Sir, you have to let us check your wound."

"It's a through-and-through. I got hours before it gives me problems, though I wouldn't mind some pain pills and antibiotics. Save me a trip back."

"Duck, you saved Sean's life." Kali's voice was raw. She pushed her palms into her eyes with a vengeance.

Eitan looked from Duck to Kali and back. "Would someone start at the beginning?"

A man shouldered his way inside the room, his well-fitting suit rumpled, loafers scuffed, and eyes weary. "What have you gotten yourself into, Peterson?"

"Duck, Charlie. Call me Duck. If you'll—"

"Hold on. Let us go where we'll have privacy and then tell me everything."

Kali refused to leave Sean, and Eitan worried about leaving her with a madman lose. He faced Kali, his back to Duck and the Detective.

"Kali, I need to tell you something about the attacker, how he knows you."

She offered a wan smile. "I know al-Zahrawi is alive. He threatened me. I don't care about that, but he went a step too far when he threatened Sean. Do what you need to and so will I."

Eitan galloped after Duck and the Detective.

"Eitan, Detective Charlie Ruiz." Duck gestured between the two. "He found Sean after the attack and thinks it may be connected to a series of murders which include the Parisher boys and a female *Princeton* officer."

Ruiz paced a moment, stuck his hands in his pockets, and then turned full face toward the two men. "Let's start with what happened tonight, Duck."

"Someone pulled a weapon on Sean. I yelled. He shot me and fled.

"If he shot you, why not finish what he came to do?"

Duck gave a disdainful glare.

They spent forty minutes reviewing what happened, Duck insisting on police protection for Sean, Detective Ruiz agreeing to the occasional stop-over. "What can our guys do a Navy SEAL can't?" Duck had to agree. When Eitan and Duck returned to Sean's room, Kali was holding Sean's hand, mouth set in a tight line, not a tear in her eye.

"Duck, when you find this gentleman, don't worry about taking him alive."

Chapter Thirty-seven

Day Thirteen, Saturday, August 19th, early morning
Englewood, New Jersey, Zeke's House

The clock read one a.m. when Rowe got home. He went for a run and then worked the weights in his garage. That made him hungry so he wolfed down a Glad container of frozen lasagna Kali had made last week and settled into his favorite Adirondack chair. There, he spent the next two hours listening to the night sounds and wondering how Krakhower was gunned down outside the FBI and nobody saw a thing.

Even without Krakhower's confirmation, Rowe would have recognized the work of Salah Mahmud al-Zahrawi. No one but the charismatic psychopath could persuade an internationally-recognized Muslim to blow a cover he spent twenty years building and put his network of brilliant jihadists at the disposal of a non-Muslim nation like North Korea.

And that was the easy part. He also hijacked two nuclear submarines and framed the West. Whatever the next step, it would be unexpected. Rowe learned last time he tangled with this madman, one hand distracted you while the other went for the throat.

His phone burred as dawn broke over the horizon. He stirred, groggy and stiff from sleeping outside, checked the caller ID.

"Bobby. You couldn't sleep either?"

"I won't sleep until America's sub is home. How's Kali?"

"Why? Something going on?"

"Get over here as soon as you can."

Rowe put the same clothes on he'd worn yesterday, mixed a cold cup of double-strong instant coffee, swallowed it in one gulp, then mixed another and jumped into his Benz. He sped through the empty residential streets and fourteen minutes later parked in front of the FBI satellite office.

James's floor was lit up like an accountant's brain during tax season. The entire team stood in hunched groups, faces tense and eyes hooded, fear palpable. Rowe waved at Tess and slumped into a seat across from his friend.

James kept clean shirts and a razor in his office, so you could never tell if he was finishing the day or starting out but today, his white shirt was wrinkled, his tie was at half mast, shirt sleeves were rolled back twice, his beard should have been trimmed long ago, and he was drumming his fingers on the desk as he snarled into the phone. For the first time since this case started, he'd tossed his jacket over a chair rather than hung it on the back of the door.

"You see it too, huh?" Tess appeared at his elbow. "Like the world falling apart's his fault."

Rowe peeked over at James's assistant. "How are you handling it?"

"He woke me at four a.m. No one wakes a grandma at that hour, Zeke. If I can wash my face and put on some lipstick, I'd be 90%."

"Go. I've got this."

She took Rowe's face between her big calloused hands and kissed him on the cheek. "You are a saint. 90%. That's all I need," and she sprinted for the restroom.

James snarled, "I need it yesterday." Usually, he hid emotion behind a neutral face. Today, the line between mellow and maelstrom was a hair-trigger. "Another dead sailor from *Virginia*."

Rowe's stomach lurched. "How?"

James threw his glasses onto the desk and rubbed his eyes. "For reasons I'll explain later, we believe *Virginia* surfaced during the window of time our satellites weren't overhead, ejected the body while taking care of other business, and submerged again."

"Body?" A heaviness descended on Rowe. He hurt for these guys, trying to save their sub, losing one of their own, but he had no doubt everyone in the crew would die before allowing *Virginia* to attack their country.

"This next is speculation, but we think *Virginia's* crew made sure the corpse would float to the surface sooner rather than later with the note in his jacket telling us they failed to switch the polarity, so will try to damage the CO2 filters."

"Messing with those filters is deadly, Bobby. A sub's air is cleaned by running it through scrubbers and charcoal filters. If those are damaged, the air fouls and the boat must surface."

The corners of James's mouth edged up. "Soon would be preferable. The longer the enemy has our sub, the more likely they break the codes."

"How many nuclear warheads on *Virginia*?"

"Who cares? The difference between having one and twenty is like falling from the fifteenth or sixteenth floor. They both kill you. When the hijackers surfaced, they called *Al Jazeera* on a sat phone."

"No one blocked personal sat phones?" Though, how would you block signals from 'somewhere' and 'someone'?

James played *Al Jazeera's* news flash. A well-dressed Middle Eastern man spoke earnestly into the camera:

> *We received this message from*
> *gentlemen who purport to be the*
> *hijackers of America's nuclear*
> *submarine. Attempts to verify the sender*
> *have failed, but we relay this out of*
> *compassion for the lives at stake on that*
> *submarine. Yaa Allah. May Allah watch*
> *over them: 'Send only Bunker Hill to*
> *North Korea or blood from the next*
> *deaths will be on your hands.'*

"That's the second time they referenced DPRK's missile launch. We're on the right track."

James slurped coffee. "You're going to find this out anyway, so I'll start with everyone's OK.

Rowe stiffened and brought a number up on his cell. "Duck. You with Kali?"

"Yeah. She's sleeping. We had a bit of excitement," and told Rowe about the shooting.

Rowe's body went rigid and bile rose in his throat. "You OK?"

"Everyone's fine." He spit the words out as though rotten food. "But they shouldn't get this close. I'm getting Sean out tomorrow."

"How's Kali holding up?"

"She's been running tests nonstop in this place called Second Life. She's mad as hell and I tell you, an angry brainiac ain't pretty. She told me not to worry about taking al-Zahrawi alive."

"She knows he's alive?"

Duck grunted. "Says he contacted her."

Rowe hung up, then dug a broken stub of a pencil out of his pocket and flipped it. His guts were churning so hard he felt the ulcer forming.

"Hunh." James lumbered out the door and returned minutes later carrying two coffees, one he dropped in front of Zeke. The coffee tasted bitter and burnt his tongue. He set it down to cool.

"Remember the call I got from London? The Brits tracked it to Penbury's office. The guards logged a complaint from Najafian about odd noises right before he called the FBI and ended up dead. Someone knew he was about to spill it."

A chill ran down Rowe's spine. "They're getting rid of loose ends—Najafian, Sean, Krakhower. No one will live who can give away the plot."

"Eitan says Paloma and *Bunker Hill* are on their way to the Sea of Japan. Any chance al-Zahrawi can get the cruiser?"

Rowe got up, paced, sat down, crossed his legs and uncrossed them a moment later. His brain buzzed, trying to tell him something. "An ultra-modern Aegis cruiser would be a hell of a bartering chip, but no—unless she's alone, which won't happen. She'll be part of a SAG—Surface Action Group—backed by the 7th Fleet. Those combined combat systems will stop anything."

Rowe's brain buzzed louder. "So what are they up to?"

James got on the phone. "SA James here. How big is the SAG assigned to the North Korean missile launch? ... Four warships—... You're kidding, right? Who the hell thinks that's a good idea? ... Need to know my ass— They hung up on me.

"Our government is taking this Al Jazeera message seriously. Suck-up with an 'f'. And by the way, where the Hell is *Virginia*, Santa Claus?"

"Gentlemen. I believe I know."

James jerked and spilled his coffee.

This time, Rowe was ready. "We need a bell on you, Otto."

"I can arrange that, Zeke. May I proceed?"

"Speak."

"*Virginia* is opening her torpedo doors."

Chapter Thirty-eight

Somewhere in the Pacific between California and Hawaii
The Bunker Hill

USS Bunker Hill CG 52 pulled out of San Diego at 0800, right on schedule. Rain threatened to the south, but a cloudless blue sky spread north and west as far as the mechanical eye reached. It took two hours to clear to sea and another four hours to reach the first stop, the Seal Beach munitions depot where they loaded Tomahawks, Harpoons, SMs, ESSMs and ASROC torpedoes for anti-submarine warfare. The senior enlisted said they'd never been aboard a ship that received a full weapons complement.

Late Saturday, the ship transited west-southwest. The weather was clear, the wind soft and seas light, with good visibility all the way to the horizon. *Bunker Hill* served as SAG commander because she had the most senior captain. He arranged a destroyer to their south, a frigate to the north, and a hidden sub on the theory the best way to find a submarine was with another.

Paloma as OOD—Officer of the Deck—stood toward the front of the Bridge, arms crossed, ears alert to calls from the Bridge crew, eyes scanning the variegated blue spreading like a silk sheet in front of her. Speed had been steady at seventeen knots for three hours.

The rumble of the engines grew louder and the vibration under her feet stronger. The current had strengthened. "Conn. Slow a knot."

"Aye, ma'am."

Paloma felt alert, every sense on edge. In her time on this cruiser, they had deployed three times. Once, *Bunker Hill* served as a carrier escort through the Panama Canal, across the equator and around the tip of South America. Another time, they trained with the Mexican Navy off Baja California. Supervising a missile launch in the Sea of Japan would be mundane if not for *Virginia* stalking the seas as foe rather than friend. This time, Paloma's training might be tested.

"Bridge, combat. We have a surface contact. EW reports commercial radar."

Paloma responded, "AIS data confirms it as a commercial vessel en route to Beijing."

The contact was cleared.

When the watch change arrived, Paloma handed off command and went to the wardroom to eat. As she munched through a chicken salad, her mind drifted to Eitan. That last morning, as they said goodbye, he had given her a timepiece he said doubled as a satellite phone. It had his private line on speed dial and he insisted she call about any odd occurrence. Paloma felt an unreasonable pang of jealousy for Sean with friends who believed in him, cared for his welfare, and dropped everything to protect him.

She finished dinner as her comm buzzed. "Ma'am. GM2. We may have a problem with the small arms assessment."

In preparation for arrival in the Sea of Japan, Paloma ordered an inventory of the ship's weapons—M-

16's, shotguns, and 9mms—available to repel borders should the need arise. Half at a time would be taken from the armory to the Helo Hanger for inspection. That ensured at any given time, weapons were accessible.

"The entire complement is in the Helo Hanger."

"Which means three bad guys can take over *Bunker Hill* simply by locking down the Helo Hanger and its three egress points—the aviation workshop entrance, the hatch from the flight deck and the one to the ship's interior." Paloma's temper skyrocketed, but she kept her voice calm. "Be right there."

She hurried to the Helo Hanger. "GMC," GM2's chief, "what's the status?"

"Going well, ma'am," he replied dismissively.

She bristled, but kept her face neutral. "Have you finished the first half?"

"XO was here." When she didn't leave, he continued, voice curt, "I gave him the status update, Ma'am."

"Does he know it's not per regulations?" She turned to a Senior Chief standing at the GMC's side. "Senior Chief. You have something to add?"

The man coughed, eyes darting from her to GMC and back. "I'll fix it, ma'am," and he fled, GMC right behind. Clearly, they considered this tasking inconsequential. Thanks to Eitan, she didn't.

She went to the gym and ran on the treadmill at a slant that changed when the ship rocked. Two miles into it, legs already burning, she got a call for a CASREP which required immediate attention. It saved her from quitting in exhaustion.

Twenty minutes later, one more signature to collect, she found a typo.

"Damn!" she said under her breath. As she stood there, wondering if it would go through, she heard a voice around the corner.

"I already told you. ...No, that's impossible. ...Don't ask me to do that... Promise no one will get hurt... Yeah, those're the coordinates... Wednesday, early."

Paloma stood silently until XO's steps disappeared. To whom would he reveal confidential information about the ship's position and time of arrival? He was annoying, but not a traitor. He must have been talking to someone with the need to know.

Saturday, August 19th, night
UCSD Hospital

For the first time since his wife's departure, Sun couldn't concentrate so he toddled down to the hospital cafeteria. He hoped to find squash or mashed potatoes, settled on Fritos, and then plopped into a booth as his mind wandered.

He liked Paloma. That was the problem. He chewed through the first bag of chips and guzzled lemonade, trying to drown out the odd taste of emotion. What if she didn't share his feelings? She kissed him, but was that gratitude? Zeke would know. And what if his sentiments for Paloma compromised his ability as an intelligence officer? He missed a significant event this afternoon—3,269,950,049 dots on his screen. If he overlooked a prime number, what else did he fail to see?

No wonder Zeke had such problems with Kali.

He slugged two antacids with a pint of milk, stuffed the last of the Fritos into his mouth and went to the restroom. There, he rubbed a soapy paper towel across his underarms and another over his face. He couldn't do anything about yesterday's clothes, but if the nurses noticed, he could make a geek-speak comment to make them giggle.

As he dried himself, the number of the sat phone he gave Paloma buzzed. "Paloma! Is everything OK?"

"Just wanted to say hi. Hey, this sat phone is neat."

She sounded happy. Sun sighed. They chatted about life at sea, the crew, the tedium. She seemed excited to talk to him which made him feel complete, like a plant that's been watered. After an animated description of a boring watch, she fell silent. Was he supposed to say something? How did phone calls work between men and women? The silence boomed.

Finally, he blurted out, "Everyone in the intelligence community believes something will happen over there. Please be careful, Paloma. This is more dangerous than it appears." Then as casually as possible, he asked, "How's Taggert doing?

She remained silent. He wanted to prod, but waited as he walked back to Sean's room.

"Yeah, well, you know, XO is away from his girlfriend." She tried to sound chipper, but failed to carry it off. Sun decided to prod.

"Anything else?"

And it all tumbled out. It boiled down to one point: Who couldn't Taggert talk to on the ship's secure communications? Sun told her again not to trust Taggert. Best case, he was stupid, worst case a traitor.

"If the ship is attacked and you can't tell from where, check these coordinates," and he gave her the numbers he had sworn on his Top Secret clearance to share with no one.

Chapter Thirty-nine

Day Fourteen, Sunday, August 20th, early morning
Englewood, New Jersey, Zeke's house

The shrill burr of the alarm dragged Rowe to consciousness. He groaned. Two hours sleep wasn't enough.

Rowe and James had spent all Saturday trying to track *Virginia's* elusive trail. Otto's 'torpedo' turned out to be more bodies, also identified as crew members. Rowe and James agreed to start fresh in the morning.

Today, Kali and Sean were coming home. He skipped a shower but brushed his teeth, dressed in work clothes, and jumped in his car.

He called Duck as he headed for James's office. "Anything going on?"

"Eitan and I packed up Sean's apartment. That fish, damn odd fellow." Duck paused. "No way would Mohammed know as much as he does about *Bunker Hill* without a mole. Taggert spends money like a drunken sailor, drools over a flashy girlfriend, and has the clearances."

He ended by telling Rowe what Paloma told Sun and signed off.

Rowe found a handicap slot, passed Tess with a wave, and plopped down in front of a sleeping James. The agent jerked awake, arched an eyebrow, and added the hand movements of pouring coffee. Rowe called Kali.

"Hey, lots of excitement last night. Everything OK?"

"Sean woke up." Her tone was excited but brusque. "We land at 11 pm. Duck's making the arrangements." Her voice cracked and she sniffled. He wanted to hold her, brush away the danger, and protect her from the evil. She blew her nose, "The doctor's here. See you soon."

Rowe felt like someone had put him in a wood chipper and turned it on. If Kali was his blind spot as James said, he needed to learn Braille.

After he finished this.

If she would have him.

Sunday, August 20th, night
Somewhere over the US

Kali managed to get loose pants and a baggy t-shirt onto Sean's frail body and sandals on his flaccid feet. She and Duck dragged him onto the plane, wrapped a blanket around him, and got a pillow under his head moments before he fell asleep. That left her with the drone of jet engines and the clatter of Eitan pecking away on his computer. He had been worried ever since talking to Paloma so Kali left him alone. She tried to read, but gave up after three pages.

A few rows back sat Duck, arm in a sling, flight attendant fluffing his pillow as he grinned ear to ear. He had a book on his tray table, pretending to read as he studied the passengers. This weekend brought perspective to her life, in no small part thanks to Duck. One moment, she wanted to strike out at anyone who attacked her son. The next, she wanted to hide where she and Sean would never be discovered. Duck said that was why he never married. What right did he have to put himself in danger when someone depended upon him?

"Hey, Eitan."

His head bobbed up and swiveled toward her, eyes soft and dreamy, glasses smudged, fingers never stopping their clackity-clack. "Hey."

"What're you working on?"

"P— Sean's problems."

Kali hoped Paloma was as smitten as Eitan. She brushed her fingers through Sean's freshly-washed hair, caressed his face one more time, and then fell asleep dreaming all this was over.

Four hours later, they popped out of the climate controlled terminal into the slam of August in New York. Even eleven at night, the air remained thick and swollen.

"Over here!" Rowe waved, two cars back along the Arrival Gate curb, handicap card on the dash, a silly grin on his face. She must be a sight in yoga pants, tube top, and sling sandals, but he looked wonderful. Same Marine green khakis, crew neck t-shirt, and sunglasses he always wore, but tonight, she couldn't take her eyes off him. His face, though tired and stressed, fed her starving soul. She shucked her luggage over a shoulder and looped Sean's duffel around her neck. Eitan lumbered along behind her, one arm around Sean's waist, carry-on in the other hand and laptop across his back. Bringing up the rear— somewhere—was Duck.

"Zeke." Her throat ached and her eyes stung. She placed both hands on the sides of his face and kissed his lips.

"Everyone in. Duck'll meet us there. As requested, Otto awaits you."

Kali slipped into the back seat with Sean, Eitan in front. Rowe asked about Paloma which made Eitan blush, how they liked California, and whether they saw any movie stars. Kali waited for him to bring up Penbury or *Virginia* or terrorists. Finally, she did.

"How can I help, Zeke? Give me something or I'll find my own stuff. I'm all Sean has. I can't—won't—let them hurt him."

Eitan started strumming his arm like a keyboard.

Zeke answered with a sigh. "Break Penbury's damn sonar shield."

"Already started. Bobby called about that yesterday. What else?"

Zeke tightened his hands on the wheel. "Find the connection between Al-alah, North Korea, and someone named Gil-dong."

The car fell silent as they zagged over to Amsterdam and turned onto Kali's street. Rowe walked in with Kali and Sean while Eitan stayed with the car. "Can I bring you dinner?"

"No. I'll find something after I get Sean settled."

As Rowe walked away, she whispered, "I love you." His step stuttered, but he kept moving. When he was gone, she shut the door and let hot tears roll down her cheeks.

"Mom. Can you help me?" She wiped her nose on the back of her forearm and rushed to Sean's room. There she found a massive fish tank filling the far wall of the room.

"Would you feed Itui? His food's in my duffle." The boy struggled to keep his eyes open.

Kali dug through Sean's carry-on until she found a plastic container with gunky brown stuff. She took a pinch and sprinkled it into the tank.

"Thanks, Mom. I love you," and he fell asleep to the rhythmic, serene swish of the eel cycling through the six-foot tank.

The peace was interrupted by a scratch and a whimper.

"Sandy!" She yanked the back door open and was assaulted by muddy paws and a furry domed head. "Hey, boy." He covered her face with his warm tongue.

"There you are, Kitten. No surprise our boy here knew you were home." Mr. Winters grinned while Sandy snorted happily. "Sorry about the mud. We were gardening."

"Why are you up so late, Mr. Winters?" She asked while brushing dirt from her blouse and Sandy's paws. The Labrador broke free and sprinted inside. The next thing Kali heard was the vigorous lapping of water from the toilet bowl.

"Waitin' on you, Kitten. Everything OK? Glad you're back," and he gave a blow by blow of Sandy's adventures. After a few minutes, the dog charged outside wagging his tail, one of Sean's shoes in his mouth. He shook it enthusiastically and collapsed at Kali's feet, shoe between his paws, licking the inside.

Which made Kali think of Sean. "I better go, Mr. Winters. Thanks. You're a wonder."

She filled Sandy's water bowl, then wiped up his muddy paw prints. Done finally, she poured a Crystal Lite and rested.

But only for a moment. "Sandy. You stay with Sean while I check my test." The dog padded happily away, but got lost halfway there, flopped down, eyes at half-mast, and fell asleep. Kali booted up her laptop and read the Team's report.

"Damn."

Penbury believed neither the Royal Navy nor the US Navy rigorously tested the sonar-shielding paint before using it so no one knew if or for how long it would work. The 'if' had been proven, so Kali tasked her team to determine the pace of the paint's degradation which would tell her when the sub would appear on sonar.

To do this, a miniature *Virginia* was placed in an adapted wind tunnel that perfectly replicated the sub's ocean environ including temperature, salinity, and pressure relative to depth. Changes in the paint were recorded.

Kali logged onto the Team's intranet and checked the data feed. Best estimate so far was the sonar shield would hold for up to six months. Her stomach tightened. No submarine paint lasted six months. What had she done wrong?

"Of course." The replica sub did what subs rarely do in the real world: It stood still. It needed to move through the water AND the water move past it. She uploaded the new script.

Now to find the connection between Al-alah, North Korea and someone named Gil-dong. She added that task to the Team's To Do list, and went to work.

"Otto—"

"Good evening, Kali. Everything went well in California?"

"Yes, Otto."

"I was worried about you." Otto tilted his round head up. "What can I do to help?"

"Let's throw a big net around these three terms, see if we can find the connection."

Without another word, Otto contacted his legion of zombie computers, much like the SETI Institute's massive network of personal computers that searched for extra-terrestrial life.

"Access all internet-accessible databases." This included libraries, emails, chatrooms, forums, newsgroups, phones, ATMs, surveillance cams, webcams, GPS, traffic cameras, WiFi, even OnStar buttons most people thought secure. Thanks to James, it also included TS/SAP government networks that collected SIGINT, ELINT, and everything INT.

Even with Otto's substantial computing power, this would take a while. James had stocked no food Sean would consider edible, so she put a light sweater on, locked the door, verified the security link to Eitan's lab—although she didn't expect a problem at two in the morning—and went shopping. The night air felt warm, but no longer stifling. She inhaled the clutter of humanity, the stench of too many cars, and the distant whiff of the Hudson—nothing like the palm trees and ocean and suntan lotion of California. She loved being back.

She took her time wandering the aisles, picking foods that would excite her nerdy son. When she checked out, the clerk took her money without a word and went back to a book stuffed under the counter. She got halfway home when her phone rang. "Eitan! You alright—"

"The electricity went off in your apartment. Probably nothing, but I called the police."

Her phone beeped. "Mr. Winters is calling. Maybe his is off too." She switched calls. "Hello—"

"Our Sandy was barking like crazy a few minutes ago, then nothing. I pounded on the door. I think I hear him whining."

"I'm on my way home, Mr. Winters. Hey, is your electricity off?"

"No," Mr. Winters sounded puzzled. "Should I check yours?"

"No—but thanks."

By now, Kali was running, her sandals slapping on the sidewalk, groceries bobbing in her arms. The bread bounced out, but she didn't care. By the time she reached her building, and then her apartment, she was sprinting. Her door stood open so she flew inside and slammed into a policeman, gun drawn.

"Ma'am—stay away! Someone ran out your back door. My partner is chasing him."

She wriggled past. "Sean! Where are you?"

A low groan came from down the hall. She dropped her groceries, ignored a splat, and ran to his room. There he lay, mumbling in his sleep. She pulled to a halt, heart beating, panting as much from fear as exertion. She patted his smooth forehead. Sixteen and already through too much. When she was sure Sean was OK, she followed a whimper to the hall closet and yanked it open. Sandy sprinted out and headed to Sean's room.

"Got him!" Mr. Winters grinned, wearing pajamas and slippers, shirt buttoned one-off, holding his cell phone with a shot of a slender man dressed completely in black right down to his gloves. He turned as he fled, showing the lithe body of a runner. A balaclava covered his head so only his eyes showed—dark pools of anger, feral and untamed.

"Would you send it to me, Mr. Winters?"

"Sure, kitten. I got your electricity on. This fella must have flipped it off."

She rubbed the old man's shoulder. "You OK?"

"Oh sure." He grinned. "Back one day and already the police are over." He yawned and shuffled into his apartment. Kali had to hold the phone with both hands to call Eitan.

"Eitan. Someone broke into my apartment. We're OK. Mr. Winters managed to get a picture."

"It includes a lot of data, Kali," and he hung up.

Kali went to Sean's room, catching Otto out of the corner of her eye in the living room, calmly churning through data, oblivious to the excitement around him.

When she reached his bedside, he was fumbling with a controller. "Are you OK?"

"Mom. Watch this," and he placed his iPod in front of her.

She watched a video of her apartment from the perspective of Sean's bedside table.

"How'd you get this?"

"Just watch, mom."

First, everything was dark. Then, Sandy started barking and footsteps moved through the house. Sandy's barks grew more frantic with each step until he yipped painfully and a door thunked. Then a body blocked the doorway—eyes those of the stranger in the photo. He opened a box and withdrew one of two syringes.

Sirens wailed along with Mr. Winters' voice, "Kali! Sandy! Is everything OK? Kali!" He pounded on the door. The stranger shoved the syringe back into its case and fled.

"How'd you get this, Sean?"

"I hooked it up to Itui when you went shopping," and he slammed through an explanation of how an electric fish powered an iPod. "I recognize his eyes, mom. It's Paloma's friend, Anchor. What's he doing here?"

All Kali wanted to know was where the hell had the protection James promised been?

Chapter Forty

Day Fifteen, Monday, August 21st, 4 am
FBI Safe House somewhere in New York

Kali called Zeke who called James who said he didn't expect Kali at one in the God damn morning. James agreed to move her and Sean and Otto—and Sandy—to a safe house until this ended. Kali packed bags, dug out one item from where it had been stored since she moved in and stuck it in her purse, talked to Mr. Winters, and an hour later, Zeke and Duck moved her to a government residence three times the size of her apartment.

When Duck left to check the perimeter, Zeke crushed her to his chest. "This house is so far off the grid, no one can find it."

Her mind leaped from the man who dropped a bug in her purse to the attack on herself and then Sean, and again in the hospital.

Al-Zahrawi always found her.

"Don't go anywhere without letting Duck know. We will get whatever you need. Meetings with your Team must be virtual."

"Otto's electricity consumption will give us away."

"Eitan's routing it through ten different locations." He took her face in his hands. "Take no chances. Al-Zahrawi is too smart."

A slow burn started in her gut at those words—*he's too smart.*

"I didn't start this, Zeke, but I'll finish it. Al-Zahrawi wants me incapacitated with fear, but that will never happen. He and his *jihadi* friends have no idea what an angry Christian mother can do when those she loves are in danger."

He stroked her hair, wishing he could absorb her rage. "When Sean feels up to talking, let me know," and left.

Otto fixed his brilliant orbs on Kali. "I sensed an odd tone in Zeke's voice."

"Ignore him. He thinks we're at the eleventh hour and he must perform the impossible."

"Are we?" As usual, Otto went right to the point.

"Maybe, but he's not the only miracle worker around here."

Sitting among the homey Ethan Allen furnishings of the safe house, Otto rolling in circles while Sandy batted at his feet, Kali could easily discount the danger of what her son had put his life on the line to prevent. She leaned back into a chair that still had the tags on it, closed her eyes to block the tears burning behind her lids, and willed her brain to stay strong.

And then got to work.

She found what she needed online at an all-night store two blocks away, changed into worn jeans and a beat-up Columbia t-shirt, asked one of the agents to watch Sandy, and ignored him when he asked where she was going. She had a credit card and one-hundred forty dollars in her purse, figured that would get the party started.

Ten minutes later, she stood at the counter and said, "I need a refresher course."

"Sure. What weapon you shoot?"

Kali awoke with a start, feeling rested for the first time in days. The morning sun beamed through the window. A tree swayed gently in the morning breeze, its bark cracked and lined, leaves limp in the dewy air. The fish tank gurgled as Itui swam and swam and swam, building up a reservoir of electricity. She rubbed a hand over her face, wondering briefly how she ended up in Sean's room, and padded to the kitchen for coffee.

"Otto." Her voice activated the AI as she settled onto the living room couch. "Anything?"

"Yes."

"Will it cheer me up?"

"I have no humor module."

"Hit me."

Otto churbled. "As we know, the locations Ankour wanted to see on the Tiger Cruise were the same as those Taggert gave his fiancée, Shalimar. To determine the significance, I hacked Taggert's email which he doesn't password protect. He told Shalimar blowing up these six locations could sink the ship. I simulated this and Taggert is correct."

That woke Kali. "Where are they?"

"The #3 generator room is outboard and includes hazardous fuel, aft steering so the rudders are destroyed, the battery shop because it shares a bulkhead with the armory and is outboard, the sonar dome, the forward pump room because it is low on the ship and operations berthing because it contains so much flammable material."

"Are you sure that would destroy the ship?"

Otto churbled. Only humans required confirmation. Otto always heard correctly and refrained from speculating unless asked to do so.

Sean called from his room, "Mom. I have to talk to Zeke."

Kali raced into his room. "What's wrong?"
"I remembered something."

Monday, August 21st, 4 pm
Cinco de Mayo Restaurant, New York

Rowe slipped into the cracked faux-leather booth at Cinco de Mayo Restaurant, Hispanic music and the buzz of customers surrounded him. Dishes clattered as waiters served food and cleared away dishes. Rowe had already scanned the restaurant for anyone out of place and found the escape routes. Now, he leaned back, phone to his ear, listening to Sean's epiphany.

"Ankour Mohammed is Gil-dong? You sure?"

"His father called him that."

Then why did Al-alah have Mohammed's email from his dad?

Sean continued as though he hadn't heard Rowe's question. "I also know why they want *Bunker Hill*, well, Ankour anyway. He's obsessed with Paloma. If he destroys her ship, he destroys her."

No wonder this plot had a split personality. Mohammed's goal had changed. He no longer cared if he double-crossed al-Zahrawi.

"Zeke—are you listening?" Rowe shook himself back to reality. Kali was on the phone. "I know how al-Zahrawi will destroy *Bunker Hill*," and Kali explained the significance of the locations Taggert shared with Shalimar.

Rowe's brain whirred. "Send me those, Kali. I'll give them to Bobby."

"Give me what?"

James slipped into the booth and motioned the waiter for coffee.

Rowe caught the agent up. "Al-Zahrawi's plan comes to a head August 30th, when North Korea launches its missile. That gives us nine days."

James sent the list to Tess with instructions to call when all locations were cleared.

"There won't be any bombs there yet, Bobby. They'll wait."

A waiter poured coffee and dropped a basket of chips between them. "You ready to order?"

"Coffee. That's all. I'll share his food."

Rowe didn't bother to say he ordered nothing. The waiter grumbled this was a restaurant not a conference room, threw a bill on the table, and left.

James drummed his fingers. "The only proof we have is a list given to an author. I need more to get the President's attention."

Rowe leaned back, both hands around his coffee cup. "*Bunker Hill* will be alone in the Sea of Japan, exactly like these guys want."

James sat up and paged through his phone. "One of yesterday's bodies is Dinar Hussabi, according to his ID. He's another NYU student in Al-alah's elite group." James texted an address. "His parents live in Lewiston NY. See if he told them anything."

"Why kill one of their own?"

James shrugged as his phone rang. "James... Thanks." He walked out with Rowe. "No bombs at those locations. The CNO refuses to talk to the XO without more proof." James started toward his car, but asked, "When's your meeting with Admiral Xibon? He still ACNO?"

"Thursday." James's eyes clouded as Rowe called Duck. "We have an errand."

Chapter Forty-one

Day Sixteen, Tuesday, August 22nd, early morning
On the road between Lewiston and New York

While Rowe drove west along the I-80, Duck googled the Hussabi's. He refused to wear the sling, saying it got in the way. Nor would he take the pain pills.

"Mr. served twenty years in the Army. Met Mrs. at the USO. County records show they lived at the same address thirty years. House is paid off, no liens. IRS records indicate they own Mac's Mechanics. Bought it ten years ago for cash and turn a small profit every year. They have a savings account, stock, and an IRA. No expenses for gardeners, maids, or manicures with nominal purchases of clothing, shoes, and that sort of stuff."

He paused to read something. "Local stories recount the couple's heroic son Dinar who serves on America's front lines as a submariner."

The two men drove on in silence, stopping at a truck stop near the intersection of the 25A and the I-90 West to fill up with gas, use the restroom, and get coffee. When they got back to the car, the rear tire was flat, as was the spare. It took a while to find an all-night gas station, but they did, paid the exorbitant fee the manager required, and were on their way.

"Things patched up with Kali?"

A big rig thundered by, its power vibrating in Rowe's chest. He considered what to tell Duck when the phone saved him. "Speaking of."

"When the formulized varnish of the sonar shield is exposed to the varying salinity, pressure, and temperatures in the ocean, as well as the movement of the currents, it degrades." She chewed something crunchy. "How fast depends on the sub's speed and travel route. My best guess is a week."

"Will Otto alert you when that happens?" Rowe asked.

"Otto isn't sonar."

"Thanks, Kali." He called James and shared the news.

"A week is just in time for the missile launch." Tess said something. "No bombs on *Bunker Hill* means someone the CO trusts is bringing them. The question is how do you reach a cruiser underway."

An hour later, Rowe took Exit 25A and elbowed Duck awake. "We're here."

Duck downed the last of his cold coffee while Rowe wound through a quiet residential neighborhood and puttered by the Kerr Street address. It was a 1960's-style, one-story brick structure with a peaked roof, freshly-painted wood shutters, and a chimney off the back. A winding sidewalk and three concrete steps led to a shining black wood door. The tree-shaded driveway stopped at a one-car free-standing garage. A pristine wood slat fence blocked Rowe's view of the backyard. The landscape was neat and trimmed and a whirly bird decorated the front yard. It looked like a nice middle-class place to grow up. How had Dinar ended up a terrorist?

"No car in the drive. Maybe in the garage."

They parked two doors down and waited. Lights winked on along the street and breakfast smells floated from kitchen windows. Car engines roared to life as people left for work. A sixtyish woman with wispy white hair smiled at a couple in their twenties, the man with his shirt off, the woman in an airy tank top. They smiled back. Two women in jogging suits walked by and a sturdily built Hispanic woman let herself into one of the homes with a key. No one cared about the two men in the Benz.

At 8 am, Rowe knocked on the door and got nothing. He called the auto shop and asked for Mr. Hussabi.

"We expect him and the Mrs. back this afternoon. Can I help?"

"Oh—gosh. We're friends from out of town. Any chance you have his cell?"

The man laughed. "Like I'd give that out."

Rowe slipped the phone into his pocket. "Let's have breakfast and take a tour."

Lewiston sat on the USA-Canadian border between Niagara Falls and the historic Fort Niagara. No matter where you were, you heard the background rumble of the Falls. Rowe breathed in the pure air. If the wind blew right, some of the four million cubic feet of water crashing over the crest every minute would sprinkle Lewiston.

They stopped at the Orange Cat Coffee House on Center Street. The hostess greeted them like long lost friends.

"Hey, good to see you two. Thanks for dropping in. I can give you a booth or a window?"

"Window, please. Maybe we'll see our friends while we're waiting." When the hostess didn't react, Rowe pushed, "Do you know the Hussabi's?"

"Oh, no. I'm only here for the Peach Festival. You two here for that?"

Rowe shook his head and Duck nodded. The hostess giggled. "Your waitress is Claudia." She gave them water and left with a peek over her shoulder at Duck. He grinned.

"Hi! My name is Claudia! Are you here for the Peach Festival?"

This time, Rowe let Duck respond. "Absolutely." He gave Claudia a dazzling smile.

"Then you might like our Peach Pancakes."

"Are they tasty, Claudia?" Duck flashed white teeth at the twenty-something waitress.

"Oh, everything with peaches is tasty!" She blushed. Duck grinned.

Rowe tried again. "We're trying to find our friends, the Hussabi's. D'you know them?"

She gave him a big smile. "I sure do. Thought they were in Canada."

"They're back today. Would you let us know if you see them?"

"Sure will. And what can I bring you from our world-famous kitchen?"

Duck looked at Rowe and back to the waitress. "Peach pancakes with everything."

Claudia grinned. "You-all are big enough to eat pancakes with everything, now aren't you?"

Duck grinned back. "But just the right size for our clothes, donchu think?"

She giggled. "Oh, for sure!" and skipped to the kitchen.

Rowe and Duck took turns going to the restroom and got back as the food arrived.

"Here you go. Steaming and tasty!"

As she arranged the plates, Rowe said, "I heard the Hussabi's son is a hero."

"Oh sure. He works on one of those submarines and fought in Iraq." She looked so impressed, Rowe saw no need to tell her submarines were nowhere near Iraq. She turned to Duck. "If you-all are going to be around this evening, be sure to come to the Ice Cream Social at the Farm Museum. Everyone goes."

Duck leaned forward and put his chin in his hands. "You too?" When she grinned, he puckered his forehead in thought. "We could stop by. Yeah."

She giggled all the way to her next table.

They stayed for an hour, but it became clear Claudia knew nothing more so they paid the bill and left. Claudia walked them to the door and hugged Duck.

From there, they walked up and down the Village streets, chatting with merchants and asking about the Hussabi's. With less than 3,000 residents, Lewiston depended upon tourism to survive. Today, summer still supreme, it pulsed with life. People going about their business while tourists sauntered down the wide sidewalks. After an hour, Rowe was convinced the Hussabi's were Mother Theresa only saintlier and the men returned to Kerr Street to wait.

The Hussabi's arrived around two pm. They were a grey-haired couple dressed in matching jeans, polo shirts, tennis shoes. Mr. Hussabi helped Mrs. out of the car and they held hands as they walked up the sidewalk.

"Mr. and Mrs. Hussabi?" Rowe called as he limped toward them. He smiled his most disarming smile, making sure his hands were at his sides. "My name is Dr. Zeke Rowe and this is my associate, Duck Peters." He wondered what they thought of two burly strangers waiting outside their home, but they smiled back with genuine warmth.

"Hello there. Nice to meet you. Are you the two asking around about us?"

Rowe grinned sheepishly. "We're friends of Dinar. Wanted to say hi."

That got even bigger smiles. "Please, come in. You drove up from New York? My goodness. Let me make coffee for you. We're just back from Canada. What a wonderful country, our northern neighbor."

They hustled Rowe and Duck inside, sat them in matching easy chairs across from a brown plaid sofa with heavy oak arms. To the side was a bookcase neatly stacked with paperbacks. Family pictures covered one clean white wall featuring a grinning youngster with eager eyes as he grew from preschool through high school. The Hussabi's chatted from the kitchen about Niagara Falls, the Peach Festival, and so many visitors.

"Dinar promised to come see us, but he's so busy. He's what they call a Machinist Mate—keeps the sub's engines running."

His wife gave a proud smile. '*Virginia*, Nuke MM'—that's what we put on the Care packages. '*Virginia*, Nuke MM' and it always gets to him."

Rowe asked, "When is he coming home?"

"Oh, you know children. He said the end of August, but what with the deployment schedule and all. You have children, Mr. Rowe? How about you, Mr. Peters? Well, we always know he means well."

They returned with a tray of coffee, cups, sugar and real cream, and a plate of sandwiches. They sat, insisted the men eat, and prattled on about Dinar.

"I got an email from him," and Mr. Hussabi pulled his laptop onto the table, pecked in a username and password, and spun the computer around so Rowe could read the message.

> *Dear mom and dad, I'm bringing*
> *friends from the sub. They want to*
> *visit Canada. I think we'll be there*
> *August 31st. I am excited to see you*
> *again. Love, your son, Dinar.*

Rowe sat back, folded his hands, and tried to figure out how to tell them.

"Oh, Dr. Rowe! You finished your coffee. I'll get you more!"

"No. That's—"

"Silly is what it is. Friends of Dinar are friends of ours," and she bustled to the kitchen, humming under her breath.

"Young man." Rowe turned toward Mr. Hussabi. The older man's eyes were deep with understanding, fear, and hope all at the same time. "You have something to say, say it. We're a military family. We know about bad news."

Mrs. Hussabi snuffled as she placed Rowe's fresh coffee on the table in front of him. Rowe stirred cream into the dark liquid until it turned the color of caramel. He put the spoon down and finally addressed the Hussabi's.

"Mr. and Mrs. Hussabi. You probably heard about the hijacked American sub? What the news doesn't know and I'm asking you to keep to yourself is it's *Virginia*." They said nothing, eyes bright with fear. "We think your son is involved with the terrorists."

Ms. Hussabi clanged her cup into the saucer and Mr. Hussabi went completely still. Rowe doubted either of them had even a passing acquaintance with danger.

Mrs. Hussabi found her voice first. "No, Dr. Rowe, you're wrong. He's going to be an officer." This came out with pride. "His professor recommended him. Akbar, what was his name?"

"Yes, I remember. Umm, Nasr Something?"

"Yes! Nasr. Wonderful man. Dinar thinks highly of him. He wrote a recommendation for Officer Candidate School. He's an important man."

Duck leaned forward. "Mr. and Mrs. Hussabi. Dr. Nasr Al-alah is responsible for blowing up *HMS Triumph*."

The couple froze, and then both started talking at once. "No, no, it can't be true." Tears filled Mrs. Hussabi's eyes. "Dinar wouldn't know a terrorist." "Dinar is a good boy."

Rowe tried every tack possible to calm the couple down and find out what they knew about the terrorists' activities, but gave up. He rose to leave while Duck planted a recording device inside a magazine.

Back in the car, Rowe pulled out onto the quiet street. "Maybe NYU is coincidence and Dinar's a hero, killed trying to deactivate the polarity."

Duck's eyes hardened, his face like flint. "Too bad about the hundreds of people destroyed by his friends. What do you make of Dinar wanting his Dad to take friends to Canada? D'you think that's the escape route?"

"Makes sense if whatever they have planned is near New York Harbor."

Something nibbled at Rowe, but he couldn't pull it out. "I'll run it by Eitan and Bobby, see if they have ideas."

Rowe parked around the corner and activated the hidden bug. The parents were hysterical, pleading with each other. Neither made any phone calls or went outside. Finally, Rowe and Duck drove back to New York arriving as the sun peeked over the horizon.

Chapter Forty-two

Day Seventeen, Wednesday, August 23rd
Englewood, New York, Zeke's safe house

Rowe woke to the sound of pounding. He stumbled out to his living room and unlatched his door while he squinted at his watch.

"9:50. Didn't we go to bed three hours ago?"

"Four. The President is on at 10, responding to accusations America must be reined in."

Rowe shook the dust from his head. "Who would think America would be blamed for getting her own submarine hijacked?" No wonder Rowe hated politics.

"The Brits." Duck flipped the TV on and started a pot of coffee while Rowe rubbed his eyes and yawned.

"Who's with Kali—"

"You better not finish that sentence," Duck said.

Rowe felt sheepish. When the coffee pinged ready, Rowe poured a cup for his friend, one for himself and sat to listen. The President gave a quick overview of events the last three weeks and then laid out America's strategy for dealing with the terrorists. He ended with words directed at *Virginia's* hijackers:

*"We are prepared to fight with every tool
in America's arsenal. Are you prepared
for that? Give yourselves up or we will
blow you out of the water."*

"Like a red flag to a bull."

The talking heads exclaimed America came across strong in the face of our enemies.

Rowe huffed. "Now the terrorists can show the world no one controls them."

"At least then we'll know where they are."

Chapter Forty-three

Day Eighteen, Thursday, August 24th, Midday
Somewhere in the Pacific, **CG52 Bunker Hill**

Somewhere west of Hawaii, *Bunker Hill* secured for heavy weather and steamed into the teeth of a forty-knot gale. The twenty-foot swells tossed the ship around like a politician's promises during Primary season, at times bouncing the hull-mounted sonar completely out of the water.

Paloma wrapped herself in the bright orange life vest and reported for watch. Thick gray thunderheads folded into the choppy angry seas. The rain tore at her hair and slashed her chapped face as she peered into the angry waters, wondering if a submarine lurked, biding its time, and caring nothing for the one-hundred-fifty plus earnest sailors who called this ship home. She laughed to herself. No one would find her ship in this squall, including Neptune himself.

A day ago, they pulled into Joint Base Pearl Harbor-Hickam for a BSF—Brief Stop for Fuel. *Bunker Hill* was on its way in three hours. The Captain didn't explain the quick departure, but Paloma knew. Although North Korea's missile would only reach the islands with a push from the hand of God, Third Fleet needed non-essential ships and people out to make room for additional ground-to-air defenses.

Hawaii marked *Bunker Hill's* last authorized contact until North Korea. Now, any radar blip would be considered a threat.

"You got cabin fever, too, Ma'am?"

She turned to see the lean muscular shape of Fire Controlman Second Class James Burlowe. He stood ramrod straight as he greeted her, rock-jawed with gunmetal eyes, a handsome man, weathered from too many days in too much sun.

She tugged the brim of her cover in a vain attempt to block the driving rain. "Nice job, GM2, firing the MK 38 yesterday."

The Captain had raised the ship's operating condition to II-AS—anti-submarine—which required extra lookouts, torpedoes armed and ready, sonar operators on duty 24/7, and live fire exercises.

Burlowe laughed. "I always look good firing at a target that doesn't evade or shoot back, Ma'am." He turned toward her, steel in his stance, fierce determination on his face. "No one's getting this ship on my watch."

His eyes were alert despite two hours of watch in a blasting rain that came down so hard it hurt your skin. Usually, that beat it out of a sailor, but not Burlowe.

"How'd you end up on *Bunker Hill*, GM2?"

"The further west, the smaller the seas, Ma'am. Katie bar the door crossin' the Atlantic, though it don't compare to Tierra del Fuego at the tip of South America. Forty degrees, fifty-knot winds, thirty-foot seas. Add in the currents and narrowness of the Strait and you have a nightmare. Sailors toss a coin to the Virgin Mary as thanks for a safe transit. I tossed nine—one for each of my lives."

The cruiser heaved. Paloma broadened her stance, but GM2 swayed easily. "I know things are dangerous, but dammit, Aegis exercises are fun."

The ship's Aegis Combat Training System had simulated an air-and-surface attack to give the crew defensive practice. They split into teams and engaged the threat with weapons of their choice. Paloma's team selected a layered defense— SM-2s and Harpoon RGM-84 Surface-to-Surface missiles to stop enemy combatant ships, 5" 54 caliber deck guns to support the SM-2s, ESSMs for incoming that got past the SM-2s, and CIWS for Hail Marys.

"You were efficient, Ma'am. I'd follow your lead anytime."

Paloma felt her face redden. "Let's hope it never gets to that."

The phone was ringing. Paloma slapped around until she found it. "FCO." She squinted. 1 a.m.

"Ma'am, Captain needs you in the Pilot House."

"Enroute," and Paloma leaped from her rack, threw her uniform of the day on and sprinted for the Bridge. The sky shone clear and the moon hung like a pale balloon at 270 degrees. The Frigate and the Destroyer copied *Bunker Hill's* speed and direction. The SAG wasn't under attack, so what was up?

The Pilot House was kept pitch dark so the navigational lights of surface ships stood out against the dark of night. The Captain beckoned her over. He was a short, barrel-chested man, with a bull voice and an unflagging affection for his crew and his ship.

"We're commencing a Transit Under ASW Threat drill," similar to yesterday's drill, but the threat existed undersea. Normally, the crew had twenty-four hours to prepare, but it appeared the Captain worried as much as Eitan.

"Paloma. Help the TAO in Combat. Create a formation with us as the Guide. Place the other ships between one and three nautical miles away at bearing zero-zero-zero to one-eight-zero degrees relative."

The Captain assumed she knew what else to do and she did. *Bunker Hill* would direct the Destroyer and the Frigate to patrol sectors generated by relative bearing and ranges to itself, search for underwater threats in the guise of a submarine, and prevent it from getting a weapons control solution on any ships in the formation.

"A visiting *Ohio*-class sub agreed to play. Combat, enter ASW training mode."

Paloma sprinted to Combat, the Captain right behind her, and backbriefed the TAO.

"Let's get that helo launched."

Quickly, the crew removed the chocks and chains securing the Seahawk. The boatswain mate of the watch announced, *Green deck*, over the 1MC, initiating what Paloma knew would be a clattering, ear-splitting roar as the chopper revved up and lifted off, though muffled in the confines of Combat. They were expected to launch a helo in fifteen minutes, but tonight it took twenty-three.

As she awaited the chopper's report, the TAO's watch team moved to the larger task of finding the sub. TAO made an announcement to the bridge to get everyone on the same page, called down to CIC to retrieve the latest intel, and reviewed emergency torpedo evasion procedures with the crew.

The Hawklink buzzed. "*Bunker Hill*, this is Redlion 616. Stand by for MAD device and sonobuoy data."

The *Ohio*-class shot a red flare.

"Torpedo in the water! Range seven thousand yards, bearing one-zero-zero."

"Evasive action! Launch ASROC!"

The simulator threw an ASROC at the sub's last known bearing, then the Helmsman performed a series of hard banks to port and starboard that left 'knuckles' in the water which they hoped the enemy fish would confuse with the ship. They also simulated the launch of Underwater Counter Measures, which included streaming nixie to simulate the noise of *Bunker Hill's* propellers and energizing MICM—magnetic influence countermeasures—to mimic the ship's magnetic signature.

The captain listened silently, feet spread beneath his stout body, hands locked behind his back as one communication after another flooded the comm lines.

After what felt like hours, TAO announced, "FINEX. Sub's gone."

The Captain nodded, face impassive. "Well done, everybody. Debrief in the wardroom."

Paloma dragged herself to the officer's mess hoping someone made coffee. Part of her wanted to go back to sleep, but a bigger portion saluted the Captain for wanting to make his crew ready for a sub attack.

Chapter Forty-four

The Virginia
Somewhere in the world's oceans

Four days put them at August 29th, the day before the hijackers' deadline, and Joey Najafian had a headache, the early warning of CO_2 poisoning. A Chief had managed to sabotage the scrubbers before one of the Kenyans stabbed him. Then, with the knife poking out of his neck, the Chief had damaged the snorkel mast before dropping dead. Without the snorkel mast, they couldn't ventilate at periscope depth and would have to surface or die of CO_2 poisoning.

Joey figured he could handle a headache.

The real sleeper must have told the hijackers about the O_2 candles, portable devices that could re-oxygenate the air if the sub couldn't surface. Luckily, the crew could only locate enough for four days.

But something worse than stale air and headaches worried Joey. He feared he'd been discovered.

Machinist Mate Dinar Hussabi had approached Joey, introduced himself as a sleeper ready to join the *jihad*. Joey persuaded him to stay undercover as backup, but then Hussabi stumbled on Joey sabotaging the mechanism that provided drinkable water. Joey convinced him he was repairing it and finished destroying it when Hussabi left. Since *Virginia* had no replacement parts, they would have to surface.

That problem paled in comparison to what Joey found out this morning. The hijackers were planning to test the weapons again, on the next unarmed ship they came across. Joey needed to disable the warheads or the delivery system—or both—and get a message to Command to destroy *Virginia*.

Through whispered meetings, the Captain told him he had a plan and to be ready. When the cook set a fire in the deep fat fryer, alarms shrieked and smoke quickly billowed into the sub. All eight terrorists raced to the galley to staunch the flames.

Joey's chance had arrived. With everyone busy, he fled to the torpedo room, jumped through the water-tight door separating the engine room from the rest of the sub, but pulled up short as he passed the reactor. For the first time since the hijacking, the door stood open. In their hurry to staunch the fire, they forgot to close it. He poked his head inside to see what they had been up to for two weeks.

There, surrounding the reactor, were bricks of C4, enough to blow the reactor and bury everything within a hundred miles in nuclear contamination.

Chapter Forty-five

Thursday, August 24th, morning
Englewood, New Jersey, Zeke's house

5 a.m. and already Rowe had finished five sets of fifty hanging sit-ups, three of thirty dead arm pull ups, and two of twenty one-handed push-ups, all with a plastic bag tied around his waist to make him sweat more.

It didn't help.

He pulled a sweatshirt over his head, laced up his Nikes, and went for a seven-mile jog to let his mind work. Even with *Virginia* against them, the Surface Action Group's three warships could take on the entire North Korean air force without breaking out of training mode, leaving *Bunker Hill* to stop the missile.

Unless the SAG was dismantled as seemed to be the plan.

He spent most of yesterday following up on the only clue from Mr. and Mrs. Hussabi. If Dinar wanted to escape via Canada, the target was on the eastern seaboard.

With nothing else to show for a day of thinking, he checked in with Kali, then James, and then got ready for lunch with Cy.

Known as Admiral Cyrus Xibon to the rest of the military industrial complex, they met when then-Captain Xibon dropped Rowe's SEAL team in the Arabian Sea to free an imprisoned American. The SEALs accomplished their mission except Rowe got himself shot, twice, and Xibon got annoyed when Rowe bled all over his clean sub. Xibon stayed in touch, often asking for Zeke's take on a situation. He claimed too many advisors were afraid to use their brains, preferring to quote experts. Rowe never suffered that malady.

Rowe showered, dressed conservatively in navy blue cotton twill pants, an off-white long-sleeved linen shirt open at the collar, tasseled loafers, and a blazer and left to meet Xibon. Despite the congested DC traffic, he got to the restaurant early and took a table in the back. At exactly noon, a tall, distinguished officer dressed in crisp summer whites arrived, cover in the crook of his left arm and a warm smile on his face. His coarse salt-and-pepper hair was short and freshly cut, his face clean shaven. He greeted the maître d' and strode over to Rowe's table with the confidence of a man who held the lineal number five—fifth highest naval officer in the country.

"Zeke. Nice to see you." He turned toward the waiter hovering at his elbow. "The usual, Mike," and the man hustled off.

Xibon placed his cover on the chair, exuding the aura of a man born to lead. "You want to rejoin, Zero? It hasn't been the same since you left."

Rowe smiled at his old friend, one of the few people who knew Rowe's nickname. It felt right hearing his throaty voice, seeing the twinkle in his eyes, the efficiency of his movements, the quiet authority in everything he did

"After the President's vainglorious bluff, you may need all the warriors you can get."

Xibon's drink arrived—seltzer water with lime—and the two men engaged in small talk for thirty seconds before Xibon dove in.

"I suspect we're not here to swap war stories." His slate-blue eyes turned dark and solemn. "I'm glad you're on my missing sub, Zero. How can I help?"

"We're closing in on it, Cy, but—"

"Wait." The word came out soft, but unassailable. "The President said we found it,"

Rowe paused, deciding the best way to explain this. "Found it, yes, when it shot two dead bodies out its torpedo tubes. Lost it when the outer doors closed." Rowe lowered his voice and explained, "You know about the sub's sonar shield?" Xibon nodded. "The inside of the tubes aren't painted so when the doors open, sonar can find our boys. We get ten seconds."

Cyrus narrowed his eyes. "But you have a solution."

"Do you remember Kali Delamagente?"

Xibon raised an eyebrow. "The beautiful scientist with the AI—what's she call it? Otto? Weren't you seeing her?"

Rowe dodged the question. "She says the shield will wear off in seven days." He fell silent as the waiter distributed the food—fish and salad, dressing on the side for the Admiral and a club sandwich with fries for Rowe.

When the man left, Xibon responded, "A lot can happen in seven days."

"I agree, and the hijackers have demonstrated a willingness to fire the warheads. We need a way to disable them."

Xibon stopped eating, fork in one hand, intense gaze locked onto Rowe. "What are you asking?"

"I need the codes, Cy," how the Navy communicated with an active warhead should the target change and a closely guarded secret. "If the hijackers launch a missile, we need the ability to tell it to self-destruct."

Rowe's phone chirped, as did Xibon's.

"Hey, Bobby—"

"*Virginia* attacked a cruise ship."

Xibon seemed to be getting the same news. The terrorists had called the President's bluff.

The Caribbean
The Carnival Dream

Half of the three thousand passengers aboard the $740-million-dollar British American-owned Carni*val Dream* were milling along the spotless deck, shooting skeet off the bough, sunbathing by the ship's sparkling pools, or enjoying a pre-prandial drink at the poolside bar to work up an appetite for the seven-course farewell dinner. Today marked the end of a five-day Caribbean cruise and they were determined to get their pound of pleasure from the final hours.

A few octogenarians ambled along the starboard bough as the cruise liner steamed home. Several pointed to a bubbly trail burrowing through the water on a course for the ship's back flank. One old WWII vet recognized it, but his warning came too late. The torpedo slammed into the cruise ship, plowed through the extravagantly-furnished staterooms, stopping only when its nose protruded from the opposite side like a tumescent tumor.

The 130,000-ton *Carnival Dream* with one hundred fifty seven-thousand horsepower could sprint at twenty-eight knots flat out, but not with a hole the size of a whale in its hull. The Captain frantically ordered, *Right full rudder, flank spe*ed but there was no way to avoid the second torpedo. This one broke the cruise ship's keel. Screams flooded the sparkling summer sky as passengers caromed off bulkheads or were crushed beneath the crumbling infrastructure.

The call went out to abandon ship. Dozens of guests didn't wait for lifeboats, preferring to leap into the warm Caribbean water. To their surprise and joy, help arrived immediately in the form of a massive gunmetal grey shape that broke the ocean's surface a hundred yards from the sinking ship. The Keyhole satellite orbiting overhead identified the domed profile with its distinctive fin and flat gray conning tower as a *Virginia*-class sub, the United States' most modern attack sub and the tenth Navy vessel named for the Commonwealth of *Virginia*. When seamen popped up from its hatch, the frightened, drowning mass of humanity cheered.

Until the chatter of gunfire erupted and the rescuers executed every man, woman, and child. When no targets remained, the sub submerged and disappeared.

The whole gory massacre took less than five minutes.

Washington DC Restaurant
Table of Adm. Xibon and Dr. Rowe

"Patch me through to *Sampson*...." Xibon had the phone to his ear. *USS Sampson* had been famous six months ago when it intercepted a drug running boat and made the biggest bust ever by a US destroyer.

"Captain? This is Admiral Xibon. I speak with the authority of the CNO. ... *Virginia* attacked a cruise liner in your backyard. ... Yes, I realize sonar shows nothing. Why is complicated... No, Captain, we're getting help for the civilians. Your job is to get that sub. Lock your sonar onto these coordinates," and he provided the latitude-longitude of the attack. "You see something, it means they're attacking. Beat them to it ....You're what?"

Xibon activated speaker. "*Sampson* is under attack."

"TAO, sonar, we have a positive contact, bearing two-seven-zero, range one thousand yards."

The Captain's voice rang out. "Incoming torpedo!" "General quarters!" "Evasive action! Flank speed!"

Xibon's hands balled into fists. "Get out of there," he pleaded through clenched teeth, but he knew *Virginia* was too close. *Sampson* would never get her engines up to full speed fast enough.

Rowe felt the color drain from his face at the thought of the sailors and their families. They proudly put their lives on the line to defend the nation, but who expected it to be America's backyard, dammit.

"It missed!" the voice over the phone cracked with emotion. Rowe slammed his hand down. Silverware bounced and water sloshed over the table cloth. "Captain, Radar. We're not the target. Sonar's picking up cavitation," tiny vacuum bubbles created by propeller rotation. Their collapse emitted an identifiable hiss. "There's a sub on the reciprocal heading from the torpedo launch throwing on speed fast. Two screws—American, at bearing one-eight-zero, range eighty-five hundred yards. It's *Jimmy Carter*."

Xibon jumped up and yelled over his shoulder as he left, "I'll see about those codes."

Rowe nearly knocked his chair over following Xibon from the restaurant. The only upside of this was if *Virginia* was in the Caribbean, it couldn't reach the Sea of Japan in six days.

Chapter Forty-six

Day Eighteen, Thursday, August 24th
***The Caribbean, aboard the* USS Jimmy Carter**

Jimmy Carter was a special operations submarine tasked with counter-intelligence work. In this case, it had been called in to play 'rabbit' so *Sampson* could practice ASW—anti-submarine warfare—tracking. This was common among US warships, to keep themselves sharp in case the real thing arrived. Since the last naval battle was the Falklands—and that was the Brits—the crew figured this would be as authentic as they ever got.

They concluded the exercise an hour ago at which time the Captain, a twenty-year veteran of three different classes of submarines, ordered all engines stop, no noise, while they waited for International Maritime Organization identifying number 246433—a Carnival cruise liner—to leave the area at which time *Carter* would proceed with assigned duties of collecting electronic intelligence, anything from wiretaps to cell phone traces to cyberthreats.

Then, out of the blue, two torpedoes slammed into the cruise ship.

"Sonar, where did those fish come from?"

"There was a blip, but it disappeared. No subs in the area," came the frightened but puzzled voice of the twenty-six-year-old Sonar Technician First Class on his second tour of duty aboard *Jimmy Carter*. "I don't even pick up screw noises," the steady, throbbing, syncopated beat made as each propeller blade cut through the turbulence from the sub's rudder and stern planes. "It must be dead in the water."

How the hell did sonar miss an enemy sub? A second later, his Sonar Tech yelled, "Torpedo in the water! Bearing zero-zero-zero, range four thousand yards."

"General quarters! Initiate evasive action."

"Initiating evasive action, aye, Sir!"

"Identity."

The Sonar Tech replied, "Screw count indicates a *Virginia* class—one of ours."

That fit a FLASH message the Captain had received. "Word is she's invisible to sonar. Fire two torpedoes the general direction where those fish originated. Let's see if we can spook her."

"Fire One! Fire Two!" "Conn, sonar, second enemy fish in the water. Range thirty-four hundred yards, bearing zero-zero-zero."

The captain barked, "String nixie and energize MICM!" This was a cable run behind the sub to simulate its magnetic hull. Attached to the end was the Nixie which simulated propeller sounds. Together, they hoped to trick the torpedo into locking onto a false signal.

"Helm, hard right rudder, course one-two-eight, full speed ahead."

The Helm repeated the order and snapped the wheel to the right. The torpedo bought the nixie's deception and exploded one hundred yards off *Carter's* left rudder. The submarine rocked violently. Lights flickered, dimmed, and reasserted themselves.

"Damage control!" Two submariners injured. Three leaks, but everything contained.

"Captain, both our fish missed."

The Captain clenched his jaw. "Put the second torpedo on speakers."

"Aye, Captain." A rhythmic churning noise flooded the room with an underlying hiss. It softened the longer they listened. "Second torpedo past and opening." It missed them.

"Prepare tubes one and two. Be ready to lock onto a signature." If the bastard fired again, *Jimmy Carter* would be ready. "Helm, left fifteen degrees rudder."

The Captain initiated a series of rapid-fire orders to find his attacker, but got nothing. After three minutes, he changed tactics. They would hide in the bottom ridge terrain until the enemy gave up and then skedaddle back to port. "Prepare to dive, twenty degrees."

The navigator responded crisply, "We are rigged to dive." "Dive!"

The alarm blared as the boat's nose plowed through the murky depths.

"Passing three hundred feet, sir... Passing four hundred fifty feet... six hundred feet."

"Level off below the thermocline," the layer of ocean where temperatures changed so rapidly, it minimized the ability of sonar to find a sub. In the Captain's mind, it balanced out *Virginia's* sonar shield. "Engines one-third."

There they hovered, well below any depth *Virginia* would expect to find them. The sea looked like tar except for a splash of whitecaps overhead. Five minutes, ten, and then thirty while the Captain imagined *Virginia* sniffing around for them. Sound gave a sub away faster than anything else and right now, *Jimmy Carter's* noise footprint was close to invisible.

The Captain whispered, "Steady course one-eight-zero. Use ship's depth versus bottom terrain to prevent our signature carrying into the deep sound channel."

"Aye, Captain."

Day Nineteen, Friday, August 25th
The Caribbean, aboard the USS Sampson

When *Jimmy Carter* reached port, the Captain credited *Virginia's* crew for his escape. "They did everything right, but a beat slow, which provided a window of escape for us. They saved our lives."

Eight hours passed before the destroyer *Sampson* got its next bite.

"Sonobuoy thirty-seven has active contact! Range nineteen thousand two hundred yards," *Sampson's* helo squawked.

"Torpedo launched! Bearing zero seven eight! It appears to be dead in the water."

The Captain frowned. Fish didn't stall. "Mark location. We'll come back."

Two ASW helos tried to box *Virginia* in with a curtain of depth charges until they ran out of fuel and were forced to return to base. After three hours and no sign of the sub, *Sampson* steamed back to the 'dead fish' marker.

"Send down a bomb bot. Let's see what we have before bringing it aboard," the Captain ordered.

An hour later, they dragged a body bag onto the deck. The Captain bent over the corpse whose throat had been cut. Pain washed through his eyes, replaced by a cold glare.

"This is Jumah Najafian—Joey." His voice trailed off. Joey was one of the good guys, popular with the crew, known for excellent work. No surprise these murderers singled him out, always faithful to Allah but an outspoken critic of the 'crazies' hijacking his religion. "Get word to Command we have him. His brother should be notified."

The *Carnival Dream* would go down in history as the first cruise ship sunk by torpedo since WWI's British-registered Lusitania, coincidentally operated by Cunard who now owned Carnival. When survivors recounted how the gunmen who mowed down civilians shouting *Allahu Akhbar*—the war cry of Islamic fundamentalism—Western journalists reminded readers Islam was a religion of peace and love. They noted Muslims decried the type of waste and debauchery flaunted on the cruise ship. *So you see,* they concluded, *blame is shared.*

Islamic mosques around the world offered prayers for the dead, explaining to the distraught families that loved ones lived a glorious life with Allah and the Prophets in Paradise, all praise and honor to their souls. In private, they wondered why Allah, praise be to his name, would allow the infidel to strike such a virulent blow in His name.

The French offered condolences to the American President, but explained this would never happen in France for they lived in peace with their Muslim countrymen. The American President didn't bother to remind the French diplomats that people from thirty-one nations died on the cruise ship, including France.

"Where's it headed, folks?" James couldn't hide his exasperation.

Rowe brought up a world map that plotted *Virginia* sightings. "Al-Zahrawi will want to keep our attention on *Virginia* so whatever is unfolding in the Sea of Japan can do so unmolested. Find high-value targets reachable from the Caribbean in five days. That includes major cities along the US East Coast, oil wells in the Gulf of Mexico and off

Venezuela, Disney World," and he listed fifteen other locations.

Conventional wisdom said the US should batten down the Capitol hatches, but no one since the Civil War had launched a naval attack on the Eastern seaboard. No one thought it possible.

James adjusted his tie. "We can't protect that many places. Narrow the list," and the analysts went to work.

Rowe shuffled to the back of the conference room and called Duck.

"Kali's fine Zero, but Eitan's trying to reach you. He's frantic."

Sun frantic was an oxymoron. Before Rowe even said hello, Sun started. "Get a SEAL team to coordinates," and he rattled off a latitude and longitude.

Rowe frowned. SEAL Teams were spread thin between the attacks on American ships and potential threats, but Sun was never rash and always right.

"I'll call Cy. Anything else, Eitan?"

"Activate the F-15."

Two hours after the attack on the *Carnival Dream*, James received a copy of a satellite message intercepted by SIGINT. It instructed *Virginia* to proceed to its final location. The sub had surfaced to receive the message; the cruise ship was extra. James set up a PUOL—permanent-until-over-location— for the Task Force within the National Counter Terrorism Center and he and Rowe moved into a nearby hotel.

Kali stayed at the safe house with Otto. The AI searched in concentric circles from *Virginia's* last location, but the constant need to recalculate for the change in the ocean temperatures, salinity, movement, and the variance of other minute characteristics proved too much even for his robust proficiency. The sub escaped.

It would be five days before the paint degraded enough to expose *Virginia*. That could be too late.

And where was Mohammed?

Chapter Forty-seven

Day Twenty, Saturday, August 26th,
FBI Safe House

Kali poked her head into Sean's room. He got up an hour ago, heated corn dogs for dinner, but fell asleep without eating them. Duck had appeared out of nowhere, carried Sean to his room, took the corn dogs, a bag of chips, two apples, eight cookies, and evaporated.

Two hours later she had a break-through. The survivors said they saw the sub, but the metamaterials should have made the sub invisible.

"Otto. Run a simulation. The paint makes subs invisible to sonar. Does the same formula make it invisible to visual?"

Otto whirred and then beeped. "No. In adapting the formula to sonar waves, it seems to have lost the ability to cloak visual."

"Access the satellite photos around *Virginia* when it attacked the cruise liner." Photos populated his desktop, but one caught his attention: *Virginia*, floating amidst the debris.

"I have something else we should share with Zeke."

"What's that?" Kali was no longer surprised Otto read her mind.

"Terror cells in Europe and North America use chat rooms for covert communications, but in North Korea, because their infrastructure is undependable, they hand-carry messages. I have been forced to find them physically via satellite images."

Kali hid a smile. "The trials of a cybersleuth."

Otto tilted his head up so his gleaming eyes focused on hers. "Why would I want to? Oh! You're accepting fate. I understand. But still, I have found something that seems pertinent."

When he told Kali what he found, she called Zeke.

"May I help you?"

Kali stopped. A receptionist on Zeke's phone? "Yes, I'm calling Dr. Zeke Rowe."

"May I take your number and have him call you?"

Kali considered that for a nanosecond. "I'll wait while you get him."

The woman sighed. "I'm sorry. He is not to be disturbed, Ms... Delamagente. I'll let him know you called."

Otto rolled over. "Would you like me to locate Zeke?"

Kali narrowed her eyes. "By all means." Did the woman think Kali was checking on dinner plans?

Within seconds, Otto found Zeke's cell phone. "I don't believe his phone is with him."

"Damn!"

"That was merely an observation, Kali," Otto continued. "I can sample lines in the near vicinity if you believe he would leave his cell close to where he is."

"Go for it."

Otto chirred, "I located his voice. Shall I get his attention?"

Kali raised an eyebrow. "Let him know the little lady would like to speak to him," and then waved her hands in the air. "Just kidding, Otto. Tell him we uncovered critical information."

She imagined the surprise to not Zeke, but the others in the room when Otto said, "Hello, Zeke. Kali and I have uncovered what she considers to be of critical importance."

After a full three seconds, Zeke responded, "Otto? I hope you have good news. This end is depressing."

"This is Kali, Zeke. First, the sub is only invisible to sonar, not visual."

Zeke grunted. "We'll put the word out."

"And, I found Ankour Mohammed's father. He's Kim Soon Young—"

"The *Wonsu* of DPRK."

The babble of voices quieted behind him and someone asked, "What's a *Wonsu*?"

"The most senior military officer in North Korea, equivalent to our top Army General. That changes everything. Mohammed's father isn't hoping to curry favor with superiors. He wants to establish North Korean dominance in world geopolitics."

Chapter Forty-eight

Day Twenty-one, Sunday, August 27th, Mid-day
USS Bunker Hill, *somewhere west of Hawaii*

SLQ32—called 'Slick 32' by operators—identified
the ship as a *Luhu*-class Chinese destroyer. It appeared after
the SAG group's frigate, destroyer, and sub detached. The
Captain explained to the crew that every available ship was
protecting American shores. *Bunker Hill* was certainly
capable of handling anything from North Korea. To his
officers, the Captain explained the hijacker's willingness to
use *Virginia* militaristically made the sub a greater threat
than the missile launch.

Then *Bunker Hill* picked up the Chinese destroyer.
The Captain called General Quarters and armed all
weapons in case the Chinese wanted payback for *Virginia's*
attack on their carrier.

"Combat, *Luhu's* position."

"Range thirteen thousand yards. Bearing zero-four-
zero, speed fifteen knots, course three-zero-zero."

The enemy continued to match *Bunker Hill's* every
rate and directional change.

"TAO. Sonar. Second contact bearing one-six-five, range thirty thousand yards! I see a periscope."

The Captain ordered, "Alter course to two-nine-zero. Let's see if it follows." The sub mirrored the direction change. The Captain smiled. "Return course to zero-four-zero." Again the sub mirrored *Bunker Hill.* "Good."

Paloma stared at the Captain. What was good about being shadowed?

Sonar reported, "It's diving... It's gone."

"Captain," the Radar Control Officer broke in. "Something was stuck to the periscope. I'll zoom in on the image." He blew up the thin strand of cable protruding above the ocean's surface.

Paloma gasped. "It's the Texas State flag."

"*USS Texas*, SSN 775, hiding in the *Luhu's* baffles where the destroyer couldn't see it, but we would." The Captain grinned. "That stays in this room."

Around 2200, the Chinese destroyer left. By 2235, Paloma fell asleep, dreaming of shaking hands with the *Texas* crew who risked their lives to let her ship know they had friends.

Chapter Forty-nine

Day Twenty-two, Monday, August 28th, evening
Washington DC, NCTC HQ

Rowe rubbed his raw eyes, nerves frayed from another day fueled by coffee. Seventy-two hours and still nothing. They missed something— Sun, James, himself— but what? He opened the file to the first page and started over.

And put it down. His brain felt sticky and he'd been running on adrenaline too long. James's team whispered in huddled groups, ties loosened, faces grey with exhaustion, desperate to solve this puzzle before disaster again struck. James stood tensely in his office, door ajar, arguing with a group of analysts. Time to catch a nap. Not real sleep, just a light doze, a smidgeon under awareness, mind edging on awake.

Five minutes later, he stood in his hotel room, in the shower, inhaling the steam, letting hot water sink into his pores and wishing it would wash the fog from his mind. He reached fifty percent when his phone rang. Bobby.

"Get back here, Zeke. We got another message buoy."

Rowe threw on fresh jeans and a shirt, ran a comb through his hair, and took a cab back. He passed through the metal detector, bypassed the elevator and pounded up the stairs two at a time to the third floor, badged the guard at the door, and rushed inside buzzing with adrenaline.

Everyone looked like they'd been poked with a pin. Rowe nudged the nearest person—Carlos. Rowe fished his name out of the fog of memory. An MIT grad who chose the FBI over Microsoft when his sister died in Desert Storm.

"Carlos. What did I miss?"

The techie's pants were rolled up off his shoes and his hair might have been combed with a pitchfork. He shot a look over the top of smudged glasses. "They found *Virginia's* message buoy in the attack site debris. They airlifted it to CENTCOM and forwarded it to us."

"Hunh." Message buoys were noisy. Smart to launch it during the attack.

Carlos grinned. "Those crazies got more than they bargained for taking an American sub. Our *Virginia* boys are pissed off."

Rowe thanked him and zagged his way to the front of the room. They'd received a message. *Torpedoes disabled. VLS in progress.*

The room erupted in cheers as a wave of energy washed over the exhausted crowd.

Rowe inched closer to James. "That'll take the teeth out of the sub's offense. We may not need those codes from Cy after all."

"Firing on a fellow warship annoys our boys." He leaned back, eyes flat as pebbles, black circles beneath them. "How do you disable torpedoes?"

"I'd go after the torpedo tube shutter door assemblies. They're protected from sabotage outside the sub, but not inside."

James swayed and reached a hand out to balance himself. Rowe could say something, but he respected a man who pushed his limits.

James flipped the note over. "They also gave us an address—604 Park Place. You and Duck track it down."

Rowe hustled to his car, awake now, and stowed his Colt under the front seat with extra ammunition clips. As he plugged the directions into the GPS, Duck jumped in. Thirty minutes later, Rowe crossed the bay with its sailboats and pleasure craft and happy people without a care in the world, then zigged over to Park Place's neighborhood.

"Al-alah took a water tour of this area."

Duck found the address on Google Earth. "It's south of Annapolis, a short drive from Washington, and walking distance to Herron Bay off Rockhold Creek. From here, you can get a lot of places really fast by boat."

After twenty minutes of exploring, Rowe turned onto Park Place. The front yards were squares of ratty grass. In the driveway of one house slouched a broken down Chevy, in another a bike rack with two bent bikes chained together. Halfway down the block, a roll-off body overflowed with yard clippings.

Rowe bobbed his head toward a one-story low-slung house badly in need of paint. "That's Al-alah's car. He should have gotten rid of it." Rowe tingled.

As they edged by the house, Rowe saw Al-alah through the bay window, sitting at a computer wearing a white dashiki, face calm, beard nicely trimmed around his weathered scholarly face, eyes focused. Rowe pretended the car stalled two doors down, got out, raised the hood and tinkered as he surveyed the area. People went on errands, visited neighbors, one accepted a FedEx delivery. No one paid the two strangers any attention.

Ten minutes passed and Rowe stood with an exasperated sigh, slammed the hood shut and let his eyes rove as though in need of help until they landed on Al-alah, still at his computer. Rowe stomped down the street, somewhat hidden in the shadow of a string of maple trees, and stopped at the sidewalk leading to Al-alah's door. He scratched his head and peered in the front window, then muttered and approached the front door while Duck snuck around the rear.

"Hello!" he called out, mixing friendly with irritation as he pounded on the battered screen door. No movement. He pounded again. "Mister! My damn car broke down! My friends are waiting at the harbor. My dal-garn cell is out of juice. I'll pay you to borrow your phone."

Al-alah ignored Rowe.

Rowe rapped again. "Hey, buddy! I see you. I'm in bad shape out here!"

Rowe caught Al-alah's eye and gestured for him to open the door.

When Al-alah shook his head, Rowe rang the bell. "It'll only take a moment, buddy. I need to use your phone is all, not have dinner with you. Hey, maybe you'll call for me. Would that be OK? Or would you drive me to the bay? It's real close."

Al-alah waived a brusque hand, *Go away*.

"I got my Triple A card. You call. Tell them what-the-hell this fuckin-address is."

A splintering sound erupted from the back of the house. Al-alah turned and lurched out of sight. Rowe heard a scuffle, a painful yelp, and then Duck's grinning face appeared at the door, one arm around Al-alah's throat and the other holding a gun to the slight man's head.

"Al-alah says come in. Where are his manners?"

Rowe limped in as Duck patted Al-alah down and threw him into the chair by his computer. The terrorist stumbled and slammed his hand into the keyboard to steady himself. Rowe pulled the curtains while Duck searched the house, and then called James.

"I'm ten minutes away. Don't let him out of your sight. He'd just as soon die for Allah as talk to the enemy. Don't let him."

Patience was someone else's virtue, but after two minutes, Rowe was bored. Maybe Al-alah would volunteer information.

"Talk to us, Mr. Al-alah Sir. We're nice. Our friend Bobby is pretty mad about the hijacked sub, one-hundred-plus dead submariners, thousands of dead on the cruise ship and carrier, and you scaring thirty thousand civilians."

Al-alah studied Rowe. "I saw you yesterday. I thought American spies were stealthy."

Rowe held his hand up. "Thanks to your friends in Afghanistan, I'm no longer a spy."

The terrorist offered a slight smile. "They must have liked you. They didn't take your hands." His gaze scooted to the computer screen. "Or your eyes."

Rowe flashed back to Al-alah's stumble. "He's deleting the hard drive."

Rowe snatched the laptop and watched helplessly as data raced by on the screen. He pushed escape, stabbed the power button, and then slammed the keyboard on the floor. The keys splattered, but it continued to whir.

His phone rang. "What?"

"Zeke. I got something for you."

Kali. Just who he needed. "Me, first. Al-alah is erasing his hard drive. How do I stop it?"

"Pop the battery out, and then bring the computer to me. I'll see what I can recover."

The computer immediately powered down. He breathed a sigh. "What's up, Kali?"

"I found where Ankour Mohammed will be August 30th. He's meeting his dad in North Korea."

That was in two days, the same day North Korea launched the missile. "You're an angel."

Rowe checked his watch. Eight minutes till Bobby arrived. He paced in a circle, and then leaned against the wall, arms crossed over his chest. Then his left foot moved, his mouth opened, and he wet his lips. Outside, a basketball bounced and a chainsaw roared. Rowe scratched first his arm, then his shoulder, and then swatted at an invisible fly.

Duck eyed his friend. "You wait much longer, you're gonna need a safe word."

Ten minutes, one second and Rowe dragged a chair six inches in front of Al-alah, eyes glued to the prisoner like a Doberman to raw meat.

"We know your plan, Nasr. We have a few questions."

When Al-alah snickered, Rowe backfisted him hard on his temple.

"The rules have changed, Professor. Yesterday you might have been winning, but not today. You want proof?" As though Al-alah answers, he continued, "I know everyone in your honors class at NYU Abu Dhabi. You started with ten geniuses. Three died on *Triumph*. Three more are on *Virginia*." Rowe was guessing, but figured he was close. "The last four will be in custody week's end. That has to put a wrench in your jihad."

Al-alah took off his glasses to inspect the lenses. "You think you know, but you don't."

"Ankour Mohammed, ne Yong Soon Young, aka Gil-dong, is the reason we're so close. He's talented, but too young for spy work." Rowe tsked. "Do you read Shakespeare? He was popular when your religion last conceived an original thought. Like all Mr. Shakespeare's characters, Mohammed has a fatal flaw: Pride."

Al-alah looked confused.

"Mohammed's pride serving Allah has become revenge against Paloma Chacone for rejecting him and you for stepping on his honor. First, you forced him to work with females and then forbade him punishing them. Those were mistakes."

When Al-alah's temple pulsed, Rowe knew he hit a nerve. He pulled his chair forward until their knees touched. Muslims hated physical contact with the infidel. The man shuddered and Rowe crowded him more.

"Turns out Anchor cares less for Islam than impressing the man who threw him out of North Korea years ago."

Al-alah flinched at the use of Mohammed's nickname.

"When he told Dad about your cell of brilliant students, Dad immediately saw their usefulness to deflect attention from his country's space-based weapon launch. In return for his son's support, he offered the approval Anchor wanted his entire life. With guidance from Dad, Anchor's goal morphed from serving Allah to regaining his personal honor."

Duck sucked his breath in. "He chose Kim Jung-un over Allah? That's harsh."

Al-alah should have been furious, but the corners of his mouth rose. Why not? He had hijacked two submarines, the West's reputation was in tatters, and an American cruiser was in his sites.

But Rowe knew where to poke his verbal stick.

"Now, this is important, Doc. I'll speak more slowly if you like. Here is why you'll lose: Salah Mahmud al-Zahrawi. He wants Mohammed to hijack *Bunker Hill*, not to assist in your jihad but to deflect attention from his own end game."

Surprise popped into Al-alah's eyes. "I know all about the warning you received. Turns out, so does Anchor and he believes you'll lose. The phone call I just got? Anchor already considers you dead. You knew al-Zahrawi was cleaning up loose ends—first Oliver Najafian, then

Norman Krakhower and Sean Delamagente—but why would he kill you?"

Rowe rolled his eyes. "Man's a psychopath. That's all you need to know."

Al-alah met Rowe's glare. "I cannot betray al-Zahrawi. You of all people understand why."

"Give me the word, you'll be as protected as a mullah's mistress." Duck shook his head. "I'll go first. Anchor is not going to blow *Bunker Hill* up. He's giving it to his father."

Al-alah lurched. "You lie. He will destroy the ship to destroy the female Paloma Chacone. Our jihad will succeed!"

Rowe waited for Al-alah to continue, but the professor's lips had become a tight line.

"We know Taggert's your mole. We've already told the captain."

Al-alah jerked. "Mohammed told you—"But he stopped.

Rowe grinned, feeling it come together. "I have only one more question: Why's al-Zahrawi want *Virginia*? Tell the truth, I'll protect you. Lie and I'll tell everyone you betrayed them."

"Stand down, Zeke, Duck." James pressed into the room, his team inches behind him. Duck grimaced, but moved away to allow the hand-off.

Rowe turned to James to update him before he took the prisoner. With Rowe's back turned, Al-alah hit himself in the mouth.

Duck yelled, "He's swallowing poison!" Al-alah frothed, eyes rolling back, crimson dripping where he bit his tongue. "Call the medics!"

No one started CPR. The ME pronounced Al-alah at 4:02 pm.

Rowe tore the house apart, checked vents, under the floorboards, in the toilet tank, even shined a flashlight down the drains, but found no hard drive backups. He couldn't stop thinking about what had bothered him since the sub disappeared: Why did al-Zahrawi need *Virginia*?

Chapter Fifty

Day Twenty-two, Monday, August 28th, Night
Somewhere over the Atlantic

The sun shone bright and pure above the stench of what imperialists called 'progress'. He was on another plane ride, this one home, where his father awaited him with open arms. The General himself had arranged Mohammed's extraction from the Great Satan and provided his son's newest disguise, the uniform of South Korea's military.

Mohammed would be glowing except for his repeated failure to kill the boy. Though chased off by police, Mohammed had returned at 1 am to find mother and son gone. A light shone one apartment down so he pounded on the door, pasted a concerned frown on his face and claimed to be a friend of Kali's, here to tell her about... well, a dead aunt. The geezer squinted at him, spit onto the ground and slammed the door. Rage boiled over and he crashed through the thin wood entrance only to find himself staring down the barrel of a shotgun. The man's hand was rock steady, gaze unblinking. He demanded Mohammed leave and pumped the shotgun. The *ch-ching* sent ice water through Mohammed's veins.

How hard could it be to follow her from her office? Except, she didn't show up for work that day or the next.

He would have continued to wait, but Nasr said Mohammed must get ready for the final step. To the youth's surprise, Nasr entrusted him with eight *mujahedeen*, more than enough to accomplish his goal, if not Nasr's.

As they kissed goodbye, Nasr said, "When you complete your task, go to NYU Abu Dhabi library study carrels every afternoon at 2 with a copy of *The Communist Manifesto*. Al-Zahrawi will find you."

As Mohammed drove away, he passed the man he recognized as Zeke Rowe and knew Nasr would die today. With Nasr dead, Mohammed would kill Paloma.

Chapter Fifty-one

***Day Twenty-three, Tuesday, August 29th, late morning
New York, FBI safe house***

Kali slapped herself, took a cold shower, and
brushed her teeth. Her face was still frightening, all dark
shadows, red eyes, and pale skin. She made coffee and took
thick mugs to Duck and her protection detail, and then
returned to work. Tomorrow marked the deadline.

As the sun cast its first luminescent glow over the
landscape, Kali sighed. "What a beautiful day, Eitan.
Normal people will have picnic lunches, take walks in the
park, and go to movies. Not try to save the world."

Eitan poured orange juice, popped open a bag of
peanut butter-stuffed pretzels, and dropped it on the table
with a half-eaten bag of cheese-flavored popcorn. "But
they'll eventually ask what they accomplished with their
lives. You and I will know.

"Chinese should be here within the half hour.
Umm. Which episode is this?" He nodded toward the
Stargate marathon he and Kali had on as background noise
while they worked. A news alert interrupted.

"A San Diego naval officer's boyfriend is wanted for questioning in her murder. She was found dead, throat slashed, after meeting him for dinner."

Mohammed's picture popped up. Eitan blanched and sweat prickled his forehead.

"Paloma is at sea, Eitan."

He gulped and bobbed his head. Kali looked— really looked—at her genius friend for the first time in days. His intelligent eyes were sunken and bloodshot, his thinning hair stuck out like porcupine quills, and his fingers were stained orange up to the second knuckle.

He dialed James on speaker. "I decrypted Barot's plan. It's quite simple—elegant even. He suggests blowing up the submarine's nuclear reactor in shallow water while the sub cannot dive. In this way, the explosion goes up, not out and down where it would be neutralized by water. I'm sending it to you and Zeke."

He yawned. "What about Taggert? Even though Al-alah as much as admitted he was the mole, I still need proof."

"Umm. He received another deposit yesterday."

James told the Secretary of Defense who told the Vice Admiral of the Strike Group that Taggert continued to receive money. Despite a heated discussion, they refused to declare a decorated officer and twenty-year member of the naval community a danger to his ship without solid proof from someone not an enemy. But, they would fax Mohammed's picture to *Bunker Hill* in case he showed up.

"Bobby, I just got the warhead codes. Otto will be prepared to use them should the need arise," though that seemed unnecessary now, thanks to the tenacious *Virginia* crew.

"Ms. Delamagente, did you order Chinese?"

Eitan piped in, "I did. Gotta go, Bobby. Food," and he disconnected.

"It's here," and the doorbell rang.

As Eitan opened the door, Kali's brain screamed a warning about first the man's scar, and then the gun aimed at Eitan.

"It's been a long time."

Eitan calmly observed the man who had once tried to kill Kali and Zeke.

Al-Zahrawi grinned. "The codes, Kalian, or I will shoot Dr. Sun?"

"All they stop is *Virginia's* weapons, nothing with *Bunker Hill.*"

Al-Zahrawi smiled. "I care nothing for *Bunker Hill*. Mohammed is working his own little plan to acquire those. Once I have *Virginia's*, I will reprogram the weapons to respond only to my new code. You will do anything I ask until I run out of nuclear warheads—and anything else she's loaded with."

Kali glanced at Eitan and he offered a subtle nod. "Send them to him, Otto."

A moment later, al-Zahrawi smiled. "Thank you. I'm sorry to do this." He turned his weapon on Otto.

"Before you end my existence, Mr. al-Zahrawi, do you mind if I ask a few questions about your religion." Kali knew from experience al-Zahrawi would be unable to resist a cerebral, intellectual conversation so while he carried on what Otto turned into a friendly conversation, Kali leaned forward so she could reach her purse under the table at her feet, pulled the 38 she'd once known like the back of her hand from her purse, and fired. She winged al-Zahrawi, who then fled. Three burly agents flew in, weapons raised. Two raced off after the terrorist while one remained.

Eitan turned toward her. "When did you learn to shoot?"

"When I realized I needed to. As Zeke taught me, words only take you so far."

She called Zeke and broke the news to him. "Al-Zahrawi stole the codes to *Virginia*."

Zeke answered, not nearly as upset as Kali expected, "I'm counting on the crew to finish what they started. What worries me more is that al-Zahrawi thinks Mohammed can get the codes for *Bunker Hill*."

Chapter Fifty-two

Day Twenty-four, Wednesday August 30th, morning
The Sea of Japan, **USS Bunker Hill CG 52**

Bunker Hill assumed its station south of the thirty-eighth parallel, between South Korea and Japan, and prepared to track the Taepodong-2 missile from Musudan-ri to its projected crash site between the Japanese islands of Tobi-shima and Awa-shima. Because *Bunker Hill* was a half-mile within what North Korea unilaterally designated a 'no sail' zone, the Communist dictatorship declared the cruiser's presence an Act of War and *Bunker Hill* bounced its alert status up to Condition II-AD, Air Defense.

The question: What would North Korea do?

Paloma trained her binoculars on what would be the green verdure of North Korea's coastline if she could see it. Overhead, *Bunker Hill's* four powerful SPY Phased-array radar scanned for air contacts. This stretch of ocean from Japan to Australia was home base to the 7th Fleet, the world's largest deployment of cruisers, amphibs, carriers, destroyers, frigates, and subs. Normally, intel would seamlessly pass from one to the other, enabling *Bunker Hill* to engage enemies through the eyes of the most forward ship.

Not today. Though every bit of intel screamed something more perilous than a communications satellite would be launched, *Bunker Hill* floated alone, its mind quiet like 7 of 9 without the Borg hive. Every available ship was busy defending America's shores or hunting *Virginia*. To Paloma, it felt worse than lonely. It felt dangerous.

But *Bunker Hill* had one trick up its sleeve the terrorists' threats had not been able to strip from its armory: the SH-60F Sea Hawk. Manned by the infamous anti-submarine Squadron Fourteen, the chopper provided a line of sight that penetrated into North Korea. Its FLIR—Forward-Looking Infrared—provided thermal imaging and infrared to see through the worst storm or fog of war, and Hawklink gave it instantaneous communication with the ship. The Hellfire missiles—a nickname for 'helicopter-launched fire-and-forget'—and .20mm Gatling gun made it a formidable ally and fearsome opponent.

Paloma took one final sweep and headed down to Combat. Sixty minutes to launch, thirty to her watch as TAO. She wanted one final check before her watch started.

"Ma'am." The Watch Supervisor greeted Paloma as she approached the LSD, Large Screen Display. Ten sets of sailor's eyes locked onto the monitors, their sole duty to detect, identify, and neutralize threats.

A blip appeared on Operations Specialist Second Class Sally Jimenez's screen.

"Incoming air contact."

Two years in the Navy, a single mother of two after losing her husband in a car crash. Jimenez's mother took care of her children when she deployed. She had worked with Paloma on each of the training exercises for this tasking.

IFF—Identification Friend or Foe—queried the blip. Paloma visualized the signal sweeping the horizon for the transponder required on every plane and ship. Once located, it spontaneously reported home country and military status. At the same time, SLQ32 analyzed the radio frequencies of the contact and SPY calculated its kinematics—altitude, bearing, and range. In this way, *Bunker Hill* identified and categorized every contact.

"Contact corresponds to IFF code SR 364849, Mode 3," or civilian. Jimenez brought up the database of commercial flights over the Sea of Japan. "Korean Air Flight 7 out of Seoul. No response."

IFF would re-query in five seconds. The tension ratcheted up. Chatter slowed.

TAO said, "EW, do you have anything along bearing two-eight-zero."

"Stand by, sir."

"Still no IFF response." From Jimenez.

The Combat Systems Coordinator—CSC— reported, "It's inside our Assessment Zone and closing."

TAO ordered, "Query them again."

The entire room held its breath. Paloma wanted to see what the TAO would do next, knowing in fifteen minutes, this would be her position.

EW came on the netlink. "TAO. EW. Signal corresponds to a private plane. No listed offensive weapons in the database."

"Captain. TAO. Weapons control solution prepared," because a private plane could be a disguised military threat. "Recommend monitoring air contact, but avoid firing until necessary."

One of *Bunker Hill's* SM-2's could knock it out of the sky in thirty seconds if need be.

The Bridge broke in. "We're picking up a VHF signal," which was unusual. "Is it from a surface contact, Radar?"

"None out there, Sir."

Paloma did some rapid calculations in her head. With the duct readings they had this morning, it could be from the plane.

TAO asked as though he read her mind, "What's the range to the plane?"

CSC: "Ninety miles."

The Bridge broke in. "We're picking up a bridge-to-bridge hail from the plane."

Jimenez: "Unidentified aircraft, turn on your IFF."

A frightened male voice came over the speakers, "We can't. Our government—North Korea—threatened all planes leaving during this time frame. We would have waited, but we have a patient who will die without treatment and his doctor is in Indonesia."

TAO paused, nodding to something the Captain said into his comm., and then, "Thanks. Good luck with your patient."

The room breathed a collective sigh, but Paloma knew this meant trouble. Forcing planes to turn off their IFF could spook *Bunker Hill* into an international incident.

Eitan was right.

Forty-five minutes to launch. Paloma left to continue rounds. She reached the quarterdeck to the *whp, whp, whp* of the SH-60 helo as it dropped a sonobuoy line northwest of *Bunker Hill*, the likely angle of a sub approach. The helo would be airborne for the duration.

She paused before climbing to the Bridge and peered east. Japan lay hidden behind a curtain of fog, its Patriot interceptor missile batteries armed and ready. They were ground zero if all went to hell. Sixty years ago, Japan was the enemy. Now, the Rising Sun had become America's ally. It didn't want the national headstone to read, 'We were ready for China, but not North Korea.'

She stepped onto the port Bridge wing. Petty Officer 3rd Class Drew Collins stood by the M240 doing maintenance, a cup of coffee steaming by his left foot.

"Ready, Collins?"

He looked at her, eyes like flint. "Yes, ma'am. No one's gonna hurt us without a ballbuster of a fight." He flushed. "Sorry, ma'am."

Paloma smiled, but said nothing. Collins gulped half his coffee in one swallow, gazing at the horizon. "Ma'am. D'you think this is how sailors felt in WWII?"

Paloma turned toward the twenty-year-old Petty Officer. No one on the ship had experienced battle, including herself. Would Collins bravely face his end? She chewed her lip, thinking how to address this serious young man.

"McCandless is a road running through the Naval Academy, named for a Communications Officer who won the Medal of Honor during WWII. When all superior officers aboard his ship died, he assumed command though grievously wounded and fired on an overwhelming force. This emboldened other American vessels and they beat back the Japanese in what became an amazing victory. He stepped into the breach."

Collins grunted. "Don't know if I'm always that brave, but I can be once."

Paloma felt a gush of emotion, but settled for a nod. "Most of *Bunker Hill's* positions are manned by untested sailors, all willing to do their best. That will be enough."

She got an update from Combat. "Thirty-five minutes." She made two hard fists to squeeze the shake from her hands.

"Captain on the Bridge!" Captain Pearson strode through the rear doors and up to the Bridge windows. Paloma had served for two years with this Captain. She respected his leadership and his instincts. A graduate of USNA and Naval Post-Graduate School, this would be his last command before retiring. He'd purchased a boat down in Florida and planned to take groups out fishing, come home evenings and sit in a rocking chair on the porch with his wife. For thirty years, he put the Navy first and meant to change that.

The Captain said, "OOD. Tell Combat I'm on my way," and left for Combat, Paloma a step behind. She'd prepared her entire career for what might happen in the next thirty minutes. If everything went wrong, it would be her job as TAO to make sure her ship survived.

Everyone worked for the TAO when the ship was in battle.

Chapter Fifty-three

Day Twenty-four, Wednesday August 30th, late morning
The Sea of Japan, **USS Bunker Hill CG 52**

"Five minutes to launch, sir."

"Arm the weapons."

By the time the watch had turned over to Paloma, she already knew everything about *Bunker Hill's* current status—not what the specs said, but the status quo. All four engines were online which meant she could order up thirty plus knots if needed. SPY was scanning at high power 360 with one sector focused on the North Korean launch. All her 400 Hz converters were aligned for maximum output. She knew exactly what her ship could do at this moment. What she didn't know was the threat.

"Two minutes."

She'd have an answer in two minutes.

"Zero minutes to launch!"

For a second, Combat was silent. Paloma imagined the Taepodong-2 lifting off the launch pad, the powerful Iranian-designed boosters catapulting the unknown payload into space. A communications satellite would establish a geosynchronous orbit over the Sea of Japan where it would facilitate North Korean communications. A weapon would ascend and then descend to its target.

Radar broke the silence. "Aegis identifies a modified three-stage Taepodong-2 missile with an Unha-2 rocket. Unable to confirm the tip is a Kwangmyŏngsŏng-2 communications sat."

The Captain snapped, "TAO, flight path?"

"It is going into orbit, Sir."

Before Paloma had time to relax, CSC announced, "TAO. Contact bearing two-eight-zero!"

Details came in from all stations. "Range two two four. Altitude thirty-four thousand feet. Bearing three-zero-zero. There are now two contacts, both inbound from North Korean airspace."

"Negative IFF. Electronic signature corresponds to a MIG-17 and a MIG-19." Old fighter planes, but still deadly.

The Captain countered curtly, "Their intention may be to fly over as a warning, threat us into withdrawing. Keep tracking them and set General Quarters."

"OOD, set General Quarters."

The 1MC blasted, "General Quarters. General Quarters. All hands man your battle stations. Proceed up and forward on starboard, down and aft on port."

An ear-shattering wail engulfed the ship. Men raced to their stations. Watertight doors and hatches dogged into place. Damage control parties added emergency equipment to their kits. All weapons were manned.

"Captain, Sir, those planes are moving awfully fast to be friendly and are aimed directly at us." Sweat broke out on Paloma's forehead. "There are now three contacts—correction, six. Aegis is preparing fire control solutions."

The Captain removed the RLEP–Remote Launch Enable Panel—key from around his neck, inserted it starboard by the Missile Systems Supervisor. Paloma did the same with the FIS—Fire Inhibit Switch—key, putting it in the panel by her console. That armed the Vertical Launch System so the SM-2s, Tomahawks, and Harpoons could be launched at a moment's notice. As Paloma turned her key, Aegis prioritized the threat values of the inbound Mig's.

The planes had closed to two hundred miles.

"Radio. Get me North Korea."

"I have them on Channel 12, Sir, through our embassy."

"North Korea, this is the United States warship *Bunker Hill*. You have aircraft approaching our position. We are abiding by international law. Do not approach closer than one hundred fifty nautical miles. If you do, we will consider it a threat and be forced to respond with all weapons at our disposal." His voice was controlled, but the hidden menace hissed.

Bunker Hill's SM-2s could reach ninety miles. The extra sixty in the threat zone was a cushion.

No response. The Anti-Air Warfare Coordinator shouted, "Six Migs inbound, one hundred eighty miles."

The Captain repeated his message and added. "This is your last warning." "TAO, verify missile upload."

"Verify missile upload, aye. Break CSC."

"Ma'am, six SM-2s armed, uploaded with current target telemetry data," which included speed, destination, range, and altitude, the plane's virtual address.

The blips crossed into the threat zone, *Bunker Hill* their bull's eye.

The Captain clenched his fists and then relaxed. Paloma watched his brain churn through what he had to do and how it would affect the lives not only of his sailors but the men in the enemy planes. In a span of seconds, his entire demeanor changed from passive surveillance to active ship's defense, as though he accepted his fate. This was his place in history, his time to stand against forces he had no part creating.

The Captain's face hardened, a thoughtful frown creasing his forehead. "Notify Command that we are under attack. Batteries release on all enemy-designated contacts."

"Batteries release. All six."

Six VLS hatch covers slapped open. Six SM-2s flew out, leaving a wake of smoke and fire. The ship shuddered. Several watchstanders steadied themselves.

The next SM-2s rumbled into position, ready. The SM-2s that just launched received midcourse guidance from SPY. The four Illuminators whirred, painting the first quad of Migs with high-frequency RF energy that made them impossible to miss, then the next two. Seconds later, the planes disappeared.

A cheer went up. Six out. Six kills.

But it didn't last.

"We have an inbound contact bearing two eight three! One of those Mig's got a missile off. ... SM-2 uploaded."

The Captain broke in. "Batteries release until I say otherwise."

With those six words, Paloma no longer required permission to respond to threats. Accountability for this fight now lay in her untested but well-trained hands.

"EW. Jam that missile."

"Jam unsuccessful. Chaff ready."

The super blooming aluminum foil-like shreds drew heat-seeking missiles away from *Bunker Hill*. Ready was good, in case her next move failed.

"Four, three, two..." Another VLS cell opened. "One bird gone! ... Missile destroyed."

Paloma had no time for relief before Radar called out additional inbound contacts. "Five, six, ten... still counting ..."

Aegis was advertised as capable of fighting off scores of simultaneous attacks, but no one had tested that claim. Today, here, they might determine its veracity or limits. She said with a calm she didn't feel, "Give me a number."

"Still identifying threats, Ma'am. Range one hundred seventy-six thousand yards. They launched while SPY was busy with the first wave. Bearing two-eight-nine. Weapons control solutions in progress." "Fifteen planes, Ma'am. Targets bearing two-eight-five to three-zero-seven. Range one hundred fifty thousand to one hundred twenty-two thousand yards," "Fire solutions identified." "Fire!"

Missile doors flipped opened, SM-2s blasted from the tubes, the Illuminators swiveled to paint targets, and the Mig's disappeared in an explosion of fire and debris.

Only to have the process begin again, a new line-up of planes bearing down with deadly intent on the lone cruiser.

One SM-2 self-destructed. "What happened?"

"Ma'am. None of the Illuminators acquired the target," which meant all four were busy. "We have one incoming at range eight-five."

Paloma did the math. There were more than sixteen contacts within the threat zone, as well as those beyond. She read about this in her classes, but no one thought an American cruiser could be overwhelmed. Why would it? Designed to be part of a Task Force, linked to other warships through comms, their combined defensive forces would be capable of defeating any threat. Today, though, *Bunker Hill* worked alone.

Worry must have shown on her face because the Captain touched her arm. "This is our *Bunker Hill*, TAO, and we have much more power than our forebears. You know how to use it."

Paloma mentally shook and turned to her console. "Time those launches better, WEPS. Get another SM-2 on that target. EW—stand by to launch chaff. Guns. Your turn." That would be Collins and Burlowe. She thought of them this morning, a little scared and a lot ready to do their jobs. "Load HECVT." These rounds had a range of ten to fifteen miles and would cover targets inside the SM-2's minimum range. "We miss one, you get it."

The ship shuddered as four more SM-2s exploded from the aft deck, their target a volley of missiles launched from the incoming Migs. They barely cleared when the tubes were reloaded. Load-and-fire time was under eight seconds. With twenty-six VLS tubes, *Bunker Hill* could launch a missile every second and illuminate one every half-second.

The converging array of threats and friendlies blurred on the Aegis displays. The sheer volume of this attack would soon put planes inside *Bunker Hill's* defense. Mathematically, with enough resources, North Korea would sink the cruiser.

She had to shake this battle up, but how?

"Four more incoming, range eight-seven miles, bearing two-eight-four!" and the next volley of SM-2s lifted off, targeted the enemy and eliminated them.

"Update, TAO!" from the Captain, his voice steel.

Paloma took a nanosecond to check the screens. "Five incoming Mig-17s and seven Su-25s. Ten—no twelve—Il-28 bombers." These again were older planes. "Tracking thirty-five total air contacts. Twenty-two Migs and air-to-surface missiles destroyed. Closest contact is eight-two miles. One-hundred twenty-two SM-2s remain. No other rounds expended," which included ESSMs, 5" rounds, and CIWS. "The North Korean satellite remains in orbit."

"If it makes a move to descend, destroy it." The Captain shared Eitan's suspicion of North Korea.

Over and over, Aegis calculated range, bearing, and fire solutions. The odor of cordite engulfed the ship, smoke flooded the fore and aft decks. Paloma's gaze darted from station to station as she updated the Captain and he reacted, voice steady, bearing rigid.

"Do it like the drills, folks—forget about the North Koreans!"

Then a five-inch gun chattered.

"Air. TAO. Report."

"One got through. Covered by Guns."

"TAO. Guns. Two rounds expended. Overshot. Bore clear. Firing again."

"Hold on, Guns, We launched ESSM." The Mig exploded, shrapnel raining down on the seas in front of them.

The Captain nodded once. "Well done."

"Surface. TAO. Track contacts with main mast cameras." The battle had reached the ship. She needed visual data in real time.

Paloma ran the numbers through her head. They were running through SM-2s like beer at a Navy football game and would run out if this pace continued. "Guns. Load the ERGM rounds," rocket-assisted rounds that go half the distance of an SM-2 with most of its deadliness.

The starboard CIWS mount trilled, followed closely by the fiery burst of exploding fuel, one more menace ended. Fear rushed through Paloma. CIWS was for close-in threats, too close for *Bunker Hill* to get away unscathed unless the gods of war themselves protected her.

They hadn't.

Bridge yelled, "Brace for impact!" And the ship bucked.

We've been hit. And then, *Where's the damage?*

DCA came on the 1MC. "Fire in the ship's classroom. Primary boundaries set by Repair Five. One sailor with third-degree burns. Two corpsmen dead. Battle Dressing Station midships on fire. Reroute all personnel casualties to Main BDS. All hands stand clear of the quarterdeck due to..." His voice cracked. He paused and then continued, "...gaping hole from fragments."

Paloma knew all the corpsmen, had met most of their families. She pushed those thoughts aside, to be dealt with later.

CIWS fired again, brought down an inbound Mig, but not before its cannon raked *Bunker Hill's* fo'c'sle. The Captain gulped. His eyes glittered with anger, his voice as smooth as ice when he asked, "Damage assessment?"

OOD's voice came over the Net, "When the plane crashed, its tail skidded across the Bridge roof. My port Bridge wing and windows are gone and an Illuminator is in the water. One wing landed on the O4 level forward and damaged the chaff launchers and the starboard CIWS mount. Minor personnel injuries. We could use a corpsman, but we'll live."

Paloma did a check off in her head. No serious injuries. No new fires or floods. Down an Illuminator eliminated 25% of the fire control system. They lost half the close-in anti-air capability and half the chaff launchers. If the enemy attack continued, that would hurt.

Paloma thought about the *USS Phoenix* CL 42, called the luckiest ship in the Navy until sold to the Brazilians and rechristened the Belgrano. When the British sub, *Conqueror*, sank it during the Falklands War, it became the only ship ever sunk by a nuclear-powered submarine.

Paloma hoped *Bunker Hill* wouldn't be the last ship ever sunk by Migs.

The Captain's steady voice asked, "Update."

She ran down the list of damages and the effect they would have on their defense capabilities.

As she finished, EW shouted. "Launched chaff!"

"Air. How did someone get that close?"

"We're doing our job, TAO. We're overwhelmed."

Air was flushed, which said a lot. When he concentrated, a dog gnawing on his leg couldn't distract him. "Thanks, Mike. Keep it up."

"The next wave is two-hundred-forty miles out."

Next! How many planes did North Korea have? Paloma felt her throat tighten. She gripped the chair so hard her knuckles turned white. The Captain winked. "We're still here. Let's keep it that way."

She grinned, tension leaking from her body as though he pulled a plug. North Korea expected them to crumble, but this Captain would fight until they destroyed him and then figure a way to continue. She stood proudly with him.

But what the beleaguered warship could handle was identified by its munitions and those were running out, even as the next wave of North Korean warplanes bore down on them.

As if he read her thoughts, the Captain said, "Backtrack the trajectories of those enemy fighters. I want to know where they came from and shut it down, even if it's based in Toksan," home of North Korea's second air Combat command and considered untouchable, "pound hell out of it. I want this attack over. I got a feeling we will see more of that satellite."

Paloma jolted. She forgot the Taepodong, but the Captain hadn't.

Two minutes later, Ships Signal Exploitation Space—SSES—came on Net 15. "Captain. Those fighters are out of two bases. One's Kang Da Ri. The second, we're working to identify."

"Now wouldn't be too soon." The Captain's voice carried an edge. "TAO. How many fighter planes does Kang Da Ri have?"

Paloma checked the latest intel numbers. "Thirty."

"We shot down more than thirty. Send them a Tomahawk, Special Delivery of the USN."

Paloma got on the 1MC. "Chief Shanifeld," the man in charge of Tomahawks and the only watchstander not busy today. That was about to change. "Dial 150."

When Shanifeld called, Paloma said, "Chief. How fast can you send a TLAM to the coordinates I sent you?"

"Is five minutes fast enough?"

She smiled. Damn fast considering this particular Tomahawk was programmed to explode into clusters, each bomblet attacking the individual planes on the tarmac. "Only if you need that long. And prepare another TLAM. I'll have coordinates shortly."

The Chief called back in three minutes. "Tomahawk ready."

"Fire!"

The Tomahawk Land-Attack Missile flew out of the VLS tube, streaked up and over the incoming wave of planes, so close to one old Ilyushin-28, it swerved and spiraled into the sea somewhere past the horizon. Minutes passed as the telemetry made minute adjustments, and then, "Direct hit!"

Paloma had no time to enjoy their success. Aegis showed a dozen planes inside the threat zone. This time, they were Mig 21s, which had to be from DPRK's vaunted 46th Air Regiment, armed with GSh-23 cannons, Kh-66 and AA-2 Atoll missiles.

She tried to hide the horror that washed through her body as she figured out North Korea's plan. The first planes had been fodder, to deplete *Bunker Hill's* inventory and analyze the cruiser's war strategies. Now, the crew tired, beaten down, defenses drained, North Korea would send their best.

The Captain crossed his arms over his chest, his face fierce with concentration. "Where is that second base, TAO? We don't have all day."

The high piercing wail of an incoming shell drowned out his voice. Paloma froze. The missile approached in slow motion, colors vibrant amidst the haze of battle, tip massive, an unstoppable strength about its attack. CWIS chattered and then Burlowe's guns, followed by the feral roar as an SM-2 flared from the ship's bowels. The enemy shell detonated five hundred yards from *Bunker Hill*. The ship lurched, groaning, as fire and debris rained down on the deck.

"Damage!" The Captain stood rock solid, face an inscrutable mask.

Reports tumbled in. Three injuries, a fire near the helo hanger. No deaths. Paloma was about to place a call and find out what was holding up coordinates for the second base when she remembered Eitan's words: *If you're attacked and can't figure out from where, check these.*

She tapped her mic. "Chief Shanifeld. Try these coordinates for the second base," and she gave him the latitude and longitude.

"Ma'am. All I see is a mountain."

"TAO?" From the Captain.

It took a moment to make sense, and then she did. Eitan gave her the location of a DPRK airbase not on any maps. Telling the Captain how she knew would end Eitan's career.

"Sir, I trust the source. Please don't ask me to explain." When the Captain said nothing, she continued. "It's a subterranean bunker. The planes shoot out the side of a mountain."

The Captain connected the dots. "Does this have anything to do with the FBI visit?"

Paloma colored. "You don't want to know, Sir."

After a moment, he gave a minute nod and asked, "I thought Thunderbird was further north?"

SSES chimed in, "There are rumors of one by Kangwon-do, fits these coordinates."

The Captain came to a decision. "Well, plug that damn hole!"

Paloma mic'd Shanifeld, "Fire when ready!"

"Stand by to fire—Fire!"

The Tomahawk leaped from the ship's deck as its solid-fuel booster ignited and latched onto its coordinates. Moments later, its fins unfurled and it hurled over the horizon. Paloma switched her attention to the Tomahawk Weapon Control System monitor which would relay images from onboard cameras. Water abruptly gave way to the peaceful verdure of shoreline and inland forests. That soon became ocean and then a mountain loomed. She felt a nervous shiver the missile would find nothing but an impenetrable rock wall, but as the craggy bluff careened forward, the camera captured a glimmer of darkness and a murky circle that must be the entrance. It exploded 4.8 yards into the mouth of the cave, sealing the exit and destroying everything inside.

"Direct hit!"

A cheer went up. The radar control operator grinned like a kid in a video arcade.

The balance of North Korea's squadron was swept from the sky. The battle ended and *Bunker Hill* won.

The sudden silence rang louder than the howl of battle. No shriek of missiles, whirr of the Illuminator, roar of gun mounts, or blast of shells. No shouts and screams of her shipmates. With the din gone, a veil lifted. Behind the fear of battle and shock of attack was relief at surviving, joy at a fight well fought, and grief for those who fought the good fight.

The calm didn't last long.

Chapter Fifty-four

***Day Twenty-four, Wednesday August 30th late afternoon
New York, New York, FBI Safe House***

"North Korea's Taepodong-2 intercontinental
ballistic missile is carrying a warhead."

Zeke no longer found it odd when Otto appeared on
his phone. He snapped his fingers and the hum of voices
behind him disappeared. "No one but the people in this
room know that."

"The deduction was simple, Zeke. I compared the
rising arc of the missile's flight path to a simulation of what
it should be if loaded with the Kwangmyŏngsŏng-2
communication satellite. It didn't fit so I checked each
stage. The payload is too long. When I modeled payloads, a
nuclear tip matched."

"We have it under control. *Bunker Hill* will shoot it
down on the descent."

"It's under heavy attack—"

Kali gasped. Eitan turned white.

Zeke jumped in. "The battle's over, though we lost
communication with the ship. The missile established a

geosynchronous orbit which imitates what's expected of a communications satellite."

Kali took a swallow of coffee and downed a handful of Fritos as she tried to understand why North Korea would attack *Bunker Hill* and pretend the satellite was benign. She gave up. "Why?"

"They're demanding two trillion dollars in war retributions from Japan or they attack."

"Trillion with a *T*?"

"Japan refused. They think and we agree this is an empty threat. *Bunker Hill* will have no problem shooting that missile out of the sky once it begins to descend. Plus, Japanese Patriots can take it down before it reaches their homeland."

"Otto. D'you know when the missile is scheduled to descend?"

"No, Kali. I chatted with the warhead, but it's not very smart. It knows only where it is."

Zeke sputtered, "Those warheads are supposed to be unhackable."

Otto churbled. "The signal node is encrypted to prevent grabbing the RF signal, but not the keyboard strokes. An amateur mistake."

Zeke's voice came out a pitch higher. He was worried. "The US will not allow a warhead to float around over our heads so we're sending the F-15 Eagle to shoot it down. I need sixty minutes to make that happen. Can you assure me this missile will wait?"

Otto churbled. "I will only know when its position changes, Zeke."

"Good enough."

Kali's head spun. Between talking warheads and space-based weapons and an F-15 Eagle, her usual morning headache exploded like a viral YouTube video. She rubbed her temples and asked, "What's an Eagle?"

"It's a warplane loaded with an anti-satellite weapon. In 1985, it brought down the damaged Russian solar observatory, Solwind P78-1, from a low-earth orbit. That proved we could defend ourselves from a space-based attack, but unfortunately, the world's fear of weaponizing space surpassed America's fear of her enemies, so the project was mothballed.

"Until yesterday when we moved one of the three remaining F-15s to Marine Corps Air Station Iwakuni, Japan. Major Todd Pearson, son of the pilot who flew the first mission, is standing by. He'll be off the ground in thirty minutes."

Otto said, "The F-15 had another success, Zeke. Have you forgotten the intrepid flight of Major Amelia Nakamura when she shot the Kosmos 1801 out of the sky?"

Kali looked at Otto. "That was a book, Otto. *Red Storm Rising*."

Otto thrummed. "It would have succeeded. I ran simulations."

Kali patted Otto and asked Zeke, "How's the missile work?"

"It carries no explosives, relies on speed of impact for detonation. The pilot will climb at a sixty-five-degree angle at Mach 1.22 and vector the warhead into the Taepodong-2's path. By the time they collide, it's traveling fast enough to destroy the target. The most we have to worry about is falling debris."

The Sea of Japan
USS Bunker Hill

"Captain. Radar Systems Controller. The North Korean missile is descending. Determining flight path. Destination is... 39° 0'20.98"N, 140°31'23.94"E. Shinjō, Yamagata."

The Japanese mainland!

"OOD. Flank Three," maximum possible speed.

"Sir, we don't have Flank Three. One of the engines was damaged."

"Give me best speed. Plot a course for Japan. TAO, notify Japan. TAO, give me a weapons control solution."

"We're too far for SM-2's, but we can use the RIM-161 Standard Missile-3," the SM-2's 260-mile long-distance cousin. They carried only one SM-3.

"How long will it take to prepare?"

"Aegis just acquired the target."

"Fire!"

"Eighty-seven seconds to impact."

While they waited, damage reports from the air attack rolled in. Five crew members killed. Fourteen injured. All fires extinguished, repairs begun.

"Ten seconds to impact... Five, four three two one, SPY picked up an explosion. We have destroyed the Taepodong—wait! SPY is still tracking a missile on that flight path."

The Captain roared, "What happened, folks?"

After a moment of stunned silence, Paloma suggested, "Intel indicates the Taepodong might carry defensive chaff."

"I think we confirmed the rumor."

Paloma had never heard defeat in the Captain's voice. She ached, knowing what it must cost him to admit failure.

He continued. "I need to let the Japanese know. They will have the same problem. OOD, tell medical to expect more injured, this time civilians."

New York, New York
FBI Safe House

"Excuse me, Zeke. The missile began its descent."

"*Bunker Hill* will stop it."

"They failed. The Taepodong-II is carrying chaff. It confused *Bunker Hill's* only SM-3 and will succeed in doing the same with Japan's Patriots. We have five minutes before impact with the island."

The Sea of Japan
USS Bunker Hill CG 52

"Sir, a South Korean helo is requesting permission to land."

The Captain's voice came over Net15. "XO?"

XO's voice came on. "I-I got a Flash about that—"

"Pilothouse," the Captain ordered.

"Go." From WEPS, offering to cover her watch as TAO, and she sprinted for the Bridge.

The Captain shouted from the debris-strewn command post. "What the hell's wrong, XO?"

One look at Taggert's face said something was very-the-hell wrong.

"I... I... my mother..." He started to cry. "It's not— they said it's not weaponized."

A tingle went up Paloma's neck as the Captain, asked, "What are you talking about?"

Taggert's mouth opened, but nothing came out. He looked at her, and then at the Bridge's fax machine. She followed his gaze.

Why did Command send a picture of her ex-boyfriend to *Bunker Hill*? She stepped toward it as the Captain asked, "How do you know, Mr. Taggert?"

"They promised it was *fiction*, you know, for my fiancée's story. Nothing else." He looked like a child who's been lied to.

Broken glass crunched behind her.

"Mr. Taggert." The voice shouldn't be anywhere near her ship. "Do you have the codes?"

XO's mouth fell open. After a few disjointed starts, he said, "N-no. I-I told you. You'll destroy the ship and all hands—"

"The alternative is I will destroy you. Those images Shalimar took? I embedded information about the bribes you received, how you planned to turn your ship over to the enemy. Once some bright intel agent figures out the steganography, this attack will become your doing."

"Steg…"

"The art of hiding electronic data within digital files."

Taggert studied his feet. "I can't do—"

There was a crack and Taggert folded, head smacking the counter as he collapsed. Anchor laughed as Paloma bent over Taggert. His eyes fluttered, head lolling into the crimson pool spreading under his thorax. She bit back her anger as she put her hand on his wound, trying to staunch the blood. He clutched her uniform.

"I didn't give him the codes, the backdoor, to the missiles—"

There was another crack and this time, a hole blossomed over Taggert's left eye. He wilted and went still. Paloma sucked in a breath and blinked back tears, their arguments now inconsequential. He was a damaged man who had reached his limits and tried to solve his problems by making a deal with the devil, but when it came down to it, couldn't betray the Navy he'd served with distinction for twenty plus years.

"Why are you here?" She asked Mohammed as she activated the satellite phone Eitan had given her.

"You and I have unfinished business."

"And that required six armed men?" she snapped, hoping Eitan was listening. Then she pasted fear across her face. "I am sorry I ended it between us," she lied. "It frightened me, getting serious—"

"I dumped *you!*" His voice was thick with emotion. "I used you. Nothing else." Spittle burst from his mouth. "In fact," and he slapped her. Hard. "I cringed sitting near you, touching you. It made me dirty to talk to you. You will spend the rest of your insignificant life as a whore. I will parcel you out to friends as favors until you are worthless for even that. Then, you die." Anchor grinned, eyes crazed. He chucked the nearest soldier in the arm, giggled something about the value of white whores. The man responded with a lecherous grin, eyes devouring her body beneath the androgynous Navy uniform.

She wrung her hands as though upset. "I'll do anything if you let the crew go."

Mohammed laughed, giddy with excitement. "You will anyway, but yes. We can arrange a trade. I want the missile codes. We have them for your premiere nuclear sub, *Virginia*. I want *Bunker Hill's* in return for the lives of your crew."

"I have no knowledge of them, Anchor," which was true. "Sir?" She turned to Captain Pearson.

"So my weapons can kill innocents?" Anger erupted from the man who convinced newly-minted eighteen-year-olds to face death with pride. "No, LT. This scum gets nothing. Ever."

Mohammed's voice: "Oh. Well, I can fix that," and he shot the Captain.

Paloma screamed, "You killed the only person who might have them."

He gloated. "Tell your president I will trade your sailor's lives for those codes."

By now, Paloma was shaking, tears threatening to overflow, but she raised her chin and looked down her nose at the man who stood there, legs spread, feet duck-toed, chin jutting forward like a boxer who's forgotten he has a glass jaw.

It was time for her first blow. "No one's going to make a trade with you, Anchor."

"I don't care." That wasn't the response Paloma expected. "Then I will gift your little ship to my father, North Korea's *Wonsu*." He scanned the room to be sure the soldiers caught his father's title. "You have no way out."

"Are you really this stupid?" She shook her head disdainfully, goading Anchor. "Half the 7th Fleet is bearing down on this position. Give up, Anchor, before you get yourself and your little friends hurt."

His face turned white with rage. "You know nothing."

"Try me," she growled.

Anchor bit. "As we speak, your nation's capital is under attack."

Paloma felt her face drain of color, saw Anchor's glee in her shock, but still sputtered, "Attack DC?" She hoped Eitan heard this.

Anchor laughed moronically. "Misinformation and misdirection. Every time you thought you understood our goal, we were somewhere else." He walked up to the splintered Bridge window and pointed northeast to the descending missile silhouetted against the sky. "When my father's missile hits Japan, your government will send everything in its arsenal to aid the Japanese people." He was breathless in his excitement. "No one will notice a sub sneaking down the Chesapeake."

Despite herself, Paloma was impressed. Clearly, someone smarter than Anchor developed this plan.

He cathedraled his fingers and tapped his upper lip. "After we destroy your Capitol, America will give us the codes to all its warships to save what remains of the country."

Paloma shivered. Where was Eitan?

New York, New York
FBI Safe House

"Otto, can you redirect the missile to fall into the Sea of Japan?"

"Of course. I can tell it to undershoot the intended target by 85.37 miles. I can also, as the failsafe you humans like to employ, tell the weapon to not arm itself."

"Do it."

Otto hummed and then red splashed across his chest monitor. "There's a problem. This is an archaic missile." He riffled. "I must go through the North Korean handler."

Kali stiffened and her temples throbbed.

"I tracked the wireless line back to the North Korean headquarters. I'm hacking the firewalls. They are sophisticated for such an old missile. The warhead armed itself. I must send a self-destruct order within the next thirty seconds, but these protocols match nothing I've seen."

Tension soaked Zeke's voice as he jumped in. "Remember you asked how I solve problems without following rules. Well, there's always an unexpected twist. Rather than looking for usual or logical, go with your mechanical gut."

Otto's processors burred more loudly than she thought they could. Numbers flew across his screen, all zeros and ones, which meant he didn't have the nano-second required to translate.

Eitan looked pale. A ragged fringe of oily hair stuck from under a 'Go Navy Beat Army' ball cap. He bounced, lips moving as he translated. "Otto got in… sent the self-destruct order. … The warhead asked for authentication. Otto… provided it. The missile is destroying itself."

Otto churbled. "Most pieces should fall into the ocean with some landing on Honshu, Sado-ga-shima, and Tobi-shima. I'm sending an open channel alert to all vessels in the area."

Kali took a breath, but jerked at a voice behind her.

"Wow. That was awesome."

Sean stood in the doorway in his pajamas, hair ruffled, cheeks flushed.

"Sean!"

"That's what I want to do, mom. I want to make a difference. Like you did. And Zeke. And Eitan. I want to matter."

Tears sprang to Kali's eyes. Didn't he know how much he mattered to her?

James broke in. "North Korea is furious, swears we turned a harmless missile into a hailstorm of lethal debris, said our counterattack is why the missile aimed at Yamagata. Japan played back a tape of the North Korean extortion demand. The two nations are negotiating on the next step, which I suspect will rhyme with North Korea promising to leave them alone for a very long time. The press is ready to excoriate us for acting like cowboys on the international stage as soon as 'all the facts are in'. We told the Japanese Emperor Otto talked the missile out of attacking. He declared him a national hero—and loves the palindrome."

Kali giggled. Leave it to the Japanese to get that.

There were congratulatory hoots all around. Kali knew there remained a lot of work to do, but for the first time in ten days, they were a step ahead. So why was Eitan so pale?

"Eitan. Is Paloma OK?"

"*Bunker Hill* has been boarded, probably by terrorists from the helo." Eitan placed a phone on the desk. "This is feed from the satellite phone I gave her before she left."

"Anchor. We blew up your missile. Give up while you've done nothing more serious than murder." Her voice carried none of the stress she must feel. Kali couldn't help but be impressed by this young woman, minutes out of a naval battle the likes of which the US last fought in WWII, her ship boarded, and she maintained the presence of mind to reach out to Eitan. What faith she placed in an odd little man she barely knew. How could she know Eitan regularly performed miracles?

"What right have you to destroy our weapon, you with your corruption and godlessness? Allah condemns you!" Anchor's voice carried a desperate edge.

"Gotcha." Zeke's voice. "He admitted the weapon is armed and he's working with DPRK."

"You have six AK 47s pointed at me. How does my corruption and godlessness help now?"

Mohammed blustered, "Tell your President he must trade or *Virginia* will destroy Washington!"

Otto interrupted. "I have a location on *Virginia*, Zeke. The SOSUS across the Chesapeake reported a contact. I have information from Nasr's computer that applies. He took dozens of pictures of a location named 'Herring Bay'."

The paint must have worn off. Kali expected Zeke to reply, but got James instead.

"Zeke's gone. He flew out of here. Does anyone know where he went?"

Sun smiled benignly as an abundance of numbers pulsed across his screen. Iran and North Korea in a complicated dance of deception, a tangled web of lies, not realizing they were puppets. But the puppet master didn't know Sun had decoded the dance.

"Excuse me, Kali. Zeke would like me to run a simulation. May I?"

Chapter Fifty-five

Wednesday, August 30th, early Evening
The Chesapeake Bay, Approaching Herring Bay

"Every available American warship is either protecting her shores or racing to rescue *Bunker Hill*." Even the lousy connection didn't hide the strain in James's voice.

"Yeah, it's a hunch, Bobby, but I'm right."

"Duck's there, isn't he? And we have a sub and a cruiser patrolling the mouth of the Chesapeake. If *Virginia's* going to set a dirty bomb off close enough to reach Washington, it must pass them first."

"Except it's already here." But Bobby had already disconnected.

He braced himself as the 108-foot wooden-hulled YP bolted south on the Chesapeake, past O'Neill Island on the right and the private docks that sprinkled the shoreline of Kent Island on the left, toward the location he should have recognized twenty-four days ago—33 44 90—the shallowest spot on the Chesapeake. The SEALs ran simulations here, hypothesizing exactly what Dhiren Barot laid out in his blueprints. These were so top secret only a handful of people outside the Teams knew and none of them thought it would happen.

Now, he had to do what his Team had never accomplished in practice: stop an attack.

North Korea had focused the world on the downed missile and *Bunker Hill's* plight. That played right into Salah al-Zahrawi's hands. The man loved misdirection and distraction. With the eyes of the world on the Sea of Japan, al-Zahrawi would even the score with the country that had cost him his reputation and his bankroll.

It might still work.

The moment Otto found *Virginia*, the bits of information playing bumper cars in Rowe's brain fell into place. He and Duck choppered to USNA's Farragut Field right off the Chesapeake, a short distance from the YP boats used to teach Naval Academy Midshipmen seafaring skills. A Navy buddy offered the assistance of Mids from the Academy's sailing team, but Rowe refused. This trip likely would be one-way.

"Faster, Duck," Rowe bellowed over the whine of engines strained to the breaking point.

"I'm maxed. This bouncing baby only goes seventeen knots."

In one sense, Rowe wished *Virginia* was going to attack Washington. Tomahawks would only kill hundreds. No. The terrorists were turning the sub into a dirty bomb. When it blew up, it couldn't sink deep enough to drown the nuclear explosion so the resulting cloud would kill thousands of civilians and devastate the area surrounding DC for decades.

Rowe, though, had his own plan, one with pretty much no chance to work but was all he came up with on the twenty-five-minute helo ride down.

Duck shouted over the engine noise. "*Virginia's* reactor is an S9G, built by General Electric. The only way to blow it is with a bomb."

Rowe grunted. "Which they have several of." Duck deftly zigged around a fishing boat trolling for blue crab. "What's the sounding here?"

The rule in a water-based nuclear explosion was ten percent neutralization for every two feet. A twenty-foot depth would defuse the explosion. According to Al-alah's records, *Virginia* would maneuver north until it reached Herron Bay, one of the Chesapeake's shallowest inlets. There it would turn to port and steam full speed into the sloping banks, beaching the sub. When the nuclear reactor blew, it would have nowhere to go but up.

Rowe needed to stop *Virginia* before it went aground.

Duck kept one hand on the wheel and with the other, rolled a bathymetric map out on the deck. "Fifteen meters."

"How far to Herring Bay?"

"Five clicks. What's your plan?"

Rowe grinned. "They gotta surface to head inland. When they do, I have a surprise."

His Naval Academy buddy who arranged for the use of the YP had thrown in a high-powered Hollis H-160 scuba scooter. It would carry Rowe's equipment with no problem, but the way Rowe intended to run it, would be out of juice in thirty minutes.

Which meant he had to get as close as possible.

He stared down river as the YP flew forward. In the distance, the *wap-wap* of helos echoed as they dropped sonobuoys by the mouth of the Chesapeake.

Duck said, "God bless those boys who messed with the torpedo tubes. At least we won't get blown out of the water."

"I hope they got the VLSs, too."

The YP plunged down the Chesapeake. Rowe used a bullhorn to warn boats off the Bay. The sightseers ignored him, but the fishermen moved toward the docks.

As soon as the YP reached latitude 38o 44' 90", Duck slowed to a stop and Rowe stripped down to his swim trunks, suited up in a rebreather, mask, fins, and a vest with his dive knives and compass, then draped a chain around his neck attached to his waist with a rope. Called a satchel bomb, it had C4 embedded along its length. Rowe scanned the choppy surface for the sub's antennae. It should be visible at this depth. He did a grid search, back and forth across the deeper center and then south to the next quadrant. Finally, *Virginia* showed up, five hundred yards ahead and just past the tip of James Island.

It had already surfaced.

Rowe went cold. Was he too late? He stared at the sub's stubby nose and calculated its position relative to the shore. No. It hadn't yet turned inland. He tossed the Hollis in the water, took a quick breath from the rebreather and flipped over the side into the Chesapeake. Without a diving suit, the cold water hit him like a bed of nettles. Rowe attached the satchel bomb to his waist so it would trail behind, jumped on the Hollis, and turned it downstream. Within moments, the cigar-shaped body of *Virginia* loomed into view.

He leaped from the scooter letting it sink to the silty river bed. He spread his arms and legs like an X and the sub's nose slammed into his body. Though underway at less than five knots, it still felt like a freight train. His head bounced off the sub as he scrabbled legs and arms around the slick rounded shape and clung with all he was worth until he steadied himself, then started to claw his way up. The sub felt clammy under his skin, the smell of fish, motor oil and waste strong in his nostrils.

After what felt like hours, he broke through the surface only to be torn loose as a flood of water sluiced from the deck over his body. He grabbed on again, fingers straining to maintain a grip, and then he pulled himself up and over the lip of the deck, the heavy six-foot chain clanging against the sub's skin. The rough Chesapeake, driven by a brisk wind, threatened his precarious purchase, but he clung until he got his bearings and managed to push to his feet.

He stumbled, flailed, then steadied himself, flipped his mask and flippers off, and decided what with the slippery deck and chain's weight, he better crawl the 377 feet.

Then, he saw the open hatch. Not one of the twelve VLS tubes. He would notice if the sub launched a Tomahawk missile. No, this marked the ingress to the sub's interior.

He froze, mind flitting back to Dinar Hussabi and the promised fishing trip with his parents. Were the hijackers going to escape before the sub blew? Not likely through the Weapons Shipping Hatch, but he checked anyway. When no one exited, he took a quick peek and a fetid sourness assaulted him. He held his nose to stop from sneezing.

And smiled. The crew had broken the CO_2 scrubbers, forcing the sub to surface for fresh air. Should he go inside? He had surprise on his side, but he didn't know where the hostages were. No, better to continue with the plan. He edged onward, shivering in the chill wind, chain clanking behind him only slightly muffled by the C4 that cushioned the metal. No doubt, the noise gave his presence away, so he better hurry.

When he reached the conning tower, he wondered if the terrorists were watching from the Flying Bridge as he scooted along the deck. It didn't matter. They didn't have time to stop him. He wrapped his arms around the smooth surface and shimmied up to a standing position. There, he clung, feeling the sub's power under his feet. Once he found his balance, he moved as fast as the slick deck allowed around the aft hatch—also open and stinking—to his destination.

The propeller.

He spread his stance, bulky satchel bomb in front between his hands, and flung it toward the propeller. If things went according to plan, it would slide down the tail and get sucked into the screw. The goal wasn't to stop the screw—nothing would do that—but foul it. The C4 would destroy the shaft seal and flood the sub. According to Otto's simulation, the sub would sink without killing the crew. But this had to be done in the center of the Bay, in twenty plus feet of water.

His plan had one hinky spot. Once the satchel bomb snagged itself in the screw, Rowe had to set the timer. He needed twelve minutes to escape, but that gave the hijackers enough time to blow the reactor.

Damn. His throw was short. He reeled the bomb in and inched closer to the sub's tail. Before he could try again, the sub shook like it had been hit by a torpedo. Rowe thrashed as his legs flew out from under him and he landed hard, catching himself from sliding into the water.

"What the—" A Tomahawk exploded from the sub's VLS tube and threw him back. It rose in a graceful arc, contrail white against the blue sky. "Weren't they disabled?"

The Tomahawk whistled a high-pitched alarm as it flew for DC. Thousands of people were there including the President and the British Prime Minister unless James had persuaded them to move. Rowe's stomach heaved as the missile arced downward and disappeared over the horizon with a muted blast. A thick gray cloud mushroomed into the air.

But no explosion. Rowe had no time to celebrate. The hijackers now knew they had only one weapon: the sub itself. As if on cue, *Virginia* turned to port.

Rowe would have to set the timer to eight minutes.

He wobbled back to his feet, slipped on the slick surface, threw his arms out to balance, and prepared his next toss. Behind him, someone shouted in Farsi. He spread his arms and flung the chain forward. It slipped down the sub's tail and stopped short of the prop. He needed to get closer. He reeled it in quickly as he took two steps forward, ignoring the agitated sounds behind him. Rowe balanced the satchel and threw again, feet sloshing awkwardly on the wet deck. This time, it worked. He set the timer and prepared to free himself and swim to shore.

A hand seized his shoulder. Rowe whipped around, kicking as he spun. When the man stumbled and fell, Rowe slammed his cupped hands over his ears and pulled out, exploding his eardrums. The attacker collapsed into the water, writhing in pain. He snatched the satchel charge like a life preserver and then uttered a wretched cry as the screw pulled him, the chain, and its deadly payload in.

By now, the sub was perpendicular to the shoreline. Rowe pulled the knife from his vest so he could cut the rope around his waist, but got no further. Someone yanked his head back. He glimpsed a leering grin as he dropped to the deck as though off balance, twisted, sweeping the attacker's feet out from under him. The man fell with a thud and scuttled backward. Rowe tried to follow, but the rope tightened around his waist as the screw pulled it into the blades. He better cut first, fight later.

Six minutes remained.

Again, the man attacked, this time throwing up his forearms like the cowcatcher on a train, trying to knock Rowe backward into the prop. Rowe spun to the side, lost his grip on the knife and heard it rattle across the deck as he whacked the man's elbow down and away, caught his head and rolled him. The man wrenched loose and slammed Rowe to the ground and the screw yanked him into the water. The attacker froze in a half-crouch and then grinned as understanding reached his eyes.

"You will die, infidel," he said in heavily accented English. "A fitting end," and he laughed like a maniac as he struggled to his feet.

No way would Rowe allow this enemy to finish his deadly work. He pulled his spare knife from his vest and realized he had a choice: Kill the man who intended to murder over a hundred crew members and destroy Rowe's homeland, or free himself.

A second later, the terrorist fell, the knife lodged deep into his left side, where the heart was.

Rowe checked his watch. Three minutes. The prop screamed as the satchel bomb wrapped tighter and tighter around the screw. Rowe splashed through the water, levered himself up, and searched madly for the knife, hoping to find it tangled in the rope. Finally, he gave up, his body still and eyes shut, as he came to grips with his fate. "I may die, but my country—Kali and Duck—they will live."

He breathed out slowly, forcing his mind to still, trying to remember even one prayer from his childhood. "Our father—"

"Zero." He barely heard the voice. "Zero! Hold the rope up or I shoot your hand off!"

Duck? He should have been on shore by now, but he sounded like he was right off Rowe's starboard. And how'd he get a lasso around his neck?

"Duck! Get out of here. It's about to blow!" Rowe choked out as he gagged on a mouthful of rancid water. Thirty seconds and everything around would be incinerated.

"I mean it, Zero. Get your arm through that loop. You got five seconds!"

A wave of water hit Rowe and he coughed violently, trying to find Duck through his clouded vision. He gripped the housing around the screw, wriggled through the lasso, and held the rope as steady as possible. A 9mm barked. Mind-numbing pain cut through his wrist, followed by a vicious yank and an ear-shattering boom. A wall of water crashed into him and he flew up, over, and lost consciousness.

Chapter Fifty-six

Day Twenty-four, August 30th
USS Bunker Hill, *Sea of Japan*

Sun stabbed a text message into the satellite phone, and then stared, waiting. Moments later, Paloma spoke softly through the phone's speaker: "You're too late, Anchor. *Virginia* was destroyed—before it attacked Washington. You no longer have leverage to trade for those codes."

Anchor chortled. "That was Nasr's plan, not mine. This vessel is a gift to my father. Try to stop me and I will destroy it and everyone aboard. I do not fear death. Give me the armory key, Paloma."

There were footsteps, a loud slap, and a grunt. Mohammed's voice reverberated in the speaker. "I dislike repeating myself."

"Catch." Paloma's voice.

Mohammed: "Place these everywhere marked on this picture. Kill anyone who gets in your way."

Paloma's voice: "That's C4. You're placing it in the spots XO marked on the DC plate. You'll sink the ship!"

Mohammed: "Paloma. Please call your crew up to the Bridge immediately. Mr. Taggert provided me the roster so I will know if someone is missing."

Paloma ordered all crewmembers to convene on the Bridge. As the crew arrived, they were hustled into the helo hanger, the only room large enough to hold everyone.

When the footsteps silenced, Mohammed said, "You are eight short."

"They are dead from the air battle or too injured to move."

"Or hiding," James's voice. "I have a hunch Chacone knows."

"Alright. I believe you. Why would you lie? Erfan. Please bring the officers from the hanger." Footsteps thumped and disappeared.

Five minutes later, the sounds of pushing and shoving as the officers arrived. A few shouted at Mohammed. One begged. Mohammed said nothing, the only sound shrieks, the chatter of machine gun fire, and Mohammed counting, "One, two, three, four..."

Paloma screamed, "Stop! I'll find them! Please!" but the shots continued.

"Six, seven, eight." The shots ended with ragged breathing. Finally, from Mohammed, "I have a job for you, Paloma, when you recover. Assist me in delivering this ship to my father."

"Anchor. I am a lieutenant. No one will listen to me."

A crack and a thump echoed through the phone, followed by another and another, and then Paloma's sobs.

"You are now the senior officer." Anchor's voice was calm.

Kali heard anguished sobs, choking, hiccupping, and deep breaths as Paloma fought to regain control.

"You will sail this ship to Wonsan Harbor, Captain Chacone. Unless there is another problem I can solve for you?"

There was a sniffle, labored breaths, then, "If those North Korean planes sank us, how would you present us to your father?"

"She's giving us time to get there and rescue what remains of her crew," Kali whispered.

Mohammed sighed. "Who would know you would fight so hard? We thought you would surrender after our first air wave, certainly after the second and third, but you kept battling. I had to stop you myself. *Alhamdulillah.* "

James broke in. "We have five ships closing on *Bunker Hill,* but North Korea has twice as many coming south and they're closer. Gen. Soon Young is screaming that *Bunker Hill* committed an Act of War and if we try to take it back, they'll sink it."

"America won't abandon the crew."

"*Bunker Hill* is two hundred miles from North Korea and twice as far from our ships. The DPRK has the fourth largest army in the world which is a lot of reasons to take them seriously."

Kali expected Eitan to be devastated, but he bounced in his chair, eyes focused, hands steady, fingers flying.

Mohammed's voice came over the phone again. "Tell your friends to stop chasing us or I blow *Bunker Hill* up."

Kali heard a whisper of movement, then *Assalaamu Álaykum.*

Otto said, "The man Mr. Mohammed sent to plant the C4 has returned. I believe he finished."

Sun 's head bobbed. "I promised her." His fingers flew, the keyboard chattered. Kali glimpsed the words "Top Secret" disappear from the monitor. Sun smiled into the miasma, his spirit somewhere no mortal man could follow, where he would do anything—including trade his freedom—to prevent a woman he barely knew and sailors he'd only met once from dying.

Chapter Fifty-seven

Wednesday August 30th, evening
The Sea of Japan, aboard USS Bunker Hill CG 52

Without warning, Nav yelled, "Sub off our port beam, a *Romeo* class."

Mohammed smiled. "Our escort has arrived."

The Captain's Indigo message, Battle Orders giving him authority to attack as needed, passed to the highest ranking officer at his death. Today, that was LT Paloma Chacone.

"Secure for battle!" No way would she allow an enemy sub near her ship.

Mohammed started to object when Nav yelled, "Torpedo in the water! Second torpedo in the water! Inbound port side!"

Mohammed looked stunned. "What? They are here to protect us! Why are they firing?"

Paloma felt like spitting on this stupid man. "Load and fire ASROC!"

"Negative, ma'am. No one's manning that station."

"Electro, get a Flash message off. Tell Command we have two fish running at us."

"Ma'am, I don't know how."

Nav added, "SHF is down anyway."

Paloma glared at Jane. "Figure it out, Ensign." She wanted to say, 'Use Bridge to Bridge,' to request what coverage the approaching US vessels could provide from three hundred miles, but she couldn't say any of that with Mohammed listening. Jane would solve it.

"All engines ahead flank! Right full rudder." Modern torpedoes cut through the water faster than *Bunker Hill* even with all its engines working, but the *Romeo* had old fish.

The Helmsman responded, "All engines ahead flank. Right full rudder. Aye, ma'am."

Mohammed yelped, "What are you doing?"

"If we don't get out of the way of those fish, how will you gift us to your father?"

Mohammed looked confused and Paloma jerked from his grasp. "Let's hope old torpedoes from an old sub are not only slow, but won't track us. Helmsman, evasive actions! Launch ADCs!" Acoustic defense countermeasures would create a cacophony of noise every time the ship's rudder shifted, hopefully confusing the torpedo.

Immediately, *Bunker Hill* swerved ninety degrees to starboard throwing Mohammed against the console. He scrambled to regain his balance. Paloma never wavered.

"Helmsman. Maintain same degrees off original course." The ship made another violent ninety-degree swing in the opposite direction to create a knuckle.

"Reverse direction!" and *Bunker Hill* veered seventy-five degrees. This would continue until the torpedo ran out of fuel or found its mark.

As it turned out, the *Romeo's* fish were no match for modern strategies. One slowed to a halt short of its target. The second swerved to chase something off the ship's starboard.

"Another torpedo in the water! This one isn't from the *Romeo*."

Paloma sighed. "Your Islamic masters turned on you, Ankour."

Mohammed turned white. "Do something!"

Out of the corner of her eye, she saw Fire Controlman Second Class James Burlowe skulking around the shattered infrastructure of the Bridge Wing, eyes focused on something below. He was missing when she called the crew to the Bridge, assumed dead. She remembered his promise not three hours ago that no one would take his ship.

Nav interrupted her thoughts. "Ma'am. The fish is targeting the *Romeo*. Lots of cavitation noises. He's digging big holes in the ocean trying to escape."

Ten seconds passed, and then an explosion rocked the battered cruiser. Air bubbled to the surface as the *Romeo* vented to the sea and a sheen of oil spread where the sub had been.

"Direct hit. The *Romeo* is gone."

Paloma stood there, confused, trying to figure out what happened, as did Mohammed. Fear flitted across his face replaced by madness.

"It does not matter if you have a friend out there, Paloma." He fluttered the plunger for the C4 at her. "If they try to take this ship back, I will blow it up. I have no fear of dying. A glorious world awaits me with Allah. Your only hope of survival is if America will trade for you once we reach North Korea."

Mohammed thought he held all the cards, but Paloma had a plan.

"Helmsman. All engines stop."

"No," Mohammed countermanded. "Continue to Wonsan Harbor." One of Mohammed's *mujahedeen* shoved the business end of an AK-47 into her chest. She slapped it away.

"Ankour, we went through a violent air battle and a sub attack. If you want to reach North Korea, we need to make sure the ship will make it."

Mohammed blinked. "You have five minutes."

The Helmsman went with two *jihadist* escorts to check the spaces for seaworthiness. That bought her rescuers five minutes.

But it wouldn't be enough. There on the horizon were the North Korean ships.

Three minutes later, the engines fell silent.

Mohammed almost wrenched her arm from its socket. "What's going on?"

Paloma yanked free and rubbed her shoulder as she stared at the dark, powerless console.

"After what we've been through, there are any number of reasons we'd stall. I need to send a repair crew to check."

Burlowe flitted through her peripheral vision again, trying to tell her something. Had he closed the fuel cut off valves outside the main engine room? He gestured in a circle with his finger as a dark figure peeked through the Bridge hatchway. Mohammed was too focused on Paloma to notice.

"I do not believe you, but you cannot escape. My father's ships are twice as close as your fleet. If America interferes, I blow up *Bunker Hill*," and he again waived the plunger that would detonate the C4 stuffed around the ship. He held up one of the ship's Hydra radios. "This is tied into the ship's wireless frequency. When I push it, poof! The ship sinks."

Sweat dimpled his forehead and his eyes were rimmed in red. He squealed with laughter. "From the frying pan into the fire, is this what your countrymen say?" A smile spread across his face. "Now, get those engines running or I start killing sailors."

"Not today, mother fucker. Put your weapon down."

The voice boomed, equal measures commanding and brutal. Paloma jerked. The warrior was massive with broad shoulders, muscles everywhere, and USMC tattooed across his neck. Mohammed spun to face him, hand raised, finger poised.

Four more SEALs appeared out of nowhere with not enough movement to leave a shadow. They arrayed themselves among the ruined consoles, automatic weapons aimed at Mohammed and the remaining *mujahid*. Paloma saw lumpy human piles where *jihadists* had stood two minutes earlier. Behind the SEALs, each with a 9 mm aimed at Mohammed, stood Burlowe and Collins. Burlowe's legs were spread, dark eyes smoldering, cords in his neck drumhead taught, a slight smile on his granite face.

One of the SEALs winked at Paloma before turning a flinty glare back at Mohammed. "Please let me shoot."

Mohammed raised his hand to show the detonator. "I have C4 throughout the ship, placed at the most vulnerable spots. If I push this, we all die, but I have the last laugh."

"What d'you think took us so long to get here?"

Mohammed took one step back and pushed the plunger—

Nothing.

His entire body shook, and then the corners of his mouth pulled up a fraction and he spun. A knife appeared out of nowhere. His arm cocked, ready to pinion her. Six H&K PM7s exploded, cutting him down before his arm began its forward arc, and Mohammed dropped like a house of cards, dead before he hit.

Paloma took deep gulping breaths to steady herself as four of the SEALs checked the corpse, put fisticuffs on the one living terrorist, and checked the rest of the Bridge crew. One SEAL approached Paloma.

"You OK, ma'am?"

She checked for a name tag, but he had none. "I thought I was dead."

He grinned, his smile a bolt of sunshine running through her body. "I can shoot a fly out o' the air at a hundred yards. This was nothin'."

Tears sprang to Paloma's eyes and she blinked them back. "Did Eitan send you?"

The SEAL grinned. "You mean Eitan Sun? The Geek God we-all pray to when our computers go down? No, ma'am. He's a myth. We just happened to be in the area."

A voice called from across the Bridge. "This man's alive!" Paloma slipped around the clutter of debris and bodies to see who the SEAL found.

"Captain Pearson."

"I got this, LT," from the SEAL leader, and loaded the Captain into a helo. Paloma was about to send the Helmsman to release the crew when they shuffled in, shaking hands with their rescuers.

The SEAL leader appeared at Paloma's side. "You did great, Ma'am, gettin' us intel—how many hijackers, how they were armed. Quick thinking for an IFNAG."

Paloma grinned at the acronym. *Ignorant Fucking Naval Academy Grad.* She knew nothing two years ago when she graduated except rules, procedures, and the Navy way. This, what she just went through, was the real education.

"You put up a hell of a fight. Impressive, the way you beat the *Romeo*, ma'am, and without ASROCs or CIC. That's a story for the boys back at base."

After a moment, he said, "We have another helo coming for casualties. It can bring a crew to sail *Bunker Hill* home." He held his radio out. "Admiral Xibon on the line for you."

"Sir, what would you like me to do? I'm the senior officer. I'll get us home or I'll turn over command to whoever you designate."

She waited, exhausted, but unwilling to let anyone finish what she started. The radio squawked. "Can you get her to San Diego, Captain?"

She observed the remnants of her crew as they straggled in from the helo hanger. "Give me a minute, sir. Electro!" the woman trotted over. Her uniform was stained, the pants ripped. Her left arm had a four-inch line of dried blood that probably hurt like hell an hour ago. She looked exhausted but relieved. "You want to stay or go back?"

"No way am I leaving. The hard part's done!"

Paloma laughed. "Then you're my assistant. Burlowe! Collins!" They hurried over. "How about you two? You earned a break."

They both shook their heads. "I'm betting there won't be any training exercises going home."

"Then I award you both battlefield promotions. Burlowe, you are XO. Collins, how's Chief Engineer sound?"

"Yes, ma'am!"

Paloma pushed her comm. "We'll be fine, sir."

The SEAL leader grinned at her. "You recognized our periscope deco in the *Luhu's* baffles? We wanted you to know we had your back."

She laughed. "The Texas flag. Nice touch."

He scratched his head. "Give us a couple of hours to check for surprises and we'll be out of your hair."

Exactly two hours later, *Bunker Hill* prepared to go home.

"Right standard rudder. Course zero-seven-nine. Clear outbound to the Pacific and head home."

Epilogue

When *Virginia's* screw seal blew, the sub flooded and started to sink. In the confusion, the crew wrestled control from the hijackers before they blew the reactor, fortuitous because the sub settled to the bottom in eighteen feet of water. In the absence of the Captain, the XO exited his men and Dinar Hussabi—the only terrorist to survive. Hussabi faked his death, bundled himself into the nuclear protective uniform kept on *Virginia* in case of a nuclear meltdown and hidden from his fellow *jihadists*. He spilled everything he knew in return for clemency and a chance at American citizenship. Thanks to his intel, James found the other members of Al-Alah's genius NYU cell and arrested them before they fulfilled their *jihads*. Many were relieved.

According to Hussabi, Salah al-Zahrawi was the mastermind behind the operation. The terrorist stumbled across Dr. John Penbury's work and saw its military importance. His attempt to meet the great scientist was rudely rebuffed. In response, al-Zahrawi eliminated Penbury's wife and bribed the scientist's largest donors into withdrawing their support, forcing Penbury to seek alternative funding. Once Penbury created the sonar shield, al-Zahrawi arranged to have Najafian discredited in his homeland, then convinced him Penbury had gone to the dark side. The formula was intended to provide a massive revenue stream for *jihads* for years to come.

Gil-dong Soon Young's enrollment at NYU was an unexpected gift from Allah. North Korea wanted a space-based weapon to flaunt their military superiority and Iran's theocrats wanted to establish their leadership over the world's six billion Muslims. When his life-long dream crashed last year, al-Zahrawi no doubt blamed Kali.

The death of Ankour Mohammed was kept secret and James planted an agent who could have been Mohammed's doppelganger at the NYUAD library every afternoon at 2 pm, with a copy of *The Communist Manifesto*. He waited two weeks for al-Zahrawi to show up, to no avail.

A search under Taggert's PayPal name—*Nevik Treggat*—came up with a chatroom he and Mohammed frequented. It contained an enormous amount of hidden data, much of it implicating the XO in the hijackings. Unfortunately, the terrorists had paid no attention to metadata which explained how the damaging evidence had been planted.

After inserting the SEALs to liberate *Bunker Hill*, the *USS Texas* launched a TLAM under the guise of rescuing the cruiser from the North Korean warships. They claimed the Tomahawk went awry and landed on a North Korean factory by accident, destroying North Korea's nuclear weapons manufacturing capabilities. Under a quickly-executed backchannel communication, North Korea agreed to withdraw the ships bearing down on *Bunker Hill*. In return, the US and Japan would keep secret that North Korea would have started WWIII if not for Otto. Mohammed's father denounced his son, calling him a traitor to North Korea.

Virginia's crew credited Joey Najafian with disabling the missile launched at the Capitol and he was posthumously awarded the Navy Cross.

After returning to San Diego, LT Paloma Chacone received a promotion to LT Commander and a week leave to recuperate. Across the continent, Dr. Eitan Sun took his first vacation in two years to explore the California coastline with Paloma. She drove. They also made a phone call to the family of Haim, the British Parisher who had died at Mohammed's hand, to pass on Obeid's words about the honor Haim showed even in the face of death.

The California Institute of Technology's Center for Advanced Research offered Sean Delamagente a full scholarship. Sean accepted, fulfilling the promise he made to Sun, and became the youngest student in the new freshman class.

James attended the funeral of the victims of the Carnival cruise liner. He assured the families if the cruise ship hadn't drawn *Virginia* from hiding, thousands more would have lost their lives. It's the little things, no matter how tragic and painful, that stop the enemy.

Rowe realized he would always be a SEAL if not by profession, by soul. Luckily, Kali concluded the world was a better place with Zeke exactly as he was. She accepted employment with the FBI to find a countermeasure to the sonar shield.

While Rowe recuperated from injuries caused when he was blown out of the water, Otto asked how he figured it out because no extrapolation of the facts resulted in Rowe's conclusions. Rowe shrugged something about hunches and instincts and going by the seat of his pants. Otto requested Kali add those characteristics to his programming so he could be more like Zeke.

As soon as Zeke was mobile, he drove to 176 Kearny wearing a shirt easily confused with the SPCA if you didn't look close enough, and knocked on Babe's door.

The same harried woman yanked open the door. When he told her about the complaints he received regarding her treatment of a dog, she said Babe disappeared yesterday and good riddance. It took Zeke ten minutes to pry the details from her. Zeke found Babe in the nature preserve by following circling raptors. The dachshund was huddled at the base of a thirty-foot precipice, two legs broken, eye swollen shut and fur matted with crusted blood. His one good eye found Zeke and his tail thumped, knowing a friend had arrived. Zeke cradled him gently in his arms for a moment and then rushed him to the animal hospital. It took two surgeries, thirty-eight stitches, and casts on both legs, but Babe recovered, his spirit unbowed, and refused to leave Zeke's side.

That was fine with Zeke. In a world where he counted true friends on one hand, he added Babe to the list.

Want More?

Find out how Zeke Rowe and Kali Delamagente met, in ***To Hunt a Sub***.
https://www.amazon.com/dp/B01K7VSPBW

Find out more about Lucy (from *To Hunt a Sub*) in the spin-off novel, ***Born in a Treacherous Time***:
https://www.amazon.com/dp/B07CTCR944

Look for Book #3 in the series:
Summer 2021

About the Author

Jacqui Murray lives in California with her spouse and the world's greatest dog. She *has been writing fiction and nonfiction for 30 years and an adjunct professor in technology-in-education.*

Sign up to be notified when Jacqui's next book is available
http://eepurl.com/cACP6T

You can find J. Murray on her blog, WordDreams:
http://worddreams.wordpress.com

And on Twitter:
@WordDreams

LinkedIn:
https://www.linkedin.com/in/jacquimurray

www.ingramcontent.com/pod-product-compliance
Lightning Source LLC
Chambersburg PA
CBHW051315250626
47155CB00007B/2327